LIFE IN MOONLIGHT

The Primigenio Tales: Book 1

By
Alison Beightol

A Schattenseite Book

Life in Moonlight
By
Alison Beightol

Cover Design: Ihor Tureh
Editor: James Millington
Interior Design: Paul Salvette

ISBN 13: 978-0-578-18460-9

Dedication

For Mom and Madeline

Acknowledgements

Special thanks go to my wonderful family who provided me with unending love, support, and plenty of caffeine while writing this book. Thank you for understanding my craziness.

Thanks to my editor James Millington whose eagle eye saw what I didn't.

And thanks to my husband Scott Baker. You gave me sanity, read and reread this book, and loved me even when I was pretty tough to take. I love you!

PROLOGUE

The Silly Thing Didn't Realize She Was Going to Be a Late Night Meal

*W*HO TO EAT, Eamon Rutherford thought as he studied the capacity crowd of Seattle's Marion Oliver Mc Caw Hall. A few of the women he saw were tempting. They were young, beautiful and sexy, exactly what he looked for in a feed.

While he looked, the marker of another vampire, a much younger vampire, somewhere in the audience caught his attention. The mystery vampire wasn't a newborn, one not yet a century old. Its marker had a quiet dignity intertwined in it, something that came with age. Usually, Eamon ignored random vampires. Being almost eleven centuries old, he had long ago learned to tune out the markers other vampires unless they were older or were a threat to him. But now that he was the oldest vampire in the world, there weren't any vampires to threaten him or match his power. From what he sensed of this vampire, they also seemed intimidated by the fact that he had noticed them. He scanned the audience with greater intensity but his phone vibrating in his jacket pocket distracted him before he could identify them. He looked down at his phone.

Irina.

That dancer, what do you see in her? There are plenty like her here, the text message read.

Eamon put the phone back in his pocket without responding. "That dancer" was the reason he delayed his return to New York and there were not any others like her. Lauryl Mellis had been the pride and problem of the Jacqueline Kennedy Onassis School of Dance at the American Ballet Theatre. Once, at a cocktail benefit for the school he attended, the student dancers were selling signed dance shoes of some of the school's notable graduates. Lauryl asked one patron in her Georgia twang, why he wanted a smelly shoe and did he plan on "jizzing" in it when he got home? Her dismissive attitude and scorn of the patrons amused Eamon but not the administration. The school powers that be often bent the rules for her, giving her chance after chance because of her talent.

Her talent and what he had seen of her stormy personality was magnetic. She would back up whatever insult or harangue with a lovely smile or a toss of her auburn hair. He'd enjoyed her from a distance, though. He never missed a performance or fundraiser when he was in New York, but he never approached her or introduced himself. She was young, still in her teens, so he waited. Then he'd lost track of her. To his good fortune, here she was on tour in Seattle.

Eamon studied the crowd a few more minutes and then flipped through the stage-bill. He passed ads, the story synopsis for the ballet, and then found what he wanted, Lauryl's picture. Gone was the teen he remembered. Instead, he saw a radiant, young woman with a dazzling smile and bright eyes.

His phone vibrated again. It was Irina but he saw no need to acknowledge his former companion. He switched it into airplane mode and returned it to his pocket. He looked back at the picture of Lauryl. The change was remarkable. She was stunning. The idea of a dancer for a companion intrigued him. All of that beauty and grace amplified as a vampire. It was a perfect combination. The image lingered in his mind for a moment and then the framework of a plan materialized.

The house lights dimmed and Eamon closed his stage bill. He tossed it onto the empty seat next to him in the box and waited as the orchestra tuned up. The cacophony of instruments merged together into a more harmonic air but the familiar sensation of a woman studying him turned his gaze back to the audience.

A young woman with light brown hair watched him from a seat below him. She was seated with two other women so he knew she would be available after the performance. She rubbed her hand over her thigh and crossed her legs. The slit in her skirt revealed a tantalizing preview of her legs. Eamon followed the line of her legs back up to her ample breasts. Her body reinforced the silent invitation in her expression. He nodded acceptance of her naïve request. The silly thing didn't realize she was going to be a late night meal.

*   *   *

THE HOUSE MANAGER had gladly granted Eamon access after the performance but it took more time than Eamon expected to work his way through the backstage crowd. He stopped twice to speak with business acquaintances but soon found himself outside of Lauryl's dressing room. Or close to outside of it. A throng of her admirers blocked the entry. The ones that couldn't fit in her dressing room hovered around the doorway, waiting for their opportunity to get in. He stood for a moment with the crowd but became bored. He looked at the mass of people and focused on their collective thoughts.

Leave, he told them silently.

One by one, they filed away and he entered the dressing room. Other dancers, all drinking champagne and chattering, surrounded Lauryl. She was seated in a chair with a blanket over her shoulders and a champagne bottle tucked between her thighs. Eamon could smell blood and his eyes tracked down to a bucket of ice water that her feet were soaking in. He looked at the bucket a moment longer and then at her face. She was lovely; lovelier than in the program picture by far.

Her pale skin was flushed pink and her green eyes sparkled with excitement. Her full lips turned in a smile for one of the dancers before she waved at them. The mass of curly hair he remembered from when he saw her in New York was scraped back in a tight bun. She laughed at something a dancer whispered to her and Lauryl pulled the pins holding her hair back out. Auburn curls dropped down and framed her face. Eamon smiled inwardly and took a few steps toward her.

"Lauryl Mellis," he said as he extended his hand to her. "It's such an honor to meet you."

Lauryl turned to him and her expression changed. Her smile

withered and her eyes narrowed as the happiness disappeared from them. She took his hand like it was covered in filth and shook it. "Thanks."

Her boredom with him was apparent but he continued on, intrigued. "I've followed you since you were a student at ABT. Your talent has certainly blossomed, as well as your beauty."

She rolled her eyes. "Yeah, thanks again."

"You're welcome."

Her frown and rigid posture intensified and Eamon knew she viewed him as one of the ballet school patrons that she scorned back in New York. He bristled slightly but his expression didn't change. As he looked into her eyes, his irritation faded into amusement. He'd play along with her. Besides, the delicious aroma of her blood continued to drift up from the ice bucket in front of him. Lauryl pulled her hand away and intensified her dismissive stare. The fact that she wanted him to leave fascinated him. Never had a woman reacted that way to him. He concentrated on her thoughts for a moment. She thought he was a rich asshole looking to get laid.

A dancer kissed Lauryl's cheeks and hugged her and then Lauryl shifted in the chair. She looked at him and then looked at the door.

Eamon almost laughed. *A not-so-subtle hint,* he thought. He'd comply. After all, he had the young woman from the audience waiting for him. "I just wanted to tell you how talented and beautiful you are. Thank you for the engaging conversation." Eamon bowed his head.

"I'll remember it always."

"So will I," Eamon said before he walked out.

Six Months Later

CHAPTER ONE

I Guess I Don't Understand
the Mind of a Vampire

"IS THAT THE final offer?" Eamon asked. He didn't bother to look up from the text message that informed him that his suits were ready in London. He fired a text back to the sales manager that he'd be in next week to get them.

The dry business details his attorney, Grant, recounted about the last meeting with the dance company's board of directors were of no interest to him. The deal would happen. He knew it. Eamon stretched his legs out in front of him and relaxed his six-foot frame.

"Can I be honest?" Grant pushed a portfolio across Eamon's desk. "Buying the controlling interest in a dance company isn't a smart investment. They've never turned a profit and they have personnel issues."

Three secretaries came into the office and prepped the large conference table across the room for a meeting. They deposited agendas, portfolios, and water glasses in front of the seats. After they finished, two of the women walked out. One lingered at the door, waiting for Eamon's acknowledgement.

"Yes, Rebecca?" Eamon asked his personal secretary.

"Can I do anything else, Mr. Rutherford?" The smile she gave Eamon revealed the tiniest invitation.

"No, thank you," he replied with a wink. She closed the door behind her and the almost imperceptible scent of her spicy perfume lingered in the air. It was faint enough that only he could smell it and it triggered the memory of her soft skin and the taste of her blood. He turned back to Grant and frowned.

"This is more than a business venture, Grant." He glanced

toward a neat stack of newspaper clippings and reached for one with a picture. The photo was of a young ballerina holding a bottle of champagne in one hand and a pair of toe shoes in the other. He held it toward Grant.

"This is why I want the dance company."

Grant leaned in closer and studied the picture. "Lauryl Mellis?"

Eamon nodded.

"She's not exactly at the top of her game. She just got out of rehab."

According to Eamon's conversations with the dance company's general manager, Lauryl had turned into a party girl after a serious bout with mononucleosis. She had used cocaine to keep her energy up so she could keep dancing without losing her spot as a principal dancer. Her drug use mushroomed from there. Or so Eamon had been told.

"I realize she's had some problems in the past. However, the director and general manager of the dance company assure me she's clean. Besides I want her for myself, not for the dance company."

"You?" Grant asked. He adjusted his wire-framed glasses.

Eamon narrowed his brown eyes at him. "You disapprove?" He placed the picture down with the others and drummed his fingers on the desk. Eamon's fangs slid down through his gums and he absently ran his tongue along the point as his irritation simmered.

Grant shifted in his chair. "Sometimes I think I understand you, Eamon. Even after all of these years." He rubbed his pant leg and held his breath a moment.

Eamon's lips turned down in a frown and his fangs retracted. His irritation lessened, but only somewhat. Grant's familiarity annoyed him. His skill as an attorney and advisor didn't entitle him to irritating behavior. He had yet to earn that privilege.

"I guess I don't understand the mind of a vampire. Or at least how you decide to find a companion," Grant admitted.

"You won't until you are one. If you ever are one."

Eamon rose from his chair and allowed Grant to ponder his

future. He walked over to a large parcel leaning against his desk and ran his hand over the thick, brown paper covering. Eamon removed the protective paper, revealing a gilt-framed, Degas oil painting. The pastel colored painting, *Two Dancers at Rest*, featured two ballet dancers in blue tutus relaxing together.

"Where did that come from?" Grant asked.

Eamon faced the painting and chuckled. "Philadelphia and a nasty divorce."

"I didn't know you were looking." He placed the portfolios and papers in his briefcase.

"This isn't for me. It's a gift for her. I thought of her immediately when I saw it." His tone of voice softened. Eamon leaned in closer to the painting, studying each of the dancers.

Grant sat forward and slammed the briefcase closed. "You're going to give her that? A painting worth millions of dollars?"

Eamon clasped his hands behind his back and focused on a red-haired dancer rubbing her foot. "Not now. After." He turned back to Grant. "And what if I did? I can't give a gift?"

A few moments passed as Grant stared at his feet. He swallowed hard. "I'm only thinking about the restructuring you'd been planning. Now with all this about that dancer, I think you're losing sight of that."

Eamon considered the restructuring Grant was referring to. It had been Eamon's desire to turn some of his executive staff into vampires in order to increase his corporation's profit margin. Having a board of vampires, with their ability to read thoughts and manipulate the minds of competitors would lessen the risks in investments. It would also allow the business entity to make even more risky investments. But it was more important to turn Lauryl so she could be his companion.

"Time isn't an issue with me. I can make those decisions anytime." Eamon shrugged and walked over to the windows. He looked down at the tiny lights far below. The streets of New York City hummed with life, life that fed his kind. "I don't like my decisions and actions questioned, Grant." He glanced up, saw Grant's faint reflection in the window glass, and smirked at the absence of his own. Grant looked over at the painting a few times before looking back at him.

"All I meant was—" Grant's grip on his briefcase tightened until his knuckles turned white as moment of silence passed.

"You do your job well. I'd hate for you to leave my service." Eamon looked down at his watch. It was close to ten. He was hungry and bored with Grant. Rebecca would be an effortless feed. It was also time to rein Grant back in. "Everyone can be replaced."

CHAPTER TWO

I Suppose We Could Dine On Some Tourists

"YOU'RE IMPOSSIBLE, EAMON," Irina said.

Eamon poured himself a glass of eighteen-year-old Glenlivet scotch and sat down next to her on the dark leather sofa in his New York City mansion. "I disagree."

Irina dipped her slender finger in the liquor and licked it off. "You're the last vampire I'd pick to take on the burden of turning a human."

"I'm tired of being alone. I want a companion." Eamon frowned. More questions about his choosing a new companion. Was he supposed to be satisfied with an endless parade of human females to keep him company as he'd done for the past four centuries? Did his age and power preclude his desire to have a vampire with him at all times? He swallowed more of the scotch. "Do you think you were burden for me?"

She twisted a lock of her sable colored hair around her finger and pretended to think for a moment. "No, but I'm nothing like the one you're after. She's complicated and not in a good way. You seem to have chosen on a whim. My friends think long and hard before turning a human."

He covered his glass with his hand when she attempted to poke her finger back into the amber liquid. "I hardly think I'm comparable to the vampires you know."

"Such an elitist." Irina leaned into him and ran her fingers through his sand colored hair. "But, my Primigenio should be, I think." She sat up on her knees and brought her lips close to his ear. "I'm by far the luckiest vampire in the world." After a pause, she licked his earlobe and placed her arms around his neck.

"*Otyets, sozdatyel', ya tyebya lyooblyoo.*"

Eamon leaned further back into the sofa cushions. Irina was a master. She alone possessed the ability to crack the indifferent exterior he maintained, just by reminding him she loved and needed him. It still surprised him. Even though they were no longer a romantic pair, his affection for her remained as her maker. Even after nearly six centuries. Hearing her call him "father and maker" in her native Russian brought a smile to his face and a sense of pride flowed through him.

"*Ya tyebya lyooblyoo slishkom, milochka*" He returned her kiss after affirming that he loved her as well. "My Russian is becoming quite rusty, darling. You should spend more time with me." Eamon leaned into the sofa cushions.

"Yes, I should. I'm afraid you're going to forget about me with your new companion." She watched him from the corner of her eye.

He noted the mocking emphasis on the word companion. "I don't think that would be possible."

"No, I'm rather unique." Irina dragged her index finger down his chest.

"That and the fact you've been part of me for over five hundred years."

She sat back. "I'm serious."

He kissed the top of her head.

Irina brushed the copy of the *Financial Times* on his lap onto the floor and stretched her petite body across him. After a moment of silence, she lifted her blue eyes up to his face. "Are you hungry?"

He shrugged his shoulders. "I could eat. Why?"

"I thought we might go out and feed together."

"That would be nice. Did you have something in mind?"

"No. Tourists in Times Square? Or maybe find a dance club. I adore that."

Eamon grimaced. "I don't."

"Where's your sense of adventure? I suppose you'll just feed from your secretary again."

He lifted his shoulders in a slight shrug. "A more relaxed feed appeals to me. Not that I don't enjoy the thrill of hunting. I do. Instead, I find eager submission is enough for me."

She shrugged her shoulders. "I prefer hunting."

"That's the Boyar in you."

Irina sat up and tipped her head to the side. "You need to get out more."

"What do you mean?"

"I mean mix with your own kind. Drop your self-imposed barrier."

He rolled his eyes. "Why?"

The last thing he wanted was his house full of vampire social climbers. Any vampire not of his bloodline would more than likely want something from him or just want to be associated with him. He wanted absolutely nothing to do with the social intrigue and politics that existed among day to day life among vampires. "You said I was an elitist."

"I'm not suggesting you open your world to everyone." She looked around Eamon's living room and frowned at the formal surroundings. "However, keeping occasional company with other vampires might do you some good."

"What sort of good?"

She opened her mouth to speak but stopped.

I'm waiting, he said in her mind.

"Too much human contact can't be good for a vampire."

"You never learned the value of humankind."

She crossed her arms over her chest. "They're food and every now and again, entertainment."

Irina had enjoyed his protection for so many years that she never learned to see the humans around her for anything more sustenance. To Eamon, they were a means to an end and not just in a nutritional way. Most of the time, they happily provided a service to or served vampires in exchange for something. Sometimes it was their life.

As a young vampire during the Middle Ages, he preyed on human fear. He found it to be a powerful motivator for servitude and loyalty. However, as humans gained knowledge and as the centuries rolled by, money and the allure of eternal life took the place of fear. The gift of being turned was what humans offered their service and loyalty for today.

"Humans are more than you give them credit for," he said as he reached for his glass. "I've tried to teach you that for centuries."

"Sometimes I think you're much too attached to them." She picked at the diamond bracelet on her wrist.

"You make them sound like pets."

"Precisely! Or farm animals." Irina turned the bracelet loose and rested her hand on his leg.

"Enough, Irina." He lifted her up and walked to the liquor cabinet to refill his crystal glass.

"What?"

"Curb your feudal leanings." He gave her a fatherly scowl.

"I have no idea what you are talking about." Irina rearranged herself on his lap when he sat back down.

"If you had your way, you'd raise humans like livestock. You've never thought much of the humans who were of a lesser station than yours."

"You're a fine one to accuse someone of being a snob."

"The situations are different entirely."

"Only because you say so." She looked him in the eye but then lowered her gaze. "But as my maker, I suppose you have the right."

"Yes, I do. Your lack of respect for humans might one day be your undoing."

Irina scoffed. "Not bloody likely." She stood up and stretched. "Well, I suppose I'll have to find something to eat by myself."

"It's not like you're a newborn. You don't need me to come with you."

"Maybe I want you to. I like having you with me." She shrugged into her leather jacket and fiddled with one of its silver buckles. "I won't have that soon."

"Find one of your like-minded friends to eat with."

Irina leaned over and kissed him. Her lips softened as the kiss turned from social to more intimate. His lips turned in a smile and she pulled back.

"Jealous," he whispered.

She stalked out of the room and he laughed. The sound of the door closing cut off his laughter. With all of the companions she had been through, it surprised him that she didn't understand his need. And yes, it was a need. Irina didn't count. Their involvement ended in the seventeenth century and his loneliness morphed into the drive to acquire as much wealth as he could. That goal had been accomplished long ago, but he was still lonely. There wasn't anything left for him to divert all of his lonely energy into. He simply wanted to fix the problem.

CHAPTER THREE

Oh, Shut Up, Anthony, You Analyze Everything to Death!

D R. ANTHONY WILSON gazed out of his office window down at the empty parking lot. Lauryl was late. Again. Her tardiness didn't surprise him but, since this was going to be their last session together, he'd hoped maybe she would surprise him and arrive on time.

He turned around and looked at her chart on his desk. It was now stuffed two inches thick with the chart notes on their sessions together. Some of the sessions were pleasant and she made excellent progress acknowledging her maladaptive behavior but some of them weren't. Anthony placed his hand on the chart.

When Lauryl first came to him, neither one of them were prepared for each other. She didn't want to go to an outpatient treatment center, so the dance company arranged for her to begin therapy with him. They'd met three times a week at first, then twice a week, and now once a week. The first thing out of her mouth when she walked in his office was "I hope you're cool and not one of those over-analytical-type doctors." She then wanted to know where his beard was because, she said, all therapists had beards and she wouldn't be able to take him seriously without one.

Anthony's intercom beeped and his receptionist whispered, "Dr. Wilson, Lauryl Mellis is here."

He walked into the reception area. Lauryl smiled and scooted past him. When he followed her in, he noticed she already was settled into the chair she always sat in. Her chair, as she called it.

Anthony took a seat across from her. "So," he began.

"Sorry I'm late."

"I don't think you are sorry. If you were, you wouldn't be late all the time."

"Okay, I'm not sorry," she said and withdrew her apology. "Is that better?"

"It's not better but it's honest." He looked at her. Her cream colored skin was now pink. "Been to the beach?"

She touched her cheek. "I guess I got a bit of a burn. It shows more on fair skin."

"You still underestimate our sun here in the northwest," Anthony said. "It's just as wicked as in the south. You should wear sunscreen."

"You sound like my grandmother," Lauryl said with a grin.

Anthony steered the conversation back to a more professional path. "Today won't be like our other sessions. Today will be a wrap up." He looked away anxiously to keep from being distracted by her when she unfastened the tortoise shell barrette holding her long, auburn hair off of her face. She tousled the thick curls a few times and then gathered them back in the barrette. "This'll also be my chance to say goodbye."

"Okay."

"It's going to be shorter, too. Not the usual fifty-minute hour."

"Sounds good."

"Great. So shoot." Anthony leaned over and turned on the little tape recorder on the table next to his chair.

So shoot. He began just about every session with those words. Lauryl stared down at her feet and then back at him. "I'm kind of sorry this is our last session. Believe it or not, I was beginning to get comfortable with this." She reached over, grabbed a pillow from the nearby sofa, and hugged the cushion against her. "I even kind of like it."

Anthony nodded. "I wish you had been that way when you first came here."

She hadn't been the most cooperative patient when she first left the hospital. She was confrontational but then sometimes she was passive. At the beginning of some of their sessions, they stared at each other, waiting for the other to give up and speak.

Every session, she won.

"I'm scared to go back," she said. "Maybe not scared, nervous though."

"Nervous is okay. You've learned to deal with your fears and problems in a constructive manner."

She twisted her shirt around her finger. "I just don't want to lose control again."

"Do you remember any of our discussions about that?"

After a few seconds, her expression brightened. "I know I don't have to have all the answers today and its okay if I don't have everything right away."

He sifted through her paraphrased quotation. "Good. Keep that in mind."

"I've got the things I learned in the hospital. I'll try to go to meetings."

Anthony knew that she wouldn't go to Narcotics Anonymous meetings but he let it go. "We've talked about more positive coping mechanisms and techniques." He leaned back in his chair and rolled a pen across the yellow legal pad in his lap. "If you feel like you need to talk to someone, you can call me. Or I can refer you to someone in Northup."

She took a deep breath in and let it out. "No, I'm fine. I'll find one on my own." Lauryl twisted a string on her jeans and peeled it apart.

"I know a couple of 'cool' therapists in Northup. One even has a beard."

"I promise. I'll be fine." She stared at him for a couple of minutes. "You're coming to see me dance, right?"

"I planned on it."

"The first performance should be in about a month."

"Let me know and I'll mark it on my calendar," he said.

With a smooth stretch and extension movement, she pulled her knees up to her chest and sighed. "So I guess you won't be my doctor anymore."

"How does that make you feel?"

"Like crap. I feel like I'm losing something."

"You're losing something?"

"Yeah, I thought I would feel whole when I left here but instead I don't." Lauryl rested her chin on her knees.

"You've gained your independence and a better understanding of yourself."

Lauryl tugged on her feet, flexing them upwards and then rotating them. "Then why don't I feel happy?"

Anthony waited for her to process her feelings. She chewed her lower lip for a second and then put her head on her knees. He counted to twenty in his head in an effort to channel his wandering thoughts.

"I'll miss you, Anthony. In some funky way, I'll miss you."

His cheeks reddened and his neck sprouted beads of perspiration. He banished his excitement that she was going to miss him. It resurfaced and he pushed it away before he lost his focus completely. He nodded.

"Me or the sense of protection and safety of this environment?"

"Oh, shut up, Anthony. You analyze everything to death." She dropped her feet down to the floor and crossed her legs.

"Forgive me. That's my job." He laughed. Her quirky humor gave him an opportunity to relax. "You can always come back here, Lauryl. No matter what, you can come back here to me." He hesitated for a moment when he realized what he said. "My office." *Concentrate*, he told himself.

"Thanks, Anthony. I'll keep that in mind."

"Are you going back to Northup today?" he asked and glanced at the small clock on the bookshelf across the office.

"When I'm done here."

"Are you going back to your same apartment?" He recalled her description of her apartment. She told him it was only clean every fourth Tuesday and that dollhouses had larger bedrooms.

"I had to have a friend go over and clean it out. He told me he was flushing the toilet for about thirty minutes," she said.

Anthony laughed and put his pen down. "Wonder what the street value of all that coke was?"

She stared down at her feet again. "I think back to then and I get scared."

"Scared is okay. Recognize it and work through it. You have control over that now. Remember that. You have control." There was a brief silence. "Is there anything else you want to say or ask?" He hated that the time was up. It had moved so quickly. Some days, time stopped. Those were days when they worked through a difficult issue or she was emotionally exhausted. Fifty minutes was like a lifetime. Today, time passed in an instant.

She leaned forward and picked up her purse. "No, I don't think so. I think I'm good." She took one last look around his office and the minimalist furniture and modern art. "Dr. Anthony Wilson, psychiatrist to the stars and IKEA shopper."

Anthony nodded his head. "Always." He took a few steps toward her and saw that her green eyes were wet with tears. "There is nothing wrong with tears, Lauryl. They can be a very healthy thing."

Tears streamed down her face and she wiped them away with her hand. "I guess I'll see you in about a month."

He put his hand on her shoulder and squeezed. "I remember when you proclaimed that you weren't going to cry in here." He offered her the box of tissues from his desk. She took one and they walked to the door.

Lauryl dabbed her eyes a few times. She stuffed the tissue in her jeans pocket and then extended her hand for Anthony to shake. He looked down at her trembling, little hand.

"This time we can hug." He opened his arms and she hugged him. Anthony squeezed her again, memorizing the feel of her slight frame against him, the smell of her hair and anything else he could think of.

"Thanks for your help, Anthony," she mumbled into his shoulder. She tried to rub away the pink mark her lip-gloss made on his Polo shirt but it ended up more ground in to the fabric. Lauryl put her hand on the doorknob and froze.

Anthony nudged her. "Go on, this is your cue. Or whatever it is you guys say."

She nodded and wiped more tears from her face. With that, she walked out of his office but not out of his mind.

The receptionist turned to him. "Your next appointment

canceled, Anthony."

"Good," he replied without hearing what she had said.

Anthony shut his door and stuffed his hands in his pockets. His caseload would be lighter now but, at the same time, he wouldn't anticipate Tuesdays at two or two-fifteen or whatever time Lauryl managed to get to the office. Anthony suffered a unique emptiness at her leaving. In five years of private practice, this never troubled him. He sat down behind his desk and stared at her chair.

Over the last four weeks, he had spent his off time thinking about her, more than he should have. His thoughts at some point diverted away from professional and turned more intimate. His attraction to her increased until it was such a distraction that he almost consulted another therapist to work through it. But he didn't. They would have tried to convince him lose her as a patient.

"It's transference and it's a no no," he said aloud. *Only if she's a current patient*, he thought. He had just discharged her. He was safe on a technicality.

CHAPTER FOUR

The New Owner Must Like Us

WITH CONSIDERABLE EFFORT and weak legs, Lauryl entered the building that housed DanceWest's offices and studios. Immediately though, she stopped and gasped softly as she looked around the reception area.

Before she left, the interiors were dark and gloomy and hadn't been redecorated since the seventies. The company couldn't afford it. Sure the Board had money to spend on performances and touring but they got by with dance space and offices required by the American Guild of Musical Artists union. One stingy board member reminded her at a fundraiser that when the Soviet Union was in existence, Russian dance studios were minimally equipped and still turned out world-class dancers. Lauryl told the board member that he could kiss her minimally-equipped, world-class ass. Now the building was new.

A full on renovation had occurred while she had been gone. Sleek modern furniture replaced the old, clunky furnishings and the walls were now a rich blue and covered with silver framed performance posters. It had only been eight weeks but she figured when a name like Eamon Rutherford was behind the order, things happened quickly. She looked at one of the large posters and leaned in closer.

It was her in the lead role in Sleeping Beauty. She placed her hand on the glass and tapped on her picture face a few times. The vague memory of the show was marred by her clear recollection that she was wired during the performance.

Lauryl's shoulders tensed and the tiny hairs on her neck rose up. The reality of her return now was taking hold. She would have to endure probing looks, gossip and probably face-to-face nastiness from some. All of the things from rehab and therapy vanished from her mind. Maybe returning wasn't such a good idea. Maybe Anthony was wrong in his assessment of her stability. She desperately wanted to dance but she didn't want to deal with being around other dancers, especially dancers she didn't like. She just wanted to come back as if nothing had happened and pretend that she was never a drug addict. Anthony told her that was impossible, irrational and even irresponsible. Lauryl didn't like hearing those things.

All of that was work that she didn't want to do and it meant that she would have to cope with situations that would be difficult at best. If it hadn't been for dancing, she would have said fuck it. Part of her still wanted to say fuck it.

Lauryl tapped on the glass again and this time the sound echoed down the hallway. She took a deep breath but it caught midway when she saw Martin, the company's general manager, standing in his doorway. She turned back to the photo.

"Me," she said.

"You," he confirmed as he walked toward her.

"How long were you standing there, Martin?"

"Not very long. I heard you walking down the hall." He stood next to her and hung his arm over her shoulder.

"The changes I've seen in the building are nice," she said. She folded her arms across her chest, hiding the red scars crisscrossing her wrists "The new owner must like us."

Martin laughed. "I'd say that's a fair statement. He's spent a lot of money correcting our problems. He keeps an eye on us, though."

"Does he ever come in?"

He nodded to a closed door at the end of the corridor. "He has an office here. You didn't hear he bought a house off the beach road?"

She shook her head.

"I figured you would have heard the gossip." Martin's voice dropped off at the word gossip.

"I didn't know that. Gray hair," she said as she touched his temples.

A frown formed on his lips. "I'm lucky I'm not gray all over. I'm betting I will be by the time I'm fifty. Either that or bald." He reached down for her threadbare dance bag.

They walked together to the rehearsal studio in silence. Lauryl swallowed back tears and chewed her lip as she searched for something profound to say for once in her life. She stopped walking and he did the same.

"You're one of the few people who's been kind to me from the very beginning to now. Thank you for that. I don't know what else to say besides thank you."

"This isn't heaven, Lauryl. No one expects you to be perfect."

"I know." She put her hand on Martin's arm and her fingers tightened a bit.

He studied her for a second. "Are you sure you're okay to come back?"

She nodded.

"You aren't your normal outgoing self."

Lauryl sighed and shrugged her shoulders. "I'm just nervous. I don't want to mess up again."

"No one holds you past against you. We're glad you're back," Martin said.

She tilted her head back slightly and closed her eyes. "Martin, you've always believed in me. Even when ABT told you that you were crazy for signing me, you believed in me. Thanks."

"You are who you are. I wouldn't change you even if I could."

They walked into the studio and she saw the new dance floor. The old, pine board floor was gone and had been replaced by a new black vinyl floor. She took a few steps in and the flooring gave slightly under her feet like fresh, green grass. Her eyes lit up and she giggled a few times before she turned back to Martin.

"Wow," she breathed.

He grinned. "Nice, isn't it? All the studios have this flooring system."

"No more splinters."

"Nothing but the best."

Lauryl took her bag from him and set it down. "What's he

like?"

"Eamon? I'd say he's hard to know. One thing, you'll know whether he likes you or not."

"Why is that?" she asked as she pulled her shoes out of her bag. She tied her pointe shoes together and hung them over the barre. Lauryl sat down on the floor and started the task of taping her toes. When the tape job on each of her toes was complete, she stood back up, pulled the shoes off the barre. She pounded the foot box of each shoe against the wall several times and then inspected her work before slipping her toe pads on along with her shoes. With practiced efficiency, her fingers tied the pink ribbons and then tucked the tails under the ribbons.

Martin put his hands in his pockets as he watched her bend and flex her feet. "You'll know. Decide for yourself at his party on Friday night."

She leaned against the barre. "A party? I don't know, Martian." Lauryl pulled her hair up in a ponytail, and braided it.

His eyes lit up. "I didn't think you were ever going to call me that. I was about to give up." He leaned against the barre next to her. "Just think about it?"

The sound of quick footsteps echoed down the hall. Lauryl shot a wide-eyed look to Martin. *Jennifer*, she thought. She stepped closer to Martin and a few moments later, Jennifer Conrad walked in.

The tan, hard-bodied dancer looked at Martin and then Lauryl. She gave her bottle blond hair a toss like a nervous thoroughbred and a sneer formed on her lips. "Well, I guess the dead can come back to life."

Lauryl's shoulders rolled back and she tilted her chin up. "Yeah, Jennifer, I'm back. Does the thought of someone taking your place bother you? Oh wait, it wasn't your place. You were just holding it for me while I was gone."

"Very good, Lauryl. You're funny even without the drugs." Jennifer pulled the Louis Vuitton tote bag from her shoulder and set it on the floor. She crossed her arms over her chest and cocked her left hip outward like a junior high school diva.

Martin shot Jennifer a frown. "Enough, ladies! I think we

should all try and get along."

"Hey, thanks, Dad!" Jennifer said.

Lauryl matched Jennifer's hateful stare. "Excuse me, bitch. You're in my way."

She shoved past Jennifer. Jennifer stumbled into Martin, sped down the hall to the front door and stopped. Dancers now trickled in a few at a time. They brushed by her, saying hello and smiling. She leaned against the wall and dropped her chin down to her chest. A few deep breaths and a few minutes later, Lauryl looked back down the hallway. Class would start as soon as Antonina came in. She walked back to the studio and stood in the doorway.

Everyone in the room turned to the doorway and an awkward silence fell over the dancers. Martin remained in the same position as before. Lauryl looked from face to face.

"It's about damn time," a voice said from the corner. Lauryl and everyone else turned to the familiar voice. A tall, brown-haired dancer stood erect and turned his nose up. He plunked his hands on his hips and glanced down at the imaginary watch on his wrist. "You forget about time!" he said with an obviously fake Russian accent.

"Todd," she breathed with relief. Her dance partner and rescuer crossed through the crowd of dancers to her. "I'm so glad to see you!"

He latched on to her arm and guided her through the crowd to the corner where he was warming up. "Come over here with me," he whispered. "I won't let the mean, nasty whore get you."

They both looked over at Jennifer.

"I had to go out on tour with her. I only wanted to kill her about once an hour," Todd whispered.

"Once an hour?"

"Well, maybe twice an hour and four times an hour on show days. Thank God it was only two months."

Lauryl laughed. "What stopped you?"

"I hear the food in jail is nasty. Nothing but starch and fat," he said, helping her stretch. "Besides, do you think I would miss seeing her face when she hears that she isn't dancing Giselle?"

"You don't think?"

"Girl, please. I know Antonina and Martin aren't going to give it to her now that you're back and things are the way that they should be." He pulled her up from her stretch. "They're going to give it to you."

At that moment, a willowy, gray haired woman dressed in a black jogging suit with a pink turtleneck walked in. A hush fell over the room. She patted the tiny pink bow securing her hair bun, strode to the front of the studio and scanned the room with an imperious scowl. She focused on Lauryl and pointed a bony finger at her.

"Ladies and gentlemen, the talent has returned. If you will be so kind as to come to the front, miss."

Lauryl walked to the front, assumed a meek pose in front of the dance mistress. Antonina wrapped her thin arms around her and hugged Lauryl.

"Welcome back, miss." After a few seconds, Antonina gave Lauryl a gentle push away and resumed her stern but noble pose. "As all of you know, our first production this season is Giselle. I don't need to remind you of the difficulty and complexity of this work so I expect everything from each and every one of you." She looked at Lauryl. "Lauryl you are Giselle. Todd, you are Albrecht, and Jennifer will be Myrtha. The rest will be posted."

Lauryl watched Todd's face as he waited for Jennifer's reaction. He danced around in delight as her facial expression turned from stunned to furious. Antonina nudged Lauryl back to her corner. Lauryl glanced over her shoulder at Jennifer, who remained locked in a stare down with Todd. He rubbed his eyes and mouthed the words boo-hoo to Jennifer, who spun around with her bleached blond ponytail trailing behind her. Lauryl glanced back at Martin, who winked at her before he walked out.

Antonina walked over to her chair by the piano and the accompanist and smacked her cane on the floor. "Line them up for me," she said to the assistant dance mistress.

CHAPTER FIVE

He's Very Excited to Have You.
Dancing in His Company, I Mean

L AURYL CHECKED HER make up in the rear view mirror, counted to three and swung her legs out of her car. She hesitated a second before standing. The last party she went to— Lauryl stopped before the memory of that night crept too far into her thoughts.

The only reason she decided to come tonight was to check out Eamon Rutherford. In some form, he had occupied her thoughts all week. She tried to manufacture some sort of mental picture of him. What he looked like, how he talked. She wondered why an outsider to the dance world would purchase a controlling interest in their company, especially since it wasn't profitable. It made no sense to her.

His Victorian-style home was the largest house on the beach road and it sat far enough off the road that you could only catch glimpses of it when you passed it. Huge, bushy trees and a serious, tall, wrought iron fence added to its sense of isolation. Eamon wanted privacy. Lauryl wondered what kind of life he led to desire such security and privacy. She stared at the camera focused on the front entryway and sighed.

"It's only a party," she whispered to herself. Those words became a silent mantra for her as she walked up the steps to his door. Pangs of nervousness poked at her as she stared at the panel of green- and blue-stained glass in the middle of the front door. She took a few more deep breaths. Why was she nervous?

The lead in *Giselle* was hers and she proved she was strong enough to come back. Being nervous and tip-toeing around only fed into what Jennifer wanted. Lauryl raised her hand to knock but the door opened. A lithe, dark-haired woman looked Lauryl over.

"I saw you drive up," the woman said. She stepped away from the door and motioned Lauryl inside. "You're Lauryl Mellis, aren't you? I'm Irina Hauer, Eamon's... sister."

"Hey," Lauryl said. She could hear the sounds of the party down the hall. A quick shout of laughter rose above the sound of piano music and then disappeared.

The curious expression on Irina's face remained. Her blue eyes gleamed. "My brother is in the living room with the other guests. I know he'll be happy to see you."

As she followed Irina down the hall, Lauryl peeked in a few of the open doors and saw that the rooms contained antiques and expensive accessories. There was a stillness and un-natural perfection to them. The rooms belonged in a decorator maga-zine. A marble bust sat on a credenza in the hallway and at the top of the stairs, she could see a large, marble clock with a gold face. Something she did not see were photographs. There were none anywhere.

"Here we are," Irina said. She placed her hand on Lauryl's arm. "It was so nice to meet you. There is wine and other drinks on the table by the French doors. Will you excuse me?" She walked away and left Lauryl standing alone in the doorway.

Lauryl saw that the room was crowded with both dancers and company supporters. A few people glanced up at her, but most remained absorbed in their own conversations. It seemed harmless.

"You made it, you brat."

A familiar arm wrapped around her waist and she turned to see Todd smiling down at her. Tension melted from her shoul-ders.

"I couldn't find anything to wear."

He handed her a glass of water and looked her up and down. "You can never go wrong with basic black. Besides, if I have to be here, you do too. I hate these things."

"Where's Rick?"

"In Seattle making nice with a client." Todd sipped his Diet

Coke. "You know he avoids these things. So, as usual, I'm solo."

"Oh." Lauryl studied the room. Martin and Jennifer were talking to someone who she didn't recognize immediately because his back was turned and she couldn't see his face. But Jennifer hung on his arm and laughed a little too loudly at whatever he said. "You and me should start coming to these mixers together."

"Jennifer isn't wasting any time. Her legs will be open for business soon," he said as he raised his glass to his lips.

"Who is she talking to?" Lauryl asked. She watched Irina walk up to the man and whisper something in his ear. Lauryl turned her back to them.

"Eamon Rutherford. Some place he's got," Todd said, looking around the room. He picked up a Faberge egg from the table and examined the lacy, gold pattern on it. "I want the chicken that laid this egg."

Lauryl rolled her eyes.

"You're so easy."

"Have you met him yet?" Lauryl asked.

Todd nodded his head and set the egg down. "Oh yeah. Earlier. He asked me about you."

"Me?"

"You," he said. "And I think you're about to meet him."

"Lauryl Mellis," a deep voice said from behind her. "I'm Eamon Rutherford."

The smooth and seductive tone of his voice caused her to close her eyes for a second before she turned around. Lauryl shook his outstretched hand. "It's nice to meet you."

His warm hand squeezed hers again before letting go. Eamon was tall, a bit over six feet, with strong, squared shoulders. His full lips curved into a suave smile. She returned his smile and stared into his unusual eyes. They weren't quite brown; they were almost amber.

"I'm glad you made it this evening. When I spoke with Todd earlier, I wasn't certain that you would be here." Eamon glanced at Todd in polite acknowledgment.

Todd leaned over to Lauryl. "Excuse me." He nodded to Eamon and then walked over to Martin.

Lauryl didn't hear or notice Todd. She continued to stare into Eamon's eyes.

"Todd is a talented dancer."

"He is. He's a good friend, too. A life saver, almost."

"It's nice to have someone like that."

His voice caressed her with its British accent and soft, baritone timbre. She usually didn't notice company bigwigs like him but for some reason he caught her attention. She couldn't shake the feeling that she'd met him before. "I think everyone showed up for your party."

"This party is unofficially for you."

"For me? Really?" She shifted her weight from one foot to the other. The black pumps she wore suddenly felt tight and awkward.

"You're the main reason I invested in this company. You're a gifted dancer."

Lauryl looked down at her empty glass. Her cheeks now burned and her lips felt like leather. What was wrong with her? She licked them twice. "We have other talented dancers."

Eamon shrugged. "Give yourself some credit, Lauryl." He squeezed her shoulder. "If you'll excuse me."

"Oh, sure, I understand."

As Eamon walked over to a couple of board members, she noted his perfect posture. He dominated the room like a king. While she talked with him, she'd almost forgotten she was at a party. The crowd in the room died away. He held her attention so well that it almost seemed like a spell. It wasn't what he said because he said so little. Something about him, his presence, intrigued her. It was odd. If he had been like any other rich asshole or company supporter, she would have only tolerated him because she had to. However, as she stared at his back, she found herself yearning for him to return and talk to her.

Eamon wasn't what she thought he would be. Yes, he was a wealthy, English business type. He wore expensive clothes and had polished manners. No doubt, his haircuts set him back several hundred dollars and were done by some BS hair stylist who had their own line of styling products. Nevertheless, there was something about him.

"Looking to impress the owner, Lauryl?"

Lauryl spun around and Jennifer, who had crept up to her, stepped away. "No, I'll leave the ass kissing to you." She took a step toward Jennifer. "But it seemed like you trying to do some real ass kissing with Eamon."

Jennifer stirred the olive in her martini around. "Whatever, Lauryl. Maybe someone should warn Eamon about your bathroom behavior. Martin never got those bloodstains out of his bathroom rug."

Lauryl gripped her empty glass, wishing she could break it and grind he jagged edges in to Jennifer's face. Or push her down. Jennifer would topple right over in the five-inch stripper heels she was wearing. Instead, Lauryl took a deep breath in, let it out, and then walked away.

Just act like nothing is wrong, she told herself.

Her gaze darted around the room and paused briefly on Martin, who was trying without success to get away from his conversation and come to her rescue. No doubt, he had seen Jennifer's attempt to start something. Lauryl inhaled deeply and blew it out before waving him off. She headed across the room for Todd. That's when she noticed Eamon watching her. He looked over at Jennifer and back to her before turning his attention to the group around him. She detoured away from Todd and headed toward the terrace doors. Fresh air might help.

A full, late summer moon shone down on the beach below the terrace. Lauryl leaned against the railing and sighed. Right now she wanted to cry, not out of sadness but from frustration. All of the confrontations and pressures were catching up to her. Tears welled up in her eyes but she dug her heel into the top of her foot to keep them from flowing. How long was Jennifer going to bring up what happened? Dealing with the past was hard enough without her throwing it in her face. Lauryl's eyes now stung with unshed tears. The only options she could think of were to cry or kill Jennifer. A couple of tears rolled down her cheek and she wiped them away. She danced in place, trying to calm down. It wasn't working, though. The dancing caused her thoughts to spin out of control. They spun back to the night of Martin's party.

Most of that day she had been shoveling spoons of coke up her nose. She stayed wired all through class and rehearsal and in her car as she drove to Martin's house for a party. As she buzzed around, she drank vodka tonics as fast as they could pour them and was, by Anthony's recounting in therapy, having a great time until Jennifer cornered her in Martin's kitchen.

Jennifer told her that Martin was planning on firing her because she was so out of control. It would seem that the liquor and the cocaine triggered some sort of paranoid rage in Lauryl. She jumped on Jennifer, beating her down to the floor. Pinned to the floor by Lauryl, Jennifer screamed that she was throwing battery charges in with the others. This part she didn't remember but Anthony told her she then grabbed a fruit knife and told Jennifer that she was going to cut up her lying, horse face. Martin managed to pull Lauryl off the bloodied Jennifer and warned Lauryl to get herself together or she was going to be in trouble. Not knowing what kind of trouble he meant and fearful that there was truth in what Jennifer had said, she took the knife and locked herself in a bathroom. The wild hair and bloodshot eyes she saw in the mirror scared her. She didn't recognize herself. She was that out of control. The only thing she knew was that she wanted to die.

At this point, she was drunk and high enough to do it. She took the fruit knife and sawed along her wrists, trying to remember which direction you were supposed to cut yourself when you wanted to die. Martin pounding on the door and Todd screaming for her to open it made her cut even faster. "I'm saving y'all a lot of trouble," she shouted back through the door. Todd kicked the door in and that was it, off to the hospital and to rehab.

Parties were supposed to be fun, she thought. Too many parties in her past changed that. She squatted in a plié and sighed again. A call to Anthony might help. He could talk her through this. Her phone was out in her car and the battery, more than likely, was dead.

The sound of the terrace doors opening caused her to shoot back up but she didn't turn around. Jennifer must be looking for another fight.

"It's not Jennifer. It's Eamon. I thought I'd check on you."

She turned around. "Jennifer is just being Jennifer."

He walked over to her and leaned on the rail. "Should I fire her?"

"What?" Lauryl's green eyes widened.

"Should I fire her?" His serious expression faded away and was replaced by a more easygoing one.

A smirk appeared on her face and she said, "No, but you can kill her." A nervous giggle bubbled out of her.

Eamon laughed.

Still laughing, she put her hand on his wrist. "I'm sorry. I shouldn't have said that."

"You know, we've met before. I saw you a few times in New York when you were a student but we met in Seattle about six months ago. I'm not surprised you don't recall it."

Lauryl tried to remember her time in Seattle. "I'm drawing a blank."

"It was difficult to get close to you because your dressing room was so crowded. When I did, I shook your hand and told you that I thought you were beautiful and talented."

"I'm sorry. I still don't remember. What'd I say?"

"You thanked me. You were busy with your friends. I was merely a face in the crowd. That's probably why you don't remember the meeting."

"Oh, crap, I'm sorry. I hope this meeting is better."

"It is. Tell me about your name. It sounds like you have some Greek blood in your veins."

"Mellis is my stage name. It's my mom's maiden name. She's the Greek in the family. My real name is Fitzgerald. My father is Irish." She touched her auburn hair. "That's where I get this from. It made me a target for teasing when I was a kid. Everyone in my family has dark hair and eyes except for my dad and me. When my sister went to college to be a nurse, she told me that my red hair and green eyes were a genetic mutation and that I was a mutant."

"It sounds like she was jealous."

"I know she was kidding. It was just a weird thing to say."

"Are you close to your sister?"

A twinge of sadness flashed across her face but she forced it away, replacing it with a more neutral expression "My family and I don't talk. I only talk to my sister every once in a while."

"I'm sorry."

"Don't be. I've gotten used to it. My parents and I haven't kept in touch since I was sixteen. They flipped out when I dropped out of school and got my GED. My grandmother paid for me to go to JKO." She gave him a sideways glance and shr0ugged. "I'm the black sheep of my family."

"They're usually the most interesting members of their families." He placed his hand next to hers.

"What about you? Are you the black sheep of your family?" The urge to touch his hand tugged at her. She stretched out her little finger out so that it skimmed his. The brief contact with his warm skin triggered a rush of excitement to flood through her.

"Yes, I suppose I am." The terrace doors opening caused them to turn around.

Irina took a few steps outside and put her hands on her hips. "Eamon, you are doing a very poor job of hosting this party. Everyone is wondering where you are." Her gaze leveled on Lauryl. "I see now why you've been distracted." Irina took a few more steps toward them. "Do you know my brother has talked of little else since we came here? He's very excited to have you." Her smile twisted. "Dancing in his company, I mean."

Irina's odd comment caused Lauryl to smile nervously. *The sister is weird*, Lauryl thought.

Lauryl looked at Eamon, who stared at Irina with an icy stare. She raised her eyebrows at him as if she were challenging him. Lauryl cleared her throat.

"I think I'm going to call it a night. Maybe do another quick lap inside and go."

"So soon?" Eamon asked, still staring at Irina.

"Oh yeah, too much party fun for me!" She waved her hands around a little. "Besides, I need my sleep. Got to be at my peak for the boss."

Eamon turned back to her and his expression softened. "Thank you for coming."

"Thanks for the invitation." She turned to Irina, who was watching her, apparently amused by something. "Nice to meet you."

"It was a pleasure."

"I'll see you around the studio, I guess," Lauryl said to Eamon.

"Without a doubt," he replied. He watched Lauryl walk inside.

* * *

HE LOOKED BACK at Irina. "You're unbelievable."

"No, I'm bored. Trying to help you is boring. And I hate pretending to be your sister. I can't wait to go back to New York."

"Patience, Irina,"

"That one is not going to be what you think." She nodded her head to the doors and placed her hand on his arm.

"That sounds like a jealous woman," he replied.

"No." She slipped her hand from his arm to his hip. "Just an observant one." Irina pinched him gently and walked back in to the party.

CHAPTER SIX

Isn't That What's-His-Name?

LAURYL FILLED HER teakettle with water and set it on the stove. Tea first and then she would think about the mess in her apartment. Clean laundry was stacked up on her sofa with several issues of *Dance Magazine*. A trail of shoes, dirty clothes, and mail leading in to her room. Dried, dead flowers from her *Giselle* performance a week ago lined the countertop.

She poured her tea and pushed aside the laundry on the sofa. The mug felt awkward in her hand. She stared at the mug of tea. Was ever going to develop a taste for this? Born and raised in the South, all she knew was sweet iced tea. Even in the winter, that was the drink of choice. Lauryl walked to her freezer, grabbed a handful of ice cubes and plunked them into the mug. They melted right away so she repeated with another handful of ice. This time the ice floated in the mug. She took a sip and headed to her sofa. *Nothing like good old sweet iced tea*, she thought as she sat down. As she reached for something to read, the phone rang. She rummaged through the pile of magazines and found it.

"Hello?"

"Lauryl, it's Anthony."

"Anthony."

"I called to see how you were."

"Are you asking as a doctor?"

"First tell me as a patient and then tell me as a friend."

Her gaze wandered around the room, as she tried to put her feelings together. "Well, as a patient, I'm okay. You were right. People are cruel, but I've only thought about coke a couple of times. No outbursts or anything."

"Just take it slow. It's your life."

"Do you have a book of those little sayings for patients?"

"They give us one when we graduate from medical school."

Lauryl laughed. "As a friend, I'm good. I'm settling back to my old life." She frowned at her disaster of an apartment. "Trying to develop a new routine."

"Can I take you out to dinner?" he asked abruptly.

"Are you serious?" she asked.

"Of course I am."

"When?"

"Right now."

"What do you mean by right now?" she replied, confused.

"I mean that I'm parked downstairs."

Lauryl walked over to her window. Anthony sat in his Jeep Liberty. He waved at her. "I can't believe you. How did you know where I lived?"

"Yeah, about that, I had the address from your medical record and Googled it. Too creepy?"

"No, not at all."

"So yes or no?"

She couldn't keep herself from smiling. "Yes. Come on up."

Lauryl looked around. Panic and embarrassment overcame her. The health department would shut her down if they ever saw her apartment. The idea of cramming everything into a closet sounded good but she would need a shovel or a broom to get everything out of sight in time. She still needed to change, too. What was more important, looking good or her apartment being presentable? She stood locked in indecision, when a knock on the door decided for her.

She opened it and Anthony smiled at her. "I hurried." He walked in and his jaw dropped but he quickly recovered his neutral expression.

"So you knew I wasn't much of a housekeeper. I told you that," she said with a defensive edge in her voice.

"I didn't say a word. If you'll clear me a spot, I'll sit down."

She grabbed her laundry from the sofa and knocked the magazines down to the floor. "I'll be right back." Lauryl disappeared into her room, kicking a couple of shoes as she walked.

Anthony studied her apartment but his eye was drawn to the dead bouquets and arrangements on the counter. "About these flowers."

"What about them?" She asked as she returned. She let her hair down from the ponytail and fluffed it with her fingers.

"Think you'll ever throw them out?"

She was oblivious to their odor. "Nope, not until the next performance."

"What?"

"It's one of my things. I don't throw away flowers from a performance until the next one. It's kind of like insurance that my next performance will be as good."

"Oh. Do you have a lot of superstitions like that?"

"I prefer to think of them as traditions but yes, I do. Like I put my left pointe shoe on first. Or I chew gum an hour before a performance." She shrugged her shoulders. "I have to do them all or I can't perform."

"As long as it works for you."

"Are you analyzing my routine?"

"No, I don't do that anymore." He stood up. "Ready?"

*   *   *

"Where do you want to eat?" Anthony asked as they drove along the beach road.

"What do you like?"

"I like just about anything. You choose though."

Food was a sore subject with her. Her diet was less than healthy but she knew she had to make some sort of effort in front of Anthony. She frowned but her attention shifted when they drove past Eamon's house. Lauryl looked up the drive to see if any cars were in the partially-hidden driveway. "That's where Eamon Rutherford lives." She pointed up to the house as they drove by.

"Who?"

"My boss. The part owner in the company."

Anthony glanced over to the mansion. "Nice place," he said, gripping the steering wheel tightly for a moment.

"Yeah, it is."

"Did you decide where you want to eat?" he asked.

Her attention drifted away from Eamon. "We could eat at Rigoletto's. It's a nice Italian place. Good food."

"Sounds okay to me."

They rode in silence until they got to the restaurant. While they waited for their table, Lauryl studied Anthony. He seemed different. Maybe it was because he wasn't in his office. She could only picture him behind his desk or rocking back and forth in his chair. Tonight he was her date, not her psychiatrist. Sadly, she couldn't remember when she was out like this last. A rush of date night jitters crept through her. She'd never noticed his broad shoulders or his artistic hands. In their sessions, she had only noticed the way his blue eyes changed colors. Sometimes they were azure like the evening sky and other times they deepened to more of a cobalt shade. In their sessions, they seemed to shift colors in response to her pain.

"Is my fly unzipped or something?"

She laughed. "No, I was just looking."

"To see if my fly was unzipped?"

"Yes." She linked her arm in Anthony's. "It's not though."

The hostess seated them and Lauryl opened the menu. Again food fear plagued her. Italian food was good for her. Carbohydrates had lots of energy, she told herself. On the other hand, she always worried about gaining weight. She didn't want to hear Todd's complaints about variations in her size. Anytime she gained a few pounds, he called her Twinkie Toes. She frowned and continued to scan the menu.

The waiter appeared at the table "Are you ready to order?"

"You are going to eat, aren't you? I hate eating alone."

Lauryl smiled. "Oh sure. I'm going to have the wheat ziti."

Anthony closed his menu. "Me too." After the waiter took their order, Anthony leaned across the table. "You look fantastic."

Her cheeks warmed and she knew that she was blushing. "Thanks."

"A lot different than when you first came to me."

Lauryl thought back to how she looked right after rehab. If she weighed a hundred pounds, she was lucky. Dark circles shadowed under her eyes and she battled periods of insomnia and hibernation. Now, she looked healthy. Not robust, she was never that. Just healthy.

"I do look different. You fixed me." Her gaze wandered around the restaurant and she stiffened when she glanced at the door. Eamon walked in with his sister and a man she didn't know. He looked right at Lauryl and then at Anthony. His eyebrows lifted slightly. Lauryl swallowed hard and tried to relax.

Anthony sat forward. "What's wrong?"

"Nothing."

His eyes followed the direction she was looking and saw a small group of people taking a seat at a table near them. "Do you know them?"

"Yeah." She noticed there was an empty seat at his table. Did he have a date? She turned back to Anthony. "It's the owner of the company." She clicked her heel on the floor.

Anthony touched her hand. "Do you want to go somewhere else?"

"Why?"

"You just seem a little edgy."

"No, I'm fine." She pushed from her mind the thought of Eamon sitting three tables away. A hand settled on Lauryl's shoulder. Eamon was now standing beside her. He smiled down at her and her heart raced.

"Hello, Lauryl. It's nice to see you."

"Hey," she said without making eye contact with him.

"Anthony Wilson." He stood and extended his hand to Eamon.

"Oh yes, the doctor." Eamon gave Lauryl's shoulder a subtle squeeze and then shook Anthony's hand.

Anthony sat back down. "I thought I'd check on Lauryl in person."

"That's nice. If you'll excuse me, I have to get back to my guests. It was a pleasure to meet you, doctor. Good night, Lauryl."

Anthony watched Eamon return to his table. "Nice guy."

"The nicest." Why did she have to see him out tonight? She wanted a dance company-free evening. Eamon and his spooky sister were the last people she wanted to see.

The waiter brought their food and Lauryl tore into hers like a wild animal. She shoveled down the heaping plate of pasta as quickly as she could.

"As a doctor, I'd have to advise against inhaling your food like that."

"I know. I could get indigestion," she said, her mouth half-filled with pasta.

"Or worse."

Lauryl kept her eyes on Eamon's table. She didn't know why. They were all involved in conversation but every so often, Eamon would glance over at Lauryl. She tried to keep herself from acknowledging him and was succeeding. Suddenly the blood drained from her face and she stopped eating. Jennifer Conrad walked in and over to the Eamon's table and sat down. At Eamon's table Eamon leaned over, kissed her on the cheek, and then went back to his conversation.

Lauryl's jaw dropped. Of all the people in town he could date, he had to choose Jennifer. She watcher her take Eamon's hand in hers and lean over closer to him. He glanced over at Lauryl again and a thin smile appeared on his face. His gaze lingered a moment and returned to Jennifer. Lauryl bit her lip until she tasted blood and turned back to Anthony, who was finishing his dinner. She gulped down the ice water in front of her, wishing it was vodka.

"I think I want dessert." *Twinkie toes be damned*, she thought.

"Really?"

"Cheesecake. A big ass piece of it." Since she couldn't have cocaine or any other illicit substance, forbidden food was going to have to take its place to blot out what was sitting three tables over.

"Cool." His phone rang and he fumbled to mute it. A frown appeared on his face. "I'll be right back." He pulled his phone out of his pocket.

While Lauryl waited for Anthony, she danced her feet under the table. She was determined not to look over at Eamon. She stopped her feet and thought about why she was so upset. Did it matter that he was out with Jennifer? No, she was out with here with Anthony and she wasn't going to let Jennifer ruin that. She took a slow deep breath and closed her eyes. When she opened them, Anthony had returned.

"Indigestion?"

"No, I'm good now."

"I'm glad. Still up for dessert or do you want to leave?"

"Hell, no. I'm eating."

On the drive back to her apartment, Lauryl was silent. Eamon dominated her thoughts. From the time he came in the restaurant until they left, he stayed on her mind. When Jennifer came in and took a seat next to him though, she almost threw up. She knew Jennifer would end up fucking him but she didn't need it confirmed. *Well*, she thought, that just shows what Eamon really likes. He's a rich tomcat and Jennifer was banging him for the money. That was what she was going to tell herself.

"Here you are, ma'am," Anthony turned the car into the parking lot of her apartment building.

"Aren't you coming up? I can make some coffee or something."

"Could you find coffee in all of that?"

"Ha. I know where everything is."

He shook his head. "I have to get back. I'm on call. I have to be within fifteen minutes of the hospital. As it stands, I'm about an hour away. And I cheated even more to finish dinner with you." He poked her shoulder. "Rain check?"

She nodded and tried to smile but couldn't quite manage it. "I guess you're leaving."

"Yep, time to make like a tree."

"You tell some dumb jokes." She fingered the door handle absently, not wanting the date to end.

"But you like them. Don't worry you'll see me again." He reached for her as she opened the door. "Lauryl."

She turned back to him and he kissed her gently. As his lips touched hers, goose bumps rose along her arms and she felt something she hadn't felt in years, the excitement of a new romance. With the kiss, Eamon vanished from her thoughts.

"Don't let him bother you," he said as he stroked her cheek. "I think that's just the way he is."

She blushed and wished Anthony would kiss her again. When she saw he wasn't, she covered her disappointment with a shy glance away. "Thanks, Anthony."

CHAPTER SEVEN

Nothing Like Make-up Sex and Blood

I'M *NOT HOME*, Lauryl thought when she heard a knock on her door.

Social wasn't a word that described Lauryl these days. Ever since she saw Eamon out with Jennifer Conrad a week ago, Lauryl's mood had been sullen at best. Contact with Jennifer every day, all day, didn't make it any better. Before class, she would recount in a very loud voice where Eamon had taken her the night before. Lauryl ignored her and stayed close to Todd. That way they could talk about Jennifer whenever they wanted.

In addition, they could make fun of her when she became tired or confused combinations in rehearsal. The best part had been when Antonina blasted her for spending too much time on her back and knees and suggested that those activities, not her "slight anemia, were the cause of her exhaustion.

Anthony hadn't called either. She was beginning to think he was merely checking up on her as her former doctor and not a possible new boyfriend. That disappointed her the most but maybe she had been reading too much into the situation. The events of the past days left her with a non-stop headache.

The knocking continued and synched with the pounding in her head. It became apparent that whoever was at the door wasn't leaving. She reluctantly opened the door when she saw who was there, her eyes narrowed.

"Hello, Lauryl." Eamon leaned against the doorframe.

"Hey." She closed the door some.

"I hope you don't mind me dropping by unannounced."

She shrugged. "Yeah, it's fine."

"I came by to talk to you. May I come in?"

She pulled the door open a bit wider and stepped aside. "Yep."

Eamon took a seat on the sofa and noticed the plate on the coffee table. On it was half a pack of saltine crackers, a green apple core, and a red apple with a few bites out of it. While he studied it, she reached down, snatched it up from the table and took it to the kitchen.

"I wanted to talk to you about the other night."

She tossed the food in the trash and the plate in the sink. "What was it you needed to talk about?" she asked as she filled her glass with water.

"I just wanted to clear a few things up."

She came back in the living room. "Jennifer made sure it was oh so clear to everyone from the corps on up."

"She sees things with a view that's different than mine."

Lauryl shrugged. "It's none of my business. No big deal."

"It is a big deal."

"How?"

"I invited Jennifer out as a courtesy. I thought it would be nice since she'd been ill."

That was a week ago, Lauryl thought. She crossed her arms across her chest. Her irritation percolated along with her hurt feelings over Anthony and the budding jealousy she felt for Jennifer. Apart from an easy lay, what did Eamon see in Jennifer? Lauryl tried to convince herself that none of this mattered but wasn't able to quite accomplish the task. She sat down across from him but didn't face him.

"However, when I saw you there, I regretted my decision." He reached over and touched her knee. "I would have preferred to be with you. I didn't mean to hurt your feelings."

She looked down at his hand on her knee. His thumb rubbed the inside of her knee with a light, teasing pressure. "My feelings weren't hurt. I told you it was no big deal," she said. The longer his warm hand stayed on her knee, the more the mix of tumultuous emotions faded. She found herself enjoying his slow caress.

Eamon took his hand away. "If they were, I'm sorry."

"I said it wasn't a big deal."

She drained her almost full glass and got up to refill it. Eamon glanced back down at the coffee table and noticed the photo album sitting in the center of it. Across the front of it, her full name, Lauryl Sarah Fitzgerald, was embossed in gold leaf. He slid his finger between the cover and the first page but hesitated before opening it. He looked up at her, as if to ask for her permission.

"You can flip through that if you want." *You were going to anyway*, she thought.

"You're certain you won't mind."

She sat down next to him and he opened the photo album. The first pages were of her as a young girl in dance classes.

"I was three in those." She nodded at the page. Those were some of the only pictures when her dancing didn't cause problems at her house.

He flipped a few more pages, going through her years as a young girl. The last photos were of Lauryl at JKO in New York. Her audition number was tucked in the album next to a picture of her and her grandmother. He closed the album and smiled at her.

"I feel as if I've known you since you were young."

"Yeah, a picture's worth a thousand words." She pushed the album away and sighed.

The penetrating gaze he leveled on her caused her to turn away. The stare wasn't unnerving, though. It was simply intense. She could feel him watching her but she couldn't look back at him, at least not yet. Then, as if he had asked her to turn to him, she turned her gaze to him.

Eamon looked into her green eyes. "You are by far one of the most beautiful women I have ever seen."

Her cheeks burned with embarrassment. The muscles in her shoulders and neck relaxed and the earlier irritation melted away. She even minimized his involvement with Jennifer. It didn't disappear completely but it lessened enough for her to enjoy being close to him. The attraction surprised her. It was unexpected and as she sat next to him, it built rapidly. She licked her lips.

Lauryl shook her head, wishing that he would kiss her or at least touch her. As soon as she thought that, she wished she hadn't. He was the owner of the company and a tomcat. She had no desire to be another local conquest. But for some reason, she found the attraction too intense to fight. In fact, fighting it seemed ridiculous.

"I've been all around the world. I wouldn't say it if it wasn't true."

She smiled shyly. "Thank you."

He touched her cheek and traced his fingers along the freckles to her lips. Eamon leaned into her, his mouth just above hers. "In fact, I think you are stunning," he said and then kissed her.

Lauryl placed her hand on his shoulder and grasped at his jacket. Adolescent excitement swept through her body and goose bumps marched up her arms. Her eyes opened slightly to see if his were closed, a throw-back to her teen years, and to her surprise they were. She closed hers again and allowed his lips and tongue to deepen the kiss. After a few seconds, she pulled back and exhaled softly.

"You're a good kisser."

"That's not all I'm good at," Eamon said.

"That I don't doubt." She leaned into him again. For the moment she was content letting his mouth control her. His kisses were like whispers that teased of his other sensual talents. Lauryl's mind spun in overload. His hand settled on her knee and then travelled up her thigh until his fingers grazed under the legs of her shorts.

She stood up and held her hand out to him. Eamon looked at it and then her face. "Yes?"

"I want to show you something," she said as she pulled him up. "It's in my room."

As she walked, she removed her clothing. By the time she was at her bed, she was completely naked. Lauryl smiled, offering her body to him. Eamon put his hands on her hips and lifted her onto the bed. He stripped off his shirt as his eyes travelled over her body. He extended her leg, kissing his way down from her ankle to her thigh. When he reached far enough, Lauryl sank her hands in his hair. She tugged it excitedly as his tongue licked past her clitoris. A moan passed over her lips and her back arched in excitement.

His smile smacked of arrogance and self-importance. Before she could clear her mind enough to be irritated by it, the teasing sensation of his hand as it traced down her leg clouded her mind again. It spurred her ardor to a new intensity before two of his fingers disappeared inside of her. Eamon leaned over her as he teased her, watching her as she let go of herself for him. Lauryl's hand dropped to his and pushed his fingers deeper. Her eyes fixed on his, and she let him take control of her. With each charge his fingers made, she twisted her neck back and forth. When his thumb found her swollen clitoris again and rubbed tormenting circles on it, she bit her lip, trying not to cry out. Another finger slid inside of her and the intensity of his thrusting increased. Her counter-pressure against him made his fingers slip in and out faster and harder.

With a desperate movement, she put her feet on his shoulders and tilted herself forward, the slight angle now making each of his teasing movements even more deliciously agonizing. The desperate need for him that rained over her was foreign. She grabbed the back of her legs, panted, and moaned. He kissed between the pale skin over her breasts. Each kiss produced a gasp from her as his tongue trailed down her stomach. He licked at her hipbones, his other hand found one of her nipples and pulled on it. His tongue licked back to her stomach and continued to the nipple. He sucked on it, teasing it with his tongue, and then caught it between his teeth.

"Oh my God," she breathed. Her hand reached out for his neck and her fingers tightened on the nape. Her fingernails dug into his skin and seemed to encourage him. Her slim hips were dancing harder and harder, faster and faster. Lauryl couldn't believe how her body responded to him. She had never felt so alive or connected. Her hand shot around to his chest and her nails dragged down his skin as her body melted against his. She grabbed him, her nails cutting his skin again. He wiped the little half-moons of blood away, grabbed her hand, and pinned it over her head. A second passed and then she let out a low moan that turned into a purr as her body let go. Each well-toned muscle spasmed and relaxed into a series of subtle shivers.

Eamon removed his fingers and licked them. He put his mouth close to her ear and whispered, "Am I forgiven?"

Lauryl blinked her eyes a few times before closing them in the shower of the endorphins flooding her body. "Oh God, yes, you are."

"I'm glad," he said and smiled. He kissed her neck, nuzzling it before gently sucking the tender, warm skin. A contented sigh came from her and the sucking stopped. "Nice isn't it?"

"Very," she breathed, the tone of his voice melting her even more. She loved the rich timbre of it. It caressed her the way his hands did.

"You'll like this even more," he whispered the second before he bit into her flushed neck.

Her eyes popped open but closed as another orgasm shot though her. His mouth stayed sealed against her neck, drawing her blood into his mouth. Her lower body shuddered and then became still. Eamon pulled away from her and studied her face, now frozen in serenity. He stood up and wiped his lips.

"Sleep now," he ordered and she drifted off.

*　　*　　*

DELICIOUS, HE THOUGHT as he surveyed her sleeping form. *Sleep well, Lauryl.*

Eamon sat on the bed next to her and focused on her sleeping mind. *I want you to remember what happened before I took your blood. Nothing more,* he said into her mind.

It took a bit of glamouring and mental manipulation but she gave into him just as he thought she would. She was stubborn but let go. He picked up his shirt, shook it out and put it on. As he buttoned it up, he paused a moment to enjoy the sensation of her blood as it buzzed through him, strengthening him. *Nothing like make up sex and blood,* he thought.

CHAPTER EIGHT

There Aren't Vampires in Real Life

"CRAP," LAURYL MUMBLED as she felt her way into her dark apartment. Once again, she had forgotten to leave a light on before she had left for rehearsal and class this morning. Now, at quarter after nine, her apartment was dark. She tripped into the kitchen and stubbed her already-battered toes on the miscellaneous clutter on the floor. The clock on the microwave gave off enough turquoise light for her to find the light switch and turn it on. She piled her coat and bag on the counter, and checked her cell phone again.

Only a message from Anthony. Eamon had not called.

It had been a week since she'd heard from Eamon or seen him around the studio. Maybe he was out of town. She kicked off her shoes and tossed the cellphone and the mail onto the sofa. *I shouldn't have slept with him*, she thought as she flopped down. She tried to read the mail but her concentration was short lived. A horrible but short-lived wave of guilt washed over her about Anthony. It was replaced by anger at Eamon. No matter where he was, he could have called. She was sure he found the time to call Jennifer. She brushed the mail off her lap onto floor and stood up.

Screw this.

The day's rehearsal and classes drained her. Her shoulders drooped. All week long, she was drowsy and sluggish, and the smallest activity left her sweaty and winded. Although, she would get a peculiar second wind in the evenings, sometimes rehearsing alone until ten or eleven. Lauryl rolled her neck and massaged the knotted and tense muscles. It was the kind of tension that a hot shower and Icy Hot couldn't relieve.

"You're getting old, Mellis." She sighed and walked into her bedroom. Maybe her career wasn't going to be as long as she thought. Even Antonina noticed her sluggishness. Every dancer's body lasted different lengths of time, the old woman had told her in class.

With her coke habit, she had knocked a few years off. At the rate she had been snorting, there was no way that it couldn't have affected her. She frowned, rolled down her leotard and examined her upper body in the mirror. A reflection never lied. Everything appeared fine. Her slim shoulders possessed the perfect amount of muscle and her back was still strong. The muscles between her shoulder blades rippled when she turned in the mirror.

The mysterious fatigue also left her moody. She had snapped at Todd, who proceeded to tell her that she was leaving the interesting category and heading over to the bitch category.

She stuck her tongue out at her reflection and sighed.

"You're earlier than usual tonight," a voice said from behind her.

The voice sent an icy blast down her spine. She remained motionless. At first, she didn't turn around because no one was reflected in the mirror. The room was empty. However, after a few seconds, her awareness increased. She could feel whoever it was as if they were leaning against her. Her eyes darted around the room's reflection before she turned.

Eamon was standing an arm's length from her.

"I'm surprised that you're home so early."

She gulped down her scream before she turned to the mirror and then back to him. Lauryl touched his arm to confirm that he was not a hallucination. She pinched the sleeve of his suit jacket and rolled the wool fabric between her fingers. Without a doubt, he was standing there. There was no way she could imagine that smug look on his face. How could he not have a reflection? She stepped to the side, hoping she was blocking it.

"I don't have a reflection, Lauryl. I haven't had one for quite some time now."

The overwhelming dryness in her throat kept her silent for a moment. "What are you doing here?" she finally managed to say.

"Why don't you sit down?" he suggested and pointed to her bed. She remained frozen, though, staring at the mirror. "Forget the mirror."

"Wh… what are you?" she stammered.

Eamon put his hands in his pockets and smiled. "I'm a vampire."

A what? Was that supposed to be some sort of joke? Nervous laughter bubbled out of her. He walked up next to her and placed his hand on the glass. The only reflection was hers.

"O-o-kay," she said. "Any time now I'm either going to wake up or whatever and things are going to be normal. I mean…there's no way this—"

Eamon cut her off by lifting her hand and placing it on his chest. "I'm real, Lauryl. This is real. It's not a dream or a hallucination."

Lauryl's knees buckled under her and Eamon caught her by the arm. "There aren't vampires in real life."

Eamon raised his eyebrows. "Tell me how I can prove it to you." His grip tightened painfully on her arm before he let her go.

"I don't know! I'm so scared that I can't think!" Tears dropped down her cheeks as she rubbed the red finger marks on her arm.

He offered his handkerchief but she refused it. Instead she wiped her tears with the back of her hand like a child. "My theatrical entrance was the wrong approach. I haven't done that in a long time and I had no idea it would frighten you so." Eamon stepped closer to her and she took a step away. He chuckled. "Lauryl, I've wanted you for quite some time now."

Lauryl's eyes widened. "For what?"

"For me." He smiled and the tips of his sharp incisors were revealed.

"Oh my God," she breathed. Her hands clamped over her neck.

"That won't help. I've taken your blood before. Tonight, I'll complete the transformation."

"Are you freaking kidding?"

"Do you want to grow old? You dread the possibility of it." He turned her back toward the mirror. "See how beautiful you are? You'll stay like this forever."

Lauryl stared at her reflection. Her face was splotchy from crying and her hair hung over one of her eyes. Why did he think this was beautiful? Her chest rose and fell like a piston with each shallow breath she took and her heart pounded. When Eamon laced his arms around her waist, her breathing regulated and her heart slowed to a thump of curiosity, instead of fear. Now accustomed to his absent reflection, the sensation of his presence, both physical and emotional soothed her. She rested her hands on his and leaned into him. As her back melted into his chest, she closed her eyes and concentrated on the queer sense of safety she now enjoyed.

He lowered his mouth to her ear. "Beautiful," he whispered.

She tilted her head back and his lips brushed against her neck. Her eyes popped open. "No!"

"Why are you fighting me?" His mouth hovered just above her neck. Tiny beads of perspiration appeared on her skin.

"Why do you want me? You hardly even know me." She pulled away from him.

Eamon stared down at her. His eyes followed the graceful line from the small of her back, to her shoulders, and finally to her neck. "Lauryl." He waited a few seconds before he reached for her again. He placed his hands on her shoulders and with the slightest pressure, they relaxed. "Let me make your life better."

The warm, almost palpable sound of his voice caused her to crane her neck to him. It erased any fears or doubts or resistance. "Better?"

"Life doesn't have to be hard. No more living day-to-day, worrying about who's going to bring up your past. No more dealing with people you can't stand for their phoniness or superior attitude. You'll be above all that."

She turned around to him. What he said sounded perfect but she knew that it came at a cost. She also knew that she could. She didn't know exactly what that cost was, but she suspected that it would be high. But even that didn't make her say no. She didn't want to say no. Everything he said was what she wanted and that attraction to him was back. Defeat poured over her as she looked up at him. Her hand balled up into a fist and she gave his chest a feeble smack. That was the only resistance she could show to what he offered. Eamon didn't move. He just waited.

"I don't want to say yes but I can't say no," she managed to say.

"Shh." He brushed the hair from her neck and kissed her cheek.

More tears slid down her face but the sadness vanished when he kissed her neck. The touch of his lips quelled any rising anxiety. His hands on her low back were strong as they held her. A sigh arrested in her chest as the sudden and brief pain of his teeth piercing her skin rocketed through her body. She cried out and grabbed his shoulder to steady herself.

"No!" she whispered.

Eamon covered her mouth with his finger.

As much as she meant no, her body said yes. Instead of trying to get away from him, she molded her body to his. She continued to push her thin body against his, grabbing at the nape of his neck. Her hands dropped down to her sides as a tingling and buzzing crept up her arms. The sharp pain she experienced at first was long gone and she only felt the slight pressure of his mouth on her neck. Between her rapid breaths, she could hear the muffled swallowing sounds from Eamon as he drained her blood. For an eternity, she felt like she belonged to him.

Soon though, those feelings vanished and her consciousness drifted further and further away. A roar like ocean waves grew louder in her ears. The room spun and blurred around her but the wonderful sense of vertigo disappeared. She tried to focus on Eamon so she could beg him to make the morphine-like sensations of her dying body continue. Lauryl tried to reach up to his face, but her hand fell away.

Eamon yanked his sleeve up and bit into his inner wrist where his radial artery now hummed with her blood. Blood oozed rhythmically out of the bite. He shoved his wrist against her mouth. "Drink right now, darling."

Her eyes rolled back in her head but she managed to close her lips around the perfusing wound. After the first swallow, she placed her hand on his arm as the blood continued to pour into her mouth. It was unlike anything she had ever known. It was serenity, power, sex, and life all swirled together in one fluid. Her mind swirled as the blood flowed through her body. The solid, grounded feeling she had always known disappeared and lighter-than-air feeling replaced it. Her mind told her she was floating as she drank. Then he removed his wrist from her lips.

Eamon touched the back of her head and smoothed her auburn hair. *Enough*, he whispered in her mind. Lauryl stared at him, puzzled over why he was taking the magical feeling away. Her brain filled with static and she stumbled over her thoughts.

His brown eyes locked with hers. "You're now part of me. My blood flows in your veins and you'll feel me just as I'll feel you. You'll hear me just as I'll hear you. We're connected forever." Eamon kissed her lips gently.

The serious expression on his face puzzled Lauryl even further. She thought he said something but couldn't be certain. Her eyes followed his sensuous lips as they moved but she didn't hear anything. All she could think about was the magical liquid she had been gulping. It was so…she couldn't even begin to describe it with words. Now even that couldn't help her fight the overwhelming sleepiness that washed over her. Exhaustion and achiness crept around her body and a chill passed over her. Lauryl blinked a few more times and closed her eyes.

* * *

EAMON EMBRACED HER and licked the last drops of her blood from the rapidly healing bite on her neck. Her frame slumped in his arms as she became unconscious. Her body would now begin to multiply his blood cells in her veins and she would stay in the near death state while her body made the excruciating transformation from mortal human to vampire. He stared down at her limp body and laughed. She'd been so frightened that she never rolled up her leotard.

CHAPTER NINE
You Can Just Suck It, Eamon!

"LAURYL, OPEN YOUR eyes," Eamon said. "It might hurt when you take a breath, but don't panic."

Lauryl's chest ached as the cool air inflated her lungs and stretched her muscles. She turned her head to the sound of Eamon's voice and searched his face. All of her muscles protested as she moved them. She opened her mouth to speak, but even that proved to be too much right now. Eamon gathered her up and held her against him. His embrace calmed her and told her she was safe. She believed she was part of him and, for a moment, she believed that he was the only thing in the world that mattered. He kissed the top of her head, and all of the vertigo and aches stopped.

"How do you feel?"

The words took a few seconds to decode in her foggy mind. "Where am I?" Her gaze wandered around the unfamiliar surroundings. The abstract shapes formed together into more concrete images and she realized she wasn't in her bed or her room. She had no idea who the room belonged to. "What happened?" she asked with an edge of fear in her voice. The events of last night slowly came back to her. Her hands trembled as she reached up to her neck. She looked up at him. "No, it didn't really happen."

"Yes, it really did."

She tried to shrug away from him, but the sudden movement brought waves of nausea crashing over her. Lauryl clutched at him and placed her head against his chest again. The slow, faint sound of his heartbeat soothed her for the moment. Tears welled up in her eyes and stung them. He smoothed her hair a few times and kissed the top of her head again.

"It's not that bad," Eamon whispered.

"What?" She pulled away from him and waves of nausea and dizziness rocked her. He reached for her but she jerked the bed sheet over her. "I can't believe you'd say that to me!"

"I want you to trust me." He reached for one of her hands, which she had bound up in the sheet.

"Don't touch me!" she snapped. "How can you expect me to trust you?" With a final tug, she pulled the sheet up to her chin.

Eamon stared at the floor and tapped his foot a couple of times before standing up. "You need to get up. We have some things to talk about and I'm sure you're hungry."

Lauryl stopped rubbing her temples. Whatever that meant didn't sound good. "Hungry? What do you mean?"

"All of those unpleasant sensations you are feeling right now: the nausea, the dizziness, and that nagging little headache. That's what I mean by hungry. In a little while, I'll show you how to stop those."

"No, tell me now!"

He opened the door and turned back to her. "No, wait and see."

*   *   *

LAURYL WALKED DOWNSTAIRS and glanced down the hall. She had no idea where Eamon was. She checked the living room, the only other room she knew in his house, but he wasn't there. Frustration nipped at her. Lauryl walked back out into the hall.

"I have no idea where you are so how about giving me a hint," she said in a modified yell.

Eamon poked his head out of a door. "I'm in here and you don't need to raise your voice."

She watched him go back in and flipped him off. She stalked in to Eamon's study and took a quick look around. One wall was a large window that overlooked the beach. Along another wall, a large book shelf filled with books reached up to the ceiling. She sat down in front of his large antique desk and sighed. He sat there as if nothing unusual had happened last night. Like he was the normal one and the rest of the world was odd. She kicked the leg of his desk.

"I hate you."

"No, you don't." He stood up and walked around to the front of his desk. "You need to feed."

"On what?" she demanded, already knowing what he was going to say.

Eamon propped up against his desk and folded his arms across his chest. "I think you know what."

"I'm not going to."

"Oh really? What are you going to do?"

Her grip on the chair arms tightened. "I'm not doing that."

"Can't you say it?" he taunted. "Can't you say take someone's blood?"

"I'll starve first. God, you're a dick."

"Will you? Do you have any idea of what you're saying? Right now you only have a headache and a few other minor complaints but as your body demands blood, your condition will worsen."

"I've been through worse."

"What you felt for drugs is nothing compared to hungering for blood."

"Maybe I'll die."

Eamon shook his head. "You're ridiculous. Get out."

She walked to the door, turned, and stared at him defiantly. Her lips trembled as she struggled for something to say. Eamon held up his hand to cut off any argument.

"I hope you'll remember all of this bravado when you're so hungry that you offer me anything to help you. With your history and lack of discipline, I give you—" He glanced at his watch. "Maybe two hours. Three at the most."

She stormed out and he trailed after her into the living room. Lauryl spun around and almost collided with his chest. "You think I don't hate you? You have no idea of how much I hate you! What kind of monster does this to someone? Who picks a recovering addict for something like this? Who just kills, kidnaps and forces them into a life like this? Oh yes, you do! I thought you were a rich weirdo or something but this is beyond that! You're a selfish, twisted fucker!" Her lips pursed in frustration when she couldn't come up with anything more to say.

"Lauryl I'm willing to grant you a certain amount of latitude in your behavior as you transition into your new life," he said through clenched teeth. "But you'll clean up your white trash, gutter mouth and behave!"

Her lips trembled and she searched for a retort.

Eamon pushed her forward and she stumbled into a chair. "Now, it would be a good idea if you just stayed away from me until you come to your senses."

"Or what?" she asked.

"You don't want to know," he said, without turning around.

For some reason, she believed him. The restrained anger that buzzed in the air was tangible. It prickled against her skin and raised the little, red hairs on her arms. It lingered even after she heard his study door slam closed. She rubbed her arms and scanned the living room. It still looked like it should be in a magazine. The room seemed staged. That made sense. He was a fake. He left out a huge part of his biography. He never lied to her. He skipped over the important things. That was a lie of omission and her grandmother always said, a lie is a lie is a lie.

She picked up a magazine, *House Beautiful*, and flipped through it. She flipped through it again but didn't stop on any particular page. Her attention span was shrinking with each passing second. She leafed through the magazine again but couldn't focus.

This is insane, she thought.

She could do this. She tried to reach back to all of the things she learned in rehab and in Anthony's office. Anthony. Lauryl frowned and panicked inside. Would she ever see him again? What would she tell him? How could she explain something like this to him? Would she end up…Her mind trailed off and she clenched the magazine until the pages wrinkled.

Her head throbbed and her tongue scuttled over the roof of her mouth. It felt carpeted with cotton. She closed her eyes and wished that she could cry. Right now, she was so thirsty she would drink her own tears. None came though. She dropped her head between her knees in an effort to ease the pounding in her head but the sound of the clock chiming in the hallway stabbed at her.

"Pace," she said. The strain in her voice caused her to jump. It sounded foreign to her. She walked around the room and settled into a track in front of the French doors to the terrace. At first, she walked with careful and deliberate steps, trying to focus and keep her thoughts organized but her steps quickened as time passed. She twisted her auburn hair around her fingers and yanked them to deflect the hunger pangs that assailed her.

Her ability to form rational thoughts dissolved. She walked out onto the terrace and as she stared at the sand and rocks, she wished for a jogger to come by. One lonely jogger. One foolish jogger out for a night time run. That's all she wanted. The more she imagined the unfortunate runner, the happier she became. It wasn't much. It was only a little want. In her mind, she could smell their sweat, feel their racing heartbeat, and most important-ly feel their blood rush.... She stopped her racing thoughts and dug her nails into her arms until blood appeared. No sooner had the blood welled up on her arm, the tiny half-moon cuts started to close.

She shook her head and walked back inside. "No! No! I am not going to do it!" She looked at the wall dividing the living room and his study. She could hear jazz music through the wall and suspected he was enjoying her agony. He couldn't see her but he knew. He had to.

She walked out in to the hall and stared at the door to his study until the oak grain lines blurred together. She could feel him, like he was pulling her to him. She tried to steady her hands, which now shook with coarse tremors. For a moment, she didn't think she'd be able to turn the brass handle so she kicked it a couple of times. When Eamon failed to respond, she forced her hand to be still enough to turn the knob.

Lauryl took a few tentative steps into the room. The air was lighter and cooler than in the living room. She hugged herself and took a few more steps toward him. He didn't acknowledge her. He remained engrossed in the document in his hand. She forced herself forward until she was in front of him. Eamon still didn't look up at her.

"Eamon?" She shifted her weight from foot to foot while she waited for him to answer. "Please."

"Please what?" he asked.

"Please?" Her heels clicked on the floorboards.

"Please what?" he repeated.

"Oh God, Eamon. Please make it stop! Help me!" Suddenly, she darted around his desk and dropped to her knees in front of him. Her fingers squeezed his thighs and she climbed up into his lap.

"Help me," she whispered into his neck.

"I'm going to." He moved her hands away from his belt. "But you need to listen to me and do as I say." He tilted her chin up. "Look at me. If you do as I say, you'll feel better."

Her arms circled him and she nodded. "I will. I'll do whatever you say."

"Remember that," he said as they walked out to his black BMW 750i.

*   *   *

"WHY ARE YOU stopping here?" Lauryl asked when Eamon pulled the car over. The sketchy neighborhood was all too familiar. Drummond Commons was where her dealer worked. Hookers and homeless people also populated the seedy area. Two gunshots rang out but none of the people on the street appeared to care. She sank down in the seat and covered her face with her hand. *This is bad*, she thought. *All I need is for somebody to see me.* She fidgeted for a second and then relaxed. The dark window tinting would shield her from curious stares.

Eamon noticed her fidgeting. "Lauryl, no one will see you or remember you. You have complete control over this situation."

She glanced back at him. "Are you reading my mind?"

"Yes," he answered flatly.

"Why?"

"Because I can."

"You're a prick."

"Perhaps but I'm not the one who is hungry. Now, pick one of these girls and I'll help you."

"You pick," she said as she watched two prostitutes on the sidewalk start to fight. They kicked and scratched at each other like two cats. One caught the other girl's face with her nails, leaving a slice along her cheek. The wound opened and blood trailed down her face. Lauryl sat forward. "Forget it. That one." She stabbed her finger against the car window several times toward the girl.

Eamon followed her finger to the girl with the bloody face. She was a petite blonde who probably was a minor. Her black miniskirt snugly followed her shape, skimming the bottom of her butt cheeks. The tops of her vinyl, thigh high boots started a few inches below the skirt's hemline. Her top had the smears of blood from where she wiped her face clean. She pulled the white half-shirt off and put it back on so the stains were in the back. Eamon pulled the car over to her and rolled down the window.

Their presence irritated the girl. She gave them the finger, but after she noticed that the BMW, she became interested in them. "Hi, honey," she said and popped her gum. She leaned against the car and looked in. When she saw Lauryl, she pointed her finger at her. "I know you, right?"

Lauryl sank back into her seat again. "No, you don't"

"Guess not," she said. She turned back to Eamon. "What do you want, handsome?"

"My wife and I are wanting something a little different; a threesome."

The girl shrugged. "C note"

Eamon nodded and unlocked the back door. "Get in."

She climbed in the back of the car and tapped Eamon on the shoulder. "There's the payment thing. You pay in advance."

"Of course," he said as he handed her the money. The one-hundred-dollar bill disappeared down one of her boots.

"My name's Jules. So I'm guessing you aren't a cop."

Eamon laughed. "No, I'm not."

She popped her gum again and turned back to Lauryl. "Are

you sure I don't know you?"

"Yes I'm sure." The snap of her gum caused her to jump.

"It's cool if I do. I mean, who am I telling, right?" She laughed and leaned forward. "You just look like someone I used to see...around."

Lauryl cut her eyes at Eamon, who appeared to concentrate on the road.

Relax, he said in her mind.

She did a double take, unsure if she'd heard him or not.

This will be over soon, he continued.

She turned to Jules and then to him. So he could use telepathy. She stared at him for a second and hoped for some sort of confirmation but he didn't look at her. He watched the road.

"There's a place we can go right up here," Jules said. "On the right."

"Fine."

They parked and followed Jules to a room. While they waited for her to unlock the door, Lauryl took several deep breaths, breathing in the smell of this girl's life. She could smell the dried blood on her face, the sweat from the earlier fight with the other hooker and something else; a faint, rubbery smell. Cocaine. That was where the girl knew Lauryl. She must know her dealer. She took another breath, this time so deep that Jules turned around. Lauryl covered her embarrassment with a shrug and walked in the room. Jules closed the door behind them. Eamon positioned himself in a corner, leaned against the wall and put his hands in his pockets. Lauryl remained in the middle of the small room, in front of the bed.

"Are you okay? You look like you're ready to freak out."

"She's fine," Eamon said "Just a little shy." He walked over to Jules and pulled her shirt off. "I'll start and then she can join us when she's ready." Eamon fondled Jules' breasts and licked along her neck.

Lauryl's mouth opened in shock. She didn't know if she was shocked by her 'husband' groping another woman or by how delicious the girl smelled. She watched Eamon continue to kiss Jules' collarbone and neck. He looked up at her and his eyes shifted some in color. The amber shade morphed into a deeper brown.

The cut on the girl's face re-opened and a thin stream of blood ran down her face. Jules wiped it away with her fingers and Eamon took her fingers into his mouth. All of a sudden, a quick, piercing pain stung in Lauryl's mouth and she tasted watery blood. She probed the area with her tongue and felt two fangs at the source of the watery blood. Her head pounded with greater intensity as she watched Eamon and Jules. She moved forward and touched her. Her skin was hot. Lauryl pulled her hand away and looked at Eamon. He continued to caress the girl's firm breasts. He whispered something in her ear and she laughed before sliding her skirt up to reveal her red thong underwear. The sound of blood pumping roared in Lauryl's ears. It died away and all that remained was the sound of a heartbeat; Jules' heartbeat.

"Don't you hear that?" she asked him, her green eyes bright with excitement.

He shook his head and turned Jules so that she faced him. The eager girl unbuttoned his shirt and kissed his chest.

"What do you hear?" he asked.

The soft, sexual sound of Eamon's voice distracted Lauryl. An inexplicable wave of jealousy passed over her and she wanted it to be her that Eamon was caressing. "Her," she said. She now stood so that Jules was in between the two of them. The heat rising off the prostitute was tangible. Beads of perspiration appeared on Jules' neck as she undressed Eamon. Lauryl took another deep breath of her.

Suddenly aware of Lauryl's presence, Jules turned as Lauryl took a predatory lunge for her. Lauryl clamped her hand over Jules' mouth and pushed her down to the bed. Jules kicked with desperation but was no match for Lauryl's new agility and strength. With a free hand, Lauryl pushed Jules' head to the side exposing her neck.

"Stop wasting time and do it," Eamon said as he buttoned his shirt.

She opened her mouth and saliva trickled down on Jules' neck. When Jules saw the fangs in Lauryl's mouth, she kicked and struggled with more ferocity.

"Do it now," Eamon told her. "This is what you wanted!"

Lauryl gave in to Eamon. She sank her teeth in Jules' neck and blood spewed into her mouth from the artery. The delicious metallic taste was like nothing she had ever known. Not even the rush of coke compared to this. Her eyes rolled back into her head as the warm liquid intoxicated her. She sucked harder on Jules' neck to make the blood come faster, but the fragile flesh tore in her mouth.

"Not so fast!" Eamon tried to separate her from the dying girl, but Lauryl smacked at his hands. "Enough!" He grabbed Lauryl by a hank of her hair and pulled her off. She tried to scramble back to her but Eamon stepped in front of her. "She's dead. You're probably going to be sick from draining her so fast!"

Lauryl sank back to the floor. "What did I do? What did you make me do?"

"I didn't make you do anything." He paused a moment. "Are you alright?"

"Yes," She looked over at Jules' lifeless body. "She knew me. I can't believe I did that."

"Don't pity her. You probably did her a favor. The only one who'll miss her is her pimp."

She stared at him, stunned by his lack of care.

"Now, let's go."

* * *

LAURYL GOT IN the car and rubbed her hands together. She had killed someone and took pleasure in it. The entire horrendous event replayed in her mind.

"I…" She broke off and retched a few times.

"I told you that you'd be sick." He rolled down her window. "If you're going to vomit, do it out there."

She leaned out of the window and did just that. Each horrible retch tore at her insides. Lauryl clutched at her stomach and moaned. When it stopped, she dropped her head against the door frame and closed her eyes.

Eamon tapped his finger on the steering wheel with a rapid

cadence and waited for her to finish. "Better?" he asked when she leaned back in the car.

"I guess so." She wiped her mouth with the handkerchief he'd thrown at her.

He didn't say another word to her on the way home. When they got to the house, he walked around to her side of the car. Not to help her out or make sure she was all right. He checked to make sure she hadn't thrown up on the side of the car. He scowled at her, shook his head and then went inside, slamming the door behind him.

She followed him inside but stopped at the stairs. Her eyes darted around the foyer as she pieced together her thoughts. Lauryl raced down the hall into his study.

"You knew! You knew how I would react. You enjoyed watching me be controlled by that."

"I have no idea what you are talking about," he said. He checked his phone and then sat down.

"Liar! How did you think an addict would react? I—"

Eamon shot up from his seat, cutting her off. "You chose what happened this evening. Through your defiance, you chose those sensations you experienced. I would think the experience would have humbled you but it didn't." He leaned across the desk toward her. "I'm sorry your experience was uncomfortable and unsettling. I'm sorry I can't control that. It will happen again unless you accept what you are and the needs you have!"

Drugs, she thought. *This is just like drugs.*

"No, you're wrong. You can control this."

"And you can control me," she said, ignoring that he was in her mind again.

Eamon sat back down. He rocked in the chair a few times and a grin appeared. Her anger keyed back up at the sight of his smile so he scaled it down. "I don't want to control you. I just want—"

"I know what you want," she said, interrupting him. "And it's not what I want."

He laughed. "That isn't what I meant. What I was going to say was I want to help you so you can adjust to life with me."

She studied his face for a moment. Was he serious? What

reason could he give her that would make her want to let him help her? Or even stay in the same room with him? She opened her mouth to speak but he cut her off.

"The reason I can give you is I'm all you have," he said. He folded his hands in his lap.

The fact he was being so cold was one thing, but invading her thoughts pushed her over the edge. "Get out of my fucking head! I can't stand that. How do you do that?"

"At last, a question of merit even though it's wrapped in foul language."

"You can just suck it, Eamon. You can't expect me to just fall in line with this. I still don't even know what the f..., heck happened to my life and me. All I know is I woke up tonight after you killed me and turned me into what you are, and then I killed someone too by drinking all their blood. Oh and you felt that girl up and basically cheered me on while I killed her." She flopped down in the chair across from him. "Have I left anything out?"

"Are you done?"

She nodded.

"I admit that I didn't give you much say in what happened to you. However, that's something that cannot be changed. If you let me, I'll make you happy. If you let me, I'll teach you how to transition into your life as a vampire." His serious expression faded and he chuckled. "'You can just suck it, Eamon.' That was funny."

Lauryl relaxed and her mood lifted briefly but then she dropped her head down. "What am I going to do? I have no clue of what to do." Her chin quivered and she covered her face with her hands.

"Your life isn't going to change that much," he began. "You and I will be married or what the outside world thinks of as married and you will now live here with me."

Her fingers separated and she peeked out. "And?"

"And," he continued. "You'll conform to the necessary restrictions I have."

"Like what?"

"Practicing self-discipline. To live like this, you must control your temper or you won't last long."

"What about my life? I'm not as easy to miss as that poor hooker. Don't you think people are going to wonder why I don't dance anymore? Or how you and I got married out of the blue?"

"Lauryl, I never do anything without planning. I've already informed Martin that you and I were married in a private ceremony and that you won't be continuing your career as a dancer."

Lauryl glared at him.

"Is there anything else you want to ask me?"

"Why me?"

"Because I've wanted you since I saw you in Seattle."

"Couldn't you just bang me a couple of times and then not call me? That's the normal thing. Why'd you have to do this?"

"As I said, I knew I wanted you. You have a magnificent strength in you. Your will drives you. The passion in you that you have little control over now will help you as a vampire, if you learn to control it. When I saw you in Seattle, I knew that you would be an amazing vampire. You're beautiful and strong, like a vampire should be."

His words confused her. She felt pride in what he said but at the same time, she was furious at his selfishness. "Yeah, I didn't want to be a vampire, though."

"You didn't say no," he said.

"Yes, I did."

"I believe you said, 'I don't want to say yes but I can't say no.'"

"I also said that I didn't want to say yes."

"We can debate the semantics of that conversation for hours but it's irrelevant now. You're a vampire and there's nothing to do but accept it."

"Okay, I accept it but I hate it. How about that?"

His eyes narrowed at her reply. "Let's move on. You'll need to feed at least twice a week. It will become easier for you and I'm sure you'll develop your own methods for finding blood. I'll help you until you're accustomed to it."

"Does that ever happen?"

"It even becomes pleasurable."

"You're joking, right?"

"No, I'm not."

She waited for him to smile, laugh, or wink but he didn't. He was serious. "Why'd you make me kill that girl?"

"So you would know the feeling of killing someone."

"Was it necessary?"

"Yes. It was."

How did you get used to something like this? she wondered. She dropped her chin to her chest and sighed. Lauryl ran her tongue over where her fangs had been. "Do our teeth only come out when we're going to bite someone?"

"No, if you concentrate, they'll come out. Or if you become excited." He watched as she gingerly poked her tongue along her gum line. "Try it."

She closed her eyes for a second and focused. The sharp canines descended almost immediately. She ran her tongue up one side and down the other of one and flicked the point. Her eyes snapped opened and she covered her mouth with her hand. "Oh my god."

"Let's see."

"No."

"Don't be shy. Show me."

She flipped her hand from her mouth.

"You shouldn't be so uncomfortable about it. It's not like I haven't seen it before."

The teeth retracted and she frowned. "I'm a monster."

"You don't look like a monster."

"That's what makes it worse!" She shifted in the seat and gave up on getting comfortable. "Your furniture sucks."

"Come here."

Lauryl stood at attention in front of him. He took her hand and she tried to shake loose from him. However, she found that she couldn't. The grip wasn't painful. It was consistent. The grip let her know that it was pointless to fight him. She allowed him to pull her down on to his lap, although she sat woodenly.

"Now, this isn't so bad."

His soft voice next to her ear melted her irritation. "No, it's not."

Eamon moved her hair away from her neck and kissed her. "This doesn't have to be hard. It's simply a matter of letting go."

"Letting go of what?" Lauryl turned her face to his. She licked her lips, parting them slightly for him to kiss her. Eamon's lips touched hers lightly at first, testing her reaction. The kiss deepened as she opened herself to him. Desire raced through her body when he kissed her before but this time, there was no comparison. Everywhere he touched tingled and hummed. When he pulled away from her for a moment, she looked at him like a greedy child, wanting more candy. He bent down to continue but stopped just above her lips.

"What am I supposed to let go of?" she whispered as she ran her fingers along his cheek. An anxious gasp came from her as his hand slid between her thighs.

"Yourself." His mouth covered hers and his hand continued up her thigh until her hand slammed down on his.

Lauryl struggled to break free of him. His hands that seemed to be everywhere but she was no match in strength. Finally, out of ideas, she bit down on his lip with her fangs. Hot blood shot into her mouth and the palm of his hand slapped her jaw. The force of the slap knocked her loose and he bolted to his feet, dumping her to the floor. Blood trickled from his bottom lip. Eamon touched it and then moved his hand. Two perfect punctures just under his lip line sparkled red. Eamon loomed over her. For a second, a surge of almost morphine like euphoria and power resonated in her. She shook her head to clear the feelings and wondered if maybe his slap had been harder than she first thought. Her mouth tingled with a feeling she could only equate to when she would rub her teeth and gums with the coke left after she had snorted up the rest. With a feline movement, she hopped onto her hands and knees.

He reached out to touch her face where he had slapped her, but recoiled and dropped his hand to his side instead. "What you're feeling is the effect of my blood in you," he said curtly. "Another vampire's blood is different than a human's blood.

Especially a vampire of my…years." He rubbed his lower lip again. The wounds were healed. The only evidence of her assault were two pink circles.

"I'm not going to say I'm sorry. I mean, what did you expect? You wouldn't let me go and I didn't know what else to do when you said that."

He sat back down in his chair. "My suggestion is not to be contrary to me," he said after a long pause.

Lauryl stood up. "I can't believe you expect me to let go of who I am just to make you happy. Until you let me come to this on my own, we're going to keep fighting."

"Not to threaten, but as your maker I can make you do or feel whatever I choose."

"Is that what you want?"

"It's what I can do," he replied. "If I wanted to, I could have you worship me and do anything to please me."

"Is that what you want?"

He lifted his eyebrows in a challenge. She stared back at him, unmoved.

"No, I want you willingly. I'll wait."

She walked out of the study and stopped after she closed the door. Would he do that to her? How would she know? *Maybe I should lock my bedroom door*, she thought.

"A lock won't stop me, darling," he called through the closed door.

I bet me telling you to go fuck yourself would.

He didn't have anything to say to that.

CHAPTER TEN

Let's Face It, Your Social Skills Suck

L AURYL FROWNED AT the empty mirror in front of her. She wondered if she would ever become accustomed to not having a reflection. *Just another one of the perks of being a vampire,* she thought sarcastically. She finished dressing and sighed. Eamon would be expecting her downstairs and she knew if she didn't show up, he'd come get her. The past two weeks she had been indoctrinated in her new routine; wake, dress and report down to him for whatever he had planned. Usually it was just feeding or sitting and watching him work on his business, although he had been promising to tell her more about being a vampire. Maybe tonight would be the night.

She hurried down to Eamon's study and stood in front of his desk.

"Good evening," he said, not looking up from the paper he was reading.

"Yeah, hey. You've been saying you're going to tell me more about what we can do." Lauryl fidgeted with her nails.

Eamon put down his reading and thought for a moment. "As a vampire?"

She nodded and found a seat. "Yes."

"I can't believe what I'm hearing. You want to know more about being a vampire?" His eyes widened in feigned shock.

She nodded. "Look, I said I accepted it so knock off the jokes and tell me more."

He reached for his drink. "I'm pleased that you want to know more about your new life."

"There's got to be more than just offing people."

"You've killed one person and that person would have been

killed by someone sooner or later."

"I haven't been able to get that girl's eyes out of my head."

"Don't be so dramatic. It was one person. You haven't killed anyone else. In fact, it's more elegant if you don't kill them."

"I don't get it."

"What I'm saying is that it's better if you remove the memory of feeding. Do you recall when you were still human and I came to your apartment to apologize?"

She nodded.

"What do you remember after you came?"

She only remembered waking up alone. "I don't really remember anything except you coming by and getting some."

"And after?"

"Nothing."

"You don't remember because I used my mind to take away part of that night. While you were lying in my arms, I was taking your blood."

Her eyebrows snapped together in a scowl. "That's f... messed up."

"On the contrary, I think it's quite generous of me. Would you like to have remembered me leaning over you with my fangs bared?"

That image came to her mind and she shivered a bit. "Not particularly." The image lingered and soon, a familiar warmth increased between her legs. Her hand slid down her thigh. She stopped when she realized that it was Eamon.

"Sorry, I was just having fun."

Lauryl scratched her face with her middle finger.

"Anyway," he continued. "I've been helping you by mentally erasing the memories of the humans you've fed from these past weeks, but you'll need to learn soon."

"I guess."

"Anything else?"

"Yeah, why don't we leave marks on people when we bite them?"

Eamon shrugged. "When we bite a human, the saliva that lingers in the wound speeds the healing process. Usually all you will leave is a bruise, which can be explained as overzealous lovemaking or a love bite."

"A what?" She cocked her head to the side.

"A love bite. A bruise left when a lover sucks on the skin." Eamon frowned.

"Oh, you mean a hickey!" Lauryl laughed. "I never heard it called a love bite. I guess for us, it fits."

"I believe it's unrelated to us."

"You really have no sense of humor, do you?"

He cleared his throat. "Do you have any more questions?"

Aggravating Eamon was fun. His nonexistent sense of humor was an easy target. She perked up and swung her legs, skimming her feet against the wood floor. "We really don't age?"

"No, we don't."

"Why don't we sleep in coffins?"

"Because we don't need to. That came from long ago when vampires hid in crypts and cemeteries during the day. You only need to shield yourself from the sun. Beds in darkened rooms are far more comfortable."

"And I already know the whole no reflection thing," she mumbled. "No changing into a bat or a wolf?"

"I'm afraid not. But your senses are enhanced dramatically now. Also your human abilities such as strength and speed have increased."

"Can we fly?"

"On an airplane."

"Crosses? Holy Water? Are they dangerous to us?"

"I was a practicing Catholic until the Church of England was created." The historical reference sailed over Lauryl's head. "When I do visit church, I attend Anglican services."

"Are any of the movie things true?"

"A few. The invitation part is true. A person must willingly allow you into their life. Once they do, you have free reign over them, especially if you've taken their blood. You can read their thoughts and manipulate them. If you concentrate enough, you can accomplish just about anything. You can even unlock doors with your mind."

"What?"

"You're capable of certain telekinetic powers. Vampires are very cerebral creatures, darling. They rely on their mind quite a bit. Stupid or dull witted vampires are few and far between."

"I'm not exactly a genius."

"You're more intelligent than you realize. You haven't uncovered the extent of your power. You're still a young vampire."

"There's so much."

"Indeed there is."

"You could help some."

"I want you to learn to use your own skills and judgment."

"Thanks for nothing," she mumbled.

"If you'd let go of some of that anger, you'd pick up these things a lot quicker."

Lauryl bit back several insults and stared at him. "How come you don't socialize with other vampires?"

Eamon loosened his tie as he walked to the sofa and sat down. "Why do I need to?"

Lauryl shrugged. "Why wouldn't you?"

"You've answered a question with a question."

She rolled her eyes and sighed. "Just answer the question."

"I see no need to socialize with vampires. I'm in the unique position of not having to rely on other vampires for survival or gain so I choose to keep to myself. I only associate with vampires of my line. They're my family and responsibility."

"That's pretty snotty of you. I mean, you could just be friends with them because you share the same experiences or whatever."

He shook his head and rolled up his shirtsleeves. Eamon dropped the cuff links in his shirt pocket. "I've been this way for a long time and see no reason to change. I'm content this way."

"Have you ever thought that maybe other vampires might want to be friends with you or get to know you at least?"

"Yes, those are the ones that want something from me."

Lauryl laughed. "It'd take them about ten minutes to figure out how you were and then they'd be gone."

Eamon narrowed his eyes. "My limited social circle is through my choosing."

She walked over to him, placed her hands on his knees, and leaned in close to him. His gaze settled on the enticing view of her breasts that her pose and blouse now afforded him.

"You just don't have any friends. Let's face it, your social skills suck."

He took her hands and ran them up his thighs until she resisted. "Maybe," he began in a soft, inviting tone. "However, my social skills were adept enough to get you on your back."

Rather than jerk back, Lauryl didn't move. Her green eyes glinted. "Too bad I was thinking of Anthony the whole time."

"And too bad I had come from Jennifer Conrad's bed to yours." He let go of her hands and she backed away. He sat in silence for a moment. "Lauryl, I shouldn't have said that."

"Yeah." She crossed her arms over her chest and hugged herself. The image of Jennifer and Eamon together wasn't one she wanted in her head but it wouldn't leave. She looked over at him. He didn't take responsibility for the nasty image. It lingered on its own.

"I have something for you." He reached into his briefcase next to the sofa and opened a red leather Cartier box. A ring with large round emerald surrounded by diamonds shined against the tan suede interior. He slid it on her finger.

Lauryl stared down at the ring. "It's beautiful."

"Just like you." He leaned forward and attempted to kiss her. She pulled away and turned her head. Unfazed, he continued, "If you don't like it, you can select something else next time we go to New York."

"No, this is great. Thanks."

"Now, that makes it official."

"Yeah." She nodded her head and sighed. The ring suddenly felt heavier on her finger. She balled her hand into a fist.

"The stone matches your eyes."

Lauryl looked away. "You shouldn't buy me things like this. You'll spoil me."

Eamon pulled her onto his lap. "I want to spoil you. I want you to have everything you want." He kissed the top of her head and played with a lock of her hair. "Will you let me do that?"

A smile appeared on her face for a moment. "Could you handle me as a spoiled little princess?"

"I think I would love you more that way."

She tried to imagine herself as spoiled and overindulged. When she did, she saw herself as Jennifer Conrad. The image brought on a nauseating feeling and she pulled away.

"I'm not a princess. It's just not me."

He took her hand and kissed it, then turned it over and kissed the palm. The maze work of scars over her wrist caught his eye. Thin, red, jagged lines ran up and down her lower arm. "Lauryl."

Regret and embarrassment tugged at her. With everything that had happened with Eamon, she had forced the memory of her past into the recesses of her mind. His inspection of her arms brought it back. She tugged her hand away, wishing she was wearing long sleeves. "Didn't you know?"

"I knew, but I didn't know you did that." He picked up the other wrist and saw the same. "I'm sorry."

"Don't be sorry for me," she said as she pulled her arm away. "Just be glad that I wasn't as good of a surgeon as I am a dancer."

"That's not funny."

"It's in the past. Nothing to do about it now."

"I'll have to keep you happy," Eamon said. He placed his hands on her shoulders and rubbed them.

Her shoulders tensed at his touch and she jerked away. Lauryl slapped his hands off when he tried to catch her. "You couldn't work hard enough," she said and bolted from the room.

Eamon was beginning to believe that.

CHAPTER ELEVEN

None of That Hollywood Crap About the Sun Reducing Us to Ashes is True

THE RIDE HOME from Eamon and Lauryl feeding was silent. Each time he looked at her, she would turn her head away from him. And each time he tried to initiate any conversation, he received one word responses or nothing at all. Eamon pulled the car into the drive of the house and turned to Lauryl. She sat with her arms crossed over her chest, pouting. He rested his forehead on the steering wheel and sighed.

"Tell me, is there anything that might make you happy? I've offered to take you anywhere in the world and you refuse. You seem committed to being miserable."

"I'm miserable because of you," Lauryl snapped.

"Me?"

"Yeah, you. I don't love you. Most days I don't even like you. You're boring."

"I just took you out," he said lightly.

"To EAT! All we do is stay in this house except for when we go out and...feed."

"You're the one who is being difficult. What is so terrible about your life?"

Lauryl's eyes widened. "I can't believe you're asking that. You took the one thing away from me that mattered. The thing I loved. But why should you care? Your life is all good. You've still got everything. You could at least let me run the dance company."

He tapped the steering wheel for a moment. "No, not right now."

Lauryl's jaw dropped. "What? Why?"

"You're not ready. I never know how you're going to behave and you make no effort to show me anything different."

Her hand balled into a fist. "Selfish," she hissed. "You only think of yourself and what you want." She raised her fist up to hit him but instead twisted off her wedding ring and chucked it at him. The ring bounced off his chest onto the floorboard of the car. She yanked on the locked door handle several times before he unlocked it. Lauryl jumped out of the car onto the pea gravel drive, her heels sinking in the tiny rocks. She stumbled forward a few steps but caught herself before she fell. She kicked off the shoes and hurled them down the drive. "These fucking shoes!" she yelled. She ran into the house and slammed the door behind her.

"Christ," Eamon said as he put his head back on the steering wheel. From the corner of his eye, he saw the ring sparkling on the floor. He scooped it up and put it in his pocket.

Why was this so difficult? Why couldn't she enjoy her life? Her statement about how she didn't even like him most days continued to play in his mind. It was remarkable how much that bothered him. His feelings were hurt. Or he guessed they were. Ages had passed since he actually experienced something akin to that. His pride was wounded and the prickly, sullen mood that was settling over him confounded him. He got out of the car and walked down the drive to retrieve her shoes.

The situation perplexed him to say the least. Women found him attractive and always enjoyed keeping him company. He'd never found someone who didn't want to be a vampire when offered the chance. Irina pursued him. Jennifer Conrad would more than likely jump at the chance to be a vampire and be with him. He suspected that she would jump at any wealthy man, vampire or not. He knew that she'd be on her back for him the moment he saw her. Eamon bent down and picked up the black Jimmy Choo shoes and stuck one in each of his jacket pockets.

"Six hundred dollars thrown down the drain," he muttered when he noticed a scrape on one of them. His phone vibrated in his pocket. Irina. "Yes?"

"How goes life with the newborn?"

"It's fine," he said. Eamon walked in the house and heard Lauryl's door slam. He threw the shoes up the stairs. "Why would you ask?"

"Because your companion is not like you at all." She laughed. "And she seems to be a feisty sort."

"She is spirited." He said as he walked into his study. He poured himself a drink and fell back into his chair. "I think she'll adjust in time though." He drained the glass in one gulp.

"If you say so."

"Goodnight, Irina." Eamon hung up and tossed the phone onto the desk.

He didn't need Irina and her taunting. For the next hour he didn't even want to think of women. Eamon frowned. Lauryl and her temper were wearing on him. All she did was argue. That wasn't what he wanted when he chose Lauryl. He wanted a companion, not a sparring partner. Now it was a challenge. Eamon took the emerald ring from his pocket and looked up at the ceiling.

"Darling, I don't like it when I don't get what I want."

*   *   *

"WHAT THE—" LAURYL muttered as she saw the book on the pillow next to her head. *The Taming of the Shrew.* She rolled out of the bed, swept the book off the pillow on to the floor and proceeded to kick the offensive little book along as she got dressed. She picked it up, carried it to the top of the stairs, and kicked it down them, smirking as it bounced down to the lower level. She bounced behind it. She curtsied to it and kicked it down the hall to Eamon's study. Lauryl opened the door, gave it a swift kick inside the room, and followed it two beats behind.

Eamon looked up in time to see the book skim across the floor and her pick it up. She held it away from her between her thumb and index finger. It flapped back and forth as she waved it toward him.

"Good. You found it. Get reading."

"Why?"

"You need to broaden your education."

"And you just happened to pick this play?"

"Shakespeare is timeless." He slid his papers to the other side of the desk. "You can sit here."

Lauryl reluctantly sat down and he opened the book in front of her. "This is going to be hard. I hated school," she mumbled.

"I know that. That's why you have to do this." He walked to the credenza where he kept his liquor and pulled out a bottle of wine. "You can make up for you lack of enthusiasm now."

He poured each of them a glass of wine and set hers on the desk. "Say thank you."

She snapped the book shut. "Thank you, Eamon, for the wine and this marvelous opportunity to learn. If you want me to read this, you'll have to leave me alone."

He snickered and sat down. "I've had my fun."

Lauryl picked up the book. The language was difficult at first but as she got used to it, the play was funny. She even laughed aloud a couple of times. She knew the reason why he'd picked this particular play. He thought he could steer her to obedience through the events in the play. He wanted her to play Kate to his Petrucchio.

She looked up at him, primed to tell him what she thought of his 'lesson'. Eamon was engrossed in whatever he was reading. After a few moments, he looked up at her and smiled. Vampire or human, he was handsome. His slow, sexy smile made her tingle and that irritated her. Even though she wanted to hate him and be scornful of everything he did for her, she couldn't when he gave her that certain look. Worst of all, she found herself desiring him more and more. It was hard to hate someone when you wanted them to be covering your body with their mouth and....

She put down the book and spun the chair around a few times. Watching the room turn from a blur to normal brought back one of the simple joys of her childhood. With each spin, her grin increased in size and on the last one, she giggled. When the chair stopped, Eamon watched her with a puzzled expression.

"Is that entertaining you?"

"I used to love it when I was a kid."

"I see. Don't let me keep you from it then."

His superior tone killed any enjoyment she found. She picked up the book. "I'm done," she said, fanning it in front of him. "I guess you'll want a book report."

"No," he said as he put down his reading. "Did you learn anything?"

"Yes, as a matter of fact I did."

"And what was that?" he asked.

"I learned Shakespeare isn't as hard to read as I thought!"

The smug expression vanished and he semi-scowled. "That's not what I meant."

"I know what you meant. You wanted me to see the error of my ways and become a perfect and obedient wife."

"Yes, that's what I wanted."

"Well, too bad."

"For who?"

"What do you mean by that?" Lauryl narrowed her eyes and tipped her head to the side.

"One day, you'll enjoy being a vampire. You'll even admit that you like me."

She laughed and shook her head. "Like you? Not a chance."

"Maybe not tonight."

"Maybe never."

"Never is a long time."

"It seems like all I have is time."

"You'll see," he predicted.

"No, I don't think I will."

Eamon finished his wine and walked to the desk. "I'm never wrong."

"Never is a long time, to quote someone," she said.

"You amaze me. You seem to delight in provoking me. I wouldn't tolerate this kind of treatment from anyone but you."

"Oh, that's a fucking honor." She ran to the door, swung it open, and turned back to him. "'I see a woman may be made a fool, if she had not the spirit to resist.'" She gritted her teeth and bolted for her room.

That line from the play stuck in her head. In her case, it was true. However, she wanted to scream after she said it. Eamon nodded in happy agreement. He even winked at her. No doubt, he was pleased at her recitation of the play.

She paced around her room for a few second, twisting a large lock of hair around her fingers and yanking on it. A few more yanks and then she sat down on her bed.

It would only be a few minutes before he came up after her.

*   *   *

EAMON CHECKED HIS watch. Two hours had passed since Lauryl's theatrical exit. She tried so hard to be dramatic, but instead, she ended up comical. Her haughty expression along with her quick strides to the door ended with an attempt to slam it behind her. She hadn't been so lucky. She shut the door too fast and it collided with her left foot, causing her to stumble. He didn't laugh then but now, why shouldn't he? It was funny. Funniest of all was the imperious expression on her face. He pushed back from the desk and went upstairs to see what she was doing.

He peeked in her room and she stiffened. Lauryl stretched across her bed on her stomach. Her feet crossed back and forth over each other, her shoes hanging off her toes. Eamon cleared his throat and her feet stopped.

"Yes?" she asked, acknowledging his unwanted presence.

He leaned against the doorframe. "I'm being patient."

The shoes fell off her feet. "Oh?"

He laughed and took a few steps closer to the bed. "I admire you, Lauryl. I really do."

"Is that so?" She noticed him staring at her legs and quickly rolled up on her knees and pulled down her skirt.

"Be downstairs in five minutes," Eamon said as he walked to the door.

"You could ask, you know."

"I shouldn't have to."

*   *   *

"DO YOU PLAY chess?" he asked when she walked into the study.

"No."

"I'll teach you. It's a very important game." He walked over to a cabinet and pulled out a chessboard and a box of chess pieces. He spread it out on a table and set up the board. "I think you'll like the game once you catch on."

She shrugged as she slumped into the chair. "Yes, I'm sure."

He sat down across from her. "Chess will teach you to think logically. It will teach you to consider your actions and their consequences. And maybe, it will curb your temper."

Eamon explained all of the pieces to her and reminded her again about thinking before acting. Lauryl learned quickly and made some intelligent moves but occasionally, she made some rash ones.

"You're not thinking," Eamon scolded. "You're too passionate with your moves." He held his hand up and smirked. "Don't misunderstand me; passion is good in some things."

Lauryl pushed a handful of hair from her face. "Will you let me play the way I want to? I'm still learning and nagging isn't helping."

"See? Passion." He leaned back in his chair and studied her face. His gaze then wandered to the rest of her body.

Lauryl tucked her legs up underneath her and looked back at him. "It's your move, I think."

"Why does my desire for you make you uncomfortable? It didn't before"

"It doesn't."

He shrugged and then moved his rook. "Check mate," he said. He noticed the time. "Come, it's time for you to go upstairs to rest. The sun will be coming up soon."

They walked upstairs and Eamon stopped in front of her door. "I'd invite you to sleep with me today, but I have things to do and I won't be in."

"Today? During the day?"

"None of that Hollywood crap about the sun reducing us to ashes is true. You can go out in the sun for limited amounts of time. However, you must exercise caution because the sun can burn us. Just very slowly."

"Amazing!"

He leaned against the doorframe. "When you're stronger, I'll show you how to do it. Then you'll see it's only a matter of concentration." He gave her a gentle nudge through the door and closed it.

* * *

LAURYL WALKED OVER to her bed and sat down. She could hear Eamon next door as he got ready for the day. She wanted to go next door and ask him more questions. However, she knew that he would hustle her back into her own room.

Why she was even excited or intrigued by anything he told her? she wondered as she changed into her gown. Each day, or night, she went through cycles of sadness or anger at him. She just wanted to make sense out of how to live like this and he was holding back a skill that might make her feel a little more…human, something that would make her happy. She kicked out of her bed and went to his door.

The room was silent now. Could he have dressed that fast? He loved his appearance too much to throw something on and go. She cracked the door open and poked her head in. The main part of his room was empty. She slipped through the door and looked around. His bed was untouched. She crept in further and saw that his Mac book was open and still booted up and his phone sat in the charger dock on his dresser. She turned a corner and saw his clothing hanging in the closet. It was more than a closet. It was the size of her old apartment's bedroom.

Hand tailored suits hung in rows, separated by their varying shades of blues, grays and black with almost imperceptible stripes of color. Each suit, with its hidden Huntsman label, was as individual as Eamon. He'd ordered his clothing from Huntsman since before the First World War. There, his secret remained protected by their ingrained sense of discretion.

When the cutter and the sales manager from the store came to call on Eamon, Lauryl found it almost comical the way the men fawned over him. They flattered his choices and advised him on what fabrics would suit him best. Eamon took extreme care and interest in the entire process. He described to the cutter and manager what he wanted and the two took notes and drew a few quick sketches. Then, after a drink and a handshake, the men gathered their belongings and returned to London with his order. One thing had impressed Lauryl while watching the entire procedure and that was how well the cutter and manager dressed. When she mentioned this to Eamon, he told her that a Saville Row employee was a walking advertisement for himself and the firm that employed him.

She examined the shelves of shoes that filled one side of the closet. Next to them were lines of silk ties placed in shallow drawers. A shelf of watches, cuff links, and glasses sat in a lighted cabinet. The costume department of the dance company had nothing on his closet. She rubbed her hand against the hanging jackets, sending wisps of his scent into the air. She leaned into the jackets and took a deep breath. A door at the end of the closet opened and Eamon walked though. Lauryl jumped away from the jackets and put her hands behind her back.

Eamon took a few steps, buttoning the cuffs of his shirt as he walked. "Oh, hello," he said. His eyebrows lifted slightly in amused surprise.

She looked at his bare, muscled chest and couldn't catch herself before a captivated smile crossed her lips. "Hey."

"I didn't expect you to be in here."

Lauryl remained silent. His hair was still damp and un-combed but he looked fantastic. He smelled even better. More than that, he smelled enticing. It was only his soap she smelled, but the sight of him with his shirt unbuttoned and his hand tailored trousers on, she found herself drawn to him. It was as if he was physically pulling her to him.

"Me either."

Eamon finger combed his sand colored hair and put his watch on. "Can't you rest?"

She walked closer to him, breathing him in. *What was wrong with her?* She wondered. He'd never been this attractive to her. She didn't know if it was the act of being caught searching for him when she was supposed to be in her room for the day or if it was some weird case of vampire lust. Whatever it was, it was incredible! "No, I can't. I came in here to ask you something."

"What?" He started to button his shirt up. He stopped when she held her hand up.

"Don't do that."

"Why not?" he asked.

"Because I don't want to unbutton them again."

Eamon backed up and leaned against the drawers. He resumed the buttoning. "I'll be late and you should be resting."

Lauryl closed the distance between them. She popped off the shirt buttons he did manage to fasten and her fingers settled on his chest. His shower-warmed skin and seductive scent invited exploration. Her hands traced over his stomach and back up to his chest. They slid back down, circled around his waist, and sank below the waistband of his pants, her nails dragging against his hips. Her eyelids drooped and she sucked in a breath as she moved her fingers around to the front and unbuckled his belt.

"There is something I need more than rest," she whispered as she opened the buttons on his pants. With a gentle tug, the zipper came down and her hands disappeared under the blue wool fabric.

Eamon lowered his lips to her shoulder. He kissed her softly before he slipped the thin silk straps of her chemise off. The filmy garment dropped down past her hips, leaving her naked in front of him. He traced his fingers up her neck into her hair. She leaned her head back and he kissed from her chin down her neck. Her skin tingled in the wake of each kiss. Lauryl raised her arms over her head and arched her back slightly.

"Let me give it to you," he whispered.

"How do you know what I need?"

"I think it's obvious," he said as he picked her up and carried her to his bed.

Once on the bed, Lauryl rose up on her elbows and looked at Eamon. Even though he was no more than ten inches from her, it felt like miles. The tiny distance between them was excruciating. The overwhelming need to have him touch her startled her. She rolled on to her stomach and glanced back over her shoulder to him, begging with her eyes. He raised her arms up over her head and covered her back with kisses. She opened her legs and drew them up closer to her. Lauryl moaned as his hands found the part of her that now ached for him. All sense of control that she maintained before disappeared and a new force took control of her.

As his fingers teased her relentlessly, she pushed her body harder against him. She turned her head to him, silently wishing him inside of her. His fingers stopped and she could feel the hard length of him next to her, lightly skimming her opening. She tried to back against him to stop his tormenting but each time she did, he pulled away from her. Lauryl dropped her head down in frustration. *What could possibly be the reason for denying her?* Her fangs dropped in and she looked back at him, her mouth slack and her lips wet with anticipation.

"Won't you please?" she whispered, her fangs visible to him.

Eamon pushed into her. She leaned back into him. Lauryl froze a moment as she processed the sensation of him inside of her, trying to experience it with each of her senses. Where his skin touched hers, a fire began to smolder. Strings of light danced in front of her eyes. Overcome by anticipation, she grabbed the bed linen and twisted as he slowly drove in and out of her.

Lauryl savored the being a part of him. It was as if he was consuming her; that she was dissolving into him. Each deep thrust tied her to him in a way she'd never experienced before. She swung her head around to look at him. The hair in her face clouded her vision but she could see the dark, sensuous expression on his face. The grip of his hands tightened slightly on her hips as he pulled her into him and the speed of his thrusting increased. Every part of her body yielded to him and his movements. Lauryl gasped and stretched her arms forward on the bed as if she was begging. In a way, she was begging. She was begging him not to end the experience of being part of him and belonging to him. She both loved and hated that. While that thought tore at her mind, the divine conclusion approached. She remained trapped between wanting to stay a part of him and wanting to go over the edge to where she had never been before. It became clear to her that she didn't have to choose. Every nerve in her body vibrated and she melted into Eamon. She experienced his body and his pleasure as well as her own. For a split second his thoughts and sensations shot through her mind. Her body fed off them and exponentially increased her own climax. She looked back one last time before she sank onto the bed.

His hands moved from her hips to her waist and pulled her into him, hugging her. Eamon kissed the back of her neck and held her close for a moment. For a moment, her hands settled on his and tried to squeeze them. Her fingers pressed lightly against his and then dropped away.

"You should sleep now, darling," he whispered.

Lauryl turned around to him and studied his face. His lips turned in a soft, sensual smile.

The need to feel his lips on her body twitched in her again, but she knew he'd insist she sleep. She touched his mouth with her finger and then kissed him. His mouth yielded to her and his tongue caressed hers briefly before he pulled away.

"No," he scolded. "Sleep."

She stretched over to his pillow. A look of contentment appeared on her face as she snuggled against the sheets. His scent in the sheets encircled her, comforting her. Lauryl looked at him one last time before closing her eyes and falling into her day sleep.

CHAPTER TWELVE

You Started to, but You Just Went with the Theory
That My Soap Held Some Aphrodisiac Power

T HE SOUND OF the clock in the hall chiming six woke Lauryl from her day sleep. She opened her eyes and stretched in the bed, scanning the room. It was Eamon's room and she was naked in his bed. The memory of this morning brought a smile to her lips. She saw her nightgown still piled where he had stripped it off. She sprinted over, snatched it up, and pulled it back on as she hurried back to her own room.

She wondered if Eamon was home. The house was quiet, but his room had been quiet last night, so she now knew that didn't mean he wasn't around. How did that happen this morning? How and why did she suddenly find him so attractive? Especially when she was irritated with him before she went into his room. As much as she hated to admit it, it was like nothing she had ever experienced before. Sex before being turned had been almost a waste of her time and energy compared to sex as a vampire.

* * *

IT SURPRISED HER to find Eamon's study door wide open. At the most, it had only been cracked open but there it was, wide open. Lauryl peeked in. Eamon lay on the sofa with the folded newspaper over his face. She hesitated before clearing her throat.

"Good evening," he said, not lifting the paper.

"Hey."

"Come in and sit with me." He pointed to the armchair near the sofa.

Lauryl walked in and sat down on the appointed seat. "Hard day?"

"Boring is more like it. Although, it started on a promising note," he said as he took the newspaper from his face.

"About that," Lauryl began.

"Yes?"

"I'm kind of confused about it."

He smiled. "It seemed straightforward enough."

Lauryl frowned. "No, I know, but I don't understand…"

"How you could find my soap so enticing?"

"Yeah. No. What?" Her eyes narrowed. "And you know that how?"

"You know how." He sat up. "Lauryl, you're attracted to me. And we're bonded together. Like it or not, I just helped you a little bit."

"Helped me how?"

Eamon stood up and walked over to his desk. "By using a little trick called glamouring."

· "What's that?"

"I removed any negative thoughts about me that you had and amplified the positive ones."

"Why?"

"I thought since you hate learning anything, be it vampire related or otherwise, that I'd do a little unorthodox teaching."

"You mind fucked me." He'd done that to her when she was human. The memory of their meeting in Seattle came crashing back.

"I suppose that's one way of putting it. You didn't seem to mind."

"Because I couldn't mind!"

"What exactly are you angry about?"

She opened her mouth to speak and stopped. "I don't know yet." It was hard to single something out.

"You'll have to have something to be angry with me about, though. I'm sure of that. Glamouring is a basic trick of any vampire. You use it for a variety of things, for feeding mainly but for other things too." Eamon loosened his tie and poured himself a drink.

She tapped her foot on the floor. "You're unbelievable. You

don't see anything wrong with what you did."

"Another vampire shouldn't be so easy to glamour. You didn't stop and think. You started to but you just went with the theory that my soap held some aphrodisiac power. You lost your train of thought as soon as you crept into my room. I knew you were there. Your markers were blazing. You didn't attempt to hide them so I took advantage of the situation." He looked at her, her lips pursed, dying to fire back at him. "You learned a lesson in a pleasurable way. What's the problem?"

"You know what, Eamon? I think you just wanted a little pussy to start your day. So you took the easy route and got it. Yeah, I learned a lesson. A good one and believe me, I'll think things through. Not because you want me to but because I want to."

"Whatever your reason, I don't care." Eamon hit the remote on the stereo and picked up the newspaper.

She nodded her head. "I know you don't care." He didn't care. He was too self-involved to help her transition to being a vampire. He only cared about himself, his business and controlling her. Maybe not controlling her but trying to force her into his idea of what a companion should be.

Eamon looked up. "Are you staying?"

Lauryl laughed and shook her head. "You're not used to hearing no, are you?"

"What?"

"Seriously, when was the last time something didn't go your way?" She twisted the emerald ring on her finger. "I mean, besides me?"

Eamon studied her for a moment and smiled. "Honestly, it's never happened."

"You have major boundary issues," she said and nodded. She knew his smile was fake. He wasn't going to let her see that he was aggravated by her question. A show of his true feelings would be asking too much.

"I suppose you learned that from the capable Dr. Wilson," Eamon said.

"I learned a lot from him." Lauryl smiled.

"I'm sure you did," he said. His tone was gaining in sarcasm.

"At least he bothered to get to know me before he tried to change me." She stood up and walked out.

CHAPTER THIRTEEN

Your Image Is That You're an Aloof, Pompous Snob

T HE WIND BLEW through Lauryl's hair as she sped down the beach road. She slid another CD into the player and hit the accelerator. The BMW M6 shot forward and Lauryl reveled in her freedom. It wasn't just the blood from the very willing, twenty-something frat boy she had fed from that made her feel so alive. Feeding afforded her a brief vacation from the critical eye of Eamon and it absolutely thrilled her. She wasn't going to let Eamon know that. Then she'd have to listen to his I told you so speech or something like it. She increased the bass on the stereo until it produced chest-vibrating thumps. Each throb that caused the window glass to shake brought a triumphant grin to her face.

She looked out at the ocean and Anthony popped into her mind. All the happiness she felt vanished. She missed him more than she missed dancing. What else would she say to him? Eamon took it upon himself to tell him that they were married and, when Anthony insisted on speaking with her, all she could do was confirm it. The hurt in his voice had devastated her. Eamon didn't care about her. So maybe she should go back to the one who did care about her. Lauryl pulled into the driveway and scowled at the front door. Behind that door was her jailer and no doubt he was going to be pissed.

* * *

"I COULD HEAR your stereo half way down the road even if I wasn't a vampire," Eamon said when Lauryl walked into his study. He took off his glasses and put down the letter he was reading. "I think I've told you about acting like an immature idiot."

She smiled to herself. "I don't think listening to the stereo loud is immature. And, I'm still pissed about the other night."

He rolled his eyes. "I think you'd better get over it and focus on not being so easily glamoured."

"Yeah, guess I should just get over being mind fucked by my husband. As long as you don't care about me and what I think, I don't care about you and what you think."

"All I ask is that you carry yourself with a little dignity."

"Can't we have any fun? I'm suffocating here!" She clasped her throat like she was choking.

"What do you call fun?"

"I can tell you what's not fun, and that's sitting at home with you. All you do is read and work."

"Perhaps you could pick up a book," he suggested.

"I need fun."

"I think you need to think about other things right now."

"Will you stop thinking for me? I'm about to crap respectability! If you make me read another book, I'll barf. I need to get out and have some plain ordinary fun."

Eamon thought for a moment. "Alright, Lauryl, we'll strike a compromise. If you make a more concerted effort to at least pretend that you care what people think of you, I'll loosen up."

Lauryl narrowed her eyes. "Do you mean it?"

"Yes, I do." He put his glasses back on.

Why was he wearing glasses? she wondered. He didn't need them. She guessed it was for effect. "Can we go out tonight?" she asked as she kicked off her shoes.

"No, I'm afraid not. I have work to do. Tomorrow night we will."

"Can't you work tomorrow night?"

"No, I can't," he said without looking up.

"Why not?"

He raised his eyes. "You're nagging and that's very annoying."

"We don't have to stay out very long."

"No."

"Why?"

He clenched the papers in his hand. "Will you drop it? I told you we'd go out tomorrow night."

She stood up and put her hands on her hips. "So what am I supposed to do for the rest of the night?"

"I suppose you'll have to entertain yourself," he said.

"Swell." She walked over to the stereo and searched through the CDs. All she saw was classical and jazz. His musical taste was nothing like hers. She liked house and dance music. After sorting through his sorry selection, she flipped through the small stack of CDs she managed to smuggle into the house. She pulled out a club mix disc and slid it in the machine.

"Nothing too loud, please," he said.

Lauryl defiantly turned the volume up. She stuck out her tongue and started to dance around. When he could no longer tolerate the music, Eamon looked up and noticed Lauryl swaying and grinding around the room. He took off the glasses again and leaned back in his chair. Her body dipped and twisted with each annoying pulsating beat. It was nothing like classical ballet and far more enticing. She swung back around and stopped when she noticed him watching her.

"I didn't think you were paying any attention to me."

"With you dancing like that, it would be hard for me not to."

"I like to dance. You know that."

"I like to watch you. You know that."

She put her hands behind her back and sat down. His eyes followed her and then he set his work aside.

"I thought you were going to work."

"I was."

"What are you going to do if you don't work?" she asked, knowing what he was going to say.

"I'm sure I can think of something. I have a few ideas."

"Forget it, Eamon."

He laughed and lifted his eyebrows. "What if I want to? What then?"

"Then you'll have to take it by force."

"How provoking," he said, smiling. "I'm not into rape so I suppose I'll just wait."

"Yes, considering how you think of yourself as this great gentleman." She slid out of the chair and stretched out on the floor in front of the fireplace.

"Off the floor," he said. Lauryl rolled away from him, ignoring him. "Did you not hear me? Get off the floor!" he said as he stood up.

She turned back toward him. "What's it hurting for me to lay here? It's not like I'm in mud."

"You're defying me. Get up."

"No!"

He stalked over to her and tried to yank her up from the floor. "Is this some sort of game for you?" he said pulling her again.

"Let go of me!"

"Get up!"

"Let go!" she yelled and bit his hand.

Eamon turned loose of her arm and she scooted away. He shook his hand and checked to see if she had bitten him with her fangs. There were no punctures, only the outline of her teeth on his palm and the back of his hand.

"Your habit of biting me is not amusing. Come here!"

Lauryl crawled under one of the end tables, far enough out of his reach to escape his grasp. Eamon threw his hands up in exasperation and bit down on his lower lip. She swallowed hard and braced herself for whatever was about to happen. He turned and kicked the chair she had been sitting in, sending it clattering across the wooden floor. She curled herself in a ball and waited for him to knock the table aside and pull her out. He didn't, though. Without a word, he stalked out of the study and the house, slamming the door behind him.

After a cautious look around, she crawled out from under the table. He was gone but now she dreaded his return.

*   *   *

WHEN SHE HEARD the door open, Lauryl stopped her game of solitaire. Eamon walked in and closed the door behind him. She glanced over at the clock and saw it was twenty minutes after three. He had been gone almost three hours.

"Can we get along now?" he asked. His tone of voice was low and controlled.

She knew the tone well. He was still angry. Lauryl resumed her game. "Are you going to leave me alone?"

"Meaning?"

She put the cards aside. "Are you going to stop nagging me?"

"Have I been nagging?"

"I'll say it a different way. Will you let me be who I am?"

"Go on," he said.

"Stop trying to make me into something I'm not."

"There are going to have to be some changes on your part. We've had this discussion before." He rubbed his eyes and sighed.

"Then we aren't going to get along." Lauryl picked up the cards and started to play again.

"Let's talk on a more serious note." He picked up the chair he had kicked earlier and sat down across from her. "I'd like these conflicts between the two of us to stop."

"Then let me go. We're never going to get along."

He knit his brows together in a frown. "What? No, that's out of the question."

"Then I guess we'll always be fighting."

Eamon drummed his fingers on his thigh. "You'll just have to forgive me for being so selfish. For this to work, we're going to have to have some sort of truce."

"Truce?"

"That's right. I want you to give me three conditions you'd like to have in order to get along with me."

"Only three?" she asked.

"Yes, so choose them wisely. Then I'll give you my three."

"You want these now?"

"Yes, please."

Narrowing down all the things she wanted wouldn't be easy. After a moment, she looked back at him. "Okay, I've got them."

"Begin."

"First of all, I'd like you to lose the smug attitude. It pisses me off."

"No vulgarity, please."

"See?"

"What if I told you it was part of my personality and I couldn't change?" he asked.

"Then I'd tell you the deal's off."

"Fair enough. Next?"

"Stop nagging me about the way I act. You knew how I was before you turned me so you're stuck with my personality. In fact, you told me that it was one of the things you liked about me. So if it changes, swell, if it doesn't too bad."

"I only ask that you behave with a little bit of refinement so we can maintain our image."

"Your image is that you're an aloof, pompous snob. I don't want people thinking that about me."

"Your third condition?

She squirmed in her chair, uneasy about the last one. "Don't be so demanding of me."

"How so?"

"Sexually. When I'm ready for you, I'll let you know. Until then, don't push me."

Eamon took a moment to consider everything she said. He nodded his head and folded his hands in his lap. "Now, it's my turn."

"Okay."

"My conditions are as simple as yours. First, I'd like it if you would at least try to show me some sort of affection. It would be nice if you behaved like a wife. That's why I chose you. Contrary to what you might think, I didn't choose you as part of some monstrous joke. Second, please try to continue your education. It's vital you do so. In the end, it will pay off. Finally, please stop being so antagonistic. You're finding more and more ways to set me off and that's not good for either of us."

Lauryl wrinkled her nose. "I didn't ask to be your wife." She made little air quotes with her fingers after the word wife. "I hate school and learning and I've told you that every time you've put a book in front of me. If you'd just talk to me and teach me things,

I'd respond better." She sighed. "The last one, I guess it depends on you."

"On me?"

"Yes. Don't give me a reason to piss you off and I won't."

Eamon studied her face for a moment before he extended his hand to her. "I would say we have a deal," he said.

Lauryl eyed his hand with suspicion before she gave it a flimsy shake. She looked down at the cards in front of her and then back to him. "I guess."

As she stared at him, she wondered where he'd been over the past few hours. She suspected he spent the time feeding but she wondered on whom. To her surprise, a twinge of jealousy poked at her. She piled her cards up and built them into a neat stack.

"Where were you?" she asked.

"Out."

"Where?"

"I went to feed."

"On who?"

He smiled at the question. "Why the sudden interest?"

She pressed her lips together and shrugged. "I'm just curious." She picked the cards up and turned them in her hand.

"An old friend," he said.

Lauryl clenched the cards until they bent. "Jennifer fucking Conrad."

He snickered and wiped his lips. "Interesting phrasing."

She jumped up and hurled the cards at him. "You douche bag! You could do anyone in this town but you just can't leave her alone. You always manage to find your way back to her skanky bed! And you do it to spite me!"

Eamon appeared unbothered by the cards flying around him. "Calm down please."

"Screw you. I'm going to my room. You should have turned Jennifer!" she yelled as she stomped out of the room.

Eamon stared at the cards on the floor. The sound of her door slamming echoed through the house. They were catalysts for one another. If she wasn't trying to irritate him, he was trying to find a way to aggravate her. He knew going to see Jennifer would infuriate Lauryl. That was the reason he did it. He wasn't accustomed to someone defying him nor did he want to try to become accustomed to it. He was going to have to discover some way though to smooth things out between Lauryl and him. She was becoming more and more independent and contrary. In addition, she was now stronger vampire.

CHAPTER FOURTEEN

Prince Charming is a Monster

ANTHONY CHECKED AT his watch for the sixth time since he had arrived at the bar. He was early and each minute that crept by added to his nervousness. He signaled to the bartender to refill his glass with tequila. He knew the alcohol was a bad choice, but he needed something, anything to keep his nerves under control. A hand settled on his back and he spun around.

"Hello, Anthony," Lauryl said, smiling.

It took him a moment to convince himself that she was really standing there. The forty-eight hours between her phone call asking to meet for drinks and now had moved along at a glacial pace, but now she was here. His palms were now damp and he tried to wipe them on his pants without being obvious.

"You look incredible, Lauryl," he said, attempting not to sound over-anxious. His eyes focused on her chest. The low cut blouse she wore gave him an unspoiled view of her breasts and his heart thumped like a sixteen-year-old boy.

Lauryl skimmed her hand down his shirt. "Thank you." She poked his chest with a gentle teasing pressure. "You don't look so bad yourself."

Anthony nodded to the empty barstool next to him. "Have a seat."

She looked at the stool and shook her head. "Let's go for a ride."

"I thought we were meeting for a drink."

"We are."

Anthony let her walk a few steps ahead of him as they walked to her car. There was something different about her walk. In fact, it seemed like there was something different about her as a whole.

She'd developed a magnetic confidence. Before she had been somewhat awkward and unsure of herself; now she radiated poise and control.

He heard a car alarm turn off and doors unlock. "What happened to the Passat?"

Lauryl's veil of self-assuredness cracked for a moment but recovered. "Eamon bought me something new."

"Oh."

They got in the BMW and she pulled out of the parking lot. "I've missed you so much, Anthony," she said, not taking her eyes from the road.

He closed his eyes for a second. Professional ethics swirled loosely in his head. He kept reminding himself that she was married now. But something made her call him. He hoped that it wasn't for a professional reason.

"I've missed you, too. I guess you must have quite a life being married to Eamon."

She gripped the steering wheel and turned the car off the road onto a bluff overlooking the ocean. "Yeah, it's some life," she muttered.

"Why are we stopped?"

"Prince Charming is a monster," Lauryl said. With a laugh she added, "I'm living a life I couldn't have imagined in a million years."

"What do you mean?"

"Nothing. You know me. Always dramatic." She took her hands from the steering wheel and held them out to him. He took hers and squeezed. "I've wanted to feel that for so long now."

Anthony shook off the confusion about his own feelings and concentrated on hers. "Are you okay?"

"Do you mean am I using? No, I'm not."

"Are you having problems with Eamon? Is he hurting you?"

She laughed. "I'm in a difficult situation, Anthony. That's all I can tell you."

He shifted in the seat. "You can tell me anything. You know that."

Lauryl shook her head. "Trust me. There are some things I

can't tell you." She pulled her hands away from him.

"Do I need to be concerned about your safety?"

"My safety? No, you don't need to be concerned about that." She stared down at the floorboard and then back at him. "Please don't be my doctor."

He realized he sounded clinical and blushed. "I'm concerned about you. You tell me all of these cryptic things and it gets my mind going." He shrugged his shoulders. "What do you want me to be?"

She leaned over and kissed him. Her tongue caressed his, making him hard. He pulled away, embarrassed by his adolescent reaction.

"Don't pull away, Anthony. You have no idea how much I've wanted this."

The sound of her words banished any resolve to remain professional. He'd longed to hear those exact words for months. He had fantasized about them with endless, pleasurable outcomes. She was married now, though. "You're married. I hate saying that, but it's true."

Lauryl started to laugh. "My marriage isn't what you think it is."

Anthony's brow furrowed for a moment. "Still, I have to try to maintain some kind of—."

She cut him off. "No, you don't. Anthony. What's the most farfetched, unbelievable thing you think you could believe in?"

"Oh, I don't know." He leaned into the car seat. "Maybe UFOs. I'm not sure what you're asking me."

"I'm asking you to tell me what is the most outlandish thing you believe in."

"I guess UFOs. It's hard to believe in something unless there's evidence."

"So if you had proof you'd believe it, no matter how weird or scary?"

After some hesitation, he nodded. "I guess I would." He had no idea where she was going with this. He watched her fidget with the key fob. He knew her body language and habits well. Being married to Eamon hadn't changed them at all.

"I want to tell you something, but I can't"

"We're back to this again," he said. His voice softened. "How about I tell you something that I haven't been able to tell anyone? Then maybe you'll feel like you can tell me."

"What?"

"It's pretty serious."

"What?"

He took a deep breath in and let it out slowly. "I'm in love with you. I've loved you since you first started coming to my office. As inappropriate as that is, I love you." He wiped his sweaty palm on his pants and touched her cheek.

She turned her face and kissed his palm. "I don't think it's inappropriate." She smiled.

"From a professional standpoint it is. I could get in big trouble. Or I could have." The feel of her lips skimming over his palm made him hard again. "You make me crazy."

Her tongue licked up from his palm to his wrist, settling on his radial artery. The sensation of her teeth, oddly sharp, caused him to pull away.

"Did I hurt you?" she asked, her eyes warm with desire.

"No, your teeth caught me a little off guard." His focus stayed on her eyes. There was something in them he had never seen before. Desire, not for him, for something else.

"Sorry." Lauryl traced her finger down his neck and then her mouth followed her finger's path.

Anthony squirmed. "They seemed a little sharp."

"Yeah, they are," she said. "I think I can show you what I want to tell you."

"That's fine."

Lauryl licked the skin of his neck and bit him.

"Oh, shit, Lauryl," he sighed. A sharp pain in his neck flashed through him but it melted into pressure and sucking. He closed his eyes for a second, enjoying the sensation of her on him. When she stopped, he looked at her. Her lips were wet with what appeared to be blood. He could smell blood. The coppery smell was unmistakable.

"Anthony, I'm a vampire." She wiped the blood from her lips

with her fingers and waited for his reaction.

He didn't know what to say. Her expression was free of any kind of sign she was joking. He reached up and touched the spot where she'd been sucking. It was wet and sticky. He checked his neck in the rear view mirror and saw two perfect punctures that closed as he inspected them. He looked back at her, her face still expressionless.

"Are you serious?"

"What do you think?"

Anthony sat and processed what had happened. What he had seen and heard. No wonder she hadn't wanted to tell him. A multitude of questions filled his head but he couldn't decide which one he wanted to ask first. He put his hand back up to his neck. The bite had closed but was still tender.

"How did this close so fast?"

She shrugged. "I'm not really sure. I just know it does. All that's going to be there is a bruise like a love bite." A giggle came from her. "Which is what it is."

"Jesus, Lauryl, there are so many things I want to ask." He ran his hand through his hair.

"Ask."

Anthony expelled a long breath. "I can't believe this. I mean, it's like beyond belief. You're really a vampire. I mean the kind that lives forever and so forth."

"Yep."

"I'm guessing Eamon's one too." He realized that was a stupid thing to say. "Yeah, dumb, I know. How old is he?"

She shrugged. "I don't know. He doesn't talk a lot about himself to me. I'm just kind of like furniture or some other possession of his."

"Is it hard being a vampire? Do you like it?"

She shook her head. "No."

"No it's not hard or no you don't like it?"

Lauryl looked down at the key fob in her hand. "Both."

"Why?" he asked.

"I hate who I'm stuck with. If I wasn't with him, I wouldn't mind it so much. But I miss having a life and I miss dancing."

Anthony nodded his head. "I guess it would be hard to dance if you couldn't see yourself in a mirror. That's true isn't it? I don't know what's real and what's a myth."

"No, that's true." She frowned. "No reflection."

He looked around the car, still struggling with this new reality. "Am I going to be a vampire?"

Lauryl laughed and put her hand on his thigh. "No, not tonight. You'll probably be more connected to me now but that's it."

That sounded perfect to Anthony. "I can't say I'm upset about that." The tiny smile that appeared on her face delighted him. "The connection part, that is."

"Me either. In fact, I'd like to keep seeing you, Anthony. I know I said it before but I've missed you. Sitting here with you makes me realize that."

"You want to keep seeing me? What about Eamon?"

"A girl's got to eat. I can be with you two or three times a week, no questions asked. He goes out to eat by himself. It's just something we do. But for me, it'll be more." A shy and tentative look crossed her face. "I mean, if you want to. I understand if you don't."

"No! Yes! Shit, I don't know what I'm saying, but you know what I mean. I want to see you and be with you."

"I was so afraid this was going to freak you out and then I was going to have to glamour you." She poked his leg with the fob.

"What's that?"

"Oh, well, it's basically messing with your mind. I would blank out your memory or whatever."

Anthony pushed on the bite again, wincing at the sharp pain. "Don't do that. I want to remember this forever."

Lauryl smiled. "Maybe one day it will be forever."

CHAPTER FIFTEEN

The Last Words Were Difficult to Say

E AMON MASSAGED HIS temples with his fingers. Perhaps Irina had been right. She predicted Lauryl wouldn't work out. How had she phrased it? This one is not going to be what you think. That was an understatement. Irina's instinct had been dead on. He should call and tell her that her prediction had been correct and Lauryl wasn't what he thought. Lauryl hated him most of the time. Her hatred was only interrupted with occasional moments of strained tolerance and then it was followed by torrents of sarcastic and sullen tantrums. He couldn't let her go because he still felt something, some intangible sort of affection for her. The fact he was her maker had something to do with it. As her maker, their bond would last forever.

Eamon pulled out his phone and dialed Irina, hoping to catch her before she went out for the evening. The last time they had spoken, she had come to the decision she too wanted a companion so no doubt she would be out prowling for a new one. Eamon hoped her choice yielded happier results.

"Hello, brother," Irina said, laughing.

"I'm surprised you're in."

She sighed. "Well, I was thinking of going out. I might have found a friend."

"Really? What's he like?" Eamon turned his chair around and gazed out the window.

"It's not a he."

"Gone over to the other side?"

"No, I've found someone who happens to be female." There was a silence and then she laughed. "Would you like it if I had gone over to the other side?"

He smiled at the idea. "It wouldn't make the slightest difference to me."

"Liar. You'd be on your plane as fast as you could have it ready."

"You're confused, Irina," he said. "Enjoy your night." He ended the call and stared out at the ocean. Another female being added to his line. Eamon hoped this companion would last longer than the last one. He disappeared within five years. Irina never said how and wasn't very emotional about his absence. Eamon suspected she'd killed him because she couldn't stand him any longer and didn't want to have to ask for permission to separate from him. She just smiled when he asked her about his whereabouts. So more than likely, he was scattered in more than one piece across London.

The slam of the study door brought his thoughts crashing to a close. The sound of the door let him know Lauryl was intent on starting an argument. He wasn't up for it, so he decided to keep his mood neutral.

"Good evening."

"Good? No. I'm stuck with you." She put her hands on her hips.

Eamon turned his chair around and folded his hands in his lap. "It wasn't a question. It was a standard greeting used by civilized society worldwide."

She seemed to be on the verge of laughter for a second. "I'll keep that in mind."

"Thank you."

Lauryl sank into a deep, theatrical bow and sat down. "You're welcome."

"What was that?"

"That," she said "was a standard gesture of submission used by civilized society worldwide. I'm surprised you didn't recognize it."

"I might have if you hadn't disguised it in sarcasm." She wrestled briefly with anger. To his surprise, she chose to smile. "What are your plans this evening?" Eamon asked.

"I'm going out to eat. Did you want to come?"

Lauryl decided to call feeding going out to eat. It sounded more acceptable to her. No matter what she called it, it was a rare thing for her to ask him to come with her to feed and he hated to pass up the honor. He did, however, have work to do. If he finished it while she was gone and if she came home in a decent mood...those were big ifs.

"No, I appreciate the invitation, though. I need to finish some work."

Lauryl shrugged her shoulders. "Don't say I never asked."

She walked out and he looked at the papers piled on his desk. Years ago when he started his business, he never suspected that it would grow into so much work. Actually, it wouldn't have to be so much work if he stepped aside and let others run the conglomerate for him. He couldn't do that though. The humans he'd hire wouldn't perform to his standards. A few months back, he entertained the idea of hiring a few and then turning them. The idea of a board of vampires appealed to him. They would possess the drive, insight and most of all the cunning to keep his business succeeding. He had even earmarked a few candidates. Lauryl sidetracked him. Her acquisition had been more important.

For her, he had to work like a human. He had to be more visible and more, well... human. With that came human emotions, which he despised. The emotion that gave him the most trouble was jealousy. He now found himself sulking or pouting over her indifference to him and her attachment to that idiot doctor. He picked up the glass of scotch in front of him and drained it.

That doctor was an annoyance. He continued to insinuate himself into Lauryl's life and she allowed it. Since he had agreed to let her have contact with him, she had become more pleasant. Whenever she talked to the doctor on the phone or "ran into him" while she was out, her mood improved dramatically. It would be a huge mistake to forbid her to have any contact with him because he still enjoyed the occasional visit to Jennifer Conrad. Lauryl hated her as much as he hated that stupid doctor. Eamon stood up to refill his drink but as he did, he froze as a feeling of terror seized him. Without explanation, the feeling disappeared.

Eamon set the glass down and his glance darted around the room. The feeling stopped as quickly as it came. The fear wasn't his. He reached out to Lauryl. It wasn't hers, either. She was off somewhere looking for her "dinner". Irina. He switched his focus and her desperate and staggering fear overwhelmed him.

He tried to connect with her but couldn't. He snatched the phone up and dialed her number, each ring lasting an eternity. After seven rings, he threw down the phone and reached out again. Irina's thoughts overran his, coming at break neck speed in her ancient east Slavic, and not Russian. Eamon desperately forced his way into her mind, but the only things he could get from her were fervent Russian Orthodox prayers. Eamon reeled with a horrendous, searing pain in his chest. His back arched and he cried out. The pain disappeared and he rubbed his chest with the sickening knowledge that something was happening to Irina. He frantically reached out to her again. He heard her call his name in his mind and then she was silent. The sensation of a knife slicing across his neck stunned him. His knees buckled and he crumpled into his desk. He pushed at the papers, trying to steady himself against the pain. And then it vanished. Irina was slipping from his mind and from him.

Eamon grabbed the phone again, his hands shaking, and dialed his attorney Grant in New York City. "Go immediately to my house and check on Irina! I think what you'll find there will be just the remains of her."

The last words were difficult for him to say. He hung the phone up before Grant acknowledged him.

The last bit of Irina disappeared. Five hundred years was now gone. He dropped his head back and closed his eyes. One of his companions, his lovers, his vampires was now dead. He didn't know what to do.

CHAPTER SIXTEEN

Holy Crap, What's Wrong

THE IMAGE OF Irina when they first met her in Paris back in 1439 flashed through his mind.

Decked out in the mink trimmed silks and brocades of Novgorod, her dark hair was crimped, curled, and interlaced with pearls the size of grapes. Ropes of the same pearls hung from her mink cap. He remembered thinking how her hair and the mink were exactly the same color and the pearls provided the only contrast. The most memorable of all was how her liquid blue eyes memorized every move he made. Her French was appalling and her clothes, although sumptuous, were provincial at best. Nevertheless, she wanted him more than the air she breathed.

"*Upir*," she had purred in his ear. "I want to give myself to you. Make me yours."

Those words still echoed in his mind the same as if she said it last night. Five hundred years were gone. All he had left were the memories he had of her. But it wasn't the same. A huge gap was now in his psyche and he had no one to fill it.

He poured himself another drink and sat down. Lauryl should be home soon. She wasn't the one who could fill the gap. He knew that. Each night she went out, he worried that some shrewd hunter would kill her. Fortunately, over the years, the population had come to see vampire hunters as insane. Most of them were, but some weren't. A few were from hereditary lines of secret hunters. Clans trained from generation to generation to hunt and destroy vampires. Those, by good fortune, dwindled to almost nothing over the years. Every so often, they would experience a rebirth of interest and even become more mainstream. In the nineteenth century, certain families of hunters even sold vampire killing kits complete with garlic, a cross, a Bible, magic potions and of course a stake and hammer. In Eastern Europe and Germany, this was a stroke of marketing genius. Unfortunately for those who bought them, these kits were nothing but a collection of superstitions packed in a travelling valise. They were harmless to a vampire. The worst it could do was anger the vampire tormented by the items. The hunters knew that, too. They weren't going to give up their business to amateurs. They would be the only ones who knew the secrets of tracking and killing a vampire.

Eamon closed his eyes and reached out to Lauryl. She remained in the process of finding her victim. Right now, he didn't want her out by herself. He concentrated on her again.

I'd like you, please, to come home to me, he whispered in her mind. *There is something wrong.*

To his surprise, she didn't argue or complain. She simply said okay. That was unusual. He took another drink of scotch and thought about Irina again. He rubbed his chest and wondered if whoever killed her had tried to stake her. That had to have been quite a surprise to the hunter when he or she saw that staking only slowed a vampire down. However, the hunter knew how to finish the job. He couldn't understand how Irina had allowed herself to get into such a dangerous situation. Was she distracted? What could have distracted her to that degree? Could it have been the girl she planned to turn? The one she said she had marked to be her new companion? That was a hunter's trick. They would lure the vampire to a false sense of security by offering themselves to them. It was dangerous though. The hunter could lose his life instead if the vampire was hungrier than normal, treacherous, or just enjoyed killing humans. If the vampire discovered the hunter's identity before, their death would be slow, painful, and creative.

The phone's vibration ended Eamon's reflection. He pressed the TALK button. "Yes, Grant."

"Um, well Eamon, are you sitting down?"

"Grant, is she dead?" he asked, closing his eyes. His shoulders tensed and his grip on the phone tightened.

"Yeah, they both are but not in a way that I would expect."

"They?" Eamon asked. He opened his eyes.

"There's another woman here with Irina. She's…like Irina."

"Meaning that she has been decapitated as well?"

"Uh huh."

"Interesting." Eamon stared out the window at the ocean. "Is there anything there that would give a clue as to the other's identity?"

"No, I checked before I called you. She either didn't bring anything or the killer took it."

"Check around their bodies," Eamon said as he rubbed his eyes. His eyes stung as tears formed in them but he forced them away. "And see if there are any odd markings or writings."

A few moments passed while Grant checked. "Nothing," he said.

"Then this isn't a real hunter. This is just a rogue. He must have followed the girl to Irina." *Another crazy person with a large knife,* he thought. He sighed and dropped his hand.

"You know what to do, Grant. Call the Cleaner and take care of it."

"You don't want to come back here?"

"No," Eamon said. He hesitated before continuing and the tears returned. "I can't. The Cleaner will know what to do. Just take care of it," he said before hanging up. He threw the phone over on the desk and dropped his head down to his hands.

Irina, you didn't deserve that, he thought. *The Romanov curse seems to have finally caught up with you, my beautiful love. No matter how far removed you were from them.*

He lifted his head when he heard the front door open and close. The sound of Lauryl singing, in a loud and very off key voice, echoed in the hall. She knocked on the study door and walked in, still singing. When she saw the expression on his face, she stopped mid-step and mid-song.

"Holy crap, what's wrong?"

"Irina is dead."

She tilted her head and blinked a few times. "Oh, God."

"Yes."

Lauryl walked over and knelt in front of him. She put her hand on his. Her soft, warm hand offered unexpected comfort. "Oh, God, Eamon. I'm so sorry. When? How?"

He looked into Lauryl's green eyes and his fingers curled around hers. For the first time, he saw something similar to concern for him. Part of his centuries-old facade cracked and the alien emotion of grief flickered across his face. He cleared his throat and paused while he mentally shoved back down the lump of emotions threatening to surface.

"Tonight. She and a friend were killed together. A hunter tracked and killed them."

"Damn," she said.

Eamon looked thoughtful for a moment and shrugged. Tonight wasn't the night to have an emotional breakdown. "Now I only have one other vampire in my line," he said.

"That's a weird thing to say. Not at all what I'd expect from someone who just lost a longtime friend," she said.

"When you've lived as long as I have, you'll understand." He forced the earlier sadness out of his mind and refocused.

"Can't you just be sad? Can't you let yourself feel that?"

"No, I can't. I'm not human, Lauryl, and I haven't been in quite some time. Human emotions are uncomfortable for me." He stood and walked over to his desk. "I don't want to discuss this."

Lauryl stood up and put her hands on her hips. "You loved her and you can't at least say 'I'm sad that she's dead'?"

He shook his head and further stuffed down his emotions. "Why do I need to say that?"

She walked over to him. "Because it's true and you feel it."

Eamon's brown eyes shifted more amber, silently warning her to stop pursuing whatever she was after. "Let this go. I told you, I don't want to discuss it anymore."

Her brow furrowed. "You wonder why I don't like you? This is a perfect example. You can't even try to show some kind of grief for Irina. Or maybe I should say you won't show it."

"No," he said, wrestling back the emotions he didn't want to hemorrhage from him. He did feel the agonizing loss. It wounded him to his core. Each word was an effort for him and his chest felt like there was a massive hole in it. Then to have her harass him over what she thought was a suitable display of grief was almost intolerable. He wasn't about to show weakness to her. She was hard enough to control without her seeing he was still vulnerable to the human frailty of emotion. That would have to remain concealed.

"I'm done talking about this now. I'll close by reminding you that this is the perfect illustration as to why you must be careful when you are out. Something like this could happen to you."

Lauryl stared at him, waiting. She threw up her hands and spun around. She walked to the door but didn't turn around.

"You know, I could have felt bad for you. I was trying to be sympathetic to you, but you made even that impossible. I'm going back out, since you don't need me or can't admit you need me."

"To where?"

She hesitated a moment and turned back to him. "To eat with an old friend," she said.

"Enjoy it because we're leaving for New York tomorrow evening and then to London indefinitely. So tell your 'old friend' good bye." Eamon's anger flared, but he concealed it before it showed. He knew she was feeding from the doctor and more than likely doing more.

Lauryl's face darkened with anger and her eyes narrowed. She shook her head, flipped him off and left.

And be thankful I don't kill that old friend because that's precisely what I want to do right now, he thought.

CHAPTER SEVENTEEN

Stupid Spy of Eamon's

LONDON ONLY MADE Lauryl's attitude worse. She sulked around their Holland Park house in the posh Kensington area and only perked up on nights she went out to feed. She treated feeding like a wonderful, complex game. She considered it exciting to adopt different names and personalities when she went out to find blood. She took great care in it. She thought Eamon would have been pleased at how she had adapted to, and even excelled at, her vampire life. He wasn't. He didn't acknowledge it at all. And that disappointed and angered her. He continued on as he had before, treating her like an employee instead of a companion.

She scanned the crowds on the sidewalk of Wardour Street. The sidewalks were full but no one caught her eye. The mix of food smells that drifted from the restaurants distracted her for a second. The aroma of curry, a favorite from when she was human, tickled her nose and brought a smile to her face. The spicy scent piqued her hunger and she focused on the humans again. The same Tuesday mix of tourists and young professionals made their way in and out of the bars, enjoying the balmy spring night. Her smile melted into a frown. If she had to eat another self-important stockbroker or German tourist, she'd scream. If things didn't pick up, she'd head over to Berwick Street to hang out in Vinyl Junkies. At least there the music was good and she'd probably find someone more interesting to eat. Then, she saw him.

He wasn't anything special. He had shoulder length, chestnut-colored hair and pale skin that bore acne scars from long ago but she couldn't take her eyes off him. The man leaned against a light

pole and put his hands in his pockets. His clothes were fashiona-
ble. Oxford Street or Milan maybe. Definitely not custom like
Eamon's. When he smiled, a deep dimple on each of his cheeks
appeared. It was infectious and soon a smile was on her face.
Their eyes locked as if they had known each other for ages. She
was looking at another vampire.

He looked like any other male in London but to her, he may
as well have had a giant sign that said VAMPIRE in big red
letters. After standing in stunned silence for a moment, she
walked directly to him.

"Hello there."

"Hey," she said. She'd never met a vampire besides Eamon.
Well, Irina, but she was one of Eamon's vampires so she didn't
know if she counted. This person was the first vampire stranger.

"Out for a bite, are we?" he asked.

"Yeah, I am" His energy became more and more enticing.
The cozy warmth exuded from all parts of him. She reached out
to touch him but just before she did, the warmth vanished. She
couldn't feel anything at all. It was as if he wasn't there anymore.

"What happened?"

"Oh that," he said. "That's just an old trick I know. Knox
Swinton." He extended his hand to her.

She shook it. "Lauryl Mellis-Rutherford," she replied, mumbling the Rutherford part.

"Sorry, I didn't get the last bit."

Lauryl squared her shoulders. "Rutherford. Lauryl Rutherford." After she said it, she glanced over her shoulder, as if she
were saying something dangerous. The people walking nearby
were oblivious to the two of them.

"That's what I thought you said, but I wanted to make certain
I heard you correctly. So you're out for a stroll and a bite then?"

"Yes, I prefer to eat alone."

"Well, I'll leave you to it."

"No!" She grabbed his arm. "That's not what I meant."

Knox looked down at her hand on his arm. "What did you
mean?"

"I meant that I eat alone not that I wanted you to go. You're the first vampire, other than my maker, I've ever met."

"Are you serious?"

"Yes, we don't mix with other vampires. You're the first I've been able to talk to."

"I wouldn't like you out on your own meeting strange vampires. You're far too enchanting."

"I don't like my husband to come with me. Actually, I don't like my husband to do anything with me."

"Really?"

"He's an asshole and I hate him." She bit her lip and wondered if she should be talking to this vampire. He could be one of Eamon's spies. London was probably crawling with people on Eamon's payroll. Lauryl narrowed her eyes at Knox. "Do you know my husband?"

"Not personally. I know of him. What vampire doesn't?"

"Do you work for him in any way?" She crossed her arms over her chest.

"Paranoid, aren't we?"

"That doesn't answer my question."

Knox smiled and his blue eyes shimmered. "No, I don't work for him."

"Good."

"Tell me, how long have you been a vampire?" Knox asked.

"Why?"

"I'm simply curious."

"About a year. How long have you been a vampire?"

Knox took her by the arm. "Walk with me."

As soon as he touched her, she could feel his markers again. He was announcing his presence to any other vampires in the area. "How do you do that?"

"I told you. It's an old trick I know."

"I think it's more than that. You can make yourself almost invisible."

They stopped in front of a pub with a red door. The sign read Waxy's Little Sister. Two women bumped past them and walked in.

Lauryl frowned. "What are we doing here?"

"You're hungry aren't you?"

She nodded.

"Well, nothing better than a pub to fix that." He opened the door for her. "After you, dear."

She hesitated for a moment and then entered. The bartender looked at the two of them and nodded a greeting. The place was quiet. In fact, it was too quiet. Not at all like what she thought a pub would be. No football hooligans smashing chairs and drinking yards of ale. It was quiet and cozy and tourist free. Music played and the random murmurs of humans as they discussed their days filled the air. The aroma of espresso mixed with ale made for a soothing combination. They went upstairs to the sofa bar and settled into a corner spot.

"So are you going to tell me how old you are?"

"I'm twenty-six," Knox said and watched the girl serving a group who chose not to use the dumbwaiter.

"You've only been a vampire twenty-six years? I doubt that."

The girl walked over to them and tucked her tray under her arm. She had freckles and a blond bob haircut. Her low-rise jeans revealed a slight paunch with a little, gold navel ring.

"Get you two something?"

"Tracy, meet a new friend, Lauryl,"

"Nice to meet you," Lauryl said.

"American. Brilliant. Want anything from the bar?" Tracy asked.

"Guinness for me and whatever she's having."

"I'm good for now."

Tracy shrugged her shoulders and left to get the beer. Knox relaxed into the sofa. "I like beer. Always have. It's a friendly drink."

"I guess." Another couple walked in and found a seat close to them. Lauryl gave them a quick nod and turned back to Knox.

"No, it is. Everyone enjoys beer. And, it is quite nutritious in its most basic form. Like liquid bread."

"Um, I guess. Look, you don't answer any of my questions and I don't feel like killing time in a pub learning about beer. I think I'm just going to split, okay?" She stood up but stopped when she heard him chuckle.

"I've been a vampire for over five hundred years. Almost six, actually. I can blot out my markers by simply concentrating. I mentally strip them away like a coat."

She turned to him and sank back down. "Almost six hundred years?"

"Yes, I was turned during an outbreak of the small pox in 1443. Not too far from here. That's why I retain a certain fondness for this area. It's home."

"Is your maker still around?"

"Alas, no. She died in the Great Fire." His face shadowed with sadness but it faded. "I still miss her."

"So you've been alone all this time?"

Tracy put the pint down in front of Knox and walked off.

"No. Unlike your maker, I tend to seek the company of our kind. I've also had a few human companions. Tracy there, for one."

"Really?" She watched the girl talk to the other couple. "How does that work exactly?"

He took a long drink and appeared puzzled. "Just like any other boyfriend-girlfriend relationship."

She shook her head. "No, not that. I mean, she knows you're a vampire, right?"

"Of course. I feed exclusively from her."

Lauryl looked from him to Tracy and then back to him. "She's okay with that?"

"What's not to be okay with?"

"You're dead. You're a vampire."

He smiled. "You say that like it's a bad thing."

"Did you tell her or did she find out? How did it happen?"

Knox tilted his head to the side and studied her. "We met at a club. There are a few underground clubs here in London where humans can meet vampires."

"No shit?"

"Tell me, Lauryl, what do you know of being a vampire?"

"Eamon doesn't tell me much, even when I ask. I don't even know how old he is. I only know that he can move in the daytime.

And then the basics."

"So he's a day-walker? No wonder he moves so naturally among humans."

"Can you go out during the day?"

"No, I can't. Not every vampire can. It is a power only a few have. Usually, only the vampires made by a day-walker can, but not always. Can you?"

Lauryl shrugged. "I don't know. I've never tried. He hasn't told me how to do it."

"Well, best not to try then. It would be painful and quite messy." Knox finished his beer. "I wonder why your husband hasn't told you very much about being a vampire."

She frowned. "I don't know. It's probably another way he can control me."

"Why?"

She shrugged again. "I didn't want to be a vampire. He tricked me. I just wanted to dance. But he had a hard on for me and now I'm a vampire."

"Really?" His eyes widened.

Lauryl nodded. That wasn't entirely accurate. She'd adjusted to being a vampire and even found pleasure in it some days. Reconnecting with Anthony gave her the happiness and peace she yearned for, but Eamon ruined that. He snatched that away with the same selfish authority he used to control the rest of her life. She didn't hate being a vampire. She hated being Eamon's vampire prisoner.

"Maybe if you knew more about being a vampire, you might enjoy it more."

"Why are you talking to me? I mean, you don't know me."

He laughed. "I've seen you out before and have wanted to talk to you. Of course, I was surprised and somewhat intimidated when I heard who your maker was."

"How did you know who my maker was?"

"Well, for one, I feel his marker in you. And vampires do like to talk. Despite your maker choosing isolation, other vampires can feel his presence and power when he is around. He causes quite a stir when he comes to town. Rather like a celebrity. He just ignores other vampires."

Lauryl found what he was saying hard to believe. Why was Eamon so popular? She frowned.

"Anyway, I wanted to talk to you because you seemed to be an interesting sort. And you're beautiful."

"This all sounds like bullshit to me." She sat forward on the sofa, ready to leave. She was done with him and his simplistic answers and chipper vampire talk.

"It isn't. At first, I thought you were alone since you hunt alone and I know what it is like to be alone as a vampire."

"I may as well be alone." Lauryl looked at her wedding ring. "Eamon hardly gives me a second thought."

"Like I said before, I don't know your maker, but I can assure you that he does give you a second thought. You have his blood in you and you're part of him. You can't change that."

"I knew you worked for him!" She shot to her feet. "Slick. You tell me a thing or two about being a vampire and then steer it back to show me what an awesome guy Eamon is and how being a vampire is super swell. Nice talking to you, Knox. If that's your real name." She pushed past Tracy and down the stairs, her heels clopping against the wood floor. She bolted through the pub door and back onto the street. The din of the road noise and people on the sidewalk drowned out her racing thoughts. She stepped off the curb and into the path of a speeding Audi. The tires screeched to a halt and she looked at the driver.

"Shit, I'm sorry," she said, her southern accent sounding through.

The man driving rolled down his window. "That's a good way to get yourself killed. You need to watch the traffic. Are you okay? What's the hurry?"

Lauryl put her hand on her chest and walked to the window. "I'm hungry and my mind isn't on what it should be on," she said.

"What should it be on?" he asked.

"It should be on finding out the name of the handsome man who didn't run me over."

"My name's Tom. And you are?"

"Lisa. Sorry about running out in front of you."

"Can I offer you a lift?"

Lauryl smiled radiantly at him. "That would be fantastic," she said as she got in the car.

As Tom put the car in drive, Lauryl noticed Knox standing in front of the pub. He nodded to her but she ignored him. Stupid spy of Eamon's.

I'm not a spy, she heard in her mind. *I'm simply someone who wants to be your friend. And you can use one.*

CHAPTER EIGHTEEN

The World as a Vampire Is Much Wider Than You Think

IN THE WEEKS following her encounter with Knox, Lauryl avoided Wardour Street. She stayed close to Whitehall and Westminster, though. The historic district charmed her and it was full of a wide variety of people. She developed a taste for MP's and staffers working late in the various ministries. Their some-times-offensive taste made a tolerable meal. They always left their offices late, horny and armed with poor judgment. However, she was tired of them and decided to return to her preferred spot. No spy of Eamon's would prevent her from eating where she wanted.

As she strolled along, part of her remained on guard for Knox. She hadn't seen him or felt him but she knew he was around. This was his home. It still puzzled her that he could "blot out his markers" like he did. It was effortless for him. She wanted to ask Eamon how a vampire could do something like that but didn't want to admit that she had met one of his operatives.

Lauryl walked past the light pole where she had first seen him and took a guarded look around. She continued on, half-looking for her dinner and half-looking for Knox. She turned from Gerrard Street on to Wardour Street and found herself in front of Waxy's Little Sister. Right away the marker of an older vampire pelted her like warm raindrops. She looked around but didn't see any vampires.

Maybe it was a trace marker, the marker a vampire left be-hind after departing an area.

No sooner had she finished the thought when she felt the even more powerful marker of another older vampire.

"Glad to see you back," Knox said as he sauntered through

the pub's red door. "This is her, Bernard," he said to the stocky, well-dressed man with salt and pepper hair that followed him.

The older vampire surveyed Lauryl. "You're as thin as a reed." He looked back at Knox. "You can tell she was a dancer."

Lauryl remained frozen in her spot. Knox stood on one side of her and the older vampire the other. Their markers were so intense together that they were almost suffocating. *Did the older vampire work for Eamon also?* she wondered.

"For the last time, Lauryl, I don't work for Eamon. I've never met him." Knox smiled but Lauryl was dubious. "This is a good friend of mine, Bernard Townsend."

Lauryl extended her hand to the older vampire and did a sloppy curtsey. She had no clue if there was some sort of vampire etiquette she was supposed to be following. "It's a pleasure to meet you."

"The pleasure is mine. Knox told me all about you." Bernard grinned at her.

"I bet he did," she said. *Bernard had kind eyes,* Lauryl thought. *Endearing.*

"Oh, it was all flattering. He was quite taken with you. I think he felt sorry for you," Bernard said.

"Why would he feel sorry for me?"

Bernard wrapped his arm around her in a paternal gesture. "I think he thought you were like a lost puppy and wanted to help you."

She tried to squirm away from Bernard. Eamon would be enraged to see another man, let alone another vampire hugging her like that. "A puppy?"

"A lost puppy," Bernard corrected.

"Shall we go back into Waxy's or should we continue on to Nightshade?" Knox asked.

"Well, first we should discover whether or not we'll have a guest with us." Bernard looked at Lauryl.

"What? I don't know where it is."

Knox patted her on the back. "We'll show you. I think you'll enjoy yourself."

Bernard's arm tightened around her shoulder.

"Yeah, okay," she said.

A black cab pulled up and the three of them climbed in the back. Lauryl was surprised they were taking a cab. Knox and Bernard had to have money. It was odd they would use something as public as a taxi.

"My dear, not everything is as it appears on the surface," As he said it, the cab driver turned and smiled a fang studded smile. "Miles is also a vampire and often shuttles us to Nightshade."

Lauryl looked closer at the cab driver. He couldn't be any older than eighteen. He still had braces on his lower teeth and a retainer on the top. His shock of red hair didn't add any age to his appearance. How ferocious could he be?

"How old are you?" she asked.

"Forty-seven," Miles replied.

"No, I mean in real life years."

"We refer to that age as chronological years, Lauryl," Knox said.

"Whatever."

"I'm nineteen."

"Oh my God, you've had braces that long?" Lauryl wrinkled her nose up.

"No, you daft cow. I've only had them a month." Miles hit the accelerator and the cab shot off. "I wanted to make a few adjustments in my appearance. I had crap teeth as a human and wanted a change. No sense in having lovely fangs in a mouth full of snagglers."

Lauryl bristled at Miles. "Since I just met you, how about you don't call me a cow, okay chompers?"

"Children, let's not argue," Bernard said.

"Well nobody calls me a cow." Lauryl crossed her arms over her chest.

"I'm certain that Miles didn't mean to imply that you were a cow. That's simply a British slang term."

"Whatever."

Knox laughed. "I'm so pleased that you came back by Waxy's. I've missed you these past weeks."

She shifted in her seat. "I didn't want to see you. I thought you worked for Eamon."

"You have trust issues that you should work on." Knox poked her arm.

"Since this happened to me, I don't trust anyone." *Especially vampires*, she thought.

"Vampires are the ones you should trust the most," Bernard said as he looked out of the cab window. "Knox told me that you don't like your maker. I find that interesting."

"Why?" she asked.

"The relationship between a maker and their offspring is typically a loving one," Bernard said.

"Mine must not know that."

Knox and Miles snickered. Lauryl shot a look at the back of Miles' head before she leaned forward and thumped him. He turned back to her and rubbed where she thumped.

"Still," Bernard said. "His bond to you is undeniable. Technically, the three of us should not even be talking to you without asking his permission."

"Are you kidding me?"

"There are very few written vampire laws but there are several unwritten ones. One being that until a maker gives you permission or freedom to function independently; you must always seek his permission to associate with other vampires. Most makers grant it immediately, but yours is known to be very possessive."

"That's putting it nicely. He's a control freak."

Bernard looked over at Knox. "I think with time you'll understand more. Unfortunately, some things only time can teach."

She shrugged and stared out the window. They were now down among the warehouses of northeast London. *What could possibly be down here?* she wondered. She felt random markers of vampires all around. She could feel them lingering in the shadows and in between the enormous warehouses along the river.

"What is down here is my club, Nightshade," Bernard said.

"You have a club?"

"Remember when I was telling you about clubs where humans and vampires could meet? Well, that's what Bernard has in

Nightshade," Knox volunteered.

"Really?"

"The world as a vampire is much wider than you think," Bernard said.

Lauryl's world was narrow. Since Irina died, there were no vampires in Eamon's and her world. Their world only contained humans. There was Grant, who she hated, the people from the dance company, the assorted humans Eamon employed, and up, until they left for London, Anthony. Now she had these vampires in her circle; vampires who owned clubs and had powers that differed from Eamon's. Vampires she didn't want Eamon to know about. She didn't care if there was some vampire law about associating with other vampires. Obviously, Knox and Bernard didn't care.

"Miles, pull around to the back so Lauryl can see where she may enter the building," Bernard said. He smiled at Lauryl. "It doesn't look like much but it's much more inside."

Lauryl agreed. They pulled behind a huge, rusted warehouse that resembled the other warehouses around. She could hear house music inside and felt vampires all around her. She noticed a doorway under a set of rusty stairs and a thin, dark-skinned man leaning against the wall. He straightened up when he saw the cab approaching.

Miles rolled the window down. "Evening, Jeremy, got Mr. T and Mr. S in the back."

"Right on," Jeremy said opening the back door. He bowed his head to Bernard and Knox as they got out and whistled softly when Lauryl swung her legs out of the cab. "Sorry, didn't know you were in there."

"Yeah, I forgot about her," Miles said. "Oy, no hard feelings, ginger."

Lauryl smiled at the goofy, red-haired vampire. "Be good, brace face."

Miles laughed. "Good one."

Bernard laced Lauryl's arm through his. "What I have here, my dear, is not only a gold mine but also a luncheonette of sorts." They walked through the door and down a dark hallway.

"Humans love vampires as much as we love them."

"More so," Knox said.

They walked through another door and the industrial hallway turned into a mahogany-paneled corridor. She could feel vampires somewhere beyond the wall where the techno music pulsed. Their markers weren't as powerful as Bernard and Knox's. The vampires in the club were newborns like her.

They continued to a door and Knox entered a code into an electronic lock. The door clicked open and the music became louder. She could hear laughter in the hall and smelled blood mixed with beer. Obviously, a vampire was feeding somewhere close by. A female vampire with long legs and strawberry blonde hair hurried down the hall toward them.

"Sorry, gentlemen, I was mired down in something in the club." The woman lowered her head to Knox and Bernard and looked Lauryl in the eye. She beamed and extended her hand. "I'm Phyl. Phyllida, actually, but no one calls me that."

Lauryl shook her hand. "Lauryl."

"I know who you are. I saw you dance about five years ago in New York. You had lovely feet and technique."

Lauryl frowned and pulled her hand back. "Oh."

Bernard put his arm around Lauryl. "Phyl was also a dancer in her human life. She danced in London before the war."

"Sadler's Wells, but I met Knox during an air raid in 1940 and that was that," she said.

She kissed Knox on the cheek and turned back to Lauryl. "I missed ballet at first but then I found that there was so much more in the world."

"Shall we?" Bernard asked.

"Is the club full this evening, Phyl?" Knox asked.

"Close enough. It's early still."

They walked down the hall and Bernard stopped abruptly, bringing the other three to a stop. "What is Micah Rollins doing in my club?"

Lauryl looked around but saw no one else.

Phyl gave Bernard a nervous smile. "Sir, he must have slipped by one of the humans on the door. I'll have him removed."

"No," Bernard said and opened the door. "Bring him in to me." Phyl disappeared and Bernard flipped the light on and walked into the office. "Please come in."

A huge saltwater aquarium with a small shark swimming in it dominated one of the walls. She walked closer to it and peered at the fish.

"That's Margaret Thatcher," Knox said. "Bernard raised it from a hatchling."

"Yes, I'm quite an aquarist." Bernard sat down behind the large desk and scanned through a stack of papers.

"I had a little ten-gallon aquarium when I was a dance student in New York," Lauryl said as she continued her assessment of the office. It was generic. There was the desk and seating around the room but nothing upscale or trendy in it. Even the computer was a clunky desktop.

Bernard chuckled. "My office is a bit low end, isn't it?"

She overlooked the fact that he continued to read her thoughts. "Sorry, I'm just used to Eamon."

"It's simply an office in a night club. I didn't see any reason to spend a fortune on it. Have a seat."

Lauryl sat down across from the desk and twisted the hem of her skirt. The evening was becoming more and more surreal. She was sitting in an underground vampire club in east London and not with Eamon. She tugged at the skirt fabric, half-excited and half-fearful. Not of the vampires she was with but of the vampire waiting for her at home.

Phyl and a large, male vampire on the security staff interrupted her thoughts. The bouncer pulled another vampire into the room. This one kicked and struggled to break away.

"Here 'e is, Mr. T. Don't know how the little wanker got in, but I'll find out." The large vampire punched the resisting vampire in the back of the head with a force that made Lauryl cringe. The blow halted any further resistance.

Bernard stood up and surveyed the punch-drunk vampire. He shook his head and clucked his tongue. "Micah, you must think I'm a fool."

"No, sir, I don't" he replied.

"Then you must think I'm weak."

Micah's eyes widened. "No."

"Then what possible reason could you have for being in my club this evening when I've told you never to return."

Micah looked around the room and hoped for some sort of help but didn't find any.

"He asked you a question, you piece of shit," Phyl said, her fangs bared. She slapped him on the neck. Her nails sliced into the skin and blood poured out.

"Patience, Phyl," Bernard chided.

"I was here because I was following a girl. A human."

"Break his arm, Reg," Phyl said.

"No!" Bernard said. "You two are far too eager this evening. Micah says that he was following a female. Perhaps. However, Micah is an ancient vampire and should've been able to prevent the human from coming in here."

"Mr. Townsend, please, I only wanted to meet her! I didn't plan on causing any problems."

"But you have, Micah. You disobeyed an order from me. So you're causing problems in my establishment. Perhaps not the same type of problems as before, but problems none the less."

Bernard nodded to the big vampire holding Micah. "Reg, would you deal with Mr. Rollins?"

"What are you gonna do?" Micah asked trying to pull away.

"I'm going to ensure that you never disobey me or return to my club again."

"No!" Micah shouted.

Knox stood up. "As Commissioner of London, I say that the sentence handed down by Bernard will stand."

Reg snatched the condemned vampire up by the arm and Lauryl heard the sickening snap of his humerus. Micah howled in pain but Reg's fist connecting with his jaw silenced him. Blood, saliva and teeth flew across the room. Micah shook his head in an attempt to restore some clarity to his addled thoughts. His jaw now moved in the opposite direction that he was shaking. Lauryl bit her lower lip and turned her head as Reg dragged Micah out.

"I'm sorry you had to see that, Lauryl. I hate mixing business with pleasure," Bernard said as he sat back down.

She looked from Knox to Bernard. "You're almost gangsters. I mean, I don't know what he did, but you settled it like you were from New Jersey."

Knox laughed and glanced at Bernard, who shook his head at Knox. "Bernard isn't the Mafioso type."

"What are you going to do with that guy?"

"Deal with him appropriately," Bernard said.

"What did he do?"

"He was a trouble maker and was making life difficult for us," Knox said.

"That's kind of vague."

"Mr. Rollins was a careless vampire. He killed humans rather than fed on them. He even had the nerve to kill one in my club." Bernard folded his hands in his lap. "And that's forbidden."

"Vampires can't kill humans carelessly. It draws attention to us. In order to survive, we avoid unnecessary attention. So we deal with those who don't think like we do. I as Commissioner seek out lawbreakers and bring them to justice and Bernard decides on sentences for crimes." Knox said.

Lauryl looked from Knox to Bernard, who seemed content to watch Margaret Thatcher swim in the tank.

"I thought there weren't many rules for vampires."

"There aren't, believe it or not," Knox said. "One would think that for as long as we have existed, some sort of codified system would have been developed but it just hasn't ever happened. Newborn vampires look to ancient ones for guidance." Knox said.

"So is Bernard like a king?" Lauryl asked.

Both Knox and Bernard laughed.

"I'm hardly a king. I'm the oldest vampire who permanently resides in London, or for that matter, the U.K. so I oversee its vampire population. I'm the Elder," Bernard said.

"You're older than Knox?"

"By two hundred years."

"So you're like seven hundred and fifty years old and not the oldest vampire in London?"

"Yes."

"Who is?" As soon as she asked, she knew. They didn't have to tell her. She knew it as if Eamon whispered it in her ear. Their blood bond told her.

"Let me guess who's the oldest," she muttered. She frowned at the shark and then at Bernard. "How old is he?"

"You don't know?" Knox asked.

"No."

"I don't either. He's older than any vampire I know of. He's rumored to be the oldest vampire in the world."

"I can't believe it." She kicked her platform shoe in frustration.

"What can't you believe?" Knox asked.

"I can't believe I have to be bound to the oldest vampire in the world. I can't stand him and I'm stuck with him."

"Ask him to let you go," Knox said.

"I've tried. The only way of getting away from him is if I just disappear."

"When you learn how, you can," Knox said, smiling.

Bernard carefully observed the interaction between Knox and Lauryl. "Knox," Bernard said coolly. The two vampires stared at each other as if they were engaged in a silent conversation.

After a moment, Lauryl reached out to Knox. "Can you teach me?"

CHAPTER NINETEEN

You're Living. Like It or Not.

"I HAVE A surprise for you." Eamon fanned an envelope in front of her.

Lauryl flung the copy of *Hello!* Magazine in her hand aside.

"I think this is something you will enjoy," he said. The smug expression on his face gave the appearance he was already congratulating himself for whatever he was going to tell her.

Her shoulders lifted in a shrug.

Eamon pulled a large vellum card out of the envelope and held it out to her. It was an invitation to a charity auction benefiting the schools of the Royal Ballet. A ripple of excitement rolled through her. She handed the card back to him and picked up the magazine again.

"I guess it sounds okay," she said with the same remote look he often gave her.

Eamon snatched the card away from her. "Perhaps showing a bit of gratitude or excitement might in order."

"Yay," she said, not even bothering to look up from the magazine.

"In your enthusiasm, I'm sure you failed to notice the date. Two weeks from tonight." He rolled his eyes and walked out of the room.

Lauryl glanced up from the magazine and smiled.

* * *

LAURYL FIDDLED WITH a bead on the new couture gown Eamon bought for her and stared out the window of the limo as they drove along. She twisted the bead and furrowed her brow as if contemplating a huge problem.

Eamon resisted the urge to invade her thoughts. "You are stunning tonight."

She stopped twisting the bead and turned toward him. Her green eyes held no emotion. "Thank you."

He stared at her for a minute before shaking his head. "I don't understand you. You sit there like you are dead."

"I am dead," she said. "Or am I? I don't know. Am I dead or undead, like they say in the movies?"

"You're living. Like it or not."

"Well, I'm living with someone I hate."

Eamon's jaw clenched. "You've got a long time to get over that." The car pulled in front of the Royal Opera House. Eamon frowned at the long line of paparazzi that had lined up. "But as it stands, you're stuck with me." He smoothed his hand over his shirtfront and looked back at her. "Now, get your negative, little ass out of this car."

Lauryl pushed back against the seat. "Why won't you let me go? You don't really care about me. I mean, why can't I live on my own? You let Irina live on her own."

"Because you're careless. You'd be dead in a month. There are people out there who know our kind exist and want to kill us, as evidenced by Irina."

"I wish I could find one of them," she mumbled as she slid across the seat. Eamon reached over before she could get out and caught her wrist. She cried out as he squeezed until her diamond bracelet cut into her skin. She looked down at her wrist and then up at him.

"Behave tonight, please." He squeezed again, this time not as tight, and let go of her.

Eamon's driver, Paul, opened the door and she tried to bolt from the car, but the blinding flashes from the photographers stunned her, halting her escape. Her eyes adjusted and she started to walk when Eamon's hand cupped her elbow. She stiffened briefly fought to hide a frown.

"Do you have to touch me?" she asked.

He leaned into her and smiled for the benefit of the photographers, who thought they were getting a shot of the elusive

Eamon Rutherford. "I'm your husband," he said as he gave her a soft shove through the door.

Once inside the Paul Hamlyn Hall, Lauryl pulled away from him and blended into the milling crowd. She could still hear his voice though. He had stopped to talk to who she assumed was a business acquaintance. The muscles in her neck and shoulders remained knotted until she could no longer hear him and then relaxed. *Freedom,* she thought as she glanced around the crowded room. A star-struck smile crossed her face when Sir Anthony Dowell and Miyako Yoshida looked up from their conversation and acknowledged her. She waved back and continued through the room. Dancers, agents, designers and other assorted dance people talked and laughed. *This might not be so bad after all,* she thought. She took a glass of champagne and scanned some of the items available in the auction.

One item caught her eye. An autographed performance poster from long ago signed by Dame Margot Fonteyn. She sighed and recalled how much she loved watching her dance on TV when she was a child. She told her grandmother that she was going to dance just like Miss Margot, as she called her. Lauryl smiled as she recalled the warm memories of her grandmother. She made a mental note of the item number on the poster. She wanted it and she didn't care how much he had to pay.

After wandering around and socializing with dancers and choreographers, Lauryl decided that she'd have to go back and sit with Eamon if she wanted him to bid on that poster. The idea of sitting with him was unpleasant but she wanted the poster. He'd want something in return, which she wasn't willing to give. That was being selfish but she was following his lead.

It still puzzled her why he wouldn't let her live on her own. She doubted it was because he thought she couldn't take care of herself. Instead she suspected that he couldn't admit he'd made a mistake with her. His pride wasn't going to allow her to be free and happy. She knew he was unhappy. They fought all the time, but he wouldn't let go. She wished she could just get rid of him or disappear herself. She stopped walking.

* * *

"PLANNING MY DEATH?" Eamon asked when he walked over to her.

His presence startled her. "I couldn't do that," she said quickly.

"No, but this is the first time in months I've seen you genuinely happy. You must be planning to do me some sort of harm for you to smile like that."

She laced her arm through his and shook her head. "I've found something I'd like to have. Would you bid on it for me?"

The sensation of her willing touch melted his brittle irritation from earlier. "What is it?" he asked as they walked to their seats.

"It's a performance poster autographed by Dame Margot. I'd love to have it." She sat down and leaned against him. After a few moments, she scratched the top of his thigh and kissed him.

Suspicion rather that pleasure pulsed through Eamon. *Something was up*, he thought. He took her small hand and folded it in his. *Perhaps he should take a brief peek at her thoughts, just to be certain*, he thought. *No, she'd feel it and it would upset her, causing her to swing back to her moody self. Trust her.*

"I'll buy you anything you want."

"Thank you." She took her hand from his, slid it up his thigh, and down between his legs.

"Are you certain you'd like to stay? I can have someone bid on our behalf. You seem to have other things on your mind."

She removed her hand coyly. "No, I want you to get it. Besides, won't it be more fun if we wait?"

"What if I don't want to wait?"

"Oh," she purred in his ear. "Force yourself."

After waiting ages for her to allow him to touch her, the last thing he wanted to do was wait. Something vague nagged at him. Something about her abrupt turnaround raised a warning flag in his mind. Nothing specific, but it was enough to distract him. He cut his eyes over to her and studied her face. A tiny, predatory glint lit up her eyes as she stared at the auctioneer. Hunger.

Her appetite approached the level of a mature vampire and that pleased him. She was no longer squeamish about feeding.

Once in a rare moment of confidence, she told him that she'd never felt so complete, so powerful. The admission came as a surprise to him. She was difficult to understand, a complex puzzle. He wondered how that idiot psychiatrist had managed to do so.

Lauryl ran her tongue over her lips and then turned to him. He looked forward but the gaze she'd now fixed on his face irritated him. It was the same predatory stare she'd watched the auctioneer with. He looked back at her and her expression softened to a more complacent one.

Better, he thought.

"Are you hungry?" he whispered.

"Somewhat."

"Let's go." He was hungry himself.

"I can wait," Lauryl whispered back.

"Now," he mumbled as he sat forward.

"No," she said and pulled him back. "I'll go and meet you back at home."

"I'm ready now. I'll have someone proxy bid for us."

Lauryl caught his hand and put it on her breast under her dress. "Stay and meet me back at home." She scooted forward and touched his cheek. "I won't be long." She kissed him softly but then her kiss deepened. He withdrew in surprise and she placed her hand back between his thighs. Eamon relaxed into the kiss.

I want to leave now, he said into her mind.

His tongue slipped deeper in her mouth and they remained in their embrace for a moment. If she said fuck me here, he would have done it. He would have glamoured the two hundred people there and stripped off the twelve-thousand-dollar gown she was wearing.

"Just give me a little time." She pulled away and caressed his cheek.

"Against my better judgment."

An inviting smile appeared on her lips and she stood up. The people behind them gave her a disapproving glare. She bent back over him almost completely exposing her breasts. "Now, don't forget me."

"As if I could." After she walked out, he turned to the people seated behind him. "We're newlyweds."

"We gathered," the man said and gave Lauryl an appreciative glance.

Eamon turned back to the auctioneer and thought about Lauryl. It would be impossible for him to sit through the entire auction, especially when all he could think about was going home to her. However, until she fed and settled her more predatory impulses, it was best to wait.

Her sudden change of attitude still bothered him. How in the span of less than an hour could she adjust so acutely? It was as if she was a different person. Eamon grit his teeth together as he thought about that. What if what she had done tonight was false? What if the affection she had shown was an act? What if that was her attempt at glamouring?

He looked down at his watch. She'd only been gone a little more than an hour. He knew she wouldn't be back from feeding. It would take her some time to find something she liked. Eamon shot out of his seat. As he stalked out into the lobby, he grabbed the first uniformed usher by the arm. The startled young man backed away from Eamon.

"Mr. Rutherford, sir. Is-is there a problem?" he stammered.

"I seem to have left my phone in my car. Is there a private phone I may use?"

Before the young man could answer, the house manager hurried over to intervene. "Mr. Rutherford, if you'll follow me, I'll be happy to direct you to a phone."

Eamon let go of the usher and followed the house manager to a private suite. The manager motioned to a chair and brought the phone over to the table next to him. "Thank you," Eamon said curtly.

The house manager, who was accustomed to being ill-treated by patrons simply nodded politely. "May I bring you a drink? Or perhaps I can inform your wife—"

Eamon held his hand up, cutting off the man in mid-sentence. "The drink..." Eamon waited for the man to volunteer his name.

"Collins, sir. Timothy Collins."

"Yes, Collins, Glenlivet." He motioned to the door.

"Immediately, sir."

Eamon dialed the number to her cell phone, but she didn't answer. He then tried the house phone. Nothing. He sat in the chair, with the receiver across his lap. The tone from the phone became annoying so he dropped it back in the cradle.

Maybe she's out feeding, he thought. What else could she be doing? He rested his chin on his palm and stared at the large arrangement of white roses on a sideboard across the room.

My companion, he thought. *She's my companion, my wife. Even if our marriage isn't a human marriage, we share the bond of blood.* His blood was in her. She might not like it but it was a fact. Trust her. He closed his eyes for a moment. Why did he have to tell himself to trust her? A soft knock on the door caused his eyes to snap open. Collins came in with a glass of scotch and placed it next to him.

"Thank you, Collins."

"Will you need anything else, sir?"

Eamon drained the glass and stood up. "No, I'm going back to the auction. I'm waiting to bid on something for my wife."

Collins bowed his head.

*   *   *

AS HE RODE back to the house, Eamon's uneasiness dissolved and was replaced by satisfaction since he had been able to get the poster the Lauryl wanted. He didn't even mind paying the seventeen thousand pounds it had cost him.

"Is my wife back, Paul?" he asked.

"I believe so, sir. She went out after I dropped her off, but I think she's back."

Eamon looked down at his watch. Two and a half hours had passed. She should be back unless of course she was playing with her victim. That was a possibility. As they pulled up to the house, he knew she wasn't home. He didn't feel her anywhere close. Eamon went inside and tossed off his tuxedo jacket. The house had a curious emptiness. It wasn't just that he was physically alone in the house. It was something more. He walked into the living room and poured himself a drink while he waited for Lauryl to come home.

After his third drink and several hours passing, Eamon's uneasiness grew. He wasn't angry. He was concerned. She had never been out this long. In addition, she wasn't the type to feed on more than one human in an evening. He walked up to her room and looked around. Nothing was out of the ordinary. The gown she had worn hung in the closet and her shoes, stockings, and undergarments lay strewn across the floor as they usually were. He could still sense her presence in the room. She wasn't very good at hiding from other vampires. He wasn't sure if she just couldn't do it or didn't care to do it. Eamon checked his watch. It was now half past four. He went into his room to get his car keys.

Eamon despised driving in London. Although, at this hour of the morning, it was tolerable. He turned onto Wardour Street and cruised down it slowly. He understood why Lauryl liked this area. Its trendy bars and clubs still sat in the West End but it edged along some areas that made the hunting easy. Drunks, tourists, and thrill seekers always made an easy meal. As he looked at the now-darkened bars and clubs, he felt no sign of Lauryl. He pulled his car over, got out, and stood on the sidewalk. The fading trace markers of other vampires brushed against him but nothing of her. He didn't even think she had been there. He got back into his car and drove along Oxford Street to Bayswater Road parallel to Hyde Park, thinking maybe she had changed her mind. He only sensed the presence of random, anonymous vampires looking for blood before dawn. They scattered as he lingered on the sidewalk, his marker frightening them away. He felt the same thing along Kensington High Street. He knew she wouldn't be there but he checked just the same.

When he returned to their house at Holland Park, he knew she wasn't home yet. The house was dark. If she had come in, she would have left every light on. He walked to the edge of the park, but felt nothing. He turned on his heel and walked back to the house.

It was now close to six. He'd finished his business correspondence and reviewed the final details of Irina's estate.

The lingering particulars of her possessions wounded him. Her New York apartment sold quickly, which was what he wanted. Grant settled the majority of the details for him. He had all of her personal things gathered up and put them in storage for Eamon in New York. Grant sent her jewelry to Eamon's apartment. One day, Eamon hoped he could go through the boxes and jewelry but he didn't think it would be anytime soon. It still hurt too much.

Eamon went upstairs back to Lauryl's room and got in her bed. He told himself that there had to be an explanation. More than likely it would involve her carelessness and lack of consideration. After tossing and turning for an hour, he finally allowed himself to fall into his day sleep.

*　　*　　*

AT FOUR O'CLOCK, Eamon awoke hoping to find Lauryl home but she wasn't. It was now beyond a late feeding or lack of consideration. His first instinct was that something had happened to her. Maybe she had met someone who knew what she was and killed her. Lauryl was careless enough. It could even happen to an old vampire, like Irina. But when Irina died a few months ago, it struck him to his core. He felt the last bit of life slip away from her like it was him. He hadn't felt anything like that with Lauryl. It was as if she'd just vanished. Eamon bolted forward in the bed.

She vanished. Lauryl walked away from him without him even giving it a second thought. That was why her mood changed so abruptly. She must have concocted some sort of scheme and used last night as a chance to put it into action. But how? She wasn't skilled enough to manage something like that. Or was she? She had come into her own since they arrived in London. The few times they fed together, she was incomparable. It was as if she was a vampire several centuries older. Her ability to glamour humans was superb. Perhaps her "I hate being a vampire" line was just a cover story, a ruse.

Eamon tried to dress but couldn't put off calling Grant any longer. "Grant, have you heard from Lauryl?" he asked as he

buttoned his shirt. He tried to keep his voice calm and unconcerned.

"Lauryl? No, she can't stand me. Why?"

"Because she isn't here." The muscles in his neck tightened
into knots as the remainder of his patience evaporated.

"What do you mean?"

What little composure Eamon had maintained snapped. "Did
I stutter, you fool? She isn't here. She left last night and I haven't
heard from her since. All of her things are here but she isn't." His
hands shook as he fastened his cuff links and threaded his tie
through his collar.

"Can she do that?"

Eamon stopped tying his tie and his jaw clenched. "Grant, I
swear if you were here, I'd kill you. Apparently, she can because
she did. Jesus Christ, you're stupid for a lawyer."

"I'm only stupid about your world. Not the legal world,"
Grant said defensively. He hesitated for a moment. "Have you
checked back in Washington?"

"No! I'm not going to call and say, have you seen my wife?
I'm leaving in an hour to come back to the states. While I'm in
transit, I expect you to be looking for her. Don't close any of her
bank accounts or credit cards. Just leave everything as it is."

"Whatever you say."

Eamon ended the call. He finished his tie and put his watch
on. Lauryl had surprised him beyond his expectations. She had
told him she couldn't stand him over and over again. She figured
out a way to leave him and she did. Now he had to find her
before she ended up dead. Although at this point, he wanted to
kill her himself.

CHAPTER TWENTY
Can't You Just Find Her Using Your Own Ways?

THE FLIGHT FROM Seattle to Northup's tiny, private airport seemed to take three times longer than it usually did. Eamon got off his private jet without a word to his flight crew and jumped in his car. The car squealed off the tarmac and shot down the road.

His thoughts had been racing since he left London. Twelve hours later, he still was mystified by how Lauryl had disappeared without even the tiniest of traces. It was like she didn't exist. Some vampires had the ability to camouflage their markers to appear almost invisible. But he thought that skill was limited to older vampires like himself. He'd never heard of any who could completely mask their presence. Even he had trouble doing it for extended periods. His thoughts drifted back to the ancient teachings of his maker, Eleanor. The only relevant information she'd given him was that humans who possess gifts of guile or cunning before being turned often learned to amplify those as a vampire. Had he underestimated Lauryl?

Eamon unlocked the front door and disabled the alarm system. He took a cautious look around the foyer, feeling for Lauryl's presence. When he felt nothing, he jogged up the stairs to her bedroom. Again, nothing. He couldn't tell if she had been here or not.

The room was exactly as she left it. He could smell the fading scent of her perfume but not her. He opened the closet doors and all of the clothing she'd left was still hanging, as it should be. Her jewelry drawer remained closed. He opened it, half-expecting it to be empty, but it wasn't. It was all still there.

She hadn't been back here. He closed the closet door behind

him and stood for a moment, considering where she could have gone. The only thing he could think of was to call Martin and see if he had heard from her. Or call her therapist.

That God damned doctor. His fists clenched and his fangs dropped down at the thought of that fool. She'd probably run to him and then they'd gone off to God knows where. He pulled his phone out and turned it over a few times as he walked to the door. As he reached for the doorknob, he stopped. Something caught his eye and he turned to make sure he had seen it correctly. In the corner, by her bed, was the easel the Degas painting sat on. It was empty.

Three quick strides across the room brought him in front of the easel. He glared at the empty wooden stand. She'd been there after all and stayed long enough to steal the painting. The gift he'd given her. Technically she didn't steal it, but she might as well have. She snuck in like a thief and absconded with it.

He shoved his phone back in his pocket and grabbed the easel. With a swift movement he collapsed the easel's legs and swung the it into her dressing table. Her perfume and lotion bottles shattered and shards of crystal flew across the room. Eamon launched the easel against the wall. The wood splintered as it impacted. He yanked open the closet door, pulling it from its hinges. With a new fury, he hurled out her clothing. Dresses and shoes flew out the door and within minutes he emptied the entire closet. The only care he exercised was with her jewelry drawer. He simply dumped the contents into his pockets and stalked out of the wrecked closet.

In his room, he unloaded his pockets onto his dresser and paced back and forth.

She left me, he thought. *The stupid bitch betrayed me for that asinine doctor.*

Eamon couldn't believe it. No one, human or vampire, had ever betrayed him. It just didn't happen. Lauryl was full of firsts for him. He looked at his watch, a quarter to ten. He dialed directory assistance for the phone number for Lauryl's doctor and then dialed it. A recording told him that Wilson's office was no longer seeing patients and all records could be obtained—.

Eamon hung up and dialed Grant.

"Grant, have our investigators begin an immediate search for Anthony Wilson, MD of Ocean Shores. I don't know anything else of the man other than he's a psychiatrist. I want no stone left unturned. I want him found." He ran his hand through his hair.

A pause ensued on the other end of the line. "Eamon, I'm not questioning, but why are you looking for him?"

"Because when I find that moron, I'll find Lauryl."

"Can't you find her using your own ways?"

"I could if I could feel her or sense her, but I can't. Simply do as I ask."

He ended the call and glanced around the room. In all of this he had neglected his hunger. He hadn't fed in four days and now was hungry to the point of distraction. If he didn't feed soon his judgment would become impaired and his strength would decrease dramatically. He dialed his phone again and a smile turned on his lips when he heard the voice on the other end.

"Hello, Jennifer. Have you missed me as much as I've missed you?"

CHAPTER TWENTY-ONE

As Long as You Aren't a Pervert

EAMON KNOTTED HIS tie and frowned as he sat back down on his bed. Tampa annoyed him. Or at least the August weather did. The heat, even after sunset, was sticky and oppressive and the wind that blew in off Tampa Bay wasn't pleasant. It just circulated the steamy air. He'd come to Tampa at the worst possible time. From mid-June until early September, it rained every afternoon. The humidity that lingered irritated him as well. Most evenings, when he woke up, steam would still be rising off the wet streets and his windows clouded with condensation.

Right now the only charm the city held was that it hid his runaway, duplicitous companion. He still couldn't sense her, though. As much as he reached out with his mind, he came up with nothing. His small team of human investigators had been a waste so far. They were only able to track Wilson to Tampa and then they came up empty handed.

One thing Tampa did have, Eamon discovered, was a high population of vampires. This seemed unusual to Eamon. Vampires usually didn't congregate in such large numbers in cities the size of Tampa. It was dangerous. More vampires in a concentrated area meant more opportunities for discovery and potential destruction. Wherever he went he could feel at least one lingering and no doubt, they felt him as well. Since he arrived, Eamon removed all of the mental barriers he maintained to keep his self-imposed isolation intact. He hoped that by keeping himself open to other vampires, one of them might be able to help him find Lauryl. He still couldn't understand how another vampire, a younger vampire, would be able to do what he hadn't learned until he reached over one hundred years of age.

As he tucked his phone into his pocket, it vibrated. He saw Grant's name on the caller ID.

"Yes?"

"Eamon, I got a call earlier from someone down there in Tampa who wants to meet with you."

"Who is it?" he asked as he walked down the stairs.

"She said she was someone who wanted to introduce herself and provide hospitality for you."

"A vampire." Eamon stopped at the foot of the stairs and looked around the foyer.

"She didn't say."

He laughed. "She didn't have to. I can tell by what she said."

"Oh. I told her I'd speak with you but I couldn't guarantee anything. She said that she knew you valued your privacy."

"Tell her I'll meet with her. Get the specifics and text me." He ended the call and checked his watch. It was only eight o'clock.

*　　*　　*

EAMON WALKED DOWN the sidewalk of Hyde Park Village, a quaint shopping area close to his house and studied the people as they filed in and out of the stores and restaurants. Being alone at home was intolerable and driving around in the dark grey Porsche Boxster the dealership sent over to him now bored him as well.

Tonight, his loneliness was more acute. In his entire existence as a vampire, he'd only experienced loneliness of this intensity one other time and that was when his maker died. It had been long ago but he still remembered her. Eleanor was beautiful. She was fair with light red hair and had the most vivid blue-green eyes. The daughter of a Roman Senator, she'd been turned around the time of Julius Caesar by a Persian slave girl her family bought to work in the house. The day walking vampire slaughtered entire family but decided to spare and turn Eleanor because of the color of her eyes. Eleanor often told Eamon that there is always something in humans to redeem them if you're willing to search for it. She found it in him. He wanted to be like her and that was enough. She said he possessed a strong survival instinct. He didn't think it was anything that noble. It was far more self-serving. He simply wanted to be a vampire.

Now, he was alone again. He chided himself for having such a small line of vampires. If he'd been like other vampires he'd encountered over the centuries, he'd have more offspring around him. He was different, though. He regarded his role as Primigenio, the Great Old One, with an intense solemnity and chose not to turn many humans. He couldn't protect them properly if there were too many, and if he was honest, he didn't have the patience for many offspring and their needs. But that was when he was a much younger and more self-centered vampire. Tonight, he wished he'd made different choices.

Eamon stopped outside of a bookstore and studied the books on display in the window. A book might distract him. Watching the people inside might distract him even more. He wasn't hungry, but he never ruled out the occasional, random feed. He stood in front of the shelf of new releases and glanced around the store. In the back, in the new age and occult books, a young woman caught his attention.

Her black hair fell almost to her mid-back and one of the straps of the oversized overalls she was wearing hung unfastened down her back. Her pale skin at the top of her curvy hips peeked out where her tank top stopped and the strap was unfastened. She caught him studying her and glared at him. A smirk appeared on his lips when she adjusted the ear buds on her iPod and returned her attention to the books in front of her.

Lovely. Her brown eyes, which burned with irritation at him, drew his attention. They appeared almost black against her porcelain skin. She was lovely, like a little gothic doll. He walked over to the aisle where she was and stood a few feet from her. The music that overflowed from the ear buds was from *La Bohème*. He shifted his position. The delicious smell of her floral perfume and natural scent drifted over to him. He took a deep breath of her, leaned an elbow on the shelf and picked up a book on Tarot cards. His view was better but no sooner than he became comfortable, she snatched a book from the shelf and made her way to the front of the store to pay.

Eamon replaced the book he had been thumbing through and moved toward a table of current events. His focus remained on the young woman. Now, even more intrigued, he followed her out of the store, but stayed a few yards behind her. Twice she stopped abruptly, sending him hurrying into doorways. The third time she stopped she spun around, pulled the pink ear buds down, and scowled at him.

"Why are you following me? I didn't steal anything," she asked with the same glare she had given him in the store.

La Bohème continued to play through the ear buds. "I was following you because I wanted the book you bought." He nodded to the bag she clutched to her chest.

The young woman eyed him up and down, narrowing her eyes. "What's the name of the book?"

Oh, she's a tough one, he thought. He concentrated on her thoughts and saw the title in her mind. "It's a book on astrology. *Astrological Forecasts for the Next Five Years for Cancer.* You got the last copy."

Her grip on the bag tightened. "Well, it's mine. You were too late tonight."

"What is your name?" Eamon asked.

"What's yours?" she countered. Her suspicious facade flaked away the longer he smiled at her.

"Eamon Rutherford."

"Amelie de la Puente." She tilted her head to the side. "You don't look like the type who is into astrology."

"Oh, I believe in the paranormal and such." Her brown eyes captivated him. "Would you like to get a cup of coffee? Maybe we could haggle over the book?" He nodded over to a restaurant with outdoor seating.

Amelie looked at the restaurant and back at Eamon. "That would be nice."

"I wouldn't want to keep you from anything."

Her cheeks turned pink. "No, you won't do that."

*　　*　　*

EAMON HELD HER chair as she sat down and took the chair across from her. "Are you an avid fan of astrology, Amelie?"

"No, not really. It's just something to read. I like off-the-wall stuff."

He glanced over the wine list. "Would you like a glass of wine?"

She shook her head. "No, but a cappuccino sounds great."

The idea of coffee in this heat sounded completely unappealing to him. He signaled for the waiter and ordered her drink and himself a scotch. "When you say off-the-wall, what do you mean?"

Amelie tucked her hair behind her ear, which exposed the slender line of her neck. "I just meant things that are less serious. Four years of academic reading gets old. I like history, but now I'm ready to read something else. It's a guilty pleasure kind of thing."

"Have you recently graduated from college?" He took a drink of the scotch the waiter placed in front of him. It wasn't good. He suspected they even watered it down.

She nodded. "BA in history from UF. The University of Florida." she added.

"That's wonderful. I like history, too."

"I graduated with high honors." She squirmed in her seat and her cheeks turned pink again. "This is boring for you, right?"

He shook his head. "Why would you think that?"

"I don't know. Just a lot of obscure knowledge and my ticket to grad school. I guess it doesn't really matter. I probably won't ever have to work."

"Why's that?"

"My dad died two months ago." Sadness passed across her face and then faded. "He left me well taken care of," she said with a frown.

"I'm sorry for your loss."

Amelie sighed and her gaze wandered around the cafe. "I'm the last of my family now. My mom died when I was born." She licked the spoon from the cappuccino and blew on the foam.

Eamon smiled as he watched her tongue lap the foam off the

spoon. "It's hard to be alone. Although they say a person adapts to it if they want to."

Amelie glanced down at Eamon's left hand. "Are you alone?"

Eamon folded his fingers in. "That's a good question. My life has become quite complicated over the past month."

"I thought you were married. I remember reading…"

"So you do know me," He smiled and picked up the scotch but didn't drink it.

"I know about your businesses. I read the papers. I've never seen a picture of you, though. You're not what I expected."

"You're not the first person to say that." He frowned into his scotch.

"No, probably not. Assumptions are wrong most of the time." She twisted a button on her overalls. "After all, I thought you were some sort of perv in the bookstore."

"A pervert?" His eyebrows lifted in surprise.

"I could…" She leaned across the table. "Feel you staring at me."

"Well, I promise that I'm not a pervert. I'm many things but not that." Eamon drained the glass and signaled to the waiter to refill it. It was dreadful but it was wet and cool and better than nothing.

"As long as you aren't a pervert," she said with a laugh. "Anyway, I kind of liked the way you were staring at me. It was intense, but it made me feel like I was the only one in the world that you wanted to look at."

"You were."

Amelie picked up her spoon and stirred her cappuccino again. He watched her retreat into what felt like self-doubt and confusion, which seemed sad and incorrect. Her lush curves and radiant, dark eyes were spellbinding. More than anything, he wanted to lean across the table, kiss her delicate mouth, and show her how beautiful he thought she was. Instead, he just placed his hand on top of hers and rubbed her fingers.

"Would you like to go for a walk? It's only half passed nine and that's too early to let you go."

Amelie turned around. "I think the stores are all closed."

"I thought we might walk by my house."

"Where do you live?" she asked.

"Bayshore. We could walk along the water if you'd like."

Amelie shook her head. "Not tonight. But you can walk me home."

"I'll drive you instead."

Eamon pulled in the drive of Amelie's house and realized that she didn't live far from him. That was a plus. He waited while she chewed her bottom lip and tried to decide if she wanted to invite him in.

"Well, this is my house." She looked at the front door and then at him. Amelie turned her key over in her hand a few times. "Do you want—" She stopped mid-sentence when his fingers skimmed down her neck. The key slipped from her hand as she caught her breath.

"Yes, I want," he whispered as he leaned over to kiss her. "I want very much."

*   *   *

EAMON ROLLED OVER in Amelie's bed and wrapped his arm around her shoulder. It had been almost impossible not to take her blood while they made love. He thought of it as making love because of the connection he felt with Amelie. Six hours, that was all the time he had known her. Their experience differed from the times with Lauryl. With Lauryl, no emotional connection existed. It was like winning a contest where she was a prize. Even that wasn't quite the case because he had to glamour her. With Amelie, he experienced simple pleasure and warmth. She willingly opened herself up to him.

"Would you mind if I asked you a question? Amelie asked.

"You can ask me anything you'd like," Eamon said.

"How old are you?" She rolled over on her stomach and propped her chin on one of the pillows.

Eamon blinked and for a moment considered whether or not to answer. "Why do you ask?"

"I don't know. I'm just curious, I guess."

"How old do you think I am?" That question bought him

some time to think of his answer.

She narrowed her eyes as she studied his face. "I don't want to guess. Just tell me."

Eamon smiled. "I'm twice your age." His chronological age was about that.

"That's not very specific." She frowned and tucked some of her hair behind her ear.

He kissed her. "Does our age difference bother you?"

"No, not at all. I'm just curious." Amelie studied his face again.

"Curiosity is fine."

She snuggled in against him. "You seem different than other men."

"Really? How so?"

"I don't know. You just are. It's weird. Again, you're not what I was expecting. I thought you'd be different."

"Different?" Eamon stroked the smooth skin of her back.

"Like super arrogant or whatever."

He chuckled. Lauryl would say he was. "It's been said that I am."

"You don't seem that way to me." Amelie kissed his shoulder.

"Maybe around you I'm not. Maybe I feel different around you."

"I hope not," she said.

Eamon had been following her thoughts. Her budding attraction to him was obvious. The attraction happened without him taking her blood or glamouring her. It was genuine. He felt her connection with him. At the same time, he felt something as well; something foreign to him. He actually enjoyed the company of Amelie. He didn't have any agenda with her. And something about this young woman allowed him to relax. He didn't have to hide who he was. Only what he was.

"You feel so good." He turned her toward him and stroked her cheek.

"Do you want to stay?" She kissed his finger as it passed over her lips.

"Unfortunately, I can't. I need to get home soon." Eamon

looked around her room. A sorority composite picture and other college memorabilia covered the walls. His gaze stopped on a cheval mirror in the corner covered by her bathrobe. He made a mental note of the mirror's position.

"You can if you want."

"I wish I could. I'd like to stay in bed with you all day but my day is already…" He thought for a moment. "Planned."

"Okay." She put her head on his chest.

He smoothed her dark hair. "I would like to see you tonight. I'm more available at night."

She nodded against him. "I'd like that."

"Good. I'll give you my number here before I leave," He thought for a moment, mulling over the idea of starting a relationship with Amelie. "And I'll give you my New York number. They can always reach me."

He tipped her chin up and her eyelids drooped.

"Am I keeping you up?"

A sated smile appeared on her lips. "Oh no. You've …exhausted me." She kissed him. "Actually I'm a night person. I'd rather stay up all night and sleep all day."

Eamon laughed softly. "Would you like to live that way?" Her confused and naïve expression made him laugh harder.

"I would if I could. You don't know how much I hate mornings. I'm not much of a sun worshiper." She motioned to her pale skin.

He hugged her, breathing in the smell of her hair. "I'm a night person, too. In fact, you might say that I hardly function during the day sometimes."

"I guess we'd make good vampires."

The irony of her statement amused him. "Yes, we would." He brushed her hair from her neck and touched his tongue lightly to the skin, savoring its delicious, salty taste. "Would you let me take your blood?" She rolled on to her back and closed her eyes. "Would you?" he asked again as his hand travelled from her neck to her breasts. He opened his mouth and his fangs dropped down, ready to take her blood.

"I'd let you do anything you wanted," she whispered.

He stared at her neck for a few seconds before he brushed his lips lightly over the skin and kissed her. "As tempting as that is, I need to get going. We can play vampire another night." His fangs retracted and he glanced at a large stuffed alligator with a toothy grin sitting on a pile of history books on her dresser.

"I'd like that," Amelie said.

"So would I." *More than you know,* he thought. Eamon got out of bed and got dressed, carefully avoiding the mirror. He reached into his wallet and pulled out one of his business cards. "Now," he said as he wrote a number down on the back. "The number on the front is the New York number. My assistant's name is Rebecca and she's very helpful. The number on the back is my cell phone number. We don't live very far from one another so I'll pick you up." Eamon leaned over and kissed her forehead. "Tonight? Around eight?"

Amelie nodded and took the card from him. "Thanks."

He kissed her again. "No, thank you."

CHAPTER TWENTY-TWO

He Was the Oldest Living Vampire and He Seemed Lovesick

E AMON PULLED UP to the house of Marta Jimenez-de Castillo, the vampire who contacted Grant a week ago, and surveyed the surroundings. The white, Spanish Colonial-style home blended well with the other large houses in the neighborhood. This was his first visit to the old money area of Tampa called Culbreath Isles. He appreciated the security and beauty of the area but the close proximity of the homes would have been the deal breaker for him.

As he walked to the door, he felt the presence of this vampire. It floated in the air and caressed him like a warm, summer breeze. The source of the marker, Marta, stood at the door. She smiled graciously at him before lowering her head in a gesture of submission.

"Mr. Rutherford, it's a great privilege to have you in my home. Please come in." Marta extended her hand to Eamon.

Eamon looked into Marta's face as he let go of her hand. A sense of familiarity poured over him and he studied her with increased scrutiny. The kinship was unusual. It was strong enough for him to notice but not strong enough for him to identify with precision. He suspected that she was part of him but he didn't know how. Perhaps she was an offspring from one of Irina's companions. His line was small so the family tree didn't have many branches.

"I'm happy to meet you, Marta. Please call me Eamon."

They walked down the hall to a large living room. Eamon sat down as she continued over to a console with liquor decanters. "Would you care for something to drink? I have a cognac you might enjoy. I also have your drink of choice, Glenlivet. Or if you prefer, I have a girl that lives with me that would be happy to satisfy any craving you might have."

In a word, Marta was beautiful. She was tall and fair with blue-gray eyes that sparkled with charm. A black rhinestone-studded clip held her blond hair up in a loose knot and a few tendrils framed her face. Although she relaxed in her seat, her demeanor was elegant. When she was human, she without a doubt had been part of a noble family. She carried herself with the grace of a queen and her regal presence came from breeding not practice.

"The scotch will be fine." He took the drink from her and swirled the amber liquid around. "Why don't you tell me why you contacted my attorney?" he asked.

"I felt your presence in the city and I felt I should pay my respects. I know that sounds a bit archaic," she said.

"I'm sure you understand that I keep to myself and avoid the company of our kind." He inhaled the aroma of the liquor. "When you're as old as I am, you aren't as easily entertained as younger vampires are." Eamon's gaze narrowed on her. He guessed her to be no more than twenty-five or twenty-six in chronological years, but he was unsure of her age as a vampire.

"I'm not that young myself. I've been a vampire for many years. Not as many as you, of course, but quite a few."

"I can tell you're from an older time," he said.

Marta laughed. Her laughter was light, almost musical. Charming and cultivated. "A time about four hundred and ten years ago. I'll answer the question you are too kind to ask."

He raised his glass to her and his attitude toward her softened. Marta was what he thought a vampire should be: beautiful, powerful, and purposeful.

"Have I pleased you in some way?" She sat down on the sofa across from him and tucked her long legs under her. One of her Chanel shoes dropped to the floor and she looked at it and then at him.

"Yes, you have by simply being yourself. It's rare that I'm around older vampires."

She played with one of the diamond hoop earrings she wore. "There aren't that many of us left. I was the oldest vampire in Hillsborough County, in Florida, for that matter, prior to you coming here so I'm the Elder. It's mainly newborn vampires here. Poor creatures that have no idea about long-term survival. They only know what they read or see on the internet. Then there's the group of humans who color the perception of what a vampire looks like and how they behave. They seem to be a mixed blessing. They're crazy enough to think they're vampires and try to live how they think a vampire should. These humans are the ones who, I think, keep the world from believing in vampires." She smiled. "I do tend to talk a lot. I beg your indulgence."

"I'm enjoying the conversation."

"I try and maintain some sort of order in the area, but vampires are hard to govern with no true law. I can only claim age as my authority and to date I've had no problem. The population remains stable and there's no problem that would make anyone question our existence."

"You've done well, my dear. Things appear to be in order." He drained the glass and stretched his legs out in front of him. He still couldn't determine how she was part of his line. Irina had never mentioned her. "Tell me about yourself."

"Me?" She shifted in her seat and kicked off her other shoe. "I was born connected to the royal house of Spain. My father was Philip the Second. My mother wasn't his wife so my father could never recognize me in an official capacity but he took care of my mother and me. I was a Habsburg in every way but name. More important, I'm part of your vampire line. You killed a French cousin of mine and took his estate and holdings. I went to visit, unaware your lovely little Russian countess and her lover lived there. She was kind enough to give me your gift."

"Irina." Sadness at the mention of Irina struck him momentarily, but finding a new member of his line brought a queer sense of relief and happiness to him.

"I felt my maker's passing and mourned her. I can only imagine your grief as her maker."

"I wish she had told me about you," he said quietly.

Marta waved off the omission. "I've done well over the years, but I've always wanted to meet you, my Primigenio. I owe my life as a vampire to you. A life I've enjoyed." She glanced down at her well-manicured fingernails. "Tell me, who is the charming young girl you've been seen with?"

"Amelie de la Puente, my new—"

"Forgive me," she said, interrupting him. "I thought that you had a companion."

"You mean Lauryl. She's the reason I'm in Tampa. I'm looking for her."

"I'd like to volunteer my services in any way that may be useful to you. I know many people in this city; humans and vampires."

"That's very kind of you."

Marta twirled one of her blond tendrils around her finger. "I know you prefer isolation, but if you ever get lonely for the company of our kind, I hope you will come and see me. My home is always open to you."

Eamon set his glass down on the table. "Marta, you're part of me and my line. I can't imagine staying in Tampa and not seeing you frequently." In finding her he recovered some of Irina. A small piece of him became whole again.

"You honor me."

"I've enjoyed our visit." He rose and she did the same.

"It's been my pleasure," she replied.

He turned to walk out but stopped. The reason he was in Tampa swept over him, causing his sense of contentment to fracture. "In all probability, Lauryl is traveling with a man by the name of Anthony Wilson. I don't know if she's turned him yet, but I wouldn't doubt it." He turned back to her. "Let me know if you hear anything."

*   *   *

MARTA STUDIED THE mild distress on his face. "I will." A gentle sadness for him tugged at her as he walked out. Even though he was with another woman, he remained obsessed with this Lauryl. Perhaps it was their blood bond but it seemed to be more. For someone who that had been a vampire so long he still fell in to the trap of human emotions. He was the oldest living vampire and he seemed lovesick.

*   *   *

DRIVING BACK TO the house, Eamon called Amelie. She wasn't at home. He left a brief message for her to call him. The sound of her voice on the voice mail would have to satisfy him. He debated calling her cell phone, but decided against it. It was Friday night and she was out with her friends. It sometimes slipped his mind that she was only twenty-two and had friends. That didn't help his loneliness. He needed companionship tonight. A psychiatrist would tell him that his loneliness caused him to be depressed. A psychiatrist. He tightened his grip on the steering wheel until his knuckles turned white. His time wasn't going to be wasted thinking about Wilson.

I should have killed him a long time ago, he thought.

Eamon pulled in to his drive and marched to the front door. The faint sensation of a vampire nearby pricked his interest. He slowed his steps and concentrated on the feeling. It was impossible to tell the exact distance, but this vampire was close. Eamon reached out to the anonymous vampire and hoped it was Lauryl. He turned to the street. A human woman walking her dogs passed on the sidewalk and the vampire's presence dissipated. He or she had gone. Eamon walked to the door. It was probably a vampire out looking to feed. Tampa had too many vampires.

He poured himself a drink and stood in front of the floor length living room windows. The lights from the city sparkled on the dark water of Tampa Bay. His life was now more chaotic than it had been in centuries. Here he was in another city that he would never have chosen all because of Lauryl. Again, he pondered the same questions that he'd thought about for months. Why had she been so miserable? How could someone be so inconsolable? He still didn't understand what specifically about being a vampire was so terrible. Her life had not changed that much. She kept saying that it was him, that he made it miserable. He doubted that. He finished his drink and was about to pour himself another when his phone vibrated. Eamon set the glass down and went into his study.

"Yes?"

"Eamon? I received a copy of the bill of sale for the Degas painting today," Grant said.

"Really?" *What next?* he thought.

"The dealer told me that a man came in two weeks ago. It was Wilson. He was stupid enough to sign his own name."

"Get the painting back and send it here!"

Eamon ended the call and stormed back down the hall to the living room. He picked up his glass and, instead of refilling it, he threw it against the wall, sending shards of crystal across the marble floor. How could she sell the painting like it was some sort of garage sale cast off? Why did she need the money? She still had all of her accounts open. Initially, he considered closing them but decided against it. If he did that, she would probably take her wedding ring to a pawnshop.

CHAPTER TWENTY-THREE

It's Not Funny to Me. It's Ironic.

THE PHONE VIBRATING across Eamon's desk broke the monotony of reading. He had been trying to catch up on his business correspondence since he awakened this afternoon but it was becoming harder and harder to concentrate. So he welcomed this interruption, even if it was from his attorney Grant in New York.

"Yes, Grant," Eamon said flatly.

"You aren't going to believe this, Eamon," Grant said.

Eamon frowned. "Try me."

"Lauryl and Wilson are opening a club in Tampa. Some sort of Goth, role-playing, trendy nightclub thing down on Seventh Avenue. I only found out about it today. It's set to open in a couple of weeks."

Eamon held the phone down at his side. Rage boiled in him but he managed to stifle it. He looked over at the Degas painting leaning against the wall and then lifted the phone back up. "I'm guessing that I'm paying for it with the money that they got when that fool sold the Degas."

"I'd say so. Five million is enough to start up a club." He hesitated for a second. "I guess that would explain what she's been doing all this time."

"Or who she has been doing." Eamon's mind raced. Whose idea was this? That stupid doctor's? He probably crossed professional and ethical lines in his head every time he saw Lauryl while she was his patient.

"What?"

"Nothing. What's the name of this club?"

"Bathory or something like that. They got a great piece of

real estate."

"Bathory?" Eamon asked and then snickered. A club named for the sadistic, Hungarian countess, Elizabeth Bathory, who history branded a vampire. Actually, she had only been a sociopathic noble with a taste for killing young girls. If the authorities hadn't stopped her, a real vampire would have. Her escapades made being a real vampire difficult during those times.

"Why is that funny?"

"Read a book once in a while, Grant," Eamon snapped and ended the call. "Damn," he mumbled as he stared at the Degas painting. So they were opening a nightclub where all the pretenders in Tampa could gather and live out their fantasies? Lauryl must be in her glory. This could either bring the world of vampires to its end or an even bigger pop phenomenon. Somehow she'd found the largest niche of vampires in the United States and nestled herself among them and their wannabe minions. To her credit, she found a way to make money at the same time. He dialed Grant's number and walked into the living room.

"I know who Elizabeth Bathory is, Eamon. I Googled her. But I don't know why that's funny," Grant said as soon as he answered.

"It's not funny, Grant. It's ironic that someone who supposedly hates being a vampire is opening a business which apparently is going to celebrate it."

"Oh."

"Yes, oh. You said this place was opening in a few weeks. Find out specifically when. Is she publicly opening this club or is the idiot Wilson doing it?"

"Both of their names are on the applications. His name first and then hers as a backer and underwriter. They pushed this through quickly, miraculously, almost."

"Grant, when was the last time anything with my name even remotely attached to it didn't happen?"

"I see your point."

"You didn't answer my question. Is she going public?" Eamon asked.

"That I don't know. I'll find out. I can't imagine Wilson being the public persona but, at the same time, I don't think she would either. She's still avoiding you."

"Obviously since she isn't here with me. All I want to know is if she plans to be there for the opening. I can't imagine her missing it. She'd go to the opening of a door if she thought it was in her honor."

"Like I said I'll find out. I'll find out everything I can and then I'll touch base with you."

"Do that."

He tossed the phone on the sofa and sank down into the cushions next to it. It was clear that she wasn't afraid of angering him or bringing a lot of attention to herself. He leaned his head back of the sofa and closed his eyes.

As the phantom scent of Amelie's perfume drifted by, he relaxed. His Amelie. She was what he needed to lift his mood. He needed to feel her warm skin next to his and, most of all, he wanted to taste her blood. That was on hold, though. He felt a lingering uneasiness about telling her the truth about him. He didn't even want to feed from her because of it. The risk of rejection wasn't worth being honest. A frown darkened his face. Being a vampire had become complicated since he decided to take a companion.

It wasn't like in the past when women were just glamorous meals. Well, some part of that remained. Marta arranged for a steady flow of beautiful and tasty young women for him to feed on in place of hunting. However, he had to do that with even greater discretion because he didn't want Amelie to think he was cheating on her. These were the perils of human dating. His down phone vibrated across the cushion. Marta.

"Yes, my dear?"

"I hate to disturb you, but I have some news."

"Would it be that Lauryl and the idiot Wilson are opening a vampire themed night club in Ybor?"

"So you know?"

"News travels fast," Eamon said.

"Yes, since it became public knowledge, our community has

been buzzing. Mostly positive from what I gather."

"Has anyone in your circle had any contact with her?"

"No, she remains invisible. This Dr. Wilson does most everything. They seem to pop into view and then disappear as quickly as they came. I can't get anyone close to him."

"I appreciate all you've done, Marta."

"*Mi amor*, the pleasure is mine. Are you staying in tonight or do you have plans?"

"I think I'm staying home with Amelie." Staying in together was becoming one of their favorite activities. He enjoyed sitting with her and talking or reading. Lauryl would have thought of that as torture. With her short attention span, she would have been bored in a matter of hours. Not Amelie, though. She would sit and watch him work, asking him questions, or telling him stories about her college years. Or she would sometimes fall asleep in his arms on the sofa. The feeling of her warm body curled against him stirred his hunger. It wasn't only his hunger for blood that increased as she slept. It was his hunger to feel the love of a companion. The love he didn't feel with Lauryl and did feel with Amelie.

"Ah, new love. I've forgotten what that's like. Well, if you change your mind, come and see us."

"Thank you, but I think I'll be content with my plans."

CHAPTER TWENTY-FOUR

Sometimes I Wonder What You Think of Me

"WHAT SHALL WE do tonight?" Eamon asked Amelie as he buttoned his shirt. "Aside from what we just did."

Amelie stretched under the sheets and propped up on her elbows. "I like doing that."

The site of Amelie lounging naked under the sheet brought a hungry smile to his face. He dialed his desire down and leaned down to kiss her. "I do, too, but you're young and I know that you like to do things in the world beyond our bed."

"Seriously, I'm happy just being with you. When I'm with you, I feel..." Her cheeks blushed.

"What?"

"I feel safe. It's weird." She looked down.

He sat down on the bed next to her. "Why is that weird?"

Amelie shrugged. "It sounds strange. I feel protected with you. Like I need to be with you. I know that sounds high school, but it's true."

"High school?"

"Yeah, you know, like I can't live without you, life-or-death kind of thing. I swore that I wouldn't be that way, but I feel that with you." She looked back up at him. "Despite me trying not to be clingy and needy."

"I don't think you're clingy or needy. In fact, I think the opposite. I'm being needy with you. That's not something I'm used to. I sometimes feel that I selfishly control your time and keep you from your friends. But I want to spend time with you." Eamon touched her cheek. Again, long forgotten human emotions controlled him. With Amelie it was easy. He didn't have to worry about appearing weak as a vampire in front of her.

Amelie sat up. "It seems that we need each other. I don't see anything wrong with that if it's mutual, right?"

He rubbed her hand on his cheek and placed a soft kiss on it. "Tell me what you want to do tonight."

"We can catch a movie, if you want."

He had never been to a movie theater on a date. He had never been to a movie theater, period. The opportunity never presented itself. He had never dated before. Amelie was the first serious dating relationship he'd been in.

"That's fine," he said.

"Really? You sound kind of unsure."

"No, a movie will be a treat."

"You sound like it's going to be your first."

"Maybe. Darling, next week there's a benefit at the Florida Aquarium. I'd like you to come with me."

"I'd love to. You don't seem like an aquarium supporter, though."

"What are they like?"

"I mean, I wouldn't think that you'd be into a cause like that."

Eamon finished his tie. "Sometimes I wonder what you think of me."

Amelie got out of bed and pulled her robe from the cheval mirror in the corner. Eamon realized he had walked into the field of the mirror's reflection and took a few steps away. He hated that mirror.

"I think the world of you," she said.

"I like the sound of that."

"I'm going to shower and then we'll go. Pick something for us to see while I'm getting ready." She kissed him and headed for the bathroom.

Eamon walked out to the living room and looked through his phone for movie times. He scrolled through, but stopped when he felt the marker of a vampire close to the house. He lowered the phone and walked to the large front window. The street was empty but the presence felt as strong as a vampire standing in front of him. Amelie's singing in the shower distracted him for a moment but his focus resumed and increased. For a second, he thought it was Lauryl. He closed his eyes and silently called out to her. The marker vanished. His concentration dissolved like the marker when he noticed that the shower was off and Amelie was no longer singing.

Vampires were everywhere in Tampa, but this was the first time he'd sensed one so close to Amelie's house. He doubted it was random. Any vampire, even a stupid one, would feel his presence and keep their distance. That convinced him his ambiguous sense of Lauryl was correct. He stared at the vacant street as he tried to reach out to her again. A car passed the house, but he felt nothing.

"Did you find a movie?" Amelie asked as she came out of the bathroom. She stopped towel-drying her hair when she saw him staring out the window. "What are you looking at?"

He turned to her and took her hand. "Nothing."

"Are you sure? You were kind of engrossed."

Yes, the idea of Lauryl close by did occupy his focus. Why didn't she answer his silent calls? What was she doing so close to Amelie's house? That troubled him. He looked around the street one last time and turned to Amelie.

"Just surveying the neighborhood and wondering about the value of the real estate."

She stood next to him at the window and nodded at the neighboring arts-and-crafts style houses. "Market's strong in this neighborhood. Houses sell for a lot. This house has been in my family for sixty-seven years. My dad grew up in it."

Eamon put his arm around her shoulder. Her breathing increased and she sniffled a few times. He squeezed her in a side hug, unsure of what to say. She reached up and put her hand on his.

"Sorry," she said.

"What for?"

"I'm bumming out our evening over a stupid question." She half-laughed and cried. "I still cry when I talk about him."

"Still? Darling, it's only been a short time since you lost your father. I don't think anyone expects you not to be grieving."

"I know, but I feel so weak and I don't want you to see me like that."

"I don't see you as weak." Eamon looked down at her. "I see you as a person who lost someone very important in her life. You loved him. He was your family." Eamon understood Amelie's grief. He still felt empty and dejected over the loss of Irina. Meeting Marta and Amelie had helped to ease the feelings, but those emotions still stung him. The more he tried to bury them, the more they resurfaced.

She nodded and wiped her eyes. After taking a few deep breaths, she managed a smile for him. "I'm going to get dressed and we can go."

He put her hand in his and wrapped his fingers around it. "As long as we're together, I'll always do my best to keep you happy."

"If anyone can, I think it's you." She kissed his hand and went to dress.

*   *   *

EAMON WALKED TO the courtyard of the movie theater and observed the crowd milling around outside. His shoulders tensed a bit. Well blended among the humans were several vampires. Their markers brushed over him lightly. He had neglected to adjust his own and it probably resembled a beacon to the young vampires. No point in adjusting now. He would simply deal with whatever reaction he generated. Eamon's gaze wandered around and one by one, he picked out the vampires. There were three Goth fledglings. No doubt they frequented Lauryl's club. For the most part, the remaining six or seven vampires were mainstream looking. A young vampire couple waiting in the ticket line stiffened when they felt Eamon approach. The male vampire turned and looked at Eamon, but when he made eye contact with him, he immediately turned back to female vampire at his side and whispered something to her. When she tried to turn to Eamon, the male stopped her.

Have no fear. I'm only here to enjoy a film, just like you, he whispered to the mind of the male vampire.

Eamon settled the addled minds of the vampires around him

and then looked at Amelie. She remained unaware, like any human would be, of the stir his presence caused. Tampa's large vampire population continued to surprise him. For the most part they did an above average job of assimilating with humans. Their makers had taught them well and they had the potential to survive for a long time.

"It's kind of crowded. We don't have to stay if you don't want to," Amelie said. She took Eamon's hand and shook it playfully.

"Why would you think that I didn't want to stay?"

"I don't know. You're watching the crowd like you're picking out potential muggers or something." She gathered her long dark hair in to a ponytail and fanned herself.

Eamon laughed. "I'm just people watching. I enjoy it." Two of the Goth fledglings circled close to him in an effort to gain his attention. He looked over at them and they bowed to him. Eamon shot them a terse glance, which discouraged their show of respect. They backed away but not before Amelie noticed them skulking away.

"Do you know them?" she asked. The two linked back with the vampire who didn't approach Eamon and she frowned.

"No. Do you?"

"No, but they kind of looked like they bowed to you."

He wrapped his arm around her. "I'm sure it was sarcastic. Perhaps they know me from my business or maybe I remind them of their parents. I don't know."

Amelie wrinkled her nose. "That's weird."

"I can't say, darling." He shrugged his shoulders, stepped up to the ticket booth and bought their tickets. He handed one to Amelie. "There are things in the world that are weird or hard to understand." Eamon kissed her. "That's what makes life interesting."

CHAPTER TWENTY-FIVE

We're Just Human

AMELIE STROKED THE black, plush "feathers" of the stuffed Emperor penguin she got at the aquarium earlier in the evening. Eamon adopted six penguins in her name after their VIP tour of the penguin habitat. She hugged the fuzzy bird and smiled at Eamon.

"Thank you for tonight. I don't know how you did it, but I loved it. I mean, going to the benefit was phenomenal, but then seeing the penguins up close like that was just beyond amazing."

"I'm glad you enjoyed it. I saw how much you liked those silly birds last week at the benefit and thought you should see them up close."

"And now I'm the mom of six of them!" She danced the stuffed toy in her lap and laughed.

"Congratulations."

"You shouldn't have done that. I know it was super expensive."

He shrugged his shoulders. "Darling, it was nothing." The total he'd spent tonight, thirty thousand dollars, was marginal. The expression on her face as the birds waddled up to her was priceless. The delight he saw in her eyes filled him with a feeling he hadn't experienced in years.

She placed the penguin on her coffee table and leaned against him. "Can I get you something to drink or eat?"

"No, thank you." He was hungry but he'd have to wait.

"How come you don't ever talk about Lauryl?"

Eamon's jaw clenched momentarily at the unexpected question. Why on earth would she ask something like that? "Why would I?"

"Did I say something wrong?"

He put his arm around her shoulder. "No. The timing is odd, that's all."

"I'm sorry. I was only curious. Most guys talk about their exes." Amelie sank in deep against him. "You never do and I wondered if you might want to."

"I never thought about discussing her with you." He sighed and she stiffened some "I don't want to bore you with her."

"I just wondered what happened between you two. Were you together long?"

Eamon hesitated a moment, pondering how to approach this and decided that it was best to tell the truth up to a certain point. "We were together about a year."

"Boy, you guys got married in a hurry."

"It seemed the thing to do at the time," Eamon replied diplomatically.

"What happened?" She stretched across his lap and looked up at him.

He glanced around her living room for a moment. "We just were two different personality types," he said after a minute. "She couldn't adjust to life with me."

"Why?"

"I suppose my lifestyle was too constricting. Certain aspects of our life together were offensive to her. And she said she couldn't stand me."

"Wow."

"I haven't heard from her in months. She disappeared one night while she and I were in London," Eamon said. It still sounded unbelievable to him.

"Disappeared? Really? How'd she do that?"

He chuckled. "Honestly, I don't know. That's too dramatic of a word. She's here in Tampa, but I don't know where. I believe she's living with her former psychiatrist."

Amelie's brown eyes widened. "Eww. That's like a major ethical breech."

"Yes, I know. I don't like the man. I never have. Even before I found out about this." Despised would have been a more appropriate description.

"What are you going to do?"

What could he do? She had already turned the idiot doctor, and he was a vampire of his line. Killing him would be out of the question. Even if he wanted to, he couldn't because he still had no idea where he or Lauryl were.

"I suppose I'll just have to let it go," he said, resigned to the inevitable.

"What's she like?"

"Beautiful and exasperating. She lives to annoy and defy me."

"Why did she stop dancing?"

"That I don't know," he lied. "Maybe she wanted to concentrate on being a wife." He started to laugh. The lie was ridiculous. The more he thought about it, the harder he laughed.

"I guess she gave up," Amelie said.

"I guess. She has a very short attention span. It's amazing that she was the caliber of dancer that she was. Her focus is quite limited."

"It sounds like she has selective attention."

"Perhaps. She's not like you at all."

"What do you mean?" She raised her head up to him.

"You two have completely different personalities. You're calm and composed. You tend to reflect on things, more like me. Lauryl is restless and impulsive. She has a temper and she loses it often."

"You two don't seem very compatible."

"If only I'd seen that back then. I thought she'd become what I wanted."

"Maybe you were over optimistic. You should have known you can't change someone."

"Over optimistic? You're being kind. I was egotistical and unwilling to see anything beyond what I wanted." Eamon hated saying those things about himself, even if they were true.

"Being kind of hard on yourself, aren't you?" She watched at his foot tapping an irritable beat on her floor.

"No," he said with a sigh. "Just honest." He took her hand in his and squeezed it. "Thank you."

"What for?"

"For letting me be honest. It's rare to be able to share my weaknesses."

Amelie kissed his hand. "You're welcome. I still think you're being too hard on yourself, though."

"I think your affection for me lets you be more forgiving of my faults." Her soft lips on his skin eased his mind and his shoulders relaxed.

"Eamon, we all have faults. What you think is a fault is also a strength. You're self-confident and determined. I'm sure that's how you've been so successful."

"My methods haven't been all together honorable."

She sighed and traced her finger over his palm a few times. "I'd be naïve if I thought they had been. You're not a saint. Neither am I. We're just human."

"Perhaps."

"You don't sound too sure about it. What else could you be?"

Eamon closed his eyes for a moment and waited for the urge to tell her the truth to pass. Before it slipped away completely, he opened his eyes and smiled. "I'm a vampire." He studied her face with interest. At first she appeared confused but then she poked him in the ribs.

"Well, you yourself said we'd make excellent vampires," Eamon said.

She returned his smile. "I did say that, didn't I?"

"You did." With a heavy sigh, he shrugged. "Well, so much for being vampires."

"We can always play vampire."

"But wouldn't it be wonderful if it wasn't just play?" Eamon brushed his fingertips over her neck, eliciting a subtle shiver from her. His hunger nudged him and obliged him to be aware of every part of her body in contact with his. He took a quiet breath in, concentrating on her scent. Her floral perfume stoked his hunger. As he concentrated, not only could he feel her heart beating, he could hear it as well. Her blood pulsed through her body and he wanted it.

"Yes, it would," she said, ruffling his hair between her fingers.

"We'll just have to be satisfied with playing."

Eamon turned his face to her inner forearm as she touched his hair and listened to her pulse throb. As he kissed the soft skin over the veins he imagined the complex flavor of her blood. His tongue skimmed over her wrist and he reined in his growing desire to take her blood. He needed someone's blood soon, but not hers.

"How do you do that?"

"What?" she asked.

"How do you manage to captivate me by doing absolutely nothing?"

Her cheeks pinked up and she gave him a shy smile. "It's you. There's something about you that must bring it out of me."

"I doubt that I have anything to do with it. You're divine. It's as simple as that."

"You say things to me that no one else has ever said. Sometimes I feel like we're the only ones in the world."

His phone vibrated in his pocket, but he ignored it. "I wish we were."

She giggled and fished out the phone. She looked at the screen and saw that it was Marta. "Marta."

"Hmm. She can wait." He clicked the ignore button and slid the phone back in his pocket.

"You could have taken that. I don't care."

He shook his head. "Like I said, she can wait. I don't want anyone interrupting our evening, especially since you're going out of town tomorrow."

"I'm not sure I want to go now." Amelie straddled his legs and put her arms around his neck. "I'll miss you too much."

"Oh no. You're going. You need to get out and see your friends and I know you're looking forward to this. I don't understand what it is you're doing, but I know you want to go."

Amelie laughed. "I'm going to Gainesville for Growl tomorrow night and then to the football game on Saturday. It's homecoming."

"What is Growl?" His eyebrows drew together and he frowned in confusion.

"Gator Growl. It's like a big, outdoor skit show concert performance thing for homecoming. It's fun." She bounced on his lap a couple of times.

Eamon remained unclear of what she was trying to describe, but suspected that it was some sort of tradition her university had. "It sounds like a college party."

"A big one. Go Gators."

"See? You need to go."

She rested her head on his shoulder. "I'm still going to miss you."

"I'll miss you as well, but think of how wonderful it will be when we see each other Sunday evening." The phone vibrated in his pocket again.

"Answer it."

With a scowl, he pulled the phone out. "Yes?"

"Did I interrupt something?" Marta asked.

"Yes," Eamon replied with an edge in his voice.

"By your short tone, I'm guessing that you're with Amelie. I apologize. Call me when you are free."

The line went dead and he stuck the phone back in his pocket. He kissed Amelie and touched his forehead to hers. "I'm sorry."

"That was the shortest conversation ever."

"Marta realized I was with you."

She nodded her head. "Gotcha."

Eamon detected the slightest trace of suspicion in her voice. At last, he thought, a bit of female curiosity. In her deep brown eyes, he noticed tiny flecks of gold mixed in with the brown. They sparkled with a new fire, the fire of budding jealousy. "Nice that even a distant relation can read between the lines."

"Distant relation?" she asked, trying to sound casual.

"Yes, Marta is a cousin several times removed. I didn't realize it until she pointed it out."

"Ah."

"I think you'd like her girlfriend. She's about your age."

"We should all get together."

"We will." He hugged her and stroked her back. "Soon."

CHAPTER TWENTY-SIX

Get the Highest Ranking Vampire Up Here

M ARTA PLACED EAMON'S scotch next to him and then sat down in the chair across from him. "I'm sorry your girlfriend is ill this evening, Eamon. However, I'm thrilled that you've come to see us." Her grey eyes turned to the doorway where a young blonde woman stood like a well-dressed statue. Marta smiled, nodded toward Eamon, and the woman padded over to him.

"Eamon, this is my human companion Isabelle," Marta said.

He started to rise out of courtesy. Before he could, the girl dropped down to her knees.

"Oh no, please don't get up." Isabelle placed her hand on his knee.

Eamon looked over at Marta, who nodded her approval. Isabelle was a beautiful offering. She had the same noble features as Marta, but not the same bearing. He took Isabelle's hand in his.

"You can get up. While you are beautiful, I'll have to pass."

Isabelle turned back to Marta, whose expression had turned to confusion. "Don't you want—"

"I'm sorry, Eamon. Have I offended you?" Marta was on her feet.

Eamon pulled Isabelle onto the sofa next to him. "Marta, I appreciate your efforts, but they aren't necessary." He caressed Isabelle's hand a moment and lowered his head close to her ear. "Why don't you go sit with Marta?" He gave her a gentle nudge and sent her back to Marta.

"You'll have to forgive me, Eamon."

"There isn't anything to forgive." He looked at Isabelle, resting at Marta's feet.

"You're very kind."

"You wanted to discuss the possibility of forming some sort of governing body for our kind?"

Marta's hand glided through Isabelle's hair. Isabelle melted into Marta's touch, stretching like a cat to meet it. "Yes, I had been giving it some thought. Even before you came to Tampa."

"You yourself said that things seemed to run smoothly without any sort of governance."

"True, I did. That's always surprised me. I'm the Elder of the Tampa Bay area and have never had any problems. The young vampires respect me."

"Most vampires are solitary and spread out geographically. Tampa is an anomaly."

"I've been here for about one hundred years now. I've seen the population of our kind grow. I'm not sure why there are so many here."

"I would have thought that you would prefer a more cosmopolitan area," Eamon said.

Marta laughed. "It's not as bad as you think. You just need to discover more of our lovely city. The large Hispanic population reminds me of home. It gives me a sense of peace."

Eamon took a long swallow of his drink and returned to Marta's idea. He wasn't sure how to approach this. The idea did have merit. As the vampire population increased everywhere, there would have to be a system of control and government. The young ones would adapt easily, but he wondered about the older ones. "How many older vampires do you know well enough to discuss this with?"

"Oh." She dropped her head back in thought. "Three. One is one hundred years older, one is about my age, and the other is a bit over two hundred."

"Where are they?"

"One is in Austin. The older one is in Chicago and the other, the one close to my age, is in Los Angeles. They're the Elders of their cities." Marta laced her hand into Isabelle's.

"Have you ever discussed this idea with any of them?" He

drained his glass and walked over to the console to refill it.

"Once or twice. Nothing in depth or serious."

"How did they feel about the idea?"

"The same as you do. I think it's just in my nature to want to make sure things are controlled and monitored." Isabelle leaned against Marta. Marta kissed her shoulder.

Eamon resumed his position across from the women. "It certainly is in your genetics. I, too, prefer to keep things controlled and monitored. However, I'm not sure how our kind will react to being subject to control and monitoring. The younger vampires should come to it quite easily. They have different ideas of what it is like to be a vampire."

"Agreed. But we won't know until we try," she said with a smile.

"Have you considered the idea of being governed won't be well received?"

"That's why I think you should be involved in this. I would think that your word would be law."

Eamon laughed. "Marta, lately that's not the case."

"I meant that by your age and status—"

He stopped laughing and shook his head. "I know what you meant. This is a very large undertaking, Marta. It's going to take planning and diplomacy. I have no doubt that you're sincere in you desires, but I need to think about this."

Wonderful, he thought. *Another complicated situation for him to deal with.* It struck him as odd that all of his problems involved or stemmed from women, his women.

"Not to change the subject, but by all accounts, Lauryl's club seems to be quite a success."

"Is that a fact?"

"Yes, from what I've been told, it's been filled to capacity every night. No sign of her or Dr. Wilson, though."

"Have you been?"

"Oh no. That sort of place isn't my style at all. Now, my lovely Isabelle would fit in much better there." She petted Isabelle again.

Eamon agreed. The girl was beautiful and would fit in at

whatever trendy club she set foot in. He smiled at her and she lowered her head. "I don't think it would be the type of place I would frequent either, but I plan to visit." Eamon had planned to go to the opening of the club to look for Lauryl but instead he opted out to take Amelie to the Florida Aquarium benefit.

Marta leaned forward some, bumping Isabelle forward with her. Marta put her arm around Isabelle's waist. "I have an idea. Let's go! All three of us. I think it would be great fun."

"I don't."

"Oh, come now," Marta encouraged. "See what your money has done. At the same time, let any real vampires hanging around there see you."

"That's not something I have any interest in right now."

Marta whispered something in Isabelle's ear, sending her out of the room. She then crossed over to Eamon. "It's already settled," she said, extending her delicate hand to him.

"Marta, really, I'd prefer to go home and check on Amelie. Since she returned from Gainesville, she's been ill," he said as he looked at her over the top of his glasses. He pulled out his phone to see if Amelie had texted him. Nothing. She was probably sleeping. He'd forgotten about how a human dealt with illness since it had been so long since he'd been ill. Poor thing. He'd send her some flowers when he got home.

She dropped her hand down and sighed. "Yes, Eamon I hear the words you say, but I think you've played the part of the lovesick vampire too long now. You've moped around Tampa waiting for one companion who obviously doesn't want to be with you. Now you're beginning to torture yourself over this current girl. What are you afraid of? That she'll reject you like Lauryl did? And what if she does? For you, is that such a loss?"

"I'll allow you some leniency in what you say to me, Marta, but don't test my limits." He stood up and looked into her eyes. Her blue gray gaze met and locked into his. After a second, though, she lowered her eyes and took a step back. "Thank you."

"I ask your forgiveness for the method I chose but not the message. In order to find a human, don't ever think you can become one again. You should know that."

"You're forgiven." The clarity of Marta's statement caused him to reflect for a moment. Out of line or not, she had a point. He was trying to relate to a human as a human and that didn't work for a vampire.

Marta walked past him and stood at the front door. "Isabelle has brought the car around I'd be honored if you join us."

Without a word, he walked out of the front door and got in the back of the black S-class Mercedes. Marta got in the front and looked at Isabelle.

"Isa, you know where this place is, don't you?" she asked her lover.

"Yes, I've already called to get us in the VIP entrance," Isabelle replied as she pulled the car out of the drive.

"That's one of the reasons that you please me so," Marta said, skimming her nails up Isa's firm thigh.

Eamon, amused and aroused by their flirting, shifted to get a better view of the two of them. "How long before you turn her, Marta?"

Marta laughed. "As soon as she asks me," she replied as her hand disappeared under Isabelle's skirt. The sedan lurched forward and sped off as Marta's nimble fingers continued to tease Isa.

*   *   *

ISABELLE TURNED IN front of Channelside and snaked her way toward Ybor City. The sidewalks were crowded with young people filing in and out of the clubs and restaurants. The random markers of vampires, obviously taking advantage of this rich hunting ground, hit Eamon. She pulled down a derelict side street paved with old, red cobblestones and parked behind a large brick warehouse. A well-muscled man sporting a mohawk and wearing a black t-shirt came out of a metal door and knocked on the car window with a large silver ring on his index finger.

"What the fuck, girl?" he said as Isabelle rolled the window down. "No parking."

"I called ahead. Dita is VIP-ing us."

The man looked at Marta and Eamon and back at Isabelle.

"If you say so." He opened Isabelle's door and she climbed out. Eamon climbed out of the back and opened Marta's door. Marta took his hand and the two of them joined Isabelle in front of the rusty door. As the large man ducked in the car, he pulled out a walkie-talkie and hit the page button.

"Send Dita to the back door. She's got guests." Without waiting for a response, he hit the gas and disappeared with the car.

"I hope you'll see your car again," Eamon said. He stared at the back of the warehouse, shook his head with disappointment and frowned. The odor of human vomit mixed with alcohol drifted by and he closed his eyes, trying to keep his temper in check. The markers of vampires close by tapped at him. He opened his eyes. He could feel them both inside the building and around the perimeter.

Marta linked her arm in Eamon's. "You're worrying for nothing, I think." She leaned in to kiss his cheek. He turned his face and instead she kissed his lips. She smiled. "I wasn't expecting that." She kissed him again. "It's nice."

The sound of metal locks sliding and giving way echoed for a minute and then the door opened. A lanky, twenty-something girl with blood red hair peeked out. She wore a heavy coating of white makeup and the contacts in her eyes were a strange, bile color.

"Izzy?"

"Yeah, it's me." Isabelle stepped where the other girl could see her better.

"You're not alone, right? You have your Mistress with you." Dita looked at Eamon and took a step back "And someone I don't know."

"Do you need to know me?" Eamon snapped. He took a step closer to the offbeat girl.

Dita shook her head and Marta placed her hand on her cheek. "Best not to ask any questions of my guest, *querida*."

"Yeah, okay," she squeaked. "If y'all will follow me." She motioned the three of them in and locked the door.

Muffled techno music from the club echoed through the dark hallway. Marta curled her finger through a belt loop on his pants.

I don't think she's here, Eamon, she said into his mind.

He looked at her. A tense smile thinly disguised his anger.

Dita opened a door and they ascended a flight of stairs. She punched a series of numbers into a keypad and the door slid open revealing a dimly lit room. Black leather sofas and overstuffed chairs covered with burgundy velvet furnished the expansive room. Large, broken mirrors with gilded frames hung on the walls and huge candle stands blazed with black and red candles. Mountains of wax piled up at their bases. Across one wall was a huge window that overlooked the club and the dance floor. He could see masses of pale-faced, darkly-clad humans bouncing and writhing to the music that poured from the sound system.

"Can I have anything sent up to y'all?" Dita asked, avoiding Eamon's gaze.

"Tell me, *querida*, who's here tonight?" Marta asked as she sank into one of the burgundy chairs.

"A couple of football players, a judge. There was a reporter from one of the TV stations, but I think she left."

"No, no, no, silly. Who like me and my handsome friend?" Marta prompted.

Dita looked from Marta to Eamon. "There are several vampires here but none like you and him." She nodded at Eamon, who had seated himself on one of the sofas looking out of the window at the dance floor.

"No? What about the owner? Is she here? I would love to meet her," Marta continued.

Eamon turned his head to Dita, who bounced from foot to foot. "She's not here. And this one has figured out who I am." He looked back to the window. He followed a female vampire leading a young man to a hallway. "She isn't going to lie because she knows she can't, but she's too afraid to tell the truth."

"Is that true?" Marta asked Dita.

"Dita, girl, you know you can't lie or hide anything from them," Isabelle said.

"Yes," she said in a shaky voice.

Eamon rolled his eyes and grew more impatient with the odd female. "Yes to what?"

"Yes, I know who you are and yes, she isn't here," she breathed before backing into a chair and sat down.

"Does she come here often? Have you ever seen her?" Marta asked.

Dita kept her eyes on Eamon. "I don't know. I haven't ever seen her. I swear. All I know is that we were all given a description of him and told to be on the lookout for him."

"Why?" Marta asked.

"I don't know. They didn't tell us that. Oh, I swear I don't know!" Dita squirmed in the chair.

Eamon's patience vanished and he glanced over at Marta. "She doesn't know anything. Get the highest ranking vampire up here."

"You heard him, Dita."

Dita looked over at Isabelle, whose expression remained neutral. She pulled the radio out of the holster around her hip and licked her dry lips. "Lucy, can Ivory come up to VIP 3?"

"What? Why?" the voice squawked back.

"Marta Jimenez-de Castillo is here with her companion. She wants to say hello."

"I'll pass the word."

"Do you know this one called Ivory?" Eamon asked Marta.

"I don't know. I've never heard of a vampire called Ivory."

"Everyone here has like a stage name," Dita said.

Eamon rolled his eyes again. He then turned back to the capacity crowd downstairs. The club was successful. The frown remained on his face until he felt the approaching presence of a newborn vampire. As it felt the powerful markers of Eamon and Marta, the vampire slowed its approach.

Don't stop now, young one, Eamon told the vampire silently. *Keep coming. I'm not going to hurt you.*

The door slid open and Ivory sauntered into the room. She was short and curvy with black hair that was pulled back into a harsh, patent strap-wrapped ponytail. She wore a black, vinyl Asian-style dress with a calf-length hobble skirt. Black five-inch lace up platform shoes completed her outfit. As confining as the outfit was, she managed to glide across the floor. No sooner than she was five steps in the room, she stopped. Her eyes fixed on Eamon and her blasé expression changed to one of fear. She recovered her composure and turned to Dita.

"Which of our guests would like to speak to me?" Ivory asked. She looked at Marta and bowed her head slightly. "It is an honor to have you here, Señorita Jimenez-de Castillo."

"Look at me," Eamon clipped.

Ivory's head snapped toward him, the shiny ponytail trailing behind. She instinctively took a step backwards and lowered her head completely. "Sir."

"I appreciate you coming to speak with us," Eamon said.

Ivory kept her head down. The ancient energy that emanated from Eamon held her captive. "You're welcome," she mumbled.

"Would you feel better if you sat down?" Eamon offered.

She nodded, still keeping her head down.

"Then by all means. And you may look up now."

Ivory sat down close to Marta with Dita and Isabelle serving as obstacles between her and Eamon. She turned and looked in the direction of Eamon, but not at him. "Thank you."

"What's your name?" Eamon asked her.

"Here it's Ivory. My real name is Sasha, Sasha Werner."

"How long have you been a vampire?"

"Seventy-six years."

"And you're the senior vampire here tonight?"

She nodded her head. "Yes, sir."

"Do you still remember your maker?" he asked.

"Yes."

"Good. Never forget where you come from." He stood up, walked over to her, and took a seat on the arm of her chair. "You were what, barely eighteen when you were turned?"

"It was my eighteenth birthday," she said quietly.

Eamon's fingers grazed her chin. *Look at me*, he said into her mind. He felt her lingering shyness and fear, but she raised her face toward his. "Do you like being a vampire?" he asked, caressing her chin.

"Yes, I do," she whispered.

"Can you imagine anyone who wouldn't?" Eamon gazed down at her. His gaze drifted over her with the same alluring sensation of his hand. He smiled at her, intensifying the hold he had over her.

Ivory/Sasha lowered her eyes. "No."

"I can't either. Nevertheless, some don't." He looked around the room again, taking in all of Lauryl's creation. "They have a sort of love-hate relationship with it. Loving it when it's good to them or suits them and hating it when it isn't."

The room remained silent for a few moments after Eamon stopped speaking and then Marta spoke. "Is this club successful, Sasha? I'm going to call you Sasha as that is your given name."

At first, Sasha remained silent and appeared as if she did hear Marta. She stared demurely at the floor while Eamon caressed her face. After a second, Eamon stopped and put his hand down.

She's asked you a question, Eamon said in her mind.

Reluctantly, Sasha turned back to Marta. "Yes, it's filled to capacity from opening to last call every night. People come from Atlanta, Miami, and Jacksonville just to check it out."

"Lots of our kind patronize it?" Marta asked.

"It depends on the night and what is going on here. Mainly it's thrill seekers and posers. They love it. They think the actual vampires in the club are actors. There are more humans that work here than vampires."

"How many, *querida?*" Marta asked.

"I'm the manager. Then there are a couple of dancers and two on security. Everyone else is human."

"Who employed you?" Marta continued.

Sasha's eyes were wide with reluctance and fear. "Sir, I don't want you to be angry at me."

"Then tell me the truth. As long as you do that, I'll consider you an ally and not an enemy."

Sasha nodded her head, signaling that she understood the meaning implied in his words.

"Anthony hired me."

"Wilson?" Eamon snapped.

Sasha's eyes widened. "Yes."

Irritation turned to anger. His fangs dropped down and his fist clenched but after a moment, he managed to assume a more composed posture. "Is he one of our kind?"

Sasha dug her nails into the arm of the chair and nodded.

"I knew it," he mumbled. A mental image of Lauryl feeding on the idiot doctor passed through his mind. He forced the offensive image away. The fear from the newborn in front of him distracted him. Eamon turned back to Sasha. Her blue eyes begged him not to be angry with her.

It's not you I'm angry with, Sasha, Eamon whispered in her mind.

She nodded. "But he wasn't when he did all of the hiring. That only just happened I think. He came in to check on the club and he had been turned."

"Thank you, Sasha," Marta said.

"I just told you what you wanted to know." She looked from Marta to Eamon. "I don't even like him. I can't say anything because I know who turned him. And who turned her."

"We're leaving," Eamon said.

Marta and Isabelle stood. "Sasha, you've been very helpful and you've done nothing wrong. My friend is troubled by what he has learned. I think you know why. Dita, be a dear and send for my car."

Eamon was already heading out the door.

* * *

THE THREE RODE in tense silence most of the way. Finally, Eamon shook his head in disgust. "I knew she would turn Wilson. I hate that he is part of my line."

"I'm sure word will travel fast that you paid a visit to Bathory."

"At this point Marta, I really don't care."

Isa turned the car into the drive. Without a word, Eamon got out and walked over to his Porsche. Marta followed him and placed her hand on his arm.

"Best not to act right now," she said with a sympathetic pat on his shoulder.

"I have no intention of acting on anything. Right now, I just need to think." Without another word, he got in his car and drove off.

*   *   *

SO LAURYL HAD turned the doctor? It really wasn't that much of a surprise. She wanted to be with him so she did what a vampire would do, she turned him. He sat back in his desk chair and looked over at the Degas painting propped against the wall. He smiled to himself for a moment but it faded when he looked up at the painting above it. The large portrait of Irina painted by Thomas Gainsborough hung centered on the wall.

He'd always loved the portrait. Not because he was a fan of Gainsborough. He wasn't. He thought the paintings were murky and lacked in detail, but her portrait wasn't. Irina's ice-blue gaze looked out as clearly as if she were standing there. In the painting, she leaned against a pedestal with a parasol in one hand while other hand fingered a ribbon on her dress bodice. Eamon stood up and walked over to the painting. He reached up to her hand, wishing he could touch her again. All he felt was the rough, cold canvas.

Eamon regretted not being able to go back to New York to take care of her in her final death, but he knew he couldn't. He couldn't deal with the pain of it. Despite what Lauryl thought, he felt Irina's death to his core and still mourned her. Even now, as he stared at the portrait, her death felt as though it had just happened. The sadness was less intense most days with Marta and Amelie but he still felt the emptiness of her loss. With the problems of Lauryl, he had been unable to search for Irina's killer. Although he doubted that he would ever find them. He didn't know any of Irina's friends because he pompously refused to get to know any of them. One day, he would find the foolish human who destroyed his offspring. He owed her that much.

He stepped back from the portrait and glared at the Degas. As far as he was concerned, Lauryl made her choice when she left. She was a hard lesson learned. He sat back down at his desk and a picture of Lauryl drew his attention. He snatched it up and frowned. It was her headshot, the one he had seen in the program in Seattle.

"Mistake," he muttered as he put the picture back. If he found her, fine. If he didn't, that would be fine as well.

CHAPTER TWENTY-SEVEN

I Think You Are Experiencing What Humans Call a Midlife Crisis

"I HAVE TO start doing things to appear more human to Amelie," Eamon said after a few moments of silence. He had only said a few words since arriving at Marta's house.

Marta sat down on the sofa in her living room. "Why?"

He took a drink of Glenlivet from his glass and frowned. "What do you mean why?"

She smiled at him. "Doesn't it seem more sensible to tell Amelie the truth rather than keeping up this illusion?"

"No, it doesn't. I'm not ready to tell her and until I am, I'll continue on as I have."

"I still feel you would be better off being honest."

"I didn't ask for your opinion."

She flipped her blonde hair and laughed. "I'm giving you a woman's point of view."

"Save it." Eamon narrowed his eyes at Marta. "I'd like you, cousin, and Isabelle to accompany Amelie and me to lunch at the Yacht Club." It was more of a decree than an invitation. He loosened his tie and ran his hand through his hair.

"Lunch? I despise going out during the day. It gives me a headache." She frowned and dug the toe of her shoe into the thick pile of the rug. "Cousin?"

"Yes, cousin. I don't care. Wear a hat. You know what I mean and I want you to do this."

He realized how he sounded and took another drink. Eamon blew out flustered sigh. "I'm sorry. I shouldn't ask like that." An uncomfortable moment passed for him as he took on a more courteous tone. "Will you please help me?"

The smile reappeared on Marta's face. "I know that took a lot for you to ask me like that. I would do anything to help you, *querido*. Maybe though, you could tell me why you're so anxious over this girl?"

Eamon moved over next to Marta. His behavior had changed since coming to Tampa. He had drifted away from micromanaging his business affairs and instead spent the time with Amelie. Meeting Amelie was the catalyst. It wasn't his search for Lauryl. Had he not met Amelie, he might have continued as he had for the past one thousand years. She turned around his life. He took Marta's hand and patted it.

"I'm anxious because this girl is different than Lauryl. I think I love her, Marta. I'm afraid to lose her." He shifted on the cushions, unable to get comfortable.

"Love her?" Marta asked. Her blue-grey eyes widened.

"Yes." He shrugged. His jacket suddenly felt tight on his shoulders. "Well, what I think is love. I'm a bit overwhelmed by this girl."

"I think you are having what humans call a midlife crisis. Although, from what I understand, you're a bit old for one as a vampire." She tapped her finger to her chin.

"Explain." He finished off the scotch and set down the glass.

She sighed. "Well, you seem unsure of how your life is progressing, which I suspect is a new dilemma for you. You're also changing who you are. You're questioning and trying to make sense of the human emotions you've long suppressed."

He sank back into the sofa and frowned. "I don't like human emotions. They make me uncomfortable."

"Mine make me uneasy as well, but I try and embrace them when they surface. As a female, I've been allowed that privilege." She put her head on his shoulder. "I certainly don't think our entire being is changed when we're turned. Our maker's blood enhances us. It doesn't destroy us. Blood builds us."

Eamon took a minute to consider what she had said before responding. "However to survive as we do, it does help to separate ourselves from our human selves. We don't even refer to ourselves as humans."

"No, we don't. I consider myself above a human. I've had the time to evolve to that point." Marta replied.

"I feel the same way and that's why I'm so confounded by it. Don't misunderstand me, I'm happy but confused by it." Eamon's shoulders stiffened, and after a moment, relaxed. The exposure of his self-perceived weakness had not been as dreadful as he feared. Marta didn't even so much as flinch. She was an easy confidante. More and more she reminded him of Irina. He looked at her and she smiled at him.

"Have you never been in love before? Even as a human?" she asked.

"Not like this. Most of my existence—and Lauryl would agree—I've only been in love with myself." Eamon took her hand.

Marta traced his fingers with hers. "What vampire isn't in love with themselves?"

"It's necessary for survival. But this girl, Marta…I think I love as much as that." He squeezed her hand. "I'd even be human again for her."

Her eyes widened. "*Dios mio*, are you serious?"

He thought for a moment. That was a bit much and he laughed. "Well, no, but I'd consider it." Eamon kissed Marta's hand as an unspoken thank you. His phone vibrated. Eamon pulled it out and saw that Amelie had sent him a text message. A+E=. <3. A smile formed on his lips as he set the message to be the phone's wallpaper.

Marta noticed his expression. "I'm assuming the message was from your girlfriend based on the silly look on your face. Nice to have a young girlfriend, isn't it?"

"You tell me," he countered.

"Yes, it is. They remind you of what it's like to be young again."

"They do." He raised his glass. "To younger women, then,"

"*Absolutamente*," she said.

"Speaking of, where is the lovely Isabelle?"

"She's getting dressed. One of the problems of having a reflection is being too attached to it. She takes a long time to get ready."

"But worth the wait?"

"Always." Her eyes sparkled and she laughed. "Look at us sitting here discussing our girlfriends! I feel like one of the boys!"

"My dear, I hardly think you'll ever be mistaken for one of the boys." Marta's long shapely legs and full breasts in no way could be considered boyish. Neither could the flirtatious charm that she poured over him.

"Thank you?" she asked. "I think I could be either offended or flattered by that statement."

"Be flattered. I meant no chauvinistic inference." He leaned forward. "And we can discuss 'men's things' whenever you'd like."

Her eyes brightened and she sat up. "I intend to."

"You're a remarkable woman, Marta. I enjoy your company." Again, he wished Irina had told him about Marta. Instead, he stumbled across her by chance and she was by far the most interesting vampire he'd met in quite a while.

"And I yours," she said as she turned to the doorway. "*Querida.*"

Isabelle padded in and kissed Marta. She then turned to Eamon, smiled, and lowered her eyes. "Hello."

"Hello, Isabelle. We were just talking about you."

The girl looked back at Marta, her eyes revealed a passing uneasiness. Marta pulled her down next to her on the sofa. "Only good things."

"So what are we doing this evening?" he asked, taking another drink.

"We thought we would go back to Bathory."

Eamon placed his glass on the table. "Why?"

"I was under the impression that you were searching for Lauryl."

"I am."

"Well, shouldn't you look for her where she's most likely to turn up?"

"Marta, have you considered that maybe I'm not looking for her as aggressively as I was before?"

She studied his face for a minute. "Amelie must have quite a bit of power over you."

"No, I'm just tired of the search. Besides, she seems content in the life she's made here and I know that she's safe. That was my main concern." Eamon's expression suggested that the discussion was closed.

"If you say so. So will you come to Bathory with us?"

"Doesn't the place bore you?"

"No, I find it amusing."

Eamon sighed. "Then I suppose we'll go."

"Excellent! *Querida*? Shall we?"

"Friday night is supposed to be amazing, according to Dita. She said that they do like performance art and stuff like that," Isabelle told Marta.

"Wonderful," Eamon muttered.

* * *

ISABELLE PULLED THE car to the back door of Bathory. The same bulky security man came out and opened her door. "Dita's coming," was all he said as he drove off.

As they watched the taillights disappear, Dita opened the warehouse door. She gave two air kisses to Isabelle, bowed her head to Marta, and then looked at Eamon. She appeared to be confused about what to do to him. She stood in awkward silence for a few seconds.

"Hello always works nicely, I've found," Eamon said.

"Hello. I've got you in the same room tonight. Come on."

Eamon looked at the leggy girl. Tonight she wore a black knit dress that had been cut apart and safety pinned back together. She still had the white makeup on, but her eyes were blue, their natural color. He walked a few steps behind her as she took them up to their VIP suite and her pace quickened. A mischievous smile appeared on his face and he stepped up next to her.

"Dita, darling, I'm hungry," Eamon whispered to her.

"What do you mean?" She walked faster.

"I mean I'm hungry." He could hear her heart accelerate with fear.

The door of the suite stopped her. "I—" she stammered.

Eamon laughed. "I'm teasing you," he said, brushing past her.

The rich sound of his laughter caused Dita to blush. He spun around and leered at her. Dita's eyes expanded to saucer size and she turned to Marta.

"Eamon, now play nice," Marta chided.

He shrugged his shoulders and sat down. "I'm only joking. You know, lightening the mood, being friendly."

Marta wagged her finger at him. "Behave." She turned back to Dita. "Is Ivory here tonight?"

"Yes, she is. There are a lot of vampires here tonight."

"Anyone interesting?" Marta asked.

"Interesting how?"

"Oh, I don't know. I always enjoy good company. Moreover, my poor friend is missing his love. She's—" Marta looked at Eamon. "Where is she?"

"Out of town with friends."

"So of course I want to keep him entertained."

"Which was precisely why I was talking to the lovely Dita," Eamon said. He winked at her and Dita's eyes widened again. "For someone who works in club run by and frequented by vampires, you certainly are timid around them."

"Only you."

"*Querida*, send up Ivory for us. We'd like to say hello."

"Sure," she said as she hustled to the door. She stopped and turned back to them. "It might be a while. They're getting ready for the show."

"Since that's the case, send me up a drink. Glenlivet, if you have it."

Dita nodded and closed the door behind her. Eamon laughed again. She was afraid of him because he was a vampire. Why wasn't she as frightened of Marta as she was of him? He wondered what the club staff knew about him. They probably knew a very one-sided story, with him as a villain and Lauryl and the idiot Wilson as the heroes. Eamon knew that he had a certain mythos about him, but Lauryl no doubt added quite a bit to it.

"Really, Eamon, tormenting that poor girl. She's terrified of you."

"For what reason?"

"I don't know. You being grouchy is not a reason. Perhaps your reputation?"

"Exactly."

"I meant as being the oldest vampire, but you raise an interesting point."

"I'm not running for office."

He stared down at the people in the club. Humans and vampires danced shoulder to shoulder on the crowded floor. In a way, this place served as the ideal hunting spot for a vampire. Willing victims were everywhere and dark places to play were abundant.

The door opened and Ivory entered with his drink in her hand.

"My dear Sasha," Marta said. "It is so good to see you again. Of course you remember Eamon?"

Sasha gave Eamon his drink and bowed her head. "How are you, sir?"

"Very well, thank you. How are you? It seems you're busy this evening."

"Yes, very."

"Won't you sit with me for a moment?" He patted the spot next to him.

Sasha hesitated but then sat down next to him. Her Lolita-style dress hiked up her thighs when she did. Eamon took an appraising glance at her legs. He was especially intrigued by the fence panel pantyhose she wore. He slipped his finger under one of the net strings and smiled. She took in a deep breath. Eamon then reached up to the high ponytails on her head and rubbed the silky black hair between his fingers. Her hair slipped through and he traced a finger down her neck. He took a long swallow from his glass before placing it on the table.

"Would you like another?" Sasha asked.

"No, not right now."

Marta stared back at him with a semi scowl. "Tell us about the show tonight." *What is wrong with you*, she silently asked

Eamon.

"Audience participation and interaction. We should have no problem getting volunteers. Should be fun."

"Like how?" Isabelle asked.

"Depending on the artist, we take a clubber and bring them on stage and use them in their bit."

"It sounds fascinating," Eamon placed mocking emphasis on the word fascinating.

Marta shot him a look. "I think it will be just that."

Sasha stood. "I really need to get back downstairs. The show's starting soon."

"Enjoy. It was good seeing you again."

"I, um, still haven't seen either one of them."

"I know you haven't," Eamon said.

"It was good to see you, Senorita Jimenez-de Castillo." She bowed her head. "Enjoy the show."

Eamon waited for her close the door behind her and then turned to Marta. "She's been glamoured. I can feel it," he said.

"I thought so, too. By whom?" Marta asked.

"Lauryl."

"Really?"

"Yes. I have no idea how she's become so skilled, but she has." His phone vibrated and he checked the caller ID. His expression softened. "Hello, my love."

"Eamon!" Amelie said.

"What are you doing?" It was difficult for him to hear her. Wherever she was, it sounded crowded. He could hear music and young voices laughing. He could also hear in her voice was that she was on the way to being drunk.

"I was just thinking about you and missing you," she said. "Hey, my friends want to say hey."

Eamon heard a chorus of drunken, young, female voices chant "Hey, Eamon" in unison.

"Tell your friends hello."

Amelie relayed the message to her friends and wave of girlish giggles followed.

"I really miss you," she said, sighing into the phone.

"I miss you, too, but I know you're having fun with your friends. You need to spend time with someone besides an old man," he said.

She laughed. "You're not old and I wanna come home and be with you. Hey, where are you?"

"I'm at Bathory with Marta and Isabelle."

"The vampire place? And you went without me?"

"You and I will come together."

"We can play vampire there."

"Wherever you want. Listen, baby, please be careful. I can't wait to see you."

"Miss you."

"Miss you, too."

Eamon ended the call and glanced back at Marta. Both she and Isabelle grinned at him. He smirked and turned his attention back to the dance floor.

"How charming," Marta said.

"He loves her," Isabelle said to Marta.

Eamon didn't respond to the teasing. He turned the phone over in his hand a couple of times and was about to say something when a spotlight hit the stage and the music stopped. Sasha sauntered onto the stage. A hush fell over the crowd and she called for a volunteer. A young man dressed in what Eamon considered normal clothes walked on stage. An employee brought out a chair, placed it downstage and he sat down. Eamon followed his gaze to the young man's cheering friends. They all appeared to be about Amelie's age and were intoxicated. He shook his head. Youth. The phone vibrated again. Amelie had sent him a picture of herself and her friends. He turned the phone in the ladies' direction.

Marta took the phone from his hand and looked at the picture. "My dear Eamon, you're so very smitten."

He tried to take the phone back from her, but she playfully pulled it out of his reach. She pulled it away a final time and placed it in his hand. Their attention turned to the stage as a monotonous, hollow voice announced, "Ladies and gentleman, vampires and humans, the beautiful, deadly Lilith!"

Eamon turned back to the stage as his senses came alive. Recognition rang through him. It was Lauryl. The club lights blacked out and from beyond the field of the single spot light, out she crept. Lean and pale, she wore a black leather bra and a pair of black boy shorts studded with rhinestones. Her hair was long, black, and straight with bangs. Across her eyes, she wore a black makeup mask and her lips were painted a deep maroon. The somber music of Dead Can Dance started and she stalked toward the nervous boy seated in front of her. As she danced around him, almost lap dancing, the boy's eyes never left her. Each time she touched him, his head lolled back and he closed his eyes. As the song came to its end, she straddled him and licked his neck. When the notes died away, she pushed his head to the side and bit him. His head dropped back, the lights went out, and the crowd went wild.

Marta, who remained by Eamon during the performance, hesitated a moment. "Is that—?"

He stared down at the dark stage. "Lauryl." Eamon didn't move. He stood and processed what he had seen.

"I thought she had red hair."

"She does."

"She certainly was a hit. I thought she would have taken a bow," she said.

Eamon turned to her, his expression asked for silence while he thought. He wasn't looking for her anymore and yet she chose tonight to appear to him. In his mind, he imagined that when he found her, he would grab her up and demand an explanation. Or kill her for her betrayal. Over the past months, he decided he couldn't kill one of his own no matter what her infraction. But now, when he was faced with the situation, he couldn't do anything. He was locked in indecision. Eamon closed his eyes and thought of Lauryl. He felt her for a second, like a breeze, and then nothing. She was gone.

"At least she's dancing again," he said with a chuckle before he sat down. "And she's safe."

"It isn't ballet, but she seems happy," Marta added pragmatically.

He stood silently, still amazed at her ability to appear and disappear at will. "Does it seem odd that she's so skilled at hiding in plain sight?"

"Yes, it does. Everything that you've told me about her is odd," she said as she inspected her manicure.

"I know." The range of emotions that flowed through Eamon surprised him. He was angry, surprised, relieved, and confused all at once. He closed his eyes and waited for his mind to settle. Marta put her hand on his shoulder and squeezed. He patted her slender hand. "I'm at a loss for what to do."

"I can see that."

Eamon looked at the picture of Amelie and her friends. He showed it to Marta. "This is what makes me happy."

"Yet you can't let go of Lauryl," she said quietly. Marta turned back to Isabelle. "Isabelle, why don't you go and find Dita?" Isabelle nodded and walked out.

"She's part of me. I'm her maker." He placed his phone on the arm of the chair and sighed. The burgundy cushions collapsed under his weight and he sank deeper into the velvety chair. "I feel that I'm responsible for her."

"And you feel that deeply. More than any other vampire I've ever seen." Marta sat down in the chair next to him. "How old are you?"

"Old." When she continued to stare at him, he sighed. "I was turned in 972."

"Do you remember your human life?"

"Portions of it."

"Was it happy?"

Eamon sighed again. "Is this therapy?"

"I'm just curious."

"As happy as a warrior's life could be during that time," he replied.

"But not happy enough that you didn't mind leaving it behind."

"I asked for this," he said as he stretched his legs out.

"Do you still remember being turned?"

"Yes, I do. I'll never forget that."

"Tell me."

"My maker's name was Eleanor. When she found me, she was already close to my age now. One night, while on a patrol, I came across her. Rather she came across me. I didn't see her until she was on top of me. As she was feeding on me, something inside of me knew that I wanted to be like her. I knew what she was. She must have been reading my thoughts because she stopped. 'Strange soldier', she said. 'You crave my existence?' I nodded and she got off me. I got up from the ground, stripped off my chain mail and helmet and left with her. The next evening, I rose as a vampire."

Marta nodded. "Were you together long?"

"Unfortunately, my maker was already tired of life. She had quite a melancholy side to her. Lauryl reminds me of her. Eleanor made me the kind of vampire I am. I can survive anything. I've been through every sort of existence. The only thing I don't like is—"

"Being alone," Marta finished for him.

He nodded. "Exactly. I have been alone off and on for the past, good God, almost eleven hundred years. When I was alone, those were unhappy times for me. After Eleanor died in 1417, I was alone until Irina. She had more of a love of hunting than a love for me, though. We could always feel each other. I felt her die. I could feel both of them until Lauryl. I have no idea how she's learned to hide herself from me."

"Her skill is a mystery to me as well. Perhaps she wanted so badly to get away from you that it enhanced her ability."

A frown darkened his face. "Well, that certainly is a pleasant thought."

Marta placed her hand on his. "*Mi amor*, forgive me. Bluntness is a terrible flaw of mine. As painful as it is, it's a possibility."

Eamon nodded.

"I think affairs of the heart are infinitely more complex than every day affairs."

"Agreed." He picked up his glass of scotch and drained it in one swallow. Lauryl said she didn't want to be with him. She meant it. She certainly felt no fear in showing herself to him. He set the glass down and sighed. "I think the project you want to undertake will be much easier than sorting out the situation I have with Lauryl and Amelie."

"You'll help me then?" She straightened in her seat.

"If you think my help will be of any use, yes."

"Wonderful! I'm so pleased!" She leaned over and kissed him on the lips, socially at first and then more passionately.

He returned the kiss and then smiled. "That doesn't help me any."

"Every once in a while, I like to see what I've been missing," she said, caressing his cheek.

CHAPTER TWENTY-EIGHT

The Things I Do for My Primigenio

E AMON PUSHED HIS black Persol sunglasses up the bridge of his nose and frowned. The sun was brighter than he was accustomed to. Even in late October the noontime sun beat down with little concern that it was autumn everywhere else in the world. He stripped off his suit jacket and rolled up the sleeves of his shirt in an effort to get some relief from the heat. The sunlight prickled his skin like a weak electric shock where it was exposed. Common sense and comfort told him to put up the top on the Boxster.

He pulled his phone out and shot a quick text message off to Marta reinforcing his desire that she and Isabelle be on time. Her reply was quick and brief.

Absolutamente.

This was quite a request for him to make of Marta, but she had acquiesced. It was even more dramatic because he'd underestimated the sun so much. Never before had he experienced such intensity. His eyes, although shielded by the polarized lenses, ached and burned. As he scanned the sky, he noticed a line of deep gray clouds out over the bay toward St. Petersburg. With any luck, those clouds would park themselves over the Yacht Club while they ate lunch. He wished that folklore was true in this case and that he could manipulate the weather. His phone vibrated. Amelie had sent him a text message wondering where he was. When he pulled in her driveway, he texted her back and told her to open the door.

Amelie opened the door, holding her phone and laughing. "You're such a nerd."

Eamon got out of the car and walked to her. "Yes, I am. But

you love me." He wrapped his arms around her and kissed her. She slid her hand down his back and sank her hand in his back pocket. "If you start, we won't make it to lunch," he murmured through the kiss.

"Okay." She picked up her purse. "Ready."

He took an approving look at her. Today she was wearing a short khaki skirt and a navy blue t-shirt that form fit her full breasts. Her dark hair was pulled up in a ponytail and tied with a bow. The outfit made her seem younger than she was, and even more beautiful. Eamon felt a surge of pride and contentment. She was beautiful and brilliant, and she was his.

"Why are you staring at me?"

Eamon shook his head. "I can't believe you want to be seen with me."

She pushed him playfully. "Oh, please."

He replaced his sunglasses. "Shall we?"

As they drove to the Yacht Club, Eamon's focus remained on the sun. Amelie wanted the top down as they drove and he didn't want to refuse her. He kept his thoughts on psychically shielding himself from the sun's rays and not on his beautiful girlfriend next to him. However, the distant cloudbank that appeared to be stalled over Tampa Bay just beyond their destination did seem promising. Clouds would allow him to loosen his focus and enjoy her.

Eamon pulled the Boxster in to the yacht club parking lot.

"Do you come here a lot?" she asked, looking around.

"No, but it's good to maintain a membership for meetings." He walked around to her door and opened it.

"Your jacket?"

He was already past his comfort level and the idea of donning the jacket again sickened him. "No, it's fine. Leave it there."

"Going casual today? Or almost." She pointed to his tie and smiled. "I like your sunglasses, by the way."

"Thank you." The purchase of sunglasses had been an interesting experience. Fearing the mirror-filled environment of a store, he had entrusted the task to Isabelle. Marta assured him they made him even more handsome. Amelie's opinion confirmed it.

Eamon saw that Marta and Isabelle were already seated on the terrace overlooking the water. He waved and silently cursed Marta's choice of tables. His irritation with Marta dissolved and was replaced by amusement. She was wearing a large brimmed hat and a pair of large-lens Chanel sunglasses. The hat brim had a circumference large enough that it shaded past her shoulders. Her champagne-colored shirt was long-sleeved and made of thin, silk jersey. The neckline dipped lower on one side exposing one shoulder. She looked like a couture-dressed eccentric. Eamon covered his mouth with his free hand and cleared his throat to stifle a laugh.

"Darling, this is my cousin, Marta Jimenez de-Castillo and her friend Isabelle Simmons. Ladies, this is my Amelie. Amelie de la Puente."

"Izzy?" Amelie asked.

Isabelle's usual stoic expression became animated. She slid her sunglasses down her nose. "Amelie, oh my God! I haven't seen you since we graduated!"

"I know!" Amelie grabbed Isabelle in a hug.

"You two know one another?" Marta asked.

Isabelle nodded. "Yes, Amelie and I went to high school to-gether."

"Well, isn't that nice?" Marta looked at Eamon and her eyes sparkled. *Who could have imagined a more divine coincidence?* she said silently.

I'm surprised you can see anything under that umbrella on your head, he replied.

You told me to wear a hat.

Is that what that is? He watched Amelie and Isabelle chat, catching up on life since high school. *Did you know they were acquainted?*

She looked over at the two girls. *I had no idea.*

He adjusted his sunglasses and glanced at the waiter who appeared at their table to fill their glasses with water.

"Can I tell you about the specials?" the waiter asked.

Marta smiled at the young man. "Oh no. I have an idea.

Choose four entrees and bring them. We'll rely on your expertise." She turned to Amelie and Isabelle. "Will that be acceptable?"

The girls nodded and went back to their conversation.

The waiter looked at Eamon, unsure of what to do. "Are you sure?"

"That's fine with me."

Marta shrugged. *It's all an act. I don't care what they bring me. Why waste time on the charade of everyone trying to decide what to eat? I know what you want to eat.* She nodded to Amelie.

Eamon scowled at her. *Human, we're appearing human.*

She nodded at the sky, which now was more overcast. *Yes, we are. That's the only reason I would be out in this ridiculous heat and sun.*

Behave. "So Isabelle, you and Amelie went to school together?" Eamon asked.

Isabelle nodded. "Yes, but she went away to college. I stayed here and went to the University of Tampa."

Amelie turned to her friend. "God, Izzy, you look even more like a supermodel than before."

Isabelle's pale cheeks turned pink. "No."

"Ah, *querida*, you're so modest. Both of you are lovely."

"What a luxury to have such beautiful lunch companions," Eamon said, keeping his focus on Marta. He sensed she was up to something.

Marta took a drink from her water glass. "Tell me how you two met. Eamon is very close mouthed about you."

"We met outside the bookstore in Hyde Park Village."

Eamon reluctantly turned from Marta. "She thought I was a pervert."

Marta's blonde eyebrows lifted over the lenses of her sunglasses. "Really?"

Amelie blushed and laughed. "He was watching me in the bookstore. I thought he was a creeper."

Isabelle laughed and Marta glanced at her, silencing her. "Eamon is many things, but not a creeper or a pervert. But I suppose you've found that out."

Eamon scowled at Marta.

"I simply meant that Eamon is a rare sort. He's not what the world thinks he is."

I'm warning you, Marta.

"Oh, I know that," Amelie said. She looked at Eamon. "I'm glad."

Marta's eyes lit up again. "I am too. I know I would not be the same person if he were."

Stop this right now! Eamon took his sunglasses off and locked his gaze on to her. Marta continued to smile and even lifted her eyebrows in a challenge.

"He's not the big bad corporate bastard he's made out to be," Amelie said, oblivious to the stare down between Marta and Eamon.

"No, that's simply a characterization," he said. "Invented by the media and my rivals."

Marta tilted her head slightly to the side for a moment before lowering it in submission.

"Sometimes appearances are necessary for survival and success though," she said as she lifted her head.

The waiter brought the food and placed it in front of them. Amelie and Isabelle switched plates and Eamon and Marta didn't say a word.

The things I do for my Primigenio, Marta said silently.

And you will always have my protection and affection in return, he replied. He replaced his sunglasses.

I'd rather have another member of your line, Marta said silently.

You will. All in good time.

CHAPTER TWENTY-NINE

With a Wink and a Taunting Smile, She Was Gone

"W̶HERE ARE WE going?" Amelie asked Eamon as they drove past Channelside toward Ybor City.

He took her hand and rubbed her fingers. "It's a surprise."

Eamon turned the Porsche on to one of the old, red-cobbled streets of Ybor City. Crowds of people lined the sidewalks and filed in and out of the clubs. Eamon turned off Seventh Avenue and stopped behind a warehouse. She gave him a puzzled look and laughed.

"Should I be scared?"

"When you're with me, you'll never have to be frightened of anything," he said softly in her ear. The rusty back door of Bathory opened and Sasha walked out, followed by the unnamed, muscular security guard. Eamon got out of his car, walked around to Amelie's door to help her out. The security guard jumped in and drove off with the car leaving Eamon, Amelie, and Sasha standing in the street.

"What's his name?" Eamon asked, pointing at the taillights of his car as it screamed around the corner.

"Trevor. He doesn't say much, especially when he is kicking the asses of drunks. He doesn't miss much either."

"That's a valuable skill to possess."

"Yes, it is. It's good to see you, Mr. Rutherford." She lowered her head in a slight bow. Her eyes looked up at Amelie, taking in all of her features. A knowing smile appeared on her lips.

"Good evening, Sasha. I'd like you to meet my girlfriend Amelie." Eamon placed his hand on Amelie's lower back.

"It's a pleasure to meet you. I have your usual room. If you'll follow me."

She motioned them inside the dark hallway and closed the door.

Amelie moved in closer to Eamon as they walked down the hall. Sasha glided through the dark and up the stairs. She was fluid, almost unnatural. Her skin was paler than Amelie's and her black hair was piled on top of her head and secured with ebony sticks.

"Have you been here a lot?" Amelie asked, her eyes on Sasha.

"A few times with Marta and Isabelle. They enjoy it more than I do." He turned back to Sasha. "You know what I like, Sasha."

She nodded to him and turned to Amelie. "May I get you anything?"

"Red wine." Her grasp on Eamon tightened.

"I'll send it up." Sasha smiled at Eamon. "Let me know if you need anything else."

Eamon gave Sasha a stern frown before she left. "I'll do that." He sat down and patted his lap. "Come and sit. I like it when you are close to me."

Amelie walked over and sat down. With a sigh, she put her hand on his chest. "I don't like her. She makes me uncomfortable."

"I think she does that on purpose. She's supposed to be playing the part of a vampire." He kissed her. "Just act like her."

"I couldn't act like that even if I tried."

"I don't think it would be too difficult for you," he said, rubbing her shoulder.

"Yeah, but walking like her would be." She stood up and looked out of the window down at the dance floor. "How come you don't go down there?"

"I prefer it up here," he said. Amelie's hips moved in sync with the music and Eamon relaxed. "It's more private."

The door opened and Dita walked in with their drinks. "Good evening, Mr. Rutherford. It's good to see you." She set the wine glass down and placed the scotch in Eamon's hand. "Dita, this is my girlfriend, Amelie." Eamon nodded to Amelie.

"It's nice to meet you," Dita said keeping her eyes on Eamon.

Amelie nodded at Dita and looked back at the dance floor. "Is it like this every night?"

"Crowded? Yeah, it is. Tonight is the floorshow so it's crazy crowded. People dig the audience participation." Dita nodded to Eamon. "If I can get anything else for you, let me know," she said, inching toward the door.

Eamon continued to watch as Amelie bobbed and swayed to the music. "I will." Dita scurried out and he took a drink from his glass. *Was Lauryl performing tonight?* Eamon wondered. For all he knew, she was in the building at this moment, maybe even right outside the door. He couldn't feel her though.

"I can't believe I'm here with you," Amelie said as she looked around the suite.

"Why is that?"

She shrugged. "I don't know. It was like the night we met. I would have never guessed you'd want a book on astrology."

"But I did."

"I know. Now we're here in this club together. A Goth vampire club just doesn't seem like you."

"You don't think vampires enjoy clubs?"

Amelie didn't catch the way he phrased his question and knelt down in front of him. "If you were a vampire, I don't think you would hang out in a place like this."

He tousled her glossy hair. "I might."

"If you were really a vampire, you would be like their king. A king wouldn't hang out with club kids." She giggled.

"A king needs a queen," he said before he pulled her up in his lap.

"Eamon," she said softly as she put her hand on his chest. "I love you."

He took her hand from his chest and kissed it. "I love you, too." Eamon held her close as he replayed the past few minutes in his head. He needed to find a way to tell her what he was, and soon. While he was lost in thought, Sasha appeared on the stage. The crowded dance floor settled and the lights dimmed. He reached out for Lauryl's presence, but only felt the mix of several vampires downstairs.

Amelie touched his cheek. "What are you thinking about?"

"I'm thinking about how I can't imagine my life without you." He kissed her fingers as they passed over his lips. Eamon cupped her face between his hands. "You're so beautiful," he whispered. Eamon kissed her, his tongue playing with hers as she closed her eyes and traced her hands down his chest. She slipped her hands underneath his shirt and lightly raked her nails across his skin. Reluctantly, she broke away.

She pulled off his shirt and kissed his chest softly at first. The kisses turned into delicate, little nipping bites as she moved from his chest to his neck. His skin tingled in anticipation just before each gentle bite and he smiled. Eamon's hands found her thighs and massaged the skin under her skirt. Amelie removed her shirt and unhooked her bra, unconcerned that they were in the club. He slipped her skirt further over her thighs and opened her legs wider for him. Her hands pushed through his hair and clasped behind his head. As he kissed her, he reached down, unzipped his pants, and flicked open the button open. Her hands dropped down from behind his head and descended to his pants. She lifted her eyes, which now burned with desire, to his.

All the things he could see in her eyes, desire, love, devotion, happiness, sliced at Eamon's control. He could smell blood in one of the adjacent rooms, which further assaulted his composure. He caressed her breasts. Her heart thumped underneath his hand. Amelie rolled her head back and her eyelids drooped. Each caress over her skin brought a fleeting pass of her perfume to him. It was the same provocative, floral, earthy scent from the night they met. He lowered his head to her neck and licked it. He took deep breath of her body and lowered his mouth to kiss her but Lauryl's unexpected marker jarred his thoughts.

Eamon's eyes fixed on the darkened dance floor and traveled along the spotlight lit stage. In a chair down stage, a young man Amelie's age took an uneasy look around. The same ominous synthesizer music as before began and Lauryl skulked out of the darkness like a cat stalking a bird. Tonight, she wore a white lace nightgown torn from the hemline up to her waist all the way around the garment, turning the skirt into strips of fabric. The gown, decorated with bloodstains and dirt, made it seem as if she had crawled from a grave in it. She wore the same black wig, but this time she didn't have her eyes covered with black makeup. The boy in the chair watched her as she snaked her way up to him. Silent alarm rang out from him but died away as soon as she glamoured him. When her hand grabbed, his ankle, he moaned in anticipation and his fear vanished.

Amelie's needy touch brought Eamon back from the spell Lauryl was weaving over the crowd and the boy in the chair. Her naked body pressed firmly against him, and her hand tried to free him from his pants. With a smooth motion, he guided her hand into his pants and placed it on him. Her eyes stayed fixed on his lap as her hand emerged with what she wanted. Amelie rocked up on her knees and seated herself on his length. A desperate little moan passed over her lips as she started to rock her hips back and forth over him. Eamon pulled her against him and thrust deeper inside of her. As he thrust, he looked back down to the stage and saw Lauryl had assumed a position behind the boy, and while her hands ran feverishly over his chest, her gaze remained fixed on the window of their suite.

Eamon stared directly down at Lauryl. He slid his hands under Amelie's round buttocks and continued to thrust. Amelie grabbed a handful of his hair, writhing and twisting as he drove deeper into her. He kissed her shoulder, desperately trying to smash the urge to take her blood, and looked back at Lauryl. Their eyes locked, each frozen in what they were doing. Lauryl broke first. She smiled slightly and winked at him before she straddled the boy and bit him. The spotlight snapped off, leaving the club dark while the club erupted in applause. Eamon felt Lauryl disappear like the spotlight. With a wink and a taunting smile, she was gone.

He shook his head and returned his attention to Amelie. From what he could feel, her thoughts were running crazy with love and absolute desire for him. He could hear her giving herself to him in her mind, pledging everything to him. Thinking of that, he pushed Lauryl from his mind and focused entirely on Amelie.

"Amelie, I need you so much," he whispered in her ear.

She grabbed the back of his neck. "I'm yours, Eamon. Always."

Amelie's statement drew his eyes to her pink, flushed neck again. He kissed her neck and nipped and pulled on the tender skin with his teeth. The salty taste of her skin only fueled his desire for her blood. He let his fangs graze over her skin. A trail of goose bumps appeared on the path where his fangs had skimmed over it. The teasing, raking sensation caused her to sigh and drop her head to the side. His tongue traced over her neck, tasting her. His desire for her and her blood was approaching the point where he wouldn't care about anything but consuming her. Eamon buried his hands in her black hair, holding her so he could look into her eyes.

"I can't fight this," he breathed, wanting her blood. The intensity of his desire for her blood was stunning to him. He hadn't wanted anyone like this. Ever.

"I don't want you to," she answered, burying her face in his neck. She opened her mouth and bit him, her teeth connecting with an eerie precision to where he would bite a human. As she started to climax, she let up from the bite. "Do it, Eamon. Bite me!" she begged as her body quivered.

She wanted him to bite her. Even though she didn't know what she was really asking for, he tentatively bit her. He quickly withdrew his fangs before her blood poured into his mouth. She cried out briefly. The sensation of his fangs piercing her skin brought on another orgasm, but soon quieted down to gasps and whimpers. The fleeting taste only teased him. The teasing turned to torment as the tiny bit of her blood circulated through his body. He had to choose and quickly. With a supreme effort, he pulled back. Amelie's body settled from vivid spasms to a fine trembling. The bite on her neck closed and healed immediately. He leaned her back and kissed her lips.

Eamon held her against him and felt her heart rate slow to a normal pace. He closed his eyes and savored the little portion of her that was now his. The soft sensation of her tongue sliding across his chest brought a deep chuckle from him. "Amelie, I've never loved someone like I love you."

She turned her face to his. "I'm yours, Eamon, body and soul."

CHAPTER THIRTY

You're for Real. You're Really a Vampire

T HE CANDLES DOTTING the coffee table flickered, distorting the shadows of the living room of Eamon's house. Amelie took a sip of wine and stared out of the large windows in the living room that faced Tampa Bay. A med flight helicopter approached and landed on the pad at Tampa General Hospital.

"My father died at Tampa General." She nodded her head in the direction of the enormous red brick complex across the water on Davis Island. "Three days before my college graduation in May." Amelie closed her eyes. "He was only sixty," she continued. "Yeah, I know you're doing the math. I was a late-in-life baby for my parents. Dad was just about to turn thirty-nine when I was born. My mom was thirty-seven."

"Lots of couples wait to have kids," Eamon said softly. He felt the depth of her sorrow but was unsure of what to do for her. So he just listened.

"He was my whole world growing up. I miss him," she added quietly.

"I can imagine." Eamon wanted to do something to ease her pain. He even thought about glamouring her to help Amelie get through the grief of losing her father, but knew that would be unfair. Her sadness tugged at him and he felt helpless.

"I'm all alone now. I don't have any family. If I were younger, I guess that I'd be an orphan." She turned around to Eamon. "I wish you could have heard the people at his funeral. Whispering, thinking I couldn't hear them. 'Oh, poor Amelie, she's all alone in the world. Poor, poor Amelie. *Pobre* Amelie. *Que lastima.*' I hated their pity." Her fingers tightened on the bowl of the wine glass. Her chin quivered for a second then stopped. "The firm that my dad worked for was nice except for one of the partners. He came on to me at the funeral." She snickered and drained her glass.

Eamon shifted his position and narrowed his eyes. "Oh, really?"

"Well, not at the funeral, but after. Talk about gross. He didn't want to take no for an answer." she said as she placed her glass down on the table.

"Who was it?" He would make sure whoever it was would not live to see many more days.

"Oh, one of the partners. He gave up." She scratched her stomach and stretched her arms over her head, shaking her hips as she did.

"His name?"

She hesitated. "Tyson Costello."

Eamon mentally noted the name. His tense expression dissolved when Amelie walked over and knelt in front of him.

"What's wrong? You look mad."

He shook his head. "Not mad. Well, yes, mad. I can't stand the thought of anyone hurting you." His finger traced along her cheek to her lips. "Especially at a time when you were so vulnerable."

She slid into his lap and laid her head on his chest. "He'd been doing it for years." She shifted her position some. "You take care me. I like that"

"I enjoy it." Eamon's hand traced along her lower back. "You need to get used to me doing it"

"Really?" She touched his face.

"Darling, I don't understand why you're surprised. I'd like you to be my wife one day." He kissed the palm of her hand, enjoying the taste.

She smiled and nodded.

"You won't mind our age difference? No more worrying about people thinking that you're my daughter or a professional girlfriend?"

"No. As long as we're together, nothing will matter."

Eamon dropped his head for a moment and wrestled with the

idea of telling her the truth about what he was. They had joked about vampires so many times that she probably wouldn't take him seriously or would think he was crazy. He definitely didn't want to tell her the same way he did with Lauryl. Turning her and forcing her to adjust wasn't a good idea. He couldn't have Amelie grow to hate and resent him too. He closed his eyes and sighed. His eyes opened when her fingers played in his hair. He kissed her fingers.

"I like it when you do that. We're going to have to talk about some very serious things, though. In order for us to be together all of the time, there are going to have to be some changes." His expression became more serious.

"You mean like you having to get a divorce from Lauryl?"

That hadn't crossed his mind. Since their marriage wasn't real, there were no legal issues for him to deal with. "No, not that." He thought for a second. "Amelie, if you decide that you want to stay with me then you'd have to make some…adjustments."

"Like personality adjustments? I don't understand." Her dark brows drew together in confusion.

"Oh no," he said, placing a gentle kiss on her forehead. "Nothing like that. But there would be some changes." He had yet to think this conversation through all the way. His gaze wandered around the room as he decided whether or not to pursue this any further.

"You seem far away." She touched his cheek. "Do you want me to go?" She tried to move, but he caught her and shook his head.

"Do you want to play vampire?" she offered in a seductive whisper as she leaned over and sucked his neck lightly. His expression softened. She pulled her shirt over her head and unfastened her bra. With a slight movement of her head, she shook out her hair so that it lay over her pale breasts like black satin. She posed for him and smiled.

Oh, my dear, that's the wrong question.

Her body was a beautiful contrast to Lauryl's. Amelie's body was soft and generous with well-defined curves and contours.

What Amelie thought of as fat or dumpy, Eamon thought was feminine and inviting. His hands always found their way to her. He also loved to watch her, especially when she was unaware. He loved how she arched her back when she stretched and pushed her breasts forward. He loved the way she tipped her head slightly to the side, unintentionally displaying her neck to him, when she was deep in thought. He also loved how her hips swung with a graceful seductiveness when she walked, a seductiveness she underestimated.

"Do you have any idea how beautiful you are?" He brushed the hair from her neck. Her delicious pale skin was now flushed pink in excitement. His desire for her burned hotter now. She would be beautiful forever, and he'd love and protect her forever. Together, they'd live the life he had wanted; a life of love and companionship.

Amelie's cheeks turned pink. She dropped her head to the side and closed her eyes. "Eamon." Her hands trailed over his stomach and down his thighs. A startled gasp escaped from her when his hand grasped her shoulder by the base of her neck.

"I want to give you everything you want. Make you happy. Take care of you." His hand dropped back to her lower back and embraced her. He couldn't wait anymore. "I love you," he added before he buried his fangs into her soft skin.

"Oh God!" she gasped. Her eyes fluttered open and then closed. She squirmed against him, tightening her arms around his neck. "This is...different. It...Oh..." Her voice melted into a purr and she ground herself against his thigh. "Hurts..." she cooed as she rose to her orgasm.

As soon as he tasted her blood, he was satisfied. Eamon closed his eyes and delighted in it. The teasing sample earlier in the week was nothing compared to this. He could taste her beauty and spirit, something he never tasted in Lauryl or anyone for that matter. She was more than worth the wait. Part of her flowed into his body and strengthened it. More than that, her blood completed him. He would do everything he could to turn her but he had to think of how to accomplish it. Amelie opened her eyes and shook her head.

She reached up to her neck and gingerly touched the wound. The wet, sticky spot intrigued her. Her fingers touched together and slipped back and forth on the blood. Her eyes were unable to focus but the liquid on her fingertips smelled like blood. She looked from the blood to his face.

"You're for real," she said. "You're really a vampire."

Eamon smiled and nodded his head.

CHAPTER THIRTY-ONE

Eamon Must Have Put a Little More Energy in Playing Vampire Last Night

A<small>MELIE OPENED HER</small> eyes and rubbed her temples. She remembered talking, red wine, and she and Eamon making love. The rest was gone. And she was in Eamon's bed. The sun was up, but she had no idea what time it was. There was no reason to get out of bed though. Another thing she remembered; Eamon would be in New York for a day or two and she'd be alone. She pulled the sheets up over her head and went back to sleep.

The next time she woke up, she turned over and glanced at the little clock on his bedside table. It was after ten. She felt better. Her hangover was gone now. Amelie noticed the note that Eamon had left for her. It was a brief mash note, which brought a smile to her face. She snuggled back into the bed, wishing he were here with her.

Amelie got up and got dressed. She pulled her shirt over her head and saw the two small bruises on her neck. *Eamon must have put a little more energy in to playing vampire last night*, she thought as she examined the bruises.

She padded down the stairs and stopped outside the door to his library. Centered in the office was an Empire desk facing of the windows to the back garden, and behind the desk was a credenza with his laptop. Books filled the bookcases along two of the walls. On the other wall was a large portrait of a beautiful dark-haired woman with ice-blue eyes. The woman was dressed in eighteenth century clothing, and by the style of the painting, she guessed it to be a Gainsborough. Next to it hung a painting Amelie knew to be a Degas. The two paintings didn't fit together.

In fact, the Degas looked as if it was an afterthought.

Amelie leaned across the desk. On the corner was a picture frame. She turned it around. The picture was a black and white headshot. It had to be Lauryl. It seemed odd that Eamon kept her headshot on his desk. Actually, it was odd for him to have any pictures of her. Then she remembered that Lauryl was still his wife. Amelie placed the picture face down and walked out of the room.

It amazed her how her energy level had improved since she woke up. She'd read the last half of a book, surfed the Internet, and watched the noon news. Now she was bored and restless. Eamon had left another note in the foyer with the alarm code and his black Centurion American Express card.

Her eyes widened as she picked up the card. She took a picture of it with her phone and sent it to her friends. Texts poured in congratulating her. One of her friends, Tatum, wanted her to come pick her up so she could help her use the card. A pang of guilt tugged at her for wanting to use the card, but it disappeared because it was what he wanted. He would spend the money on her himself if he was here. He'd do anything for her.

The way her relationship with Eamon had blossomed still surprised her. Only a few months had passed, but it was like they had been together for years. It felt natural to be with him, like they were meant to be together. Just being with him left her with a sense of contentment. They didn't have to do anything or go anywhere. Some of their best times involved laying on the sofa together reading or listening to music or talking. She didn't even mind when he worked while she was at his house.

Without warning, Amelie experienced an inexplicable wave of loneliness for him. She wanted to feel his hands on her body or hear his voice. It felt like a need. A day or two without him now seemed like an eternity. She paced, hugging herself. After a few seconds, she went back upstairs to his closet and put on one of his shirts. She could smell his after-shave faintly on it and she took a deep breath, imagining Eamon was here with her. It was a silly substitution, but it somehow eased her longing.

She tied the shirttails in a knot and went to roll up the sleeves, stopping when she saw his monogram, EDR, on the left cuff. She touched the monogram affectionately and wished it was him before she rolled the sleeve up.

Amelie texted her friend Tatum. She'd take her up on the shopping offer at the International Plaza after all. Amelie would milk this distraction from her loneliness for as long as she could.

*　*　*

AMELIE AND TATUM picked up their orders from the Starbucks counter and sat down.

"We're definitely eating at Too Jay's, right?" Tatum asked. The curvy blond pointed at her watch. "It's this fat girl's lunch time."

"Yeah, but first I want to go to the bookstore. And you're not fat, okay? I don't know why you say that." Amelie scowled at her friend.

Tatum was what some men described as thick. She had the same defined curves that Amelie had, but her hips and butt were rounder. It was a constant source of self-deprecation for Tatum and Amelie hated hearing it.

"Whatever. Just make sure lunch is on the agenda." She took a drink of her coffee and leaned back in her chair. "Before we go any further, tell, tell, tell, Ami. What's going on with Eamon?"

Amelie blinked. "I told you, we're dating. Well, dating seriously now." *And I love him*, she added silently.

"Yeah, I know. I hardly ever see you. He seems to monopolize your time." Tatum's phone rang, but she silenced it and then looked back at Amelie.

"We spend a lot of time together. What's wrong with that?" Amelie frowned at Tatum. "Man, Tate, before I started seeing Eamon, you complained about me being alone."

Tatum shrugged. "I've never seen you so into someone before. Even back at UF." She hesitated for a moment. "Isn't he kind of old?"

Amelie took a long drink of her cappuccino, swallowing her rising irritation. "Nope."

"Don't get me wrong, Ami. I'm glad you're happy or whatever, just be careful."

"Be careful of what?" Amelie asked. She placed her cup on the table and glared at her friend.

Two well-dressed, dark-haired men walked by. Their gazes lingered on the two women before they continued on their way. Tatum smiled at one and clucked her tongue. "Damn. Nothing like a hot Cuban guy to get your heart pumping."

Amelie gave the guys a second look and shook her head, unable to see Tatum's attraction to them. They were nothing like Eamon. They didn't have his perfect posture or broad shoulders. And they didn't have his presence. They were ordinary. "Back to what you were saying."

"Oh, yeah. Beware of rich, old guys. You know. They have issues usually." She took the lid off her cup and finished the coffee.

"You know this how?" Amelie rubbed the shirtsleeve where his monogram was hidden. "And stop calling him old."

Tatum stopped nibbling the edge of the cup. "I just do. I've had experience."

The worldly, superior look Tatum gave her gnawed at her. "No offense, Tate, but you're a fucking caterer, not a therapist or relationship guru."

"Easy, Ami!" Tatum held her hands up. "I'm only making sure you're okay. And anyway, I've come across my share of rich, old guys in my work. Rich, foreign, old guys at that."

Amelie took in a deep breath and blew it out. If Tatum called Eamon old one more time, it was going to be a short outing. "For the last time, he's not old. Can you just let me enjoy this? I love him and he loves me." Tatum's eyes widened and Amelie shook her head at her. "Don't question it or undermine it. For the first time since dad died, I'm happy. I don't want to have to explain or defend what I'm doing."

Tatum studied Amelie and nodded. "I'm sorry. I didn't mean to be a bitch. I just worry about you." She took Amelie's hand and shook it. "You know I love you."

"I know you do. I love you too."

"Now," Tatum said as she stood up and nodded toward the

department store a few yards away. "Neiman Marcus is right there and is just begging for us to wreck it." She rubbed her stomach. "And then let's eat."

* * *

AMELIE STOOD ON her porch and struggled to get her backpack off her shoulder, shimmying it down her arm, trying to find her house key. She put down the bags in her hands and dug through the backpack. "Put the stupid key on a ring and this won't happen," she muttered.

"Amelie."

Amelie swung around toward the voice behind her. She recognized her right away from the picture on Eamon's desk. It was Lauryl.

"I'm guessing that you know who I am." Lauryl took a step toward Amelie and smiled when Amelie took one away from her. "Find your key and let's go inside."

"How did you—"

"Know where to find you?" Lauryl offered. "You're not hard to find. I followed Eamon."

Amelie opened the door, picked up her things and looked at Lauryl, who hung back. "Are you coming in?"

Lauryl smiled. "I like to be a good guest and wait to be asked." She brushed past Amelie and sat down on the sofa.

"Why are you here?"

Lauryl scanned the inside of the bungalow. Her eyes focused on the diploma hanging prominently on the wall. A nerd. No wonder he liked her. "I wanted to talk to you about Eamon." She crossed her legs and looked at Amelie. The shirt she wore belonged to Eamon. "I'm sure you know that don't like him very much. I know he's told you that."

Amelie fidgeted. "He doesn't talk about you much."

"Really?"

"If you don't like him and you aren't with him, then why are you here?" Amelie asked.

Her green eyes sparkled. "What do you know about Eamon? I mean, do you really know anything besides the superficial bullshit he tells people."

Amelie stood up to open the door, but Lauryl was next to her grabbing her arms. "Let go of me," Amelie pleaded.

"You're going to listen to me, Amelie. You don't know anything about Eamon because he hasn't told you anything." Lauryl pushed her back into the chair. "I'm going to tell you the truth." She grabbed Amelie's hair and yanked her head to the side. A knowing laugh erupted from her when she saw the bruises on Amelie's neck. "Eamon's a vampire. Like me and by the looks of it, like you're going to be."

"I think maybe you should go," Amelie whispered.

"He's a monster. He did this to me without even asking. One night he appeared in my room and did it."

"I-I-I don't understand," she stammered.

Lauryl rolled her eyes. "That's when he made me a vampire!" Amelie stared at her blankly.

In a vicious, smooth movement, Lauryl jerked her up from the chair and dragged Amelie down the hall. "Show me where your room is."

Amelie pointed to the doorway and Lauryl shoved her through it. Lauryl followed her in. The familiar scent of Eamon smacked into her, throwing her off guard. The memory of Eamon making love to Amelie gnawed at her. A flash of jealousy shot through Lauryl like lightning and she felt the intense tug of the blood bond between Eamon and her. She spied the cheval mirror in the corner and pushed Amelie in front of it.

"This is how Eamon showed me." Lauryl grabbed Amelie's shoulders. "Now what do you think?"

Amelie's jaw dropped. Lauryl was standing behind her, but there was no reflection. "No way. There is just no way," she mumbled as she put her hand on the mirror face. She swung around to make sure Lauryl was there. Lauryl smiled, revealing her fangs, which caused Amelie's knees to buckle.

Lauryl brushed Amelie's hair away from her neck and Amelie frantically tried to move her hands away. "You know, I could kill you right now." She lowered her face to Amelie's neck and smiled as the veins thrummed. "Or, I could turn you myself and bond you to me instead of him. But that wouldn't hurt Eamon enough."

Amelie steadied her breathing. Her chest only rose and fell in short quick breaths. She opened her mouth to speak but nothing came out. She tried again and the words came out. "Just don't kill me."

"No," Lauryl said. "That's too fast and too easy." She placed her other hand on her shoulder and stared at Amelie in the mirror. She could smell Eamon's aftershave on the shirt Amelie was wearing and the memory of him screwing Amelie at Bathory flashed through her mind. Jealousy followed close behind. This was whom Eamon loved, if he could love. Lauryl suspected he truly felt something for this girl. Something different than what he had felt for her. Anger fed into her jealousy. *Why didn't he feel that way about her?* she wondered. Lauryl fought the jealous feelings back.

"When you see him, if you see him, tell him I came by." Lauryl let go of Amelie. "I'll leave you alone. You've got a lot to think about. The mirror trick is fun. I know why he enjoys it so much." Lauryl snickered and then was gone.

As soon as Amelie heard the front door close, she exhaled the breath she was holding and fainted.

CHAPTER THIRTY-TWO

She Wasn't a Vampire. Yet.

AMELIE STRETCHED AND turned her head toward the mysterious yet soothing aroma. A strange, metallic scent played in the air, rousing her from her sleep. The scent grew heavier, becoming more enticing. She opened her eyes and rose up on one elbow.

Her surroundings were unfamiliar, but that didn't disturb her. Her clothes weren't hers either. The high-end, designer dress didn't come from her closet. She sighed and scanned the room for the source of the incredible fragrance filling the room and intoxicating her senses. The smell was now familiar. Not an everyday scent, but one she knew.

A soft coo came from the corner of the room. She sat forward and her eyes adjusted to the dim lights. As they did, she was drawn to a squirming bundle of blankets on a chair. A chair she knew was in Eamon's living room. A squeak and then a squeal came from the pile of blankets. Amelie rolled to her feet. The smell, which she now recognized as blood, came from the blankets. She ran her fingers through her hair and then took a few tentative steps toward the chair. The closer she got, she could hear the sound of a heartbeat. She rubbed her chest, ignoring her skin's cold temperature. Nothing else mattered except the delicious, wiggling bundle in the chair.

Amelie licked her lips and halted her approach at the sensation of two long incisors now in her mouth. Her tongue touched the points with increasing curiosity. She closed her eyes and took in a deep breath, appreciating the erotic, pinpoint sharpness of them. A smile spread across her lips as she opened her eyes. Next to the chair stood Eamon.

His gaze traveled from her face to the baby in the chair, who by now had shoved a tiny hand through the blankets. Eamon sat down on the arm of the chair and silently pulled her forward. Amelie stood in front of him, her chest rising and falling with quick breaths. She wasn't aware of anything else in the room. Only Eamon, herself and the baby.

She reached down, her fingers digging through the flannel for the baby's skin. She traced her index finger over its chest and up to its neck. A warm pool formed on the crook of its tiny neck. As she pushed her finger through the pool, the metallic odor of the blood exploded into the air again. The warm pressure from Eamon's hand on her shoulder stirred her from her trance. She looked at him, before dropping to her knees.

Amelie cradled the baby, holding it close to her own face. She closed her eyes and inhaled the baby's delicious scent. How could something so small and so insignificant be so vital? How could it promise so much?

Blood, a voice whispered into her mind.

Yes, that was it. She nodded and lowered her head to the child as if to cuddle it, but instead buried her fangs into its slim neck. Her lips covered the baby's neck. As the first surge of blood entered her mouth, the infant began to wail and shriek. Life and power poured into her. The rapid, fluttering heartbeat of the dying baby angered her as she pulled off her mouth and held the limp bundle away from her. The rush of power was short lived, though. Eamon moved behind her, his breath warm on her neck.

"This is what we are," Eamon whispered. "This is what you will be. A slave to your hunger for death. You're bound to me forever."

She looked down at the bloodstained blankets marked "Property of Tampa General Hospital" and let the baby fall in a heap to the floor. "No," she said in a tear-choked whisper.

"Yes," he whispered as he bit her shoulder.

Her eyes squeezed shut. A hand cupped her chin and turned her face up. Amelie opened her eyes and screamed. Lauryl stared down at her, smiling. Eamon pulled his mouth away and licked at the wound on Amelie's shoulder. He leaned forward, pulling

Lauryl's hand from Amelie's chin. He pressed his bloody lips to her palm.

"You'll learn to accept it and love it in time. Ask my wayward Lauryl."

Amelie shook her head furiously.

"Now I'll have you both. You're mine."

Amelie bolted upright in her bed, flailing her arms to keep Eamon and Lauryl away. She took a more lucid look around. Her room was empty and she heard her radio playing. It was a nightmare; a horrific, vivid nightmare. She rubbed her neck and shoulder, feeling for any bites and ran her tongue along her teeth, sampling the sharpness. They were all normal. She looked around the room again. It was her room at her house. She wasn't a vampire. Yet.

Amelie fell back in her bed. There was no way she could go back to sleep now. The images from her dream kept replaying in her mind. Each time she visualized Eamon as a vampire, her heart pounded, and not with pleasure. He was a killer. A monster. When she pictured the Eamon she knew in her mind, it was difficult for her to believe what he really was. But it was true. Or what Lauryl showed her was true. She rubbed her neck.

All of the times they had "played" vampire, they weren't playing. At least he wasn't. Tatum was right. He did have issues. This went beyond issues, though. She remembered when she asked him how old he was. He told her that he was twice her age. No kidding. He said he hardly functioned during the day. Yeah, that was true too as well. He was a monster. A charming, well-dressed monster. That made it even worse.

Her phone rang with Eamon's ring tone. She sat up and stared at the pink phone, as if it could somehow reach out and grab her. Did Eamon have powers like that? Amelie snatched the phone up and turned it off. Before she did, she noticed that it was three fifteen.

Eamon must be home, she thought. *And he's looking for me.*

CHAPTER THIRTY-THREE

Choosing to be a Vampire Wasn't Like
Choosing to be a Democrat or a Teacher

EAMON CURSED UNDER his breath and tucked his phone back into his pocket. It disturbed him that he had been unable to reach Amelie since returning to Tampa. All of his calls and text messages had gone unanswered. That wasn't like her at all. Something was wrong. Now, he wished he hadn't gone to New York, even if the trip had provided the opportunity to buy an engagement ring for her.

It was a lovely Edwardian piece he found in an estate jewelry store in Greenwich Village. It wasn't where he usually shopped for jewelry. He preferred Cartier or Bulgari to bring him a selection and choose from the privacy of his office or home. Nevertheless, the actual shopping and choosing of the ring brought him a feeling of closeness to Amelie. He knew she would love it. Delicate filigree carving and scrollwork decorated the platinum band and a two-carat, mine cut diamond sat in an ornate setting.

When he pulled in to her drive, her black 1965 Mustang was there, but the house was completely dark. Right away, his suspicion that something was wrong was confirmed. He could feel Lauryl's presence with the same intensity as if she were standing at the door. It leaned on him, and tension crept up his back and into his shoulders. The idea of Lauryl close by immediately raised red flags in his mind, especially after what had happened at Bathory. Her markers rained on him from everywhere around the house.

Damn her, he thought as he walked up the porch steps.

Eamon listened for any sounds inside the house before he

knocked. The faint sounds of a floorboard creaking and of tiptoeing distracted him, and Amelie's almost out of control anxiety and fear filled the air. Eamon stepped over to the window and tapped on the glass.

"Amelie, I know you're in there. Please let me in." He could feel her standing just to the side of the window. A few moments passed and neither of them moved. Again, he tapped on the window.

"No, Eamon," she finally said. "I'm...I can't let you in."

"Why not?"

"I know what you are," she said softly.

"And now you're afraid of me," he said. His eyes darted around the porch as he imagined what Lauryl had told her. "I don't want to have this conversation through a window. Will you please let me in? I swear I will not hurt you."

"No."

"Amelie, please let me in for a few minutes. I have the right to know what she told you."

She unlocked the door but didn't open it. Eamon opened the door, took a few steps inside and looked at her. Amelie stared down at the floorboards, avoiding his gaze.

"I guess it is a myth that vampires need to be invited in."

"No, that's true, but you invited me in long ago, darling." A large silver cross hanging around her neck caught his attention. "Wearing a cross for protection is a myth," he said with a sad smile. "I promise I won't hurt you."

She nodded and continued to glance around the room. "I don't know what you can say."

"What did she tell you?"

"The truth. Actually, she showed me."

He scanned her neck for any new marks, fearful that Lauryl had taken her blood. He only saw the fading bruise from his bite.

"Anything else?"

"Wasn't that enough?" she asked. Amelie stopped looking around the living room and faced him.

"I would never, ever hurt you," Eamon said. He wanted to reach for her to comfort her, but he knew that if he did her fear would increase.

"What about the other night?"

"Do you mean when I took your blood?"

"Yes." Amelie reached up to her neck. She touched the bruise gently, pressed her fingers on it for a few seconds, and let her hand fall back to her side.

"I didn't hurt you. I did that so we could be together," he said.

She shook her head. "You're trying to kill me."

"No. If I had wanted, I could have turned you and not given you a choice."

"Like Lauryl."

Her reply stung him. Again Lauryl was reaching out and causing misery. "Yes. But I don't want you to hate me. I don't want…I can't have the same thing happen with you."

"I don't know what to say," she whispered.

Eamon reached into his pocket and removed the ring box. "This is for you." He placed it on the sofa table. "I'm giving you a choice. If you choose not to be with me, I swear I won't harm you. I'll leave Tampa and you'll never see me again. But please don't let Lauryl influence your decision."

His rage and sadness battled beneath his calm exterior. He stared down at the ring box, hating the situation he was now in. He hated Lauryl even more for putting him in it. *Why was being a vampire such a terrible thing?* he wondered. There were those who didn't think it was so terrible. Lauryl's club proved that. "Life with me would not be as you think. And don't believe what those tell you." Eamon pointed over to the small stack of vampire books she had been reading. "As you can see, vampires aren't myths or folk tales."

Amelie sighed and took a timid step toward him. "I have questions."

Eamon ached to touch her. "I wish you would ask them. I'm here. I want to answer them."

"Not now. I need to think."

"This isn't an academic problem, Amelie."

"I know, but I want to make my decision on my own."

He pressed his lips together. "I don't suppose you could give me an idea about which way you are leaning?"

She smiled. "I'll let you know my decision either way." Amelie picked up the stuffed penguin and hugged it.

Her smile eased his mind slightly and allowed him to relax. He took a step toward her, the smile withered, and the frightened expression returned. Her mistrust of him, even if it was fleeting, wounded him. Another surge of anger toward Lauryl pulsed through him. Eamon turned away from her.

"Do you love me, Amelie?" he asked as he walked to the door.

Tears welled up in her eyes. "I've never loved anyone as much as I love you."

"I feel the same way. I'm in love with you." Eamon hesitated at the door for a few seconds. "I just want you to know that," he said and closed the door behind him.

*   *   *

AMELIE STARED AT the door. Part of her wanted to bolt it shut and part of her wanted to throw it open and run out after him. Now she knew Lauryl caused the nightmare she had. She didn't know how, but it made sense. Did they really drink baby blood? She had no idea. Only he could tell her that, and she wasn't ready to ask or hear the answer.

How do you possibly decide if you want to be a vampire? Choosing to be a vampire wasn't like choosing to be a democrat or a teacher or something like that. Once you made your choice that was it. Moreover, what was the thought process that got you to your decision? Did you weigh the pros and cons, or did you go with what your heart told you?

Amelie backed up to her sofa and sat down. From the corner of her eye she noticed the velvet ring box sitting on the table. She picked it up and held it between her hands. It undoubtedly had a diamond ring in it, which meant one thing; he planned to ask her to marry him.

CHAPTER THIRTY-FOUR

Gosh Eamon, I Want to be Like You
When I Grow Up

O N THE BRIEF drive back to his house, Eamon called Marta but only got her voice mail. She was probably spending time with Isabelle and didn't want to be disturbed. *When I need you most, you're unavailable,* he thought. He fired off a text message, instructing her to call him immediately.

His thoughts shifted to Lauryl, or Lilith, as she called herself at that ridiculous club. What a perfect name, the name of the willful and problematic first wife of Adam. Lauryl was indeed that. Even when he wasn't searching for her, she still managed to reach out and cause mayhem. Was that her special talent as a vampire?

The possibility of losing Amelie settled in his mind. She might not choose to be with him. The thought ripped through him. He'd be alone. Well, not truly alone. Marta would fawn over him and continue to send over a non-stop string of beautiful women to take his mind off of Amelie. They wouldn't help. They wouldn't be the little gothic doll he loved. He tightened his grip on the steering wheel and floored the accelerator. His thoughts flew as fast as the car as he raced past his house down Bayshore Boulevard.

The intensity of his potential loss was more stunning than what he'd felt with Irina. Possibly because with Irina it was a final death. She was gone forever and, while it was painful, he accepted that. With Amelie, he'd have to live with the knowledge that she was out there living her life without him. That was unacceptable, but what if he was forced to accept it? He didn't know if he could.

How was it that everyone around him had a companion who loved them? He appeared to be destined not to have that. Even when he truly loved someone, he couldn't have them. Or that was how it seemed.

He sped down Bayshore Boulevard until he reached Gandy Boulevard and turned around. His thoughts calmed and he drove back to his house at a sensible speed.

Eamon jumped out of his car and stalked to the door, ignoring the annoying vampire presence that lingered close by. This one was too close. He stopped and gripped the key ring in his hand. He knew the marker well. It was Lauryl.

"I know it's you, Lauryl," he said as he resumed his approach to the door.

"Nice car," she said, referring to the Porsche.

"Thank you. The dealership thought I would enjoy it." He spun the key ring around his finger as he walked along.

"How was your reunion?" she asked from the shadows.

"You know God damn well how it was." Eamon turned around. Fury rolled through his body. After all these months, she was here in front of him. His shoulders tensed and his right hand curled into a fist. He stared into her eyes, thinking that she would back away or lower her head in submission, but she didn't. She simply stood there.

"It was the only way that I could hurt you." She leaned against his car.

"Why?" he demanded in a loud voice. He pointed to the front door. "Inside."

"You can't order me around like that, Eamon." The skirt of the light-weight, cotton floral dress she wore blew in the warm breeze and a white satin ribbon kept her auburn hair off her face.

Eamon found her innocent appearance both charming and nauseating. He grit his teeth. "Won't you please come inside, Lauryl? I'd like to talk to you."

Lauryl pushed off the car. "You're much more attractive when you're nice."

Eamon trailed after her into the house. Lauryl stopped in the foyer and folded her arms across her chest as she checked out the furnishings. He brushed past her into the living room, still unable to believe that she had the nerve to show up now. He poured himself a drink and sat down. Without looking at her, he nodded to the chair opposite him.

"Sit down and tell me why you are here because I cannot think of a single reason for you to show yourself to me."

"You mean you aren't happy to see me?" Lauryl took a seat in the chair he pointed to.

Happy? Hardly, he thought. "I might have been pleased a few months ago, but not now."

"Oh, I think you are," she said, inching her skirt up over her knees. "After all, I am your offspring." As she stared at him, she sniffed the air. "I can smell your girlfriend."

Eamon raised his eyebrows and smiled. "Can you?" He was accustomed to Amelie's lingering floral scent but took a second to appreciate it.

"She's pretty, Eamon. Smart. Big boobs. That's what you like." Her lips twisted in a smirk. "She looks…fat to me."

"You're jealous," he muttered. "I don't think she is the least bit fat." The two stared at each other for a few minutes before he spoke again. "Again, why are you here?"

"Oh, I've been around. We've seen and felt each other." She tipped her head to the side. "Like the other night."

"Yes, the other night. Was that the final straw?"

She sighed and closed her eyes for a second. "Yes." She opened her eyes and stared down at her pink polished toes. "I hate the connection I have to you. I hate that no matter where I go or what I do, my mind goes back to you."

He smirked before draining his glass. "It's our blood bond, albeit a blood bond you betrayed. I told you that you would always be a part of me."

"That doesn't mean that I have to like it."

"Really? You're capitalizing on our bond with your club. You used my name to get what you wanted. You've improved and honed your abilities to a point that astounds both Marta Jimenez de Castillo and me."

She dropped her head back against the chair back. "I didn't

mean being a vampire. I meant being connected to you."

"As long as I live, you'll be part of me." He tapped his finger on the side of the empty glass. "I always knew that your skills would blossom."

"They come naturally. What do you want me to do?" She shifted in the chair and sighed.

"I want you to tell me why you did that to Amelie?" Eamon stood up and walked over to refill his glass.

"I told you," she said. "I wanted to hurt you. To make you feel a little of what I've felt." Her green eyes narrowed at him.

"I think you hurt me when you vanished. You hurt me when I found out about the God damn doctor!" Eamon stopped and pulled back on his growing anger. He rubbed the back of his neck. "Believe me if you wanted to hurt me, you got your wish!"

"You weren't too hurt. You found yourself a nice, young girlfriend that you've marked to be your next victim. She seems more receptive to your needs of a robot companion. I'm surprised you missed me."

"Was that what this was? Some sort of ridiculous test for me? I didn't know where you were or if you were safe. As your maker, I was devastated. Whether you believe it or not, I feel an affectionate connection to you. Maybe not love like I thought it would grow to but I do feel something. And yes, I found someone else, someone who loves me."

"Not anymore."

Her words stabbed into him. He set the glass down and spun around. He closed the gap between them with a few strides and loomed over her. The urge to grab her by the throat pushed at him but he stuffed it down. "I wish I had listened to Irina. I don't know what I saw in you."

Lauryl flinched and pushed back in the chair to get away. "You couldn't have me in a normal way. I never even gave you a second look that night I met you in Seattle! And then in Northup, you always had to semi-glamour me for me to pay any attention you." She shook her head. "You were so hung up on the chase and the conquest that you never even gave a thought to whether or not we would get along."

Eamon walked to the window. "I should have never bothered with you."

"I wish! Your selfishness made you do it. Now, you've made a mistake that you can't fix."

He stared out across the dark waters of Tampa Bay toward the city. "Don't be too certain of that. There's never a mistake that I can't fix." The anger he had been nursing began diffuse with each passing second. He knew he couldn't kill her. She was his only direct offspring left. He placed his hand on the window pane and leaned forward. He could feel her thoughts racing, wondering whether he was going to kill her and wondering why she came here in the first place.

He closed his eyes for a moment and gathered his thoughts.

"I know what you're thinking, but you don't need to be afraid of me. I'm not going to hurt you." Eamon turned around. Lauryl was a vampire of his blood and would have been a companion if he'd understood what Lauryl needed. But that was irrelevant now. Still, he had to protect her, no matter what. After standing silent for a moment he chuckled.

"Why are you laughing?" she asked cautiously.

"I'm laughing at my life," he said, now laughing harder. His phone vibrated in his pocket. "Yes, Marta?"

"Eamon, I got your text. I was otherwise occupied," she said with a giggle.

"Yes, I thought so. This is a bad time for me." He cut his eyes at Lauryl.

"Amelie is there?"

"No."

"Not L...." she stopped before saying her name.

"Exactly. I'll call you later." He hung up before Marta could say any more.

"You love that iPhone," Lauryl pointed to the phone in his hand. "You love it like a teenager does."

"So?" he said before replacing it in his pocket.

"It just doesn't fit. You're nothing like what people think a vampire would be."

"Should I be writing with a quill and ink pot? Not have electricity?"

She smiled and relaxed. "No, you're fine the way you are. Your whole look is dead on. You blend. I guess that's how you've lived so long."

Eamon returned her smile but then his expression became serious. "I'm curious about something, Lauryl. How were you able to hide yourself so well from me? Not only me but Marta as well."

Lauryl pushed back in her chair and sighed. "When we were in London, I met some vampires on Wardour Street who told me all the things you didn't."

"Is that right?" He recalled his misguided theory that if he withheld information about her powers as a vampire, she'd remain dependent on him.

She sat forward. "You're like a rock star to vampires. You do know that, don't you?"

"So I've been told," Eamon replied.

"Vampires bow to you big time. When you were at Bathory, the entire place practically vibrated from your energy and the stir you caused. Then when you would come with Marta, vampires would pour into the place. I mean they were scared shitless of your power but you still brought them in." She pulled her legs up to her chest. "And I could feel you calling to me."

"Yet you never answered," he said.

"No, I couldn't. I mean, I could, but I didn't want to."

Eamon studied her face for a moment. She really didn't want to be with him. She preferred being anywhere but with him. He could have kept her beside him one thousand years and she would have been unhappy. His heart sank. The only reason she was here now was their blood bond. Maybe she felt some sort of kinship to him, but it was nothing like he wanted. She would never feel anything beyond what any vampire felt for their maker.

"I understand what you're telling me, Lauryl. I can't expect you to come back to me and live some sort of fantasy life." He sighed. "I suppose I should apologize."

"Why apologize? It can't change anything."

Eamon refilled his glass and sat down. "I suppose you're

right," he said in a defeated tone. "But I do owe you an apology." He dropped his head back and closed his eyes.

Lauryl nodded her head and stared at the floor. "I'm sorry for what happened with Amelie."

His eyes popped open. "Thank you, but as you said, an apology won't change anything. Amelie might have reacted the way she did even if I'd told her."

"You really love her," she said.

"I do."

"No, like in a song kind of love. I've seen the way you look at each other."

"When?"

"Oh, around and of course at Bathory. You never looked at me like that."

"As for Bathory, I'll just say we were overcome by the moment. In retrospect, it was in poor taste."

She shrugged her shoulders. "Maybe I had it coming to me. I don't know. It was weird. You watching me dance as I watched you f…, make love to her. It bothered me to see you with someone else."

"I see that."

"What do you think of Bathory? Or the Bat, as I call it," she asked sheepishly.

Eamon thought for a second. The urge to chastise Lauryl for her financial risk rose up in him, but he tamped it down. He wanted to be diplomatic and not critical. Although there really wasn't anything to be critical about, other than the way the upfront money was obtained.

"Quite honestly, I'm pleased. At first, I was angry, and then I was appalled, and now I think it has its own niche. You've done well. I assume it was your idea and not your friend's."

"Who, Anthony? No, it was all my idea. I got it from when we were in London. There are a couple of clubs like it there. When I found out there were a bunch of vampires in this area, I decided to come here."

Eamon scowled.

"You don't like Anthony, do you?"

"I've never liked him. One doesn't like a rival. Would you like something?" he asked as he started to refill his glass.

"No, I'm good." She watched him top off the glass and sit back down. "It was his idea though to sell the painting for the upfront money for the club."

He lifted his brows as he took a drink. "Another reason not to like him."

"I loved that painting. We just didn't have the liquid cash to get the property. So he sold it." She tucked her feet under her.

The night he gave her the painting was the happiest he had ever seen her. She was speechless, a rare occurrence. He set it up in her room and she spent hours just staring at the blotchy dancers, like she was deciphering each brush stroke and getting lost in their dancer's world.

"Well, have no fear. The painting is in my library. I certainly wasn't going to let that idiot liquidate something like that."

"Is it really? Thank you."

He started to laugh. "I didn't say I was going to give it back to you." Her happy expression deflated. "I'll consider it. I know how much you enjoy it."

Her smile returned and lit up her face. "Thank you, Eamon." The thank you came out with the Georgia twang she worked so hard to keep hidden. He smirked. "What?"

He shook his head. "Nothing. You're welcome."

Lauryl looked around the room for a second. "Your place is amazing. You always seem to have the coolest houses."

"Not all vampires live in spooky castles, crypts, or haunted houses," he said.

"I know, right? Most of the people who come to the club think they do."

"You encourage the stereotype."

"I think it works for our advantage, don't you?"

"Without a doubt. Think about it. Of all the older vampires you know, how many dress and act like the people who frequent your club?"

"So far I haven't found any."

He winked at her. "Precisely. Those of us who have lived a

long time know that it is best to blend in."

"How long is long time?" she asked.

Eamon hesitated a moment. She had pestered him countless times about his age and how long he had been a vampire. He never gave her a straight answer. Now, it didn't seem that big of a deal. He could tell she thought he wasn't going to answer her question or answer it vaguely, as he had in the past, but why keep it a secret?

"Well over one thousand years."

Lauryl blinked. "Wow."

Eamon raised his glass to her. "Well put."

"I had no idea."

"That's why I don't let my age become common knowledge. It's better for others just to speculate. They can feel I'm old and powerful. I don't need to tell them."

After taking in the astounding piece of information, Lauryl stared at him for a few seconds before she smiled. A quizzical expression formed on his face and she giggled. "Gosh, Eamon, I want to be like you when I grow up."

He laughed along with her. "I think you might."

They stopped laughing. "You know what? I think this is the most we've ever talked, or at least talked without arguing."

"Funny how that happens. Perhaps now we can be friends?"

"Yeah, I guess so." They stared at each other for a few seconds. She twisted her skirt around her finger and sighed. "There must be something in Amelie's blood that's changed you."

He shrugged. *It wasn't in her blood*, he thought. It was just her. "I've only taken her blood once so I doubt it."

"I hate to keep going back to this, especially since I'm the one who screwed it up, but you need her in your life."

Eamon dropped his head back and groaned. "Enough. I can't change the situation so I'm going to let it be. Whatever she decides, I'll have to accept. I learned the hard way with you. You don't force someone to love you or force someone to accept this life." He finished off his drink and set the glass on the table. "Besides, Marta has me involved in a project that should keep my mind off of Amelie."

Lauryl's eyebrows lifted. "A project? What kind of project?"

"Oh, something that some older vampires are going to meet about and consider," he said and waved her off. He knew she'd pelt him with more questions anyway.

"Like what?"

"You don't need to know everything."

"I'm just curious. Especially since you used didn't want anything to do with other vampires."

He ignored her odd phrasing. "This is a favor to Marta. Like I said, it will give me something to occupy myself with."

"Are you sure you don't want to tell me?"

"Yes, I'm sure."

"You know, as the owner of a very successful vampire club, I should know so I can keep you informed of anything that might develop."

Her attempt at sounding serious amused him, but he didn't smile. "How would you know what you were looking for?" he asked.

"That's what I'm talking about! See you've proven my point!"

"Sometimes I think you talk simply to hear your own voice because that makes no sense. When the time is appropriate, you'll find out."

"Oh, okay," she said, frowning.

Eamon glanced at his watch. It was after midnight now. "Why aren't you at Bathory?"

"I took the night off. Anthony's there."

"You must have a great deal of confidence in him. More than I would, at least."

She laughed. "He's not that bad."

"That's not saying much." What would a psychiatrist know about running a club? For that matter, what did Lauryl know? Somehow it was working, though.

Lauryl's expression morphed into a more pensive one. "I think I feel the same way about him as you do about Amelie."

"Really?"

She nodded. "I think I had fallen for Anthony way back in therapy, which was messed up, I know. Messed up or not, it works."

"I supposed I ruined your blossoming romance," Eamon said. He had sensed Wilson's attraction when he saw them together that night at dinner. He ignored it, thinking that the doctor was no competition for him. Once again, his arrogance blinded him. Eamon sighed and rubbed the back of his neck.

"Yeah, but it worked out anyway."

"Well, I'm happy that you have someone. I can't say I'm happy he's of my line, but I'm happy for you." He thought for a moment. "Tell me, how did he react when you told him you were a vampire?"

"He was shocked at first, and then he was thrilled. He couldn't wait for me to turn him." She shrugged. "Anthony loves being a vampire."

"Who would have thought?"

"Yeah, I know. I guess I was the only reluctant vampire."

The psychiatrist surprised him. He thought for sure he would have been a self-loathing, mopey vampire. To his credit though, he turned out to be like everyone else. He embraced it.

Eamon's phone vibrated. It was Marta again. "*Bueno.*"

"Is she still there?"

"Yes. We're talking. We seem to be able to do that now that we're no longer together."

He looked at Lauryl, who was mouthing the words "should I go". "Hang on," he said, lowering the phone. "No, because I might not see you again for months."

"Eamon, bring *la niña perdida* with you and come to my house," Marta said.

Lauryl stood up to leave. "I think I should go."

Eamon's patience blew up. "Both of you stop it!" he said. "Lauryl, sit back down. I don't want you to go."

Lauryl sat down like an obedient dog.

"Marta, Jesus Christ, what's the urgency with you tonight? If I can get over to you, I will. Tonight hasn't been a stellar evening and I'd like to have a moment to process things."

"I'm sorry, Eamon. Forgive me. I didn't even think about that," Marta said. "I don't know what has happened, but my home is open to you when you're ready."

Eamon ended the call and looked back at Lauryl. Her green eyes were soft and concerned. A tiny smile formed on her lips. As he stuffed the phone back into his pocket, he closed his eyes for a second. "I'm sorry about that."

"Next time let it ring," she said softly.

The gentle tone soothed his frayed nerves for the moment. "I suppose I should."

"What did she want?"

"Well, there were several items on her agenda." He pinched the bridge of his nose and closed his eyes. This night had been the most stressful he had in a long time. He yearned for the times when he didn't have stress. Those were gone. They ended when he decided to take a companion.

"Like? You don't have to tell me if you don't want to."

He frowned and got up to get himself another drink. "She wants to know what's going on between you and me. I'm sure that she also wants to know when we can discuss the project I was talking about earlier, and finally she'll want to know what happened earlier when I called her." Eamon returned to his seat and crossed his leg over his knee.

"Oh."

He drained the glass and looked at her. He didn't want to be alone right now so he may as well take advantage of Lauryl's good mood. "Would you like to take a ride?"

"Where to?"

"Culbreath Isles to see Marta." He knocked the empty glass against his shoe.

"Are you serious? You want me to go with you?" She sank back in her chair.

"Why not? She won't let up until she's inspected you."

"I guess so."

CHAPTER THIRTY-FIVE

I Did Have Rare Periods
When I Did Like You, You Know

LAURYL KEPT HER focus on remaining as they drove through South Tampa to Marta's house. Once in a while she would steal a surreptitious glance at Eamon. It didn't take a genius to guess what was troubling him. She knew he was agonizing about Amelie. She could feel the black cloud lingering around his marker. He could spout all of the inner peace, what-will-be-will-be, mumbo jumbo that he wanted. She knew he was devastated. She reached over, turned on the stereo, and Dancing Queen by ABBA blared from the speakers. She looked at the radio and the MP3 player synched with it.

"Whose music is this? You don't listen to ABBA."

He turned the volume down. "It's Amelie's. That's her iPod. She left it in the car and let me keep it."

Lauryl picked the iPod up and scanned through the playlist. "You listen to it? You listen to this music?"

He turned to her. "Yes, I do. She put together the playlist for me. I suppose that it's a version of a mixed tape." Eamon frowned and turned back to the road.

Lauryl continued to scroll through the playlist. Amelie's taste in music was close to her own. It surprised her that Eamon listened to it. Some of the songs were sappy and functioned as sort of an iTunes love note to him. The girl was slick; nerdy, but slick.

"Kind of nice that you all live so close to each other."

"Uh huh," he mumbled. "Although Amelie may as well live on the moon now."

Lauryl felt another twinge of guilt. She had never seen

Eamon so morose. He didn't even bother with his usual vague, smug smile. He just frowned. It was a frown like she'd never seen, even worse than when Irina died. More than likely, his mind was spinning overtime with possible ways to fix the situation, or make at least make it tolerable.

Lauryl ached for him. It surprised her, but he was truly devastated. Maybe she could help. She couldn't undo the mistake. Maybe she could fix it. "I can go talk to Amelie if you want."

Eamon shook his head. "No, I don't want anyone to have any contact with her. She needs to make the decision on her own. Besides, I don't think she'd let you in her house, let alone listen to you."

Lauryl's shoulders drooped. The nightmare she'd glamoured Amelie with was a little over the top. She sighed and wished she'd listened to Anthony when he tried to talk her out of going to see Amelie. "You live close to Marta though, right?"

"Yes, about ten minutes away." He looked over at her. "Where do you live?"

"Me? Channelside."

"I'm guessing that you live in one of those oddly-colored condos," he said, referring to a block of condos painted in various "tropical" colors.

"Good guess."

"Did I pay for that?" He frowned again and added, "Not that I mind, I suppose."

"No, Anthony bought it."

Eamon's gaze drifted down to her left hand. Her ring wasn't there. "Where's your wedding ring?"

"My ring?"

"Yes, you know. The ring I gave you with the emerald and the diamonds."

She looked at him for a second and smiled before pulling the chain around her neck from under her dress. The three-carat emerald and diamond ring hung from the chain. "No matter what you think, I wouldn't sell it." She dropped the ring back under her dress. "I did have rare periods where I did like you, you know. I probably like you now."

"That's good to know." He pulled up to the gate to Marta's neighborhood. The guard waved him through, and Eamon continued on to Marta's house. He turned the Porsche into Marta's drive and got out.

Lauryl got out of the car and stepped back against it.

"It's just a house where a friend lives. No one's going to hurt you, Lauryl. Relax." He took her hand and pulled her gently to the door. Isabelle opened it.

"Hello, Eamon." She lowered her head.

He turned her chin up to him. "Hello, Isabelle. We've come to see Marta."

Isabelle looked at Lauryl, her jaw dropping slightly at the sight of her. "Come in, she's in the living room."

Eamon pulled Lauryl in with him. Marta came out of the living room. Her eyes sparkled at the two of them.

"I'm pleased that you've come, Eamon. And I see you have brought *la perdida* with you."

"Lauryl, may I present Marta Jimenez-de Castillo. Marta, this is Lauryl Mellis. Or is it Wilson?" he asked, looking down at Lauryl.

"No."

"No?" Marta asked. She took a step closer to Lauryl.

Lauryl could feel the energy pouring off Marta. She never understood why she only felt parts of Eamon's intense energy, but could feel other older vampires' energy like furnaces. She swallowed hard. "No, it's not Wilson."

"Ah, well, that's cleared up." Marta surveyed Lauryl. "She is beautiful Eamon. I like her like this, not as she dresses when she performs at Bathory. She is very provocative there, though."

Marta's probing stare ran all over her body. The way she was talking about her, as if she wasn't there, stripped away her confidence. Maybe because it was in front of Eamon. She stepped closer to him.

"She is lovely." He pulled her into the living room, sat her down on the sofa, and then sat next to her.

Marta sat down across from them. "First, let me offer you something to drink. Would either of you care for anything?"

He turned to Lauryl and she shook her head. "No, not at the moment."

"Isabelle," Marta called. "Come in here, *querida*."

Lauryl liked the way Marta pronounced Isabelle's name. Eee-sa-bell. The girl came in and sat on the floor in front of Marta. The human was like a pet for her, or a slave. A willing human who wanted to be a well-cared for meal. Marta played with the girl's hair. Lauryl watched Eamon from the corner of her eye. He sat with his typical air of nonchalance, observing Marta pet and play with Isabelle.

"As you can see, Marta, my night has been interesting," Eamon said.

"I see that."

"It started off less than stellar though. Amelie now knows I'm a vampire and is frightened of me. I tried to convince her I wouldn't hurt her, but she's conflicted, to say the least."

"Oh, Eamon, I'm so sorry."

"That's why I called you earlier this evening. When I got back to my house, I found I had a visitor." He nodded at Lauryl.

"I—it was my fault Amelie found out. I did that," Lauryl said. She frowned at Eamon.

He gave Lauryl a forgiving smile. "Anyway, since I've given Amelie the final say in whether or not she wants to be with me as a vampire, it would seem that I might have more free time to devote to your project."

Lauryl again perked up at the mention of the project. "Are you going to tell me?"

"I suppose."

Lauryl inched forward, waiting for them to let her in on their secret.

"So," Marta began. "I can let my friends know that we want to discuss our idea?"

"No, you may tell your friends that you want to discuss your idea," he corrected. "This is your project, Marta. I'm only a supporter." He absently reached for his phone to check for any messages. As soon as he pulled the phone out, he knew that there wouldn't be any. He glanced at the A+E= <3 wallpaper and dropped it back in his pocket.

"But you think it is a viable idea?"

"I wouldn't support it if I didn't. I don't think you need my name on it, though. You're strong enough and persuasive enough to make this happen."

Marta looked over at Lauryl, who was listening carefully to what they were saying. Marta turned back to Eamon. "Well, I just like the protection of my Primigenio."

"What?" Lauryl asked.

Marta rolled her eyes and nodded at Eamon. "My Great Old One, Our First Born." She crossed her legs and sighed. "*Querida*, do you know nothing of being a vampire?"

"Not a Spanish one," Lauryl replied.

Eamon spoke up. "Darling, that isn't a Spanish term. It's a universal term applied to very old vampires, or vampires who are the head of their line."

"I didn't know," Lauryl said, shrinking into her seat with embarrassment.

"No need to be embarrassed." He smiled at Marta. "You have my full support."

"Thank you." Marta turned back to Lauryl. "The project we're working on is the formation of a governing body for our kind. At the moment, there isn't one."

"Oh, I thought you were it, Eamon," Lauryl said.

"No, I'm not. I'm only the guardian of my own line." Eamon closed his eyes for a second. "And I have enough trouble doing that."

Marta nudged Isabelle over to Eamon. She sat on his lap, kissed him gently, and then moved the hair from her neck.

"*Mi amor*, don't offend me by refusing my gift twice," Marta said before he could say anything.

Eamon stared into the inviting eyes of Isabelle. He placed his hand on her breast and kissed her hungrily. He slid his hand from her breast to her neck and tilted it closer to him. His tongue traced down her neck and he bit her. As her blood poured into his mouth, and she began to ride him through his pants. Eamon placed his hands on her slim hips and met her body move for move.

"Oh God!" she whispered. Her motions became more furious as he withdrew his fangs from her. Her head lolled back, and she shivered as he licked the last drops of blood from her neck.

Eamon put his mouth close to Isabelle's ear. "Thank you."

She kissed him again and put her head on his chest for a moment. "You're welcome."

Isabelle slid off his lap and resumed her spot and Marta's feet. Marta kissed the top of her head and played with her hair.

He took in a deep breath and blew it out. A satisfied smile formed on his lips.

"She has that effect on a vampire," Marta said.

Lauryl, who witnessed the entire incident, looked from Eamon to Marta to Isabelle. *Unbefuckinglievable*, she thought. She found herself wishing it was her on Eamon's lap. She crossed and uncrossed her legs and rubbed her knees, trying to clear that thought from her mind. As soon as she did, the vision of Amelie on Eamon's lap while he did her replaced it.

"Thank you, Marta, Isabelle," Eamon said. "That was what I needed; just to be a vampire." He winked at Isabelle.

"Yes, I think so. Don't you agree, Lauryl?" Marta asked.

Still stuck in the memory of Eamon and Amelie, it took a moment for Lauryl to acknowledge Marta's question. "What?"

"I asked if you agreed that my lovely Isabelle was what our Eamon needed."

"Um, yeah, that would be the thing he would need." She looked over at Eamon and shook her head.

Eamon laughed. "Lauryl thinks I'm a—"

"Poon hound," Lauryl finished for him.

"Exactly." Eamon stretched his arms over his head and then rested one around her shoulder.

"No, *querida*, he's simply a healthy vampire. If you were honest with yourself, you would agree and hope your companion is the same." Marta flashed a brilliant yet condescending smile at Lauryl.

Lauryl nodded.

"Oh, Eamon, I think Lauryl has seen the light!" Marta said

with a giggle.

"I won't be the lucky beneficiary, but progress is progress."

"Well, that's a shame. On a lighter note, Lauryl, how is your club doing?"

Lauryl straightened in her seat. "It's cool. I don't think there's been a night where it wasn't full with people lined up waiting to get in." Lauryl was proud of Bathory. It was an overnight sensation. Anthony even said it was profitable. Its success surpassed both of their expectations. And there she could still perform. Not like she did before, but she could still dance. The best part about it, though, was it provided the easiest way for her to feed.

"Congratulations. I think it's fascinating and I'm pleased it's here."

"Yeah, me too."

Marta showed a profound loyalty to Eamon. She took her bond to him deadly serious and showed contempt to anyone who stood against him, including her. Knox and Bernard warned her about that. They told her she had the most powerful maker in the world for a companion, and that other vampires might easily do their best to send her right back to him. Lauryl hadn't taken their advice. She continued with her plan and found no barriers until she got to Tampa. That's where she came up against the vampires who worked for Marta. They'd been on her and Anthony nonstop. Fortunately, for her, what she learned from Knox allowed her to elude not only them, but also Marta and Eamon as well.

Eamon stood up. "We should be leaving."

"I hate to see you go, Eamon. I would love to continue talking to our little *impresario*." Marta motioned to Lauryl.

"Oh, she'll be around. Won't you, Lauryl? Perhaps she'll bring the good doctor with her?"

Lauryl hesitated before she stood. "No, I'm not bringing him around. You hate him."

"*Querida*, you are going to have to come to the realization that we're all like a family. We might not get along but we are connected and need one another."

Lauryl looked at Eamon for a second. The bland, slightly amused expression on his face had returned. She never learned to decipher what it meant, and she was sure he meant to keep it that way. "Maybe. I don't know."

"You see, Marta? She doesn't trust me."

"She should," Marta said firmly.

A little too firmly for Lauryl.

CHAPTER THIRTY-SIX
I'm Pleased That This Has Gone So Well

E AMON ADJUSTED HIS position on Marta's sofa again. The
wait for her guests continued to strain Eamon's patience
with each passing minute. He tapped his foot against the marble
floor and scowled. Marta gave him an apologetic smile, which
managed to melt some of the impatience, although he remained
irritated. Vampires, much like people, had different personalities
with all sorts of quirks and foibles. Older vampires were no
different. In fact, they were worse as their idiosyncrasies had been
galvanized over long periods of time. It would seem punctuality
was not a trait that mattered to these vampires. Many vampires
considered clocks and time irrelevant to them so they just
disregarded them. Let the humans worry about time. Lauryl had
embraced that philosophy with vigor. However, she never paid
much attention to time before he turned her.

"Do your friends own watches, Marta?" Eamon shifted again.
Lauryl laughed but covered her mouth when Eamon glanced her
way.

"I'm not certain, Eamon. I can't imagine what is keeping
them."

Eamon dropped his head against the chair back. "Rudeness
would be my guess," he muttered. He turned back to Lauryl.
"Was the good doctor not interested in joining us?"

Lauryl shook her head. "He's at the Bat. He doesn't like politics."

Eamon shrugged. "Whatever."

"Whatever?" Lauryl laughed. "I don't think I've ever heard
you say that."

"Nor I," Marta concurred. "Our dear Eamon's speech usually is free of colloquialisms."

He gave both of them dismissive glances and again checked his watch. Ten more minutes and he was leaving. He wasn't going to sit here and have his time wasted by a few self-important, younger vampires. He shifted his position again and opened his mouth to say something when he felt the presence of four vampires. Lauryl and Marta turned to Eamon.

"It's about bloody time," he said when the doorbell rang.

Isabelle stuck her head in the room and waited for Marta to acknowledge her. "Do you want me to answer it?"

"No, *querida*. It's my party. I'll do it." She kissed Isabelle on the cheek as she brushed past her.

"Can I get anyone anything?" Isabelle asked.

Lauryl shook her head and Eamon just smiled. Without a word, Isabelle turned and closed the door behind her. A few moments later, Isabelle returned with a glass of scotch and handed it to him.

"You are a delight, Isabelle," he said, taking the glass. His hand brushed hers and lingered on her wrist.

"Thank you," Isabelle said. As she lowered her head, she gave him a demure smile.

Eamon took a drink. "I wish you'd look at me. I always enjoy looking at you."

Isabelle raised her eyes to him. "Thanks."

Lauryl saw Eamon ogle the girl and shook her head.

I'm simply lonely, he said in her mind.

He took another drink and placed the glass down on the table. Marta returned, accompanied by the four vampires. Eamon didn't bother to acknowledge them physically or mentally. He continued to study Isabelle as she crept out of the room.

Marta took the social initiative. "Eamon, may I present my friends? This is Jonathan Tyler, my senior most friend."

Eamon looked over at the man standing next to Marta. He was tall, thin and pale with a head of spiky blond hair. *He was dressed well*, Eamon thought. Nothing out of the ordinary or Goth. "How do you do, Jonathan? I'm Eamon Rutherford," Eamon did not rise. He extended his hand to Jonathan.

"It's an honor, sir. I was quite excited to come and meet you when Marta called me." Jonathan turned to Lauryl, who had drifted to Eamon's side. He extended his hand to her. "And you are?"

Eamon cut off Lauryl's response. "Not important now. Marta, if you would continue."

Marta ignored Eamon's rudeness and continued. "*Querido*, please make yourself comfortable." She placed her hand on Jonathan's arm and nudged him to a chair. "Eamon, this is Anna-Maria Torres, from Los Angeles."

Eamon smiled indifferently at the petite, dark-eyed vampire standing next to Marta. He easily sensed Marta's deep attachment to her. In fact, he suspected Marta was her maker. His smile became sincerer and he tipped his head to the side. "Come closer, dear."

She walked closer to him and bowed her head. He took her hand and stroked her thin fingers. He heard the words *My Primigenio* in her mind as he looked in her eyes. Yes, she was part of his line.

He brought her hand to his mouth and kissed it. "I rarely meet one of my own line. It's a pleasure to meet you."

Anna-Maria looked back at Marta, who beamed with approval at her. "Thank you. I'm honored."

"Please. Have a seat," Eamon said and gestured to Lauryl's seat. Lauryl tensed up at being ejected from her place. He looked up at her and reminded her silently about behaving.

"Finally, may I present Vivian Strayer and her companion Eliza Hemphill?"

Eamon studied the two youngest vampires. The olive-skinned brunettes could have been sisters rather than lovers. "Ladies, it is a pleasure to meet you both." He extended his hand, they each shook it, and semi-curtsied to him. "If everyone would take a seat," he prompted. The last two vampires scurried for seats and then he stood up, bumping Lauryl as he did.

"I would like to introduce everyone to my dear friend, Lauryl Mellis. Her companion Dr. Anthony Wilson, couldn't be with us as he's at the club he and Lauryl own in Ybor City."

Eamon looked over at Marta, who stood behind Jonathan. Her position was inappropriate and annoyed him. To observers, it appeared she was more supportive of Jonathan than of the father of her line. Eamon scolded her silently before returning his focus to the reason for their meeting.

"My friends, I'm here tonight only as a moderator for the discussion tonight." Eamon looked around the room, briefly making eye contact with each vampire. Everyone remained in some sort of star struck silence. It was just as Lauryl told him. They regarded him as if he was some sort of rock star. And he loved that. "I'll turn this over to our charming hostess."

Marta walked over to Eamon. "I know you all have traveled today and aren't interested in a long, drawn-out conversation, so I'll be brief," she said. "As you know, I have for some time felt the need for a governing body for our kind. In this room are the oldest vampires in the country and I feel we are the ones to make this decision and implement it."

Jonathan, who had been watching Lauryl, turned toward Marta. "Europe has been considering this as well. As our population increases, the need for organization and control is becoming a necessity."

"This is why we should be proactive. With the exception of Lauryl and Eliza, we are the oldest vampires in the United States. We are the most capable of providing this governing force," Marta said.

"What are you proposing, Marta?" Jonathan asked.

Marta gave him a dazzling smile. "I'm open to suggestions."

"Would it be an absolute leadership or a body of leaders?" Jonathan asked.

"Oh, *mi amor,* no one vampire could or should have that sort of responsibility. It should be a governing body, don't you think?"

Eamon looked up from his thoughts. Marta's charming, semi-concealed manipulation wasn't going to fool anyone. It was enjoyable to watch, but it wasn't going to fool anyone.

"Jonathan, perhaps the four of you could all serve as members of this vampire government," Eamon said.

"Four is an even number. If all the votes are equal, decisions could end in a tie," Anna-Maria said.

Eamon turned to her. "I would be the tie breaker."

"Think of this as a round table of sorts," Marta said. "No one vampire would be any more important or have more sway than another,"

"Not to cause a problem, but two of the four vampires here in this government descend from the same Primigenio. And he's the tie-breaking vote. How can we insure that one line would not be self-serving?" Jonathan looked over in Eamon's direction. "I mean no disrespect, but I think you can see my concern."

Marta started to speak, but Eamon held up his hand and she stopped. "My friend, I have no interest in this. I told you, I'm here to support a descendant of mine. That's all. I had no idea Anna-Maria was also of my line. That came is a happy surprise. My suggestion to you, if you still have reservations, is to bring in more vampires. Perhaps choose representatives from the North East and the North West to bring the number to six members."

"Sir, I don't mean to question anyone's motives. I'm only making sure that all voices are heard." Jonathan nodded at Marta and Anna-Maria. "I don't have the birthright and breeding of Marta and the protection of her and Anna-Maria's Primigenio. I'll just say I am speaking for the less posh vampires."

"What we have is amazing, yes, that's true. However, you have age and the strength that comes with it. And the respect," Marta said.

"Vivian, you're awfully quiet," Jonathan said. "Usually you're not so sedate."

Vivian dropped Eliza's hand. "I'm thinking, Jonathan. This is huge. Not just the thing Marta is talking about, but sitting here in this room is someone even you should be in awe of." She stared pointedly at Eamon.

Lauryl leaned in and poked Eamon in the arm. *What did I tell you?* she said in his mind. Eamon furrowed his brow at her and she sat back.

"While I appreciate your admiration, my dear, I would expect you to carry on as if I were any other vampire." From the corner of his eye, he saw Lauryl roll her eyes. "Jonathan, I respect your concerns and I'm sure Marta and the others do as well. I would have the same ones in your position. But again, I have no desire to use this as a way to become some sort of master vampire of the world."

Lauryl burst out laughing. All the vampires in the room turned to her and stared. She looked at Eamon and tried to stop but she couldn't. "I'm so sorry, y'all but I just got an image in my head of Eamon like superman wearing a crown and had to laugh." She covered her mouth with her hand and snorted a few times before settling down.

"Ignore her," Eamon said. "She tends to be inappropriate."

"We'll recruit two more vampires for our group. Jonathan, will you do this for us?" Marta asked.

"Yes, of course. I'm for this, Marta. You can count on my support." Jonathan nodded his head to Eamon. "And of course my fealty."

Anna-Maria hesitated a second. "I'm in as well."

Vivian nodded and walked over to Marta. "You know you always have my support." She kissed her cheek and hugged her. Vivian then crossed over to Jonathan and shook his hand. He pulled her into him and kissed her cheek. "You're a dog," she mumbled playfully as she walked over to Anna-Maria. "*Niña*, we're all together in this, *verdad?*"

Anna-Maria hugged Vivian. "*Siempre*. Always." Both Anna Maria and Vivian looked at Eamon, who watched them. "May we?"

"Of course." He stood up and hugged each of the women.

"I'm pleased that this has gone so well." Marta smoothed her blonde chignon.

"Did you expect a problem?" Jonathan asked, reaching out to kiss Marta's hand.

Marta shook her head. "Well, one never knows when vampires gather."

Jonathan nodded his head at Lauryl, who sat in Eamon's seat and looked bored. "What's the story between Lauryl and her maker?"

Marta clucked her tongue and gave Jonathan a cautionary

look. "They're no longer together but I wouldn't approach her in his presence. Eamon tends to be quite territorial about his offspring, perhaps to a fault."

"I sense a story." He smiled at Lauryl when she looked up at him.

"One better left untold," Marta said, patting his arm. He started to walk in Lauryl's direction and Marta caught him by the elbow. "You were warned."

"I'm just going to talk to her about her club," he said innocently.

*   *   *

EAMON WATCHED MARTA walk away from Jonathan as he continued to talk with Anna-Maria. His eyes tracked Jonathan's approach to Lauryl but chose not to say anything to her. He would watch and wait.

Marta leaned against Eamon and sighed. When he didn't acknowledge her, she sighed again. He put his arm around her and continued his conversation with Anna Maria. When he finished and Anna-Maria walked away, he hugged her.

"What's wrong?"

"Nothing. I'm surprised at how things went this evening." She looked at the other vampires.

"Why is that?" The sound of Lauryl's laughter drew his attention back over to her and Jonathan.

"I just am."

"You just are? Well, you've been discussing this with your friends since before I came here so it came as no surprise to them. And you've known them for quite some time."

"Yes, those things are true."

"Perhaps you should hang on to your surprise until this is finalized. It will prevent you from becoming complacent." He watched Eliza and Vivian whispering to one another.

"Should I be worried?" Marta asked.

"No, but be cautious. You have to wait for Jonathan to recruit two more vampires, and then you have to meet with them. Then you must begin the work of connecting with younger vampires" He checked his phone and put it back in his pocket. "But you should know that."

"You remind me of a teenager." She reached into his pocket and pulled out the phone. "Yes, I do know what you are telling me. I just hope you continue to help me."

Eamon kept his eyes on his phone. "For as long as I'm able to." He reached out for the phone and she pulled it away.

"How long do you think you would last without this?" she asked.

"Until I got home. I have another in my desk."

The smile faded from Marta's face and she handed the phone back to him. "What do you suppose Lauryl and Jonathan are talking about?"

"I don't know or really care."

"Really? You don't care? If you say so."

"I do say so." Eamon continued to watch Lauryl and Jonathan talk. He knew what Jonathan was doing but assumed Lauryl to be astute enough to see it as well. "She's now the good doctor's companion. I simply care about her well-being. Not her sexual exploits."

Marta shrugged her shoulders. "So she makes a friend. Lucky her. She could do worse."

"Are we done for the evening?" He checked his watch and saw that it was only eleven o'clock.

"You can't be serious."

"I am. The work of the meeting has been accomplished. There's no reason to stay." And he had no desire to remain with a room full of vampires. Even if three of them were of his line.

Marta leaned in to him again and wrapped her arms around his waist. "I want you to stay."

"What for? Your friends are here."

"Because I do. I hate you being alone, left to your thoughts."

Eamon laughed. "I should never have told you that. Perhaps I'm practicing for what might be. It's beginning to look like I'm going to be alone." That was the first time he'd verbalized his doubts and it kicked him in the stomach. He hadn't heard from Amelie in a month and suspected that he wasn't going to. He frowned and looked over at Lauryl. She smiled, trying to make him smile back. The frown remained and he looked back at Marta. "I remember a time when being a vampire was easy."

"You seem to have developed a taste for women who aren't as enamored with our kind as we are."

"Well, one seems to have adjusted. The other I have no idea about."

"Ask her."

He shook his head. "No, I told her that it would be her decision. I'm not changing that."

"Suit yourself. You refuse to let me send Isabelle over to talk to her when that might shorten your unhappiness."

The muscles in Eamon's neck and shoulders knotted. He rubbed his neck and sighed. "Does Isabelle want to be a vampire?"

Marta thought for a moment. "Yes, she does."

"You hesitated before you answered."

"She wants to make the choice as to when."

"You feed from her frequently, though."

"Yes, I do. Almost exclusively from her."

"You're fortunate." He wished that had been the case with Amelie. Lauryl broke away from Jonathan and walked over to him. "Yes?"

"I wanted to see what was wrong. You seem like something is bothering you." She looked at Marta, who continued to hang on him.

"I'm ready to leave."

Marta tightened her grasp around his waist. "Really? I thought I'd take everyone over to Bathory. Jonathan wants to see it."

"I'm sure he does. You don't need me to come."

"I want you to." Lauryl linked her arm in his.

The sensation of Marta and Lauryl flanking him brought a sensual smile to his face and for a moment, his mind drifted off on a fantasy involving the three of them. "No, as much as I would enjoy spending the night holed up in a private room with you beautiful ladies, I think I'll go home."

Marta laughed and pulled on his arm. "Would it be more inviting if I included Isabelle? I know you think she's beautiful."

Was he that transparent these days? "I'm thinking more of Anna-Maria." The petite brunette looked over at from across the room and smiled.

Lauryl let go of his arm. "Are you serious?"

Eamon and Marta stared at her.

"I was," Marta said.

"I'm going home." Eamon leaned over and kissed Marta on the cheek. He looked back at Lauryl. "Tell Dr. Wilson I said hello." He kissed her on the cheek and was pleasantly surprised that she didn't pull away. "Goodnight, darling."

"You're really going?" Lauryl asked.

"Yes. Ladies, Jonathan, I have to leave due to some business I have to take care of. I'll no doubt see you all soon." He winked at Anna-Maria and then left.

Lauryl turned back to Marta. "Do you want to come with us to Bathory?"

"No thank you, *querida*. But I know my friends will want to. Vivian, Eliza? Would you care to accompany Lauryl and Jonathan to Bathory? I think you'll find it quite entertaining."

The two vampires and Jonathan walked over to Lauryl and they all headed for the door. As they were walking out, Lauryl took Marta's hand. "Cheer him up. He needs it."

Marta nodded to Lauryl and closed the door. She turned back to Anna-Maria. "I suppose you are wondering why I didn't send you off on their excursion."

"I don't question you, Marta."

Marta wrapped her arm around Anna-Maria's shoulder. "We are otherwise engaged."

*　　*　　*

EAMON SAT AT his desk and drained the scotch in his glass. For a moment, he wished he could feel the intoxicating effects of the liquor he was so fond of. It would be nice to be able to forget the chaos and pain of his life, even if it was only temporarily. Alas, it had been too long for him to remember what that felt like. Now he drank for the taste. He refilled the glass, but pushed it away from him.

He wondered if Marta had been serious with her offer of her and Anna-Maria joining him in bed. Marta was an enigma. She did what she thought was necessary to keep the status quo, even if it involved sex. Her human life probably taught her that. Women had no real power so she probably learned at an early age to use her beauty and desirability to get what she wanted. It amused him that she had taken him on as sort of a personal project. She'd do whatever she needed to make sure he was stable and happy or as happy as he could be. He sat back in his chair and frowned at the picture of Lauryl.

He meant to take off his desk, but just hadn't gotten to it. Why had she been so hesitant to join Marta with him? For all of her loud, gutter talk and erotic dancing in her club, she was a prude. Even though she hated to admit it, he knew that she harbored a bit of jealousy toward Marta and her attachment to him. He told her that eventually she'd like him. He tilted his head back and closed his eyes for a moment. The markers of older vampires caught his interest.

A few moments later, the bell rang. Marta and Anna-Maria.

Eamon opened the door and the two ladies smiled invitingly at him. "This is an unexpected pleasure." He stepped aside from the door. "My dear Anna-Maria, welcome to my home."

"We just came over to make sure you weren't drowning in despair." Marta rubbed against him like a cat as she walked past.

"You didn't go to Bathory with the others?"

Anna-Maria turned to him. "No, we were more concerned about you."

Eamon sat on the sofa. "I'm fortunate to have such caring ladies in my line. Caring and lovely." Marta sat next to him on one side and Anna Maria the other. He put his arms around them. "However, I feel that I'm going to have to say no to whatever delights you offer me."

Marta frowned at him. "Are you serious?"

"Marta, I'm completely serious. I'm not going to lie and say that I wouldn't love spending the rest of the night with you two, but I just can't. I love Amelie and I can't do that to her."

"Sir," Anna-Maria began. "I feel the love you have for this human and understand. We simply wanted to take you mind off the pain you feel."

Eamon kissed her. "You're very sweet, Anna-Maria."

Marta sighed. "There is only one thing you can do to correct this problem with Amelie."

He rolled his head back to Marta. "And that is?"

"Ask her."

"I can't do that, Marta."

"Yes, you can. Aren't you tired of not being in control of this situation? Right now you seem in a state of limbo. You have no idea of what is going to happen. If you ask her, you will know one way or another."

Eamon reflected on what Marta said. "So you think I should ask her?"

Marta nodded. "Ask her."

CHAPTER THIRTY-SEVEN

I Can't Lose Another Person in My Life

A SK HER.
Marta's words from last night rang in Eamon's mind. It was easy for Marta to make such simple statements, Eamon thought with a scowl. He understood she was only trying to help him, but it wasn't that easy. Or was it? No more promises like the one to Amelie, he told himself. Not having control or influence over a situation was too difficult for him. This situation would be difficult for any vampire.

Eamon stopped at a traffic light and noticed Amelie's iPod. Lauryl tried to take it from him but he refused to let it go. Right now that was all he had of her; the music she loaded into that iPod. He turned the music on and pulled forward when the light changed.

Ask her.

*   *   *

AMELIE CHUCKED HER copy of *Smithsonian* on to the coffee table next to the other unread magazines that had piled up while she had been gone. She had stared at the same article for an hour but couldn't focus. Restlessness had overpowered her since before she left for Gainesville two weeks ago. Spending time away from Tampa didn't help her. Her friends there hovered over her like mothers. They took her out and tried to set her up on dates, but she refused. She wouldn't tell them what happened between her and Eamon. She only told them that she had a lot to think about if they were going to stay together. When she packed to leave, they wanted her to stay, but she couldn't. All she wanted to do was get back to Tampa.

She missed Eamon.

Yes. She missed him. She ached for him. Nothing she did took her mind off of him. Amelie wanted him back in her life but was afraid to reach out to him. What if he had moved on? After all, she was the one who sent him away. That fear controlled her.

Amelie stood up and stretched. She turned the light off and noticed a car parked outside. Her eyes adjusted and she recognized the dark gray Boxster. Eamon. She could see him leaning against the fender.

Her heart pounded. After a few seconds, she realized her heart wasn't pounding with fear. It was pounding with excitement. The ache of loneliness disappeared. She parted the sheer curtains and stood in the window.

I have missed you so much, she thought.

Amelie hurried to the door, opened it, and moved back to the living room. A soft knock came from the door facing.

"May I come in?"

The splendid, sexual sound of his voice caused her knees to buckle with her first step. She steadied herself and walked to the foyer. "Yes."

Eamon took a few cautious steps inside, closed the door, and looked over at her. Her eyes were shining with tears. "The last time I saw you, you had tears in your eyes. I hate to think I made you cry so much."

She laughed and wiped her eyes. "I'm happy. I...Oh my God, I've missed you!"

He nodded and walked over to her. Each step he took, he waited a few seconds before the other. "Not as much as I've missed you."

Amelie rushed to him. His arms closed around her and she sighed. "I thought I'd never feel your touch again."

Eamon tilted her face up. "You only needed to ask." He bent down and kissed her. As his lips touched hers, she melted into his arms. He kicked the door closed and picked her up. "This past month has been the longest I've known." He carried her down the hall to her room and placed her on her bed.

Amelie rocked back on her heels. "I couldn't find the words. I have so much to ask. I've missed you so much."

He loosened his tie and pulled it off. "I'll answer every question you have."

"After. I need you close to me now."

She reached up and unbuttoned his shirt, exposing his chest. She placed her hands on his skin and sighed with happiness. Her hands trailed up his to his neck and back down his body. When they got to his waist, she stopped. He smiled and guided her hands below the waistband. Eamon stepped out of his pants and laid her down on her bed. She was soft and warm underneath him.

Amelie touched his face. "I need you." She took his hand, placed it over her heart, and slipped it between her legs. Her eyes never left his as he surveyed the warmth and wetness of her. Her heart raced as he continued to kiss her. Her nails scraped over his shoulders.

"I need you, too." Eamon removed his fingers. Her legs opened wider for him and she drew her knees up. She took him in her hand and lifted her hips to him. He pulled his mouth away from hers.

"I've missed you so much. I know I keep saying it, but I have." She reached up for his face.

"Let me show you how much I've missed you." His tongue explored her mouth like it was their first kiss. Her body came alive everywhere his fingers touched. Goosebumps rose on her smooth skin and she shivered with anticipation. She raised her legs and wrapped them around his waist. Eamon's hand found her breast and caressing it, pulling, and teasing the nipple. He placed his lips on it and sucked it gently before increasing the intensity. His tongue licked up to her collarbone and her heart raced again. To her disappointment, Eamon diverted his attention from her neckline. His finger sought the same wetness but she grabbed his hand. Her hips bumped against his in suggestive desperation and he finally gave her what she wanted.

Amelie froze and savored the sensation as he slid into her. She had forgotten the intense pleasure she felt when he filled her body. After a few seconds, her hips rolled and they matched each other's movements. For every deep stroke, she forced her hips against him, meeting him. Her thighs tightened around him and she crossed her ankles to hold onto him. Her pace picked up and she lost herself in the moment of renewing their connection. Her memory of him was nothing compared to the actual sensation of him touching her. She closed her eyes and felt the increasing heat of her approaching orgasm. Eamon wrapped his hands in her hair and pulled lightly as he continued to thrust into her.

"Eamon," she whispered. Her nails dug into his shoulders and stopped before drawing blood.

"Yes, darling," he said close to her ear.

"Never leave me," she said, turning her face, exposing her neck to him.

"I won't. I promise."

*   *   *

AMELIE WATCHED EAMON from the corner of her eye. He was propped on his elbow, running his hand along the curve between her waist and hip. He had stayed obviously clear of her neck, despite her trying to get him to kiss her there.

"Did you want to drink my blood?" she asked quietly.

His hand stopped. "I did. Not from hunger, but to be closer to you."

"Oh," she said, trying to sound casual.

"I'm not going to take your blood unless you ask me to."

She sat up and faced him. "I want to talk about this. I'm ready to ask you some things."

"I'll answer anything you want."

"I wanted to talk to you last night when I got home from Gainesville, but when I drove to your house, I guess you had company. There was a black Mercedes in the drive."

"Ah yes, Marta and her offspring Anna-Maria had dropped by."

"So she's not really your cousin," she said.

"No. She is the offspring of one of my former companions who met a final death."

"Oh."

"I couldn't tell you the truth then, darling. I wasn't ready."

Amelie nodded. "When I saw you had company, I came home."

"I wish you would have called me."

"It's okay." She fidgeted with her fingers, unsure of what to ask next. "This is really weird to talk about."

"Just ask, darling."

"Is it going to hurt? I mean when you do it. I know you've done it before, but I don't remember."

"No, none of it will be painful. Amelie, I love you and wouldn't do anything to cause you pain."

"How often will I need to drink blood?"

"Two or three times a week in the beginning."

She nodded. "Do you know a lot of vampires?"

The serious expression on his face morphed into a smile. "My dear, this city is thick with them. That club, Bathory, is a hangout for them. The young woman who took us to the VIP suite, Sasha, is a vampire."

"Oh." Amelie took a moment to process everything. It was incredible that Tampa, the city she had been born and raised in, was full of vampires.

"Yes, this is an odd place for such a high population of vampires. You would think somewhere like New York or Los Angeles but never Tampa."

"How do you go out in the daytime? I didn't think vampires could go out in the sun?"

"I'm what's known as a day-walker. Not all vampires are day-walkers. More than likely, you'll be one. Traits and strengths like that are passed through blood like human heredity. I myself don't really understand how I can do it. It's just an ability I have. I can psychically shield my body in a way other vampires can't. Perhaps all vampires can do it but haven't realized the power."

"Can you read my mind?"

"I can. I try not to do it because I've found that those I love don't like it. I'm having a hard time breaking the habit."

"Can you make me do things? Or think things?"

"Yes. I can."

"Have you ever?"

"No."

"Oh," she said. "I think Lauryl has."

His eyes narrowed. "What do you mean?"

"After she came to see me, I had this really vivid nightmare. I don't usually have nightmares, and it seemed like too much of a coincidence." She bit her lip. "You don't drink baby blood do you?"

Eamon frowned. "I don't drink any person's blood under the age of eighteen. It's an unspoken law not to take the blood of, or turn anyone who is a minor. And yes, that does sound like something Lauryl would do."

"You loved her once."

"In retrospect, I don't think I loved her. She was more of a challenge or infatuation."

Amelie hesitated a moment. "Am I an infatuation?

"No."

"How old are you? Really?"

He looked down and then into her eyes. "I was turned in July of 972."

"Oh," she whispered. She took a long look at his face. The things he had seen. All of the history he had experienced. His face revealed none of it. He was like any other man.

"I'm the oldest vampire in the world."

"That's amazing!"

"Yes, I suppose it is." He caressed her cheek.

Her expression brightened suddenly and she shot out of bed to her dresser. She pulled the black velvet ring box out and showed it to him. "You left this."

He took the little box from her and set it on the bed. "Did you open it?"

She shook her head. "No, I wanted to wait for you."

Eamon sat up. He picked her left hand up and kissed each of her fingers gently. "Amelie de la Puente, I love you more than I have ever loved anyone. I want you to be my wife and companion." He flipped open the box, plucked out the ring, and slipped it on her finger.

"Yes Eamon, I'll stay with you and love you for as long as you want me."

"I'll love you forever," He looked from the ring to her eyes.

"Then I want you to make me what you are."

"You're certain?"

"Over the past month I tried to imagine life without you and I couldn't. I don't have any family or anything to hold me back. When I was in Gainesville, I just knew. I knew I wanted to be with you. I want—" Her words were silenced by his bite. At first it stung, like a needle prick. Then the pain dissolved. She only felt his mouth on her neck and the gentle and rhythmic sucking.

Eamon stopped feeding and licked the blood from her neck. The punctures' oozing slowed and closed quickly. He kissed the bite and hugged her.

"Is that it?" She fingered the bite with curiosity.

A soft chuckle came from him. "Yes, that's what it is in its plainest form, without the aid of glamouring or sex."

"When do I become a vampire?"

"Not until I take all of your blood and give you mine."

"How long do I have to wait before we can do it?"

"There's no waiting period. Whenever you choose, we'll do it."

"Now?"

"Why now? What's the hurry?"

"I want to be with you. Anything I have to do, I want to hurry up and do it so we can be together."

"I want that as well, but I haven't made any arrangements." His phone continued to buzz in his pants on the floor. "I want this to be special."

Amelie watched his pants shake. "It will be special. I know it."

"I do want you to know I'm in the middle of some vampire political intrigue right now with Marta so we might not be as alone as I would prefer," he said as his pants vibrated again. "Damn," He reached for the phone and saw he had two missed calls from Lauryl and text messages that read CALL ME BACK NOW!!! 911 and THIS IS A FUCKING EMERGENCY!!!!

"Is everything okay?" Amelie asked.

"Lauryl. I need to call her, darling. Something seems to be wrong." Eamon dialed Lauryl number and frown when she answered. "What is it, Lauryl? Your timing is legendary."

"Eamon, I'm fucking freaking out! There's a crazy guy with a bunch of people here in the club!"

"What? Calm down, please. What has happened?"

"Sasha said that this guy said that he knew that we were real and that he was going to kill us like he killed Irina!"

"He's there now?" Eamon snatched up his pants and pulled them on.

"Yes, he's downstairs. Trevor and the other security guys are watching him and his group."

"Get all of the vampires together in your office. I'll be right there."

He ended the call and dialed Marta's number. He pulled his shirt on and stepped into his shoes. Amelie, stared at him, her eyes were wide as she listened to his conversation. "Marta, stop what you're doing and meet me at Bathory immediately. Don't question me, just do it." He shoved his phone in his pants pocket.

Eamon looked at Amelie and then stopped. "Darling, there seems to be a problem at Bathory. Apparently a human has shown up and is threatening to expose us and kill us. He's already killed a vampire of my line. I have to go and see what's happening."

Amelie shook her head. "I don't want you to go! What if something happens to you?" She reached out for his arm and he put his hand on hers.

"Nothing will happen. I'm going to see what the problem is. Besides, this isn't the first time I've come up against someone like this lunatic." He squeezed her hand.

Her grip on him tightened. "If you're going to go, then I want you to turn me now!"

"Darling, you're worrying for nothing." He stroked her hand. "Like I said, I've dealt with people like this before. I'm still here. They're not."

Amelie let go of his arm and sat back. Her expression turned from frightened to solemn. "I can't lose another person in my life."

Eamon looked into her dark eyes, feeling her wild apprehension. He concentrated on her fears, minimizing them until they were gone. "I'll be back. I promise."

"But…"

"I promise," he said. He kissed her tenderly.

Amelie nodded. "I guess."

When she smiled, he kissed her again and left.

CHAPTER THIRTY-EIGHT

I Would Like You to Stop Speaking Until I Specifically Speak to You

WITHIN TEN MINUTES, Eamon pulled his Boxster into the vacant lot behind Bathory next to Marta's Mercedes and looked for her. She walked out of a shadow and knocked on his window. Eamon jumped out of his car and tossed his phone back inside.

Marta smiled. "This must be serious for you to let go of that."

"This is deadly serious, Marta. The bastard who killed Irina is inside threatening to expose and kill every vampire he knows of."

She took a step backwards and her gray eyes darkened. Her jaw line tensed before her fangs popped in. She took a deep breath and closed her eyes for a second before speaking. "That would certainly explain the fear I sense around the building."

He reached out to Lauryl. She was safe but frightened. They heard the footsteps of a human approaching the door. A moment later, it slid open. Dita peered out. The glassy-eyed expression on the girl's face revealed she was in a state of shock.

"Dita, take us to Lauryl." He brushed past her with Marta behind him. When Dita didn't move fast enough, Eamon pulled her back in by the arm. "Dita, darling, now." He gave her a push and she nodded.

As Dita started to walk down the hallway, she appeared to recover her scattered and panicked wits. Her quick, shallow breaths caused her to become light headed. As her knees buckled, she reached out to the wall to support herself. Eamon caught her by the arm and helped her back up.

"Thanks." Her breathing became steadier when she made eye contact with him. Dita continued down the hall. She stopped at a keypad and entered the code. The door locks clicked. She looked back at Eamon and Marta. "We still have another door to go."

The security in the club impressed Eamon. The building itself was a maze. With all of the keypad-controlled locks, it would be difficult for someone to get into an area they shouldn't be in. As he followed Dita, the overpowering scent of blood captured his attention. Somewhere in this darkened hallway a large amount of blood had been spilled. Marta put her hand on his hip and moved up closer to him.

I know, he told her silently. *There's a dead human in this hall.*

A young woman lay crumpled on the floor. The acrid scent of gunpowder under the blood hit his nose. No warmth rose from her body and the blood that had pooled around her was now a sticky, coagulated mess. He turned to Dita.

"Dita what happened? Does she work here?"

"Uh huh." She nodded. "It's been a bad night."

"To say the least," Eamon said.

They stopped in front of another door and Dita entered the security code. At first, it wouldn't open and she squeaked. Dita shook her hands and closed her eyes, trying to think of the code. Eamon put his hand on hers and guided it up to the keypad.

Try again, he told her silently.

The door clicked and opened. "Lauryl, they're here." Dita pointed at Eamon and Marta.

Eamon looked at Lauryl, who sat next to Anthony holding his hand. He ignored the presence of Wilson and continued to scan the room. Sasha stood in a corner along with a leather-clad dancer. "Now, what has happened?" They all started to talk at once and Eamon held up his hand, silencing them. "Sasha, what's happened?"

"It's my club!" Lauryl said.

"And you're the youngest vampire here!" Eamon flashed Lauryl an icy stare.

"This guy came in around 12:30 with a small group, which isn't uncommon. They milled around and asked to speak to Lauryl. They asked for her as Lauryl, not Lilith. Mina told them she wasn't available and turned to walk off. That's when the guy who I guess is the leader grabbed her. He told her that he knew who the real vampires in the club were, and that he was going to kill them. She signaled for security to grab him, and then one of the nuts in his group shot her in the stomach."

"Shot her? Didn't that panic the club patrons?" Marta asked.

"No, they were in a side hall and the guy who shot her had a silencer, or whatever you call them, on his gun. Mina got on the handset and was talking to me when she fell out in the hall. I ran up here to Lauryl and Anthony, and I guess that's when she called you." Sasha's chest heaved and her hands shook. "Poor Mina. She almost made it to Lauryl's door." Her voice dropped. "She was dead when I came past her."

"Thank you, Sasha," he said. "Where are the security personnel?"

"Downstairs keeping an eye on the guy and his mob." Lauryl fidgeted with her nails.

"Is Trevor the head of security?" Eamon asked Sasha.

"Yes."

"Get him up here and let's have a look at this person and his associates." Eamon looked at Lauryl. "I assume that you can watch the security cameras from your office," he said.

Lauryl nodded and typed on the laptop on her desk. When she couldn't get it to open the program, Anthony helped her. Eamon rolled his eyes at the two of them and waited for them to log into the camera system.

"Just a second, Eamon, it's coming," Anthony said.

The system came online and twelve different views emerged. Eamon and Marta crowded around the screen. Sasha reluctantly pushed between them. She checked each of the views and stopped.

"That's the guy." Sasha pointed her finger at the screen.

"Bring it to full screen, please," Eamon said.

The image expanded and they all leaned in further. An unassuming man in his forties wearing a dark trench coat and a fedora glanced around nervously. Another man dressed in jeans and a t-shirt walked up to him, and they started to talk. After a few seconds, they both looked up at the camera. Fear passed over their features and they walked out of camera range.

"Does anyone recognize him?" Marta asked.

"Or has he been in before?" Eamon asked.

Before anyone could answer, the door opened and Trevor entered. "He's walking around mumbling something about killing you like he did Irina. It's like that's become a mantra for him," Trevor said. "I'm talking to you and you." He pointed at Lauryl and Eamon.

Lauryl continued to fidget. She looked at Eamon. "He must be pissed at you."

He turned toward her, blasting her with a frown that caused her shrink back. "Trevor, has this person ever been in here before?"

"Inside the club? Nah. He's paced around outside a lot, though. I've got a butt load of pictures of him. I've taken at least one every time he's been around."

"Which of them shot the girl?" Eamon continued.

Trevor spun the laptop around. "This guy. In view seven."

Eamon turned the computer back around. The man was unremarkable. He appeared more like a bored suburban husband instead of someone who had just shot and killed a girl. Eamon took in a breath and let it out. "Ladies and gentlemen, it would appear that a small group of hunters has marked Lauryl and me. Because you're connected to this club, you're in danger as well."

"I could easily fuck this guy up," Trevor said. It wasn't a boast or macho posturing; it was a fact. Trevor stood six and a half feet tall and was rock solid. He knew no fear. Not even of the vampires he met, including Marta and Eamon.

"Without a doubt, Trevor, however you could get killed. Your skills are far too valuable to be lost like that. No, this is a problem for those who can't be killed by shooting." Eamon walked over to the sofa and sat down. "And this is personal. This person killed a vampire of my line, a former companion."

"He killed my maker," Marta said.

Eamon watched Marta. Her fierceness was still under the control of her polished demeanor. However, he suspected she'd consume the hunter and then tear his bloodless body apart if given the chance. "Before we do anything, we have to formulate a plan."

Marta sat next to him and crossed her arms over her chest. "I am all ears."

Eamon checked his watch and saw that it was now 01:48. "I assume you close at two."

"Yeah," Lauryl said.

Eamon faced Trevor. "Tell your associates to start thinning the crowd. Turn the lights on, but don't let the leader or any of his compatriots leave."

"The customers are going to bitch," Lauryl said.

"They won't when I tell them," Trevor said. He walked out of Lauryl's office without another word to.

"I know he's hoping for someone to complain," Sasha said.

"He enjoys his job, especially the enforcer aspect of it." Eamon said. He noticed the leather-clad girl standing next to Sasha. He hadn't seen her before. She was dressed like one of the dancers in the glass boxes along the dance floor. "Who are you?" he asked with polite curiosity.

The girl's eyes darted around and she pointed to herself. "Me?"

He smiled. "Yes. What is your name? And please don't give me the name you go by here. Tell me your given name."

She looked at Sasha and then at Lauryl and Anthony. "Carissa Rosado."

"Carissa. That's beautiful. I'm sure it's better than...." he trailed off.

"Luna," she finished.

Eamon nodded. "Yes, much better. I'm Eamon Rutherford. This is my friend Marta Jimenez-de Castillo."

Carissa bobbed in a short curtsey. "*Mucho gusto.*"

"*Me encanta,*" Marta said.

"Lauryl, you have beautiful employees," Eamon said.

Lauryl rolled her eyes. "Can you turn your pussy radar down for a sec and think about the nut that's downstairs?"

"My pussy radar?" he asked. "Anthony, haven't you been

able to curb her use of foul language?"

"She's got her own personality, Eamon," Anthony said, rubbing her shoulders.

"Yes, she does." Eamon ignored the urge to start in on Lauryl. He instead rested his hand on Marta's thigh. "It's been quite some time since a human threatened me."

"This is the first time since coming to Tampa. I thought I left all that behind when I left Europe."

"You two are nuts!" Lauryl pulled away from Anthony. "You're sitting there talking like this is some kind of trip down memory fucking lane!"

"I understand that you're frightened but there's no reason to behave like that, Lauryl," Eamon said. "In fact, the more out of control you get, the easier it is for you to get hurt." She opened her mouth to respond but the expression on his face quieted her down. "I am thinking, contrary to your incorrect assessment."

"You two are like fire and ice," Marta said. She smiled at Lauryl and crossed her legs.

"Yeah, guess which one is which," Lauryl mumbled.

"I would like you to stop talking until I specifically speak to you," Eamon said curtly.

Lauryl pulled away from Anthony again. "You aren't my father."

"No, I'm not. I'm your maker and the Primigenio of this line, which is far more important," he bit out. All eyes in the room turned to Eamon. "Something you've never shown the slightest respect for. Even now you're doing your best to show all the insolence you can to me."

"Eamon," Sasha interrupted. "She's young and stupid." Sasha looked at Lauryl, who stared dumbstruck at her. "I just have to say this. You're an idiot. Your maker is one any vampire would adore and worship. Maybe in time you'll see that, but I doubt it. I know you're a young vampire but you won't last long if you keep this up." She turned to Anthony. "And you, Jesus Christ, you're complacent. You let her do anything, act any way she chooses because you're so into her. Yeah, she's your maker but you're clearly more dominant" Sasha threw her hands up and shook her head. "*Mein Gott, sind Sie Dumm. Ein was fur Abfall! Beide von Ihnen.*"

Eamon and Marta hid smiles at Sasha's statement. Lauryl, on the other hand, wasn't pleased.

"I don't know what you just said but they're smiling so I'm sure it's some kind of insult," Lauryl snapped.

Sasha moved closer to Eamon. "I apologize, Eamon, Marta. That was uncalled for but I just had to say that. She and Anthony are the only ones here who haven't dealt with a hunter and they're the most cavalier acting. Maybe not Anthony, but he's blind." She turned to Lauryl and Anthony. "I apologize for calling you dumb but not for saying both of you were a waste. You have so much to learn." She walked back over to Carissa. "Fire me, I don't care," Sasha muttered.

"No one's being fired," Eamon said. "Anthony, would you please check and see if the club is empty?"

Anthony checked the camera views. After a few minutes, he turned the laptop around to Eamon. "Looks about empty. The lights are on."

"Excellent." Eamon walked over to the desk and studied the camera views more closely. "There appears to be four of them. I suspect they all have long knives. Hence the long coats in this miserable, muggy weather." He studied the four on camera as they paced around the room. At least three of them were. The one in the hat stood staring at the camera. "Are the two on security vampires?" Eamon asked.

"Yes," Anthony and Sasha answered in unison.

"So it stands at eight vampires and a human against four humans." Eamon crossed his arms over his chest. "This should be fun. Sasha, call Trevor, and let him know we're coming down." He looked around the room. "No one touches the one in the hat but me and Marta."

Carissa shyly approached Eamon. "Sir?"

He turned around to her. "Yes?"

"I'll bet the blond bouncer, Egon, is going to want to take out the shooter. Mina was his."

Eamon wondered what prevented him from killing the man

outright. "Thank you, Carissa. I think we'll leave the shooter to...
what was his name?"

"Egon," she said. "That's really his name."

"Egon. What is the other one's name?"

"Augy. Augusto."

"Thank you."

Carissa bobbed in another curtsey. It was out of place for a
girl who was dressed head to foot in black leather to be curtsying.
He glanced down at her towering high-heeled shoes and stopped.

"Ladies, if you feel your shoes might interfere with this, now
would be the time to take them off."

Sasha and Carissa took off their shoes off and tossed them
toward Lauryl's desk. Eamon noticed Lauryl was already
barefoot. He wondered if she had even worn shoes tonight.
Finally, he looked back to Marta, who shook her head at him.

"I have worn heels for as long as I can remember and have
done many things in them. I'm not shedding them in this place."

"Suit yourself."

Lauryl pushed past them both and mumbled. "The floors are
cleaned every night."

Marta snickered and Eamon caught Lauryl by the arm. "This
is very serious. I don't know what the vampires you met in
London told you, but these humans are here to kill us."

"I know. I'm the one who called you, remember?"

He let go of her arm. "Do you know how they are going to try
and kill us?"

"No, I don't."

"By separating us from our heads. That is why they're carry-
ing swords or long knives."

She blinked a couple of times. "I thought it was just for effect."

"Yes, the effect of killing us. You can only kill a vampire by
cutting off their head or bleeding them out."

"Fuck." She wrapped her hands around her neck and walked
away. Her pace quickened as she hurried over to Anthony.

Beautiful yes, intelligent, no, he thought as he headed downstairs.

Trevor and the two vampire bouncers stood outside of the

door where the hunters were trapped. Augy and Egon leaned against the wall, but straightened up when Eamon and Marta approached.

"All four of them are in there," Trevor said. "They all wound up in that room for some reason. The only one not shitting bricks is the one in the hat."

"Thank you," Eamon said to Trevor. "Gentleman, I'm Eamon Rutherford and this is Marta Jimenez-de Castillo. No doubt you know us through Lauryl and Anthony." He shook the two vampires' hands and then turned back to Egon. Eamon peered into the eyes of the tall, muscular blond vampire. Something in this vampire's marker struck Eamon. Something unpleasant. "*Sind Sie wie alt?*"

Eamon's seamless switch to German triggered a smile on Egon's lips. "*Vierundsiebzig Jahre alt,*" he replied.

Seventy-four. A newborn. "*Waren Sie eine Nazi?*" Eamon continued.

The smile on Egon's face faded. "*Selbstverständlich.*"

"*Lassen Sie Mich schätzen, Waffen SS?*" Eamon asked.

"*Ja, Sir. Aber die ist die Vergangenheit,*" Egon said quietly.

"Interesting. I'm glad your Nazi inclinations are in the past."

"Yes, sir. Now I only want to kill the human who killed my girl." Egon's cut jaw line clenched and his blue eyes became icy. Egon's English only held the slightest trace of a German accent. It was only audible now because he switched from German to English so quickly.

Eamon turned back around and, one by one, looked at Marta, Sasha, Carissa, and finally Trevor. "Black the lights out and then take them."

CHAPTER THIRTY-NINE

Suicide by Vampire

THE LIGHTS GOING out and the doors to the dance floor opening happened with sublime coordination.

The four hunters froze in terror.

The air temperature dropped subtly as the vampires overtook the room. The breeze created by their movement disappeared with the same suddenness as their motion. The smell of adrenaline, fear, and urine blended in the air. Only the vampires detected the first two. Time stopped as Eamon watched the others pursue the stunned humans.

Anthony cut through the darkness with the skill and ease of a vampire far beyond his years, sending the hunter he and Lauryl had marked to the floor. Lauryl leapt across the room and landed in between the legs of the man as Anthony consumed him. She ripped through the denim fabric of his jeans and buried her fangs in his femoral artery. The man let out a terrified scream that melted to a whimper when her hand groped his penis. Anthony grabbed her hand and knocked it away.

Eamon stood motionless as Trevor strolled up to the human closest to the door and swept his legs out from under him. Trevor yanked him back up by the collar of his trench coat and spit in his face. The hunter kicked and squealed like a pig. Trevor silenced him with a vicious head butt that dropped the man to the floor. The dazed hunter climbed back on his knees and swayed, unable to find his equilibrium. Trevor put his gorilla-sized hands on each of the hunter's temples and wrenched the man's head around full force so now he faced backwards. The hunter thudded to the ground and Trevor rained a torrent of kicks down on him.

Egon hung back as the gunman pulled the 9mm Glock from

his back waistband and pointed it blindly in the dark. Egon walked up to the gunman without a sound. The human turned sharply and his arm collided with the blonde vampire. The gun fell from his hand. The sound of the weapon clattering across the floor was unnaturally loud.

"*Sie werden dummen Menschen sterben,*" Egon whispered.

"W-w-what?"

"You're going to die, stupid human."

He grabbed the man by the arms and lifted him a few inches off the floor. The gunman's feet scraped and skidded across the floor as he kicked furiously. Egon laughed and pulled off the human's arms. Blood exploded from the sockets. The human screamed in agony and Egon chucked the arms to the side. He pulled the human toward and buried his face in his neck.

Augy, Sasha, and Carissa batted their hunter around in a killing game. They pushed him from one to the other, each biting and feeding from him for several seconds before passing him to the next. Sasha drank deeply from his carotid and slapped the man on the butt before sending him over to Carissa. The petite vampire kissed him, fed from the opposite side of his neck, and shoved him over to Augy. He wasn't as playful. He bit a chunk from the man's wrist and exposed the radial artery. Augy clamped his mouth over the blood fountain and took his share of the foolish human. Each time the hunter got pushed to the next vampire, blood would spray out as the man waved his arms, trying to catch his balance. The girls clapped and tried to catch the shower of blood like raindrops on their tongues.

The leader of the pseudo-hunters was the only human not under attack. Eamon rushed him with Marta a step behind. He stopped in front of the man, causing him to take a blind step backwards. Marta flanked around him and flew onto his back, knocking off his hat and glasses. She jerked his neck to the side and began to drain him. Eamon's face twisted in anger and he raised his hand.

"Stop!"

Marta looked up from the pudgy neck of the hunter, fangs wet with blood. "*Por que?*"

"Because I want to talk to him."

"*Tu eres afortunado, humano*," she whispered with a malevolent smile before she slid down his back. "You're lucky for now."

The hunter tried desperately to slow his breathing and control his fear. The screams of his comrades as the other vampires descended on them tore at his composure, but somehow he didn't show it. He was more stoic.

After a moment, Eamon put his hands behind his back. Here in front of him was the murdering human who'd taken one of his vampires. Rage rolled below Eamon's tolerance level. Only his curiosity held him back. This commonplace human had destroyed part of him. It seemed improbable.

"Human, how dare you threaten me?" Eamon's voice held centuries of threat in its baritone timbre as it resonated through room. The other vampires peeked up for a moment, transfixed by his voice, but returned to draining their victims when the hunter failed to respond.

"Answer him, you miserable waste of skin," Marta snapped.

Eamon glanced over at her and back to the man. "You've committed the gravest of errors, human."

The hunter recovered his voice. "You deserve to die."

From across the room, Lauryl looked up from the femoral vein she had been feeding from and focused on Eamon and the man. She sprang to her feet and was on her way to Eamon's side when he turned her back mentally. She hesitated, but went back to the dying hunter she and Anthony shared.

"I have lived and thrived for over a millennium. When you're dust, in a rotting box, I will be here."

"It doesn't change the fact that you're a monster and deserve to die. All of you do."

Eamon scoffed. "I'm a higher life form. My kind has evolved leaps and bounds beyond yours." Eamon pushed the fleshy man backwards. The hunter stumbled a few steps in the dark. Marta shoved him back in front of Eamon.

"I killed one of you. One of your vampires." The human's voice sounded more angry than frightened.

Marta reached for him, but Eamon shook his head. The waft

of air from Marta's hand passing close to his neck caused the hunter to swat blindly in the dark. She leaned next to his ear.

"You're going to die, *cerdo*." She faded back before his waving hands connected with her.

Eamon walked a small circle around the jumpy human. Each of his steps produced an ominous thud. Each time Eamon took a step, he could hear the human's heart raced. Eamon followed his desperate thoughts. Irina had chosen his girlfriend to be her new companion, and the pathetic man couldn't or wouldn't accept it. He and his friends ambushed Irina and the girl, raping and killing them. Then he heard a name that rang familiar. Bernard Townsend. He heard the name again, and something about money and a trip to London. How did this human know Townsend?

"Is Townsend a monster as well?"

The human sucked in a startled breath at the mention of that name. "Yes," he answered with false bravado.

"You lie poorly, human. How do you know him?" The scent of adrenaline wafted through the air again. Eamon reached back into the human's mind, but found that the memory of Bernard Townsend was fading. There was no clue as to Townsend's motivations. Now, the human was only thinking of his dead girlfriend and his failings as vampire hunter.

"I'm the first of many hunters who are coming for you," he said, his voice shaking.

"You are no hunter, human. How you killed Irina is beyond me. And your death, as well as your comrades, will mean nothing."

"I kept one more human from becoming a vampire. That means everything to me."

Eamon stepped forward on the hunter's glasses. Their sickening crunch as he ground them under his heel brought a fanged smile to his face. "It also means your death."

Eamon's hand shot out and seized the hunter's fleshy neck. The human clawed at Eamon's hand with no effect. Eamon shook the man a few times. Humans were so easy to kill. No matter how hard they tried, they still were no match for a vampire. Especially him. This one was no different from the hundreds of hunters who had tried and failed before him. Eamon tore away the side of the hunter's neck with one well-practiced twist, shredding his carotid artery. Marta was on him again. Eamon licked the blood from his hand and took a step back from the spew of blood. The blood spray waned as Marta consumed the rest.

Marta raised her eyes from the dead human to Eamon. "*Como venganza por* Irina."

He nodded. "Yes, revenge for Irina." He closed his eyes for a moment and gave his little Russian countess a final thought as the smell of the dead hunter's blood floated up. *Good-bye, my love.*

CHAPTER FORTY

I Love You, My Lovely, Little, Gothic Doll

E AMON STRIPPED OFF his blood-saturated shirt and used the unstained corner he found to wipe his mouth. He disliked fighting for this very reason. The uncontained energy and ferocity yielded messy results. However, it was unavoidable in a vampire's life. Not so much in modern times as in the past, thankfully.

The vampires had torn through the group like paper. Eamon wondered how the hunters had found one another. He suspected the Internet. Openly seeking people who had lost a loved one to vampires wasn't a sane thing to do. Instead of soldiers or true hunters, they were a group of soft, social loners who only fought or hunted on a computer screen or a game board. How did they know that they were vampires? That disturbed him. Bernard Townsend figured into the discovery somehow.

Stupid humans. One lucky kill didn't make them real hunters.

The lights flipped on and Eamon looked around at the bodies on the floor and the amount of spilled blood. Most of the blood had been consumed, except for the hunter Trevor killed. That man was lying in a heap like a forgotten life-sized doll. His neck hung at a peculiar, un-natural angle. He was more than likely a gelatinous sack after Trevor had kicked the remaining life out of him.

Eamon looked over at Anthony and Lauryl, who were surveying the carnage as well. Anthony wiped his chin and cleaned the corners of Lauryl's mouth gently and kissed her before kicking the dead man at his feet face down. More and more the doctor surprised him. Sasha had been correct. He was the more dominant one. He would grow to be a powerful vampire if Lauryl let him. Eamon knew though that she would eventually submit to

Anthony and do what he wanted.

Marta walked up behind him. Her hands traveled up to his shoulders and then back to his waist before encircling him. "Once again, something was easier than I thought."

"This was like fighting children, Marta. These weren't vampire hunters like we've experienced. This was a group of amateurs who lost their girlfriends to vampires. They did have an unusual supporter, though."

"Who? This Townsend person you mentioned?"

"Yes. Bernard Townsend, an old rival of mine," Eamon's voice dropped some as he recalled his last encounter with Townsend in London in 1801. Eamon shook off the unpleasant memory. "Well, he's not much of a rival. He's several centuries younger and much less powerful."

"Why on earth would he send humans like these after you? It's comical, not threatening."

"Townsend probably played up the fact that they had killed an old vampire or outright glamoured them. He must have maintained some control of the hunter we killed. His mind going blank when I discovered his connection to Townsend was too much of a coincidence."

"But why?"

"I have no idea why he's renewing his rivalry with me after all these years."

"The governing board? Jonathan said that Europe was already at work on it."

"Possibly." Eamon thought about Townsend. He'd never been more than a poor excuse for a petty autocrat. He'd always envied Eamon's age and power. Eamon was already over four hundred years old when Bernard was turned in London.

"Do you think he wants to usurp control of Europe and America?"

"I can't say for certain, but that sounds like something he'd try." He frowned at Marta. "This is precisely why I prefer to keep to myself."

"*Mi amor*, power struggles are common, even among humans."

"I don't want power, Marta," he said flatly.

"Perhaps, but your age is your power. And covetous vampires want that. They want to be the oldest and most fearsome."

Eamon frowned. "Well, until I choose otherwise, I will continue on as such."

"Undoubtedly. But I think the days of you keeping to yourself are over. Everyone knows you are the oldest vampire. It's time to act as such."

"Did I not just say that I don't want power?"

"Eamon, until vampires form a stable governing unit, there will be power struggles. My prediction is that you'll inevitably be drawn into these struggles unless you're visibly present in all of this."

Marta's blue-grey eyes met Eamon's, but not in a challenge. He took solace in the familiarity conveyed in her gaze. He was left with the unhappy realization that his days of isolation were over and his line would now need active protection and watching. His line would also need to be expanded. Tonight was not the time to begin all that needed to happen. He'd start with Bernard Townsend and move from there.

"I'll begin inquiries about what Townsend is up to."

Carissa, Sasha, and Augusto were taking the wallets from the bodies. Eamon bent down and pulled the wallet from the hunter's pocket. He flipped open the worn brown leather wallet and looked at his driver's license. Daniel Sanchez. He continued to search and found a picture of Daniel, and who Eamon assumed was his girlfriend, in Times Square. He turned it over and read the back.

Ceci and me NYC.

You should have let Ceci go with Irina, Eamon thought as he put everything back in the wallet and tossed it to Augusto.

Trevor walked over to Eamon and Marta. "Are we done?"

"Yes, I believe we are. Thank you for your help." Eamon shook the human's hand.

"Just doin' my job, man," he replied. "Augy, go upstairs and bring down—"

"*Kein ist sie meine!*" Egon shouted, his face contorted with rage.

"He says she's his," Eamon said.

"Then you get her, you Nazi douche bag," Trevor muttered. "We've gotta get this stuff gone." Egon stalked out of the room, kicking one of the corpses as he walked by. "Fucking nut job vampire," Trevor said as he grabbed one of the bodies by the arms and dragged it to the center of the room.

"Why don't we let the gentleman from security finish this?" Marta suggested. "Lauryl, would you show us the bar?"

Lauryl stepped around the corpses and led the way to the main bar. She turned the lights on as she entered and waved everyone in.

Carissa jumped over the bar, filled a couple of pitchers of water, and set it out. She found some clean bar towels and put them down next to the pitcher. "In case anyone wants to clean up."

Sasha and Marta wiped their hands and faces and spot cleaned any areas they saw on each other. Lauryl sat on one of the stools and looked over at Eamon, who was balling his ruined shirt up.

"Losing that shirt is pretty tough to take, isn't it?" she asked with a smile.

He gave her a disapproving frown, but then softened. "You know that I'm fond of my clothing."

"You want a t-shirt?"

"No, thank you." He set the shirt on the bar and faced Anthony. Whether he liked Wilson was not important anymore. He was a vampire of his line and Eamon owed him his protection. The doctor had more than proved himself in this fight. He also made Lauryl happy. Eamon extended his hand. "I appreciate your help in this. You show promise."

Anthony hesitated a moment before shaking Eamon's hand. "Thanks. I appreciate the compliment."

Eamon let Anthony's hand go and looked at Lauryl. "He loves you."

Lauryl smiled shyly. "I know. I love him, too."

Two young vampires of his blood in love. He fought back a brief urge to roll his eyes and instead quietly appreciated the situation. "On second thought, I would like a t-shirt."

Carissa rooted around behind the bar and tossed him a black t-shirt. He unfolded it and grimaced when he saw the club's logo printed in red on the front and the word *Változás*, Hungarian for turned, on the back. After frowning at it for a moment, he pulled it over his head and smoothed his hair.

"I wish I could take your picture," Lauryl said. "Because no one would ever believe you were wearing that."

"I think the pained expression on his face would be a nice photo as well," Marta said.

"I think he looks hot," Sasha said.

"Me too," Carissa agreed.

Eamon nodded. "Thank you, ladies."

"Well Eamon, your little coterie of vampires seems to think you look nice. It would appear that you have enlarged your line with the lovely Carissa and Sasha. They seem quite loyal to you."

"I'm not their maker." Eamon checked behind the bar for a bottle of Glenlivet.

"Mine is dead," Carissa said eagerly. "He died twenty years ago."

"Mine is gone as well," Sasha said. "He never left Germany."

Eamon put the bottle down and studied the two orphans. The two had fought for him without the least hesitation. They didn't even need to be asked. They fell right into the ranks and put their lives on the line for him. It wasn't much of a threat, but it was still quite a show of loyalty. If they were orphans and wanted him as a maker, he'd do it. It was an easy way to gain vampires without having to bother with turning them.

"If you'd like, I'll be your protector. However, I'll tell you all that there will be another joining our group." He poured himself a glass and offered the bottle to the others. "Amelie has agreed to be my wife."

"You waited until now to tell us?" Marta asked, hugging him.

"There was another matter we had to deal with." Eamon kissed her cheek.

"Yes, but a quick update would have been nice," Marta said. "I'm so happy for you."

Lauryl leaned over and touched his hand. "I couldn't be happier for you."

"Thank you," he said as he raised her hand to his lips and kissed it.

"Y'all are perfect for each other in a nerdy way. The way we weren't," she said. "I'm perfect for Anthony because he knows all the sneaky, psychiatrist ways to keep me in line and he knows all of the shitty parts of me."

"Poor Anthony," Eamon said with mock concern.

"Shut up!" Lauryl snatched her hand away and smiled.

Eamon drained his glass and turned to the others. "Well, I'm calling it a night. I'd like to stop at my house before returning to Amelie. I'll arrange a gathering after she joins us. That way we can celebrate our union as well as my good fortune of gaining the two newest members of our line." Sasha and Carissa grinned at him. "Then we can have the adoption ceremony and make it official. For now, though, you'll have to allow us our time to be together." He nodded to the room and left.

*   *   *

AMELIE PICKED UP the clock. It was close to four-thirty. She looked down at her phone to make sure she hadn't missed a text message. It was the same as the last time she checked. What kind of business could keep Eamon out until four thirty? Vampire business. Some sort of problem at Lauryl's club was all he said. The familiar sound of the Boxster's engine slowing in front of her house erased her concern. She jumped up and went to the door.

"I was worried," she said.

Eamon wrapped his arms around her and kissed her. "Just a lot of nonsense."

"Bar fights or something?" she asked.

"Something like that."

"You weren't wearing that when you left," she said. Amelie touched the collar of his shirt before she kissed his cheek.

"No, I stopped off at my house to change. I was a bit of a mess."

Amelie buried her face in his chest. "You smell so good. This is so cliché, but I love a man who smells good. Whatever it is you wear, I love it. It's not overpowering like some men. It's just subtle and well, sexy. It suits you."

"I think you're biased." He chuckled.

She shook her head. "No way."

Eamon held her back a bit and looked at her. He'd be content to stay isolated with her, discovering the millions of intricate details about her that he knew existed. Then he had an idea.

"What?" she asked. "You've got a strange look on your face."

"No," He tilted her head to the side and inspected his bite, which had healed into a bruise, and kissed it. "I'm thinking how lucky I am."

Amelie's cheeks blushed. "I think that every time I see you."

Eamon picked her up, carried her into her room, and placed her on the bed. He loosened his tie and pulled it through his collar. "You have a passport, don't you?" he asked as she unbuttoned his shirt.

She nodded. "Why?

"I thought we'd go to London tomorrow." He leaned in and kissed her.

"Okay," she said.

"Okay?" That was it? No endless list of questions or complaints like Lauryl? Amelie just accepted what he said.

"Yes."

"So you'd like to go to London?"

"Of course. It's with you." She kissed his chest.

"I love you, my lovely, little gothic doll."

"What?" she asked.

Eamon smiled "That's what I thought you looked like in the book store the night we met."

About the Author

Alison Beightol is a registered nurse and studied history at the University of Florida. These days she works as a real estate agent. For as long as she can remember, Beightol has had an affinity for vampire stories, romance, and gothic tales that keep her up at night. She lives in Gainesville Florida with her daughter, two boxer dogs, two cats and her husband Scott M. Baker, who is also a writer. Beightol fills her free time with writing, travelling to lesser known historical sites and searching for the ultimate pair of shoes.

You can find Alison on Facebook at Alison Beightol, Author or by email at maddy56@ufl.edu. She loves to hear from readers!

www.ingramcontent.com/pod-product-compliance
Lightning Source LLC
Chambersburg PA
CBHW070809180626
46818CB00001B/173